ruthless redemption

EDEN SUMMERS

FOREWORD

A full list of content warnings for Ruthless Redemption can be found on the Eden Summers website.

1

———

LAYLA

I slap my palms against the inside of the car window as a scream sears my throat.

My brother is outside, a few yards down the alley, pummeling his fists into Matthew's chest. His face. Smashing. Beating.

"*Stop.*" My shriek reverberates through the Lincoln's interior while I fight harder against the glass, then wrench at the door handle. "*Cole. Stop.*"

I'm locked in here. Trapped by the order of the man my brother's attempting to beat to death right in front of my eyes.

"Shut up," Bishop snarls from the driver's seat. "I can't fucking think with your wailing."

No. I won't.

I don't want Matthew to die today. Not like this, anyway. If he's going to leave this world it will be by my hands.

I bang harder. Scream louder.

Matthew charges, shocking me into silence, ramming his shoulder into Cole's chest. He grapples my brother backward in a bear hug, gaining control as Hunter watches them from a few feet away, his gun aimed in their direction.

Then they stop.

From devastation to inaction in the space of seconds, and I can't understand why.

"Shit," Bishop mutters under his breath.

"What?" I shove forward in the back seat. "What's happening?"

"Langston pulled a gun on your brother."

My heart nosedives to the pit of my gut. "Do something." I shove at Bishop's shoulder. "Let me out. Let me stop this."

"Shut the fuck up so I can listen." He lowers his window and hoists his head outside.

I can't hear the exchange. Even if my pulse wasn't a thunderous staccato, I'm not sure I'd be able to comprehend the words. There's nothing but my panted breath and the *thump, thump, thump* of my frantic heartbeats.

"If he's dead, she's dead, too," Bishop yells. "I don't have a fondness for the bitch like he does."

I don't fear for my life. What frightens me is Bishop's ignorance as he attempts to intimidate my brother. Nobody threatens Cole. At least, not if they plan to live.

Matthew glances over his shoulder to us. Our eyes meet in a clash of emotion. I see his determination. His power. And beneath the already swelling cheekbone and blood on his lip, I glimpse a man with regrets, too.

Good. I hope he chokes on remorse.

He's made every moment we spent together an agonizing memory. Each blink of remembrance is a knife through my chest.

At the time, I'd been stupid enough to think we were falling in love. That our connection was driven by fate. The reality was, the only thing molding us together were his lies. His manipulation.

I despise how easily I succumbed to feeling wanted.

Matthew returns his attention to Cole and retreats a step, raising the gun in the air. He makes a show of surrender as he lets the weapon fall limp in his fingers. They're talking. Maybe arguing. I can't tell. And with each mouthed word, my stomach twists a little more.

I don't want him informing my brother of the mistakes I've made.

I need to get out of here.

I have to go home.

I slide back in my seat and clench a fist to bang it against the side window. I pound hard enough for the bones in my hand to ache. I don't stop when Bishop threatens me. I keep pummeling as the showdown continues, my brother's expression morphing from a glare to a taunting grin.

What the hell are they talking about?

I bang and thump and hit until he starts toward the Lincoln, sparking delirious relief inside my burning veins.

I've made a plethora of bad decisions that Cole will forever hold against me. But the epitome of my nightmare is about to be over. I can return to my dismal existence—home, the place that once seemed like hell, yet now resembles a refuge when pitted against my current situation. I'll slink into isolation to lick my wounds. I'll become a goddamn hermit.

Cole stops on my side of the car, parallel with the driver's seat, and glances at Bishop. "Lower her window."

I straighten. Pause. *Panic.*

I don't need the window lowered. I want the door opened. There's no time for temporary measures when our enemies are near. The men who played a role in killing my husband are in the hotel beside the alley, looking for me. The men who I now know are Matthew's brothers.

My window descends an inch, allowing a breath of the outside world to sweep in.

"Layla," Cole greets in a condemning tone. "This is quite a mess you've made."

"I know." I give another pointless tug of the door handle. "I'm sorry. I'll explain on the way home."

"I don't need an explanation."

There's something in his statement that chills me. Something callous and cruel.

"You don't?" I glance at Matthew standing a few feet away, my gaze connecting with eyes devoid of emotion. He's not enraged that I'm about to leave him. Not annoyed. Or bitter. Or heartbroken. He's a blank slate, only marred by the damage my brother inflicted on his face.

"Please let me out." I return my attention to Cole. "Salvatore and Remy are—"

"You're not getting out, Layla."

I stiffen.

Everything slows—my concept of time, my thoughts, the world

around me. Everything except my pulse, which does the opposite, its frantic beats threatening to cause heart failure.

"What do you mean?" I grip the edge of the window. My fingers claw as I fail to lower the barrier. "What's going on?"

"Do you remember what we discussed the day of Benji's funeral?" His voice hardens as he steps closer.

I ignore the question, tugging violently on the glass. "Open the door." I don't want to talk about the funeral. Or my late husband. I don't want to do anything other than get out of this car.

"You begged me for peace," he continues. "You pleaded for me to leave the Costas alone for the sake of Stella and Tobias. And I complied. I delayed honor and retribution for you. For your recovery, as well as the children's. But I also told you there would be a price."

My blood turns from red-hot to stone-cold, the icy dread splintering painfully through my limbs. "Open the door, Cole." My fingers ache from my aggressive grip on the glass. "Don't do this."

"I made it clear there would be a price to pay for such a sizeable favor."

"No." I raise my voice. Shake my head. "Please."

"It's time to pay up, sister."

"*No.*" I rattle the window. Kick the door. "Let me out."

"I'm not always going to be around to fix your mistakes. You need to learn to clean up the mess you create."

My mind continues the screams my parched throat can no longer achieve.

I tug and pull and thrash against the door. I thump and punch and shove.

My brother ignores my plight. Everyone does.

Cole stares down at me, devoid of empathy. Bishop remains silent in the front seat. And Matthew—the man who stole my heart through deception and fraud—watches with his traitorous lips set in a thin line.

I clench my teeth as I glare through my heartache.

I want him to suffer. But more than anything, I want to wake from the nightmare of the last twenty-four hours and not be the victim of his lies.

"Listen to me." Cole leans closer to my window. "You need to understand the situation you're in—"

"*I understand,*" I plead. "I know the mistakes I've made."

"Like always, you have no clue. The men you've spent your time with—"

"*The men you're threatening to leave me with,*" I shriek.

His nostrils flare. "It's not a threat, Layla. This is happening. You're pulling yourself out of this on your own. What you need to be aware of is who will be by your side while you do it."

"I already know who they are." My eyes burn from the overwhelming frustration. "I'm well aware Matthew and Bishop used to be Italian mafia. I've met Lorenzo Cappelletti."

Cole gives a placating smile. "Then I'll assume you know the role they played in increasing Lorenzo's empire and the lengths they went in an effort to achieve success. And I'll guess that you're also aware these men are the reason Baltimore is now under the control of the Italians."

The chill digs deeper, sinking into my bones, freezing my marrow.

No, I wasn't aware. This insight is yet another notch to add to the tally of things Matthew kept from me.

"If you think I'm a monster," Cole murmurs, "then you'll find yourself in good company, because the atrocities instigated by the Butcher Boys of Baltimore far outweigh my own."

The moniker rips through me. Shreds.

"No." I shake my head, my stomach revolting.

I've heard tales. Myths. None of those horror-filled stories could be about the man I've fallen for.

"Yes, Layla." Cole straightens and steps back. "You found your way into the devil's bed. Now it's up to you to get yourself out of it."

2

MATTHEW

My jaw aches. My cheek, too. But nothing hurts more than having to witness the devastation tightening her beautiful features.

I'd warned her I wasn't a good man. I never claimed to have a soul.

Her mistake was thinking my crimes would be comparable to those of her people. That the wrongdoings of a small underworld crime family in Portland would be somehow similar to the monstrosities I committed to gain Lorenzo unfathomable power.

The shock in her eyes lets me know she now understands.

"Cole." Her voice is pure fragility. "Please don't do this. Even if you don't want to take me home, just let me out. Don't leave me a prisoner."

"You're a prisoner of your own making. One that will no longer be funded by family money." Her brother takes another retreating step. "You can pay for your mistakes from now on."

I clench my teeth, almost regretting the deal we made.

Almost.

"*Please.*" Tears glisten in her eyes, but not a drop spills free. "You can't do this to me."

Movement shifts in my periphery. The shadow of a body enters the open hotel window Layla and I had previously climbed out of.

"Salvatore," I state in warning to those around me, finding my brother's gun already aimed in our direction. *"Get down."* I haul Cole across my body, using myself as his shield.

Shots reverberate through the alley. Bullets whiz past.

Layla screams. Cole ducks.

Hunter returns fire from behind us.

The noise is deafening as I lunge for the passenger door and yank it open. "Get around the other side of the car. We'll cover you."

Cole complies as I climb into the Lincoln and Bishop hits the gas. We cruise forward, Layla's brother doing a crouching run beside us to where his vehicle waits at the mouth of the alley.

"Let me go with him," she begs through the window. "Let me out."

Never.

"It isn't safe." I don't trust her with a brother who could easily give her up. She's mine to protect now.

We nose up to Cole's vehicle and he climbs inside, Hunter doing the same, before they both slam their doors. The town car violently reverses, clearing our path to escape as bullets ping off the back of the Lincoln, smashing a tail light.

"Hold on." Bishop clings to the steering wheel. Our tires screech with rapid acceleration. "Am I heading for the airport?"

"Yes." I grab my cell from inside my jacket and dial the pilot's number, my ass sliding from side to side on the seat as we speed through the parking lot and onto the main road. He answers on the second ring. "Get the jet ready. We'll be there in fifteen. I don't want any delays."

"I'll need to schedule it with traffic—"

"Get it done." I disconnect, return the device to my pocket, then lower my sun visor. I use the makeup mirror to gain a glimpse of Layla in the back seat, her bowed head and slumped posture threatening to reawaken emotions long since hibernated. "Are you okay?"

She raises her gaze, meeting my reflection with a scowl. There are no words. No actions. Just hard eyes that scream of loathing.

"We'll get you out of Denver," I vow. "You'll be looked after."

"I don't want your help. Leave me at the airport. I'll find my own way home."

"That's not an option." I can't win her back when she's not by my side. "We can discuss the future once we're settled at a safe house."

Her lip curls, her vehemence increasing, but she doesn't argue. Instead, she drags her gaze out the window while we continue weaving through traffic, Bishop slamming the horn like it's an arcade button.

We reach the airport without a sign of Cole or Salvatore. Thankfully, there are no cops on our tail, either.

Bishop takes us to the gates leading onto the private runway, escorting us inside as soon as they're opened by airport staff.

We stop by a hangar in front of the jet already waiting on the tarmac. The ignition is cut. Silence descends. Nobody moves.

It isn't until a guy pauses at the driver's door, waiting to take the Lincoln off our hands, that Bishop looks at me in recrimination. "Are you sure this is the right move?"

I don't need specifics to understand he's talking about Layla.

He wants me to leave her behind. To dump and run.

"It's the only move." I shove from the car and open her door for her to get out.

She doesn't.

She remains seated, staring straight ahead. She doesn't even look at me.

I'm not sure if I should be livid or impressed that rejection is high on her priorities even though her life is in danger.

"We need to get out of here." I pull the door wider.

She crosses her arms over her chest, refusing to acknowledge me. She's all defiance and spite. Hostility and fury.

I'd be fucking turned on if I wasn't concerned for her safety.

"Believe me, you'll have more than enough time to make your resentment known once we reach our destination," I mutter under my breath. "But if you don't move your ass, I *will* carry you."

Her chin rises, her mega-watt scowl turning to hit me head on. "Touch me and I promise you won't live to regret it."

A thrill skitters through my veins. If she isn't careful, she'll learn the hard way that defiance isn't the best strategy against me. "Then get out of the fucking car, *amore mio*. We need to disappear."

Her jaw tightens as she continues to stare me down. Seconds pass. My pulse increases.

I want an excuse to grab her. Touch her. Force her to me and make her see sense.

"Where are we going?" Finally, she scoots from the back seat and moves to stand before me, her shoulders straight with authority.

"Somewhere safe." I slam the door behind her while Bishop climbs from the other side of the vehicle.

I stalk beside her toward the jet whirring on the tarmac, the stairs lowered, the pilot already waiting in the cockpit.

I pause at the first step and indicate with a wave of a hand for her to proceed before me.

She plants her feet. "I'll follow."

No, she'll run, and I'm more than tempted to let her just for the opportunity to give chase.

She has no idea of the dangerous response she's spurring to life inside me. If she knew, her expression would be less defiant and more fearful.

"Move." I hold her gaze, daring her to defy me.

She's undaunted, maintaining my stare for numerous heart-beats. "You're such an asshole." She reaches for the hand rail and climbs the slim staircase to disappear inside.

"Asshole?" Bishop murmurs as he stands by my side. "I don't think she fully grasps the description her brother gave."

"Don't cause shit for me." I keep my focus on the top of the stairs.

"Cause shit for *you*?" He gives a derisive huff and takes the first step. "My bad. Here I was thinking you were the one fucking me over with your drama."

The slumberous itch of remorse attempts to niggle its way into my chest.

We fought hard to get away from this lifestyle. To distance ourselves from the devil's to-do list.

Now it looks like I've dragged us back in.

But this is temporary.

I follow him into the jet and jerk my chin in greeting at the copilot who waits at the entrance to the cockpit. "Get us in the air, Malcolm. The sooner, the better."

"Will do, sir." He drags the staircase inside and shuts the door behind me, enclosing us in a volatile capsule of aggression and hatred.

Bishop starts down the aisle. "I'll reach out to Irene and make sure the house is stocked and cleaned before we arrive."

"Ask her to provide any necessities for our guest."

He nods, passing Layla who sits on a window seat in the middle of the cabin.

The coastal safe house has everything Bishop and I will need—clothes, toiletries, weapons. But I don't want Layla left wanting. I'm impatient for her forgiveness. And the looming deadline to regain her love is already a tightening noose around my neck.

I've got thirty days. Yet I want to believe I can achieve it in one.

I take the seat beside her, ignoring her stubborn silence as the jet begins to move. I plan my defense while we remain in a holding pattern near the runway and indulge the quiet she obviously craves as we leave the ground.

She needs time for her adrenaline to weaken, and I give it to her, allowing her turmoil a chance to settle while we ascend and turn toward the East Coast. I watch her, though. From the corner of my eye, I note the ragged rise and fall of her chest. Her hands rest in her lap, the position seeming like a deliberate show of calm if it weren't for her constant picking at her fingernails.

"Have you eaten?" I ask.

She keeps her gaze straight ahead, unflinching. Mute.

"We've got a lot to discuss, *amore mio*. I know you're—"

"You know nothing," she grates. "You don't know what you've done. And you sure as shit seem ignorant to how I hold you accountable, otherwise you'd quit pretending we're not enemies."

"I'm well aware of the role I've played. I'm only asking for an opportunity to explain."

"I'm all out of opportunities. You can go to hell as far as I'm concerned."

I'm already there. "I didn't—"

"*Don't. Talk. To. Me.*" She enunciates the demand slowly. Vehemently.

I clench my molars. *Fine*. I'll give her more time.

We spend the rest of the flight in silence, her tense posture unfaltering until we land at a small private airport in South Carolina.

As soon as the copilot opens the door and lowers the stairs, Layla climbs over me like a caged animal finally gaining freedom and exits the jet before I can release my belt.

By the time I step into the sunlight at the top of the staircase, she's already seated in the waiting Lincoln on the tarmac. There were no protests. No acts of aggression. Only a one-track mind to get as far away from me as possible.

I slide into the back seat with her, the quiet continuing from all parties as Bishop drives us toward the beach, the unfettered sunshine and slight warmth in the air doing nothing to soothe the animosity Layla exudes.

She wants me dead.

Rightly so.

I lied. Deceived. Manipulated. But she did, too.

The wreckage of our relationship lays at both our feet.

"Irene has cleaned the house and stocked the kitchen." Bishop meets my gaze in the rearview mirror. "Do you want me to stop to pick up anything else before we arrive?"

"No." I'm sure there are a million things I need to organize but my priority is getting Layla alone. The longer her malevolence festers, the more impatient I become.

I stare out the window, never more thankful for the partial isolation of my coastal property than I am right now. The closest neighbors are half a mile down the road. Layla can let loose and rail on me all she likes without fear of being overheard.

And she *will* let loose.

I can already feel her building detonation.

"Home sweet home." Bishop pulls onto a cement drive, pausing before the property gate to tap in the security code, and then we proceed inside.

We stop before the two-story waterfront house with its sleek architectural lines and L-shaped staircase leading to the upstairs veranda. The property hasn't changed since we last escaped here two years ago. There are no cobwebs or remnants of autumn leaves. Irene has kept the place immaculate with all the curtains now drawn from the massive panes of unfettered glass, ready for us to arrive.

Layla doesn't react to the multimillion-dollar property.

It isn't until the car stops and the ignition is cut that she drags in a long breath, releasing it in a heave.

"I have a question." She gives me a sideways glare. "Only one. And that's all I want from you."

"Ask." I tense, anticipating her interest in the negotiation I had with her brother. I won't lie to her again. But distancing her from that truth will work in my favor.

"How did you get my things?" She holds my gaze, her eyes narrowed slits. "The items from my purse after I was mugged. How did you get them? *When* did you get them?"

Shit.

She's gone straight for the jugular of my deception.

Bishop clears his throat. "I paid someone—"

"No." There's aggression in my voice as I interrupt. A harshness born from frustration over my biggest mistake. I appreciate his willingness to take the blame, but her fury is my punishment to bear. "I can handle this. Layla and I will meet you inside."

Bishop stares at me through the rearview mirror, silently warning me of the hostile situation that's about to erupt.

I'm fully aware of my fate, asshole.

"Go." I jerk my chin. "We won't be long."

He sighs and climbs from the car, shutting the door behind him.

Layla straightens, as if steeling herself against being alone with me when this used to be her fucking preference.

"He paid someone?" Her tone is flat, lifeless, along with her expression. "Paid them for what? To find my purse? To retrieve it from a dumpster?"

"He didn't pay anyone." I unclasp my belt, preparing to chase after her. "I did. And it wasn't a search or retrieval mission."

Her brow furrows. She may have been born into a vicious family but apparently, her upbringing wasn't harsh enough for her to assume how low I would stoop for information.

"I paid someone to steal your purse, *amore mio*. I arranged for you to be mugged."

She remains rigid.

The detonation I anticipate waits in a holding pattern while she blinks.

Once.

Twice.

Then the shock wears off with the thinning of her beautiful lips and a fast swallow. She keeps her devastation tempered, the buffered reaction punishing me more than her rage ever could.

"You wouldn't tell me who you were." It's a fucking lame excuse. "You used a burner phone. The name you gave the restaurant was fake. I had nothing to—"

She snaps her gaze from mine, flings her door wide, then slides outside, smacking the door shut behind her. She doesn't run. Doesn't flee in a whirlwind of emotion. Instead, she holds her head high and strides for the house, climbing the staircase with grace and dignity.

I shove from the car. "Layla, wait."

She doesn't.

"*Layla.*" I stride after her.

She needs to understand my reasoning. The necessity.

She reaches the veranda and yanks open the front door, then slams it in her wake.

Fuck. I clench a fist, preparing to punch my knuckles through the car window. I anticipate the contact. Already hear the shatter of glass. Feel the distracting pain. It's a whirlwind of relief just waiting on the edges of my consciousness.

But I can't break. I won't succumb to the easy option.

I've worked hard to overcome my impulses. I'm better than that now. At least, I'm meant to act like I am.

Problem is, I'd fucking planned to tell her. I had every goddamn intention of laying my cards on the table. Then Remy sent me a text about the shooting and I'd realized too late that my time was up.

I would've explained where I came from. Who my family was —the ones who raised me only to destroy me. I intended to outline all the underhanded tactics I'd used to keep her close. To win her over. To make her mine.

Then my brother fucked me.

I climb the stairs and stalk my ass inside.

The tiled entry sparkles. The scent of lemon cleaning chemicals taints the air. I prowl my way along the cobweb-free hall and into the pristine open living area, every single pane of the floor-to-ceiling glass scuff free.

The perfection mocks me. It fucking pokes at my inferiority, screaming how unworthy I am.

Bishop stands in the kitchen, his ass leaning against the island counter as he takes a bite of a half-eaten apple.

"Where is she?" I ask.

He jerks his head toward the far hall leading to the bedrooms. "I told her to take the room next to yours."

I divert my path in search of her. We're going to talk this shit through. I'll justify my actions or die trying.

I pass my bedroom, then continue to hers and stop before the closed door. I raise my hand to knock, the gentle fall of the shower pattering in the distance. There's something else, too. A sniffle. The faintest whimper?

Fuck. Is she crying?

Her pain is an arrow through my chest.

"I told you this would happen." Bishop comes to stand at the start of the hall. "I warned you."

I brace my clenched knuckles against her door and hang my head, not daring to look at him for fear of lighting the fuse to my temper.

"I said she would bring drama." He approaches. "That she'd be a fucking complication. Now look where we're at—in the middle of a war that's not ours with loot that will get us killed."

"She's not loot." Anger mixes with my self-loathing, the potent concoction warming my veins. I fight to hold myself in check, to calm the devil within.

"Then what is she? What the fuck have you dragged us into?" Bishop keeps approaching. Keeps taunting. If he's not careful, he'll bear the brunt of the madness waging war inside me.

"What have *I* dragged us into?" I push from the door and swing around to face him. "None of this would've happened if you'd done your job in the first place."

"You're blaming this on me?"

"Why wouldn't I? All you had to do was find out why she was spying on Emmanuel at that fucking restaurant. You had one goddamn job."

He raises a brow, his lips slowly curling in a threatening smile. "Why don't we take this outside? I'll give you the fight you're itching for."

My chest hums, my soul empowered by the offer of violence.

Pain is exactly what I want. The crunch of bone. The thrill of carnage.

"I'm not fighting you," I snarl.

"Why? You worried I'll kick your ass?"

If I thought he could overpower me in my current state, I'd welcome the threat. I'd accept the hospitality of his beating and hope he knocked me out cold. But the opposite will happen.

"No." I dig my fingers into my palms, wishing the need for brutality would lessen. All it does is build. Morph. Punish. "I'm more concerned I won't stop until I kill you."

He straightens. Sobers.

He knows I'm not exaggerating.

He squares his shoulders, tightens his jaw. "If that's the case, you shouldn't be anywhere near her."

The caution pokes my self-loathing higher, making it dance with my rage.

I'd never hurt her… not physically… at least, not by my own hand.

Fuck.

All I've done is hurt her.

Emotionally. Physically. I arranged to have her mugged, which left her injured. I've destroyed the ties that bind her to her family. I've devastated her confidence and shattered her trust.

Have I ruined her just like Emmanuel ruined me?

"Take a walk." Bishop's expression tightens. "Clear your head. I don't know what the fuck you said to Torian to have him handing over his sister, but we'll discuss it later. Right now, you need to pull yourself together before this situation gets more out of hand. Scaring her isn't going to work in your favor."

"She isn't scared of me." I've caused frustration, hatred, loathing, disgust. But never her fear.

"No, but she should be."

Another muted sniffle comes from her room, stabbing more jagged arrows through my chest.

She has to understand my motives.

She needs to fucking listen.

"Walk, Langston. I'll keep an eye on her until you return."

3

———————

MATTHEW

I WALKED.

I gave her time.

Three fucking days to be exact. I played the role of personal chef, supplying every meal to her bedroom only to be forced to leave it on a tray in the hall because she wouldn't unlock the door.

She won't talk to me. Acknowledge me.

I left her a new toothbrush, shampoo, and soap, yet I get nothing in return. Not even a grunt or a curse.

I'm sure she knows it's driving me insane.

During the day, I spend hours sitting on the floor in my room, my back to our adjoining wall, listening to her occasional footsteps as I drink scotch from the bottle.

The nights are worse. That's when I sit in the darkness of the deck, my attention firmly affixed on her silhouette through the sheer curtains behind the French doors leading to her room.

I'm starved for the sight of her. I need to see those emotive eyes. Hear that haunting voice. Every minute that ticks by is another wasted moment creeping toward my deadline to win her back.

She can't stay in that room forever.

Bishop's footsteps approach down the hall, his unimpressed glower at my bedroom door seconds later. He eyes the liquor bottle beside me as I sit on the floor, my head resting back against the wall.

He sighs, long and judgmental. "How long do you plan on moping?"

Moping? Seems this asshole is still looking for a fight. "If I'm not mistaken, you're the one who told me to give her time."

"So you heard me?" He crosses his arms over his chest and leans a bicep against the doorframe. "For the last two days I've been wondering if the message got lost in translation and you actually thought I told you to act like a punk-ass bitch."

He's definitely itching to get pummeled.

"We've got employees wondering why the hell you disappeared. They've got questions I can't answer, motherfucker. You need to start returning calls."

I clench my teeth, glare, and grab for a bottle I already know is drained.

"I'll ask again," he mutters. "How long do you plan on moping?"

"How long do you expect to keep breathing if you continue to test me?" I drag myself to my feet, the liquor bottle dangling in my hand.

He snickers. "There he is. The son of a bitch we all know and love."

I stalk toward him, shoving past to enter the hall and continue to the open living area.

He follows, joining me in the kitchen as I dump the bottle in the trash. "I think it's time we had a chat about why she's here. Don't you?"

And have him judge me more than he already has? No thanks. "I've got things to do." I make for the hall again only to have him block my path.

"What things?" He narrows his gaze. "You've got that look in your eye."

"This look means I'm done waiting. She can't ignore me any longer."

"If that's the case, do you want me to go out to stockpile first aid supplies? Because you're going to need them if you go in there half cut with the devil on your shoulder."

The devil has never been on my shoulder. That fucker resides in my soul.

"I'm sure she's put her isolation to good use," he adds. "Her claws will be sharp."

The thought of those claws isn't a deterrent. If anything, her touch, blood-drawing or not, has the opposite effect. I'd let her hurt me. I'd encourage it if it meant she'd acknowledge my existence.

"Look." He raises his hands in surrender. "Why don't I start dinner? We both know I'm a one-trick pony, so we're stuck with spaghetti, but at least that way you can take a cold shower, sober up, and figure out what the fuck you're going to say to stop her from stabbing you."

"She's not going to stab me. And I'm not drunk." The liquor was merely medicinal, each sip taking the edge off days of building frustration. "By now she should've realized I'm the only one who can help her. She just needs to listen—"

"Help her do what?" He backtracks around the island counter and pulls a saucepan from a cupboard. "Fix the mess you created?"

He's right. However, that doesn't mean I'm wrong.

I'm all she's got, and the fact she hasn't run by now means she's fully aware of it.

The neighbors might not be close, but they're within walking distance. She could've fled there for help. My bet is that she knows the only things the outside world can give her are temporary measures—a phone call, a short supply of cash.

"Yes," I admit. "I'm the only one who can fix the mess I created."

Bishop moves to the fridge, making a mass of noise as he claims ingredients, then dumps them on the counter. Something else enters the mix. A far-off sound coming from the hall leading to the bedrooms.

I cock my head, hearing it again. A muffled whir.

Did she flee her hiding place?

I stalk for the hall, hungry to see her, to speak to her, only to find her bedroom door closed as usual.

"Layla, are you in there?" I speak to the painted wood.

Her response is a squeak of mattress springs as the whir repeats down the hall. The washing machine? She snuck out to wash her clothes?

If only she'd fucking asked. I would've bought her every item under the sun. Shirts. Dresses. Underwear. She doesn't have a fully stocked wardrobe like I do, but it was only a matter of voicing a fucking request.

"Layla." I pause, willing the devil inside me to calm. "You've had enough time on your own. Tonight, you eat with me."

There's another squeak of mattress springs. I picture her shoving from the bed to stand tall, her chin high with defiance, her face unbelievably mesmerizing as it tightens in anger.

"Layla?" I test the handle and taste victory when the lever lowers. Did she forget to lock the door? "I'm coming in."

"Don't," she warns. "I'm not eating with you."

I grin, sinking in to the sound of her voice, loving her strength even though her tone is one hundred percent vehement.

"You've had three days." I continue to plunge the handle, then inch the door open a crack. Anticipation is a motherfucking drug as I creep the barrier between us wider and wider, seeking her out, my vision eagerly scanning past the disheveled four-poster bed to find her standing tall and proud on the other side.

My pulse increases, the dull throb turning into a heavy beat at the sight of her in nothing but a towel.

She's a vision, the peach glow of sunset streaming in through the sheer curtains, the light kissing her perfect skin. I thought maybe she'd look drawn or tired after what I've put her through, but it's the opposite. A warrior glares back at me, ready for a battle I would much prefer to have while we're both horizontal. Legs entwined. Mouths frantic.

"Get out," she seethes.

"You've had three days. Neither of us can afford any more. We need to make plans."

Her chin hikes. There's no protest. She knows I'm right and hates me for it.

"Not tonight," she grates. "I have no clothes."

"I can see that." I rake my gaze from her indignant stare to her beautifully bare shoulders, all the way over her towel-covered curves that stop where the bed blocks the remainder of my view. Then I leisurely trek back up again, appreciating everything I've been denied for the last seventy-two hours.

"Where are your clothes?" I feign ignorance to fill the silence.

"In the washing machine. You may not have realized, but I've been left in here without any luggage. Not even fresh underwear."

"You only had to ask. I've never left you wanting in the past."

Her scowl deepens at my innuendo. "I won't eat with you. You can bring the food to my door like usual and leave me alone."

"Don't get me wrong—I'm a slave to your affections, but I won't be to your demands. Tonight, you either eat with me or don't eat at all."

She scoffs an irate laugh. "Well, I'm afraid your company would only slaughter my appetite. So if you're forcing me to make a choice, I'd rather starve in isolation than in your presence."

My blood boils, only this time it's no longer from frustration alone.

Her defiance is an aphrodisiac. Her lies are like heroin.

She still wants me. I refuse to believe otherwise.

"Then let me raise the stakes by pointing out that the person you can't stand the sight of is also the one who stands between you and the only clothes you have." I smile, smug. "A little civility will go a long way."

Her eyes flash with rage.

"I'll leave you to your solitude, *amore mio*. When you change your mind and want to discuss borrowing my cell to call your daughter, just let me know."

Her face crumples. It's a split second of vulnerability before the warrior expression returns. "You're a manipulative prick."

Yes, I am. But I'm also the victor in this scrimmage.

"And you're still the most beautiful woman I've ever seen." I step back into the hall. "I'll call you once dinner is ready."

4

MATTHEW

I RETURN TO THE LIVING ROOM, BREATHING IN THE SCENT OF GARLIC and basil, then exhale exhilaration and victory.

I should've forced her hand days ago. If only I'd known taunting her was the way to encourage communication.

"He returns without a scratch." Bishop shoots me a two-second glance as he opens a packet of pasta. "Color me surprised."

I divert my path to the cutlery drawer to begin setting the table. "She's eating with us tonight."

"That's going to be a hard pass from me, brother. I won't be hanging around to ingest your dramatics. You two can duke this out on your own."

Even better. I don't want an audience.

He doesn't understand my infatuation. How could he? He never plunged to the level of darkness I did. He doesn't need a lifeline like I do.

The things we did for Lorenzo didn't affect him the way they did me.

He took the brutality in his stride while each murder chipped away at my humanity until I was hollow. The more sterile I became on the inside, the more my outward facade morphed. I could schmooze and seduce without flaw. Lie and manipulate without hesitation.

Killing was no different.

With every criminal act, I learned to dissociate from the kid I once was. To despise the world and everything in it.

Until her.

She made me feel again. Lust returned. Longing surfaced.

"When are we going to discuss why she's still with us?" Bishop adds salt to the bolognese sauce, then stirs the pasta.

"Later." One hurdle at a time.

I need to retrieve the knives I stabbed into the backs of those I trust one by one. I can't have everyone despise me at once.

"Stalling isn't a good look for you." He turns and grabs bowls from a cupboard. "Whatever you've done, you're only compounding the issue by not telling me."

"I'm not stalling." I stalk for the table to lay two place settings. "There's nothing to worry about." Just as long as I win her back.

"For once, you're not a good liar, Langston. You're losing your touch."

I return to the kitchen, disregarding his attempt to goad me into a confession. "How long until dinner, asshole?"

"A few minutes."

I grab a bottle of wine from the fridge and pour Layla a glass. It isn't until I place her drink on the table that I realize liquor is a necessity to curb my rampant tongue, and return to the kitchen to retrieve the bottle and another glass.

"You're on edge." Bishop strains the pasta without looking at me. "What is it about her that messes with you? Is it the sex? Or the thrill of her family legacy? Because I can understand how excep-tional fucking can drive a man to his knees, but this—"

"Nothing about her messes with me." It's another lie. One hundred percent fiction.

Absolutely everything about her tinkers with the cogs of my soul.

He slams the strainer into the sink, his forehead etched with a severe frown. "Lie to me one more time, motherfucker. See where it gets you."

He's right. He deserves better. "Let me get through tonight and I'll explain everything."

His eyes narrow. "Are you lying to me again?"

"Tomorrow, we'll talk." I place the wine bottle and glass on the table, then head to the island counter, ignoring his scrutiny. "And I'll return all my missed calls."

I'll right this derailing train. Just as soon as Layla is back on my side. In my arms.

His only response is to snatch one of the bowls from in front of me to start serving the spaghetti. "You might want to call your woman. Dinner's ready."

My woman.

The title strokes my ego. If only it were true.

"*Layla.*" I raise my voice. "*Dinner.*" I keep my back to the hall, my ears alert for the first sign of her submission, my blood simmering.

Three bowls are filled with pasta, and still, I don't hear a shift of movement.

"You sure she's coming?" Bishop rinses the pot and places it in the dishwasher before moving to the stove with his wooden spoon.

"She's coming." She'll join me, even if I have to drag her to the table by that damned towel. I won't go another day with my actions hanging over my head. I'll make her understand.

The faintest click sounds from the hall, then the soft pad of bare feet on tile leisurely approaching.

I grin, keeping my back to her arrival. "See?"

Bishop glances at me, his gaze then diverting over my shoulder. "*Jesus fucking Christ.*" He drops the spoon to the counter, the spaghetti sauce splattering over the marble as his jaw snaps shut.

She's done something. Instigated some sort of defiance to temper her battered ego.

I'm so fucking tempted to look.

Instead, I keep my attention on Bishop, trying to determine what sort of threat she poses.

I don't care if she found a makeshift weapon. She can threaten me all she likes. I'd actually enjoy a sparring match.

"A little help here," he mutters, reclaiming the wooden spoon to shove it into the spaghetti sauce. "I'm over this shit."

I succumb, hating how it takes such little encouragement to turn and look at her.

To look at absolutely *all* of her.

She saunters toward the dining table, entirely naked, her hair loose around her shoulders, her arms comfortably at her sides.

Not one stitch of clothing covers her delectable flesh. She's bare to me. To Bishop. To *anyone* who might happen to walk along the beach and glance up at the wall of glass she currently walks before.

"Which seat is mine?" She stops before the table, her expression haughty, her tits perky.

At one time, I would've enjoyed this performance. When she was mine, I reveled in the hunger she awakened in other men. I fucking thrummed every time someone glanced in appreciation at the enviable prize on my arm.

Now she's just another thing I've lost, and the blatant display acts like a knife between my ribs.

It's the perfect power play.

"*Leave,*" I snarl at Bishop.

"If you think for one second that I'm not trying to get my ass out of here as fast as fucking possible, you're an ignorant piece of shit." He slaps a spoon full of bolognaise onto his pasta, then snatches a fork. "Enjoy your fucking meal."

Layla blinks back at me, composed and confident as Bishop storms from the room. She's so fucking beautiful, her chin high with poise, her lips curved in spite.

It's a facade. One I fall victim to regardless.

She's always been hesitant when it comes to exposing her sexuality. Weeks ago, she'd been a skittish kitten when a member of the hotel staff walked in on us in the bath.

This is all an act. A well-planned strategy to push me off-balance.

I finish serving our meals and grab the bowls. I pretend I'm not approaching pure temptation and sidle up beside her, deliberately getting close enough for my suit jacket to brush her arm as I place her meal down in front of her.

"I feel overdressed." I keep my voice in check, no lust or frustration evident as I pull out her chair. "You should've warned me. I could've followed the dress code."

"It's not too late," she drawls. "And it's not like your appearance can disgust me any more than it already does."

I fake a snicker. "I don't think now is an appropriate time to remind you of how hard you make me." I walk back around her, pausing on her other side to lean close to her ear. "And besides, I prefer this dynamic. Having you exposed and vulnerable while I'm fully dressed is a fantasy I never knew I had."

"That's where you're wrong. You're no longer in a position to make me vulnerable." She sidesteps to take her seat. If it weren't for the way she quickly grabs for the glass of wine, I'd almost believe her confidence.

"And why is that?" I place my bowl on the opposite table setting and slide into my chair.

"Because my vulnerability has only ever been exposed by people I care about, and you're no longer on that list."

This time, my chuckle isn't only fake—it's forced. "You've switched from love to loathing in such a short space of time, *amore mio*. Are you doing okay with the whiplash?"

She gives me a viperous smile and takes another sip of wine. "Thank you for your concern, but I'm doing just fine."

This isn't the conversation I planned to have. The mood and tone are all wrong. Yet I can't stop lapping up her venom. Each taste brings exhilaration.

My desire for her is already mutinous. Barely manageable. My palms sweat with the need to touch. I have to taste her. Breathe her in. Even with her vicious energy.

I incline my head and grab my fork. "Well, I appreciate you joining me."

"Are you under the misconception I had a choice?" Her tone is friendly even though the question drips with resentment.

"There's always a choice."

She bats her lashes. "As much as I'm enjoying this display of truly deplorable acting, we both know you took away my power to decline your offer when you mentioned my ability to call Stella."

I raise my brows and nod thoughtfully, spinning the tines of my fork into the spaghetti. "So I guess what you're saying is that you *are* still vulnerable to me."

Her facade falters with the brief flare of her nostrils.

She concedes a pawn in this provoking game of chess.

I raise my fork and take a bite, filling my mouth to lessen my victory grin as our gazes remain locked.

She doesn't eat though. She merely sits there, more than likely tweaking her mental strategy as she remains silent.

"I appreciate the eye contact, *amore mio*." I grab my wine glass and take a sip. "I'm not sure how I could remain a gentleman with such an exquisite temptation seated before me if it weren't for those hypnotic eyes."

"Let's not continue the sham that you've ever been a gentleman, Matthew. We both know you're nothing but a monster." She cocks her head and frowns. "Or should I say *butcher*?"

I take another sip—slow, drawn, smooth.

I won't hand over one of my chess pieces so easily. "Both are fitting. Although, I will argue that I've always been a gentleman to you."

"No, you've always been a liar."

"We both lied, Layla. We're even in that regard."

She scoffs and settles back into her chair, crossing her arms beneath her breasts, plumping them, attempting to use temptation to her advantage.

I don't look. Not directly. I let those luscious mounds taunt my periphery, the tease of nipples making my mouth salivate as I fork another mouthful of food.

I chew and swallow. Chew and swallow. I allow the silence to wrap her in a false sense of security while she remains poised on her mantle of superiority.

She's getting to me, though. With each poisonous retort, I fall victim to the brain fog of lust. I crave her capitulation. I need her to admit that she feels more for me than the animosity she's portraying.

What we had can't be extinguished by a few mistruths. Especially not when we were both duplicitous.

"I hope you're not getting cold." I fork more food and make a strategic surrender, lowering my gaze from those fathomless eyes to leisurely trek downward. I skate my attention from her lips to her collarbone, then farther to those perfectly ample breasts.

I can still taste the salt of her skin. Can still remember the deliriously soft texture.

She would moan whenever I sucked her nipples. She'd shudder.

Now, though, her breathing is calm. Measured. The only sign I'm having any effect on her is the wash of goose bumps that awaken under my gaze.

"I'm fine." Her civility wavers, her tone gaining a hint of annoyance.

"Are you sure?" I gradually return my attention to hers with a slight lick of my lower lip. I don't need to pretend I'm attracted to her. *Tempted* by her. That part of our relationship never held a hint of deception. "I could give you something to wear."

She grows an inch with my offering.

Are you handing over another pawn, amore mio?

She lowers her focus to my jacket and gives a subtle clearing of her throat before returning her gaze to my face with the Stepford act falling back into place. "That would be appreciated."

I lock my jaw, determined not to cluck my tongue as I steal her rook.

She came out here ready to instigate war and backtracked before swords clashed.

"Like I mentioned earlier, you only had to ask." I place down my fork, then slide a hand over my tie to slowly loosen it from around my neck.

She watches with interest, eyeing my shirt, no doubt anticipating the rich fabric resting against her shoulders. Would she appreciate my scent against her skin, too?

She remains still, her brows furrowing as I raise the tie over my head and slide it toward her.

"You're welcome," I purr.

I witness the moment my intent sinks in. When she realizes the only clothing I'll afford her is a thin slip of fabric.

Her tightly restrained anger is a work of art.

A masterpiece.

Her cheeks hollow. Her lips lose their color. She reaches for her fork, her fingers white with the tightness of her grip.

Go on, amore mio. *Bite. Sink those teeth into me. Let me have your rage.*

"I don't understand the hesitation?" I drawl. "You wanted something to wear, so put it on."

Her glare is gradual. From picture-perfect princess to viperous hellion in long, stretching heartbeats. She raises her feral stare, nailing me with undiluted fury. "I changed my mind."

"Put it on, Layla." I add an edge of malice to my tone. I'm more than happy to do this her way. We can fight, then fuck, then put this bump in the road behind us. "*Now.*"

She doesn't move. The only action she takes is to narrow her eyes, intensifying her hatred.

"Interesting." I reach into my suit jacket, pull my cell from the inside pocket, and place the device on the table. "After sauntering out here in your current state, I thought you were willing to do whatever it took to speak to your daughter."

"You're a fucking bastard."

I shrug. "And you're a tempting goddess. We use what we have." I slide my fork into the pasta and twist. "Now put on the tie."

Her evil eyes attempt to burn me to the ground as she glares and glares and glares some fucking more. I'm sure she's about to grab her bowl and lob it at my head when she snatches the slip of fabric from the table and tugs it over her head, muttering a string of unintelligible delight under her breath.

She's gorgeous when outraged. Turbulent and unpredictable.

She might not realize it, but I've never cared for her more than I do right now. I'd protect this spitfire with my life. I'd carve her name into my skin to let the world know she owns every inch of me.

The tie settles between her breasts as she gathers her hair out from beneath the material and resettles the strands behind her back, her glower pinning me the entire time.

"It looks good on you." I grin. "Now eat."

"No, thank you," she grates.

"Would you prefer if I fed you? Because I will." My pulse spikes with possibility. I'd sit at her side, her hair in my fist, a fork in the other. I'd feed her gently. Patiently. And with every insolent remark she made, I'd whisper in her ear all the punishments I had planned once her belly was full.

"I already told you I'd lose my appetite if I had to share a meal with you."

"Don't tell me I misjudged your intelligence." I raise a brow. "I thought you were smarter than this."

"Meaning?"

"Denying what your body needs hurts nobody but yourself. You'll lose strength and focus. Malnourishment will only make it harder for you to find a way out of your situation. What you should actually be doing is taking every possible action to increase your chance of success... That is, if you want to get out of your predicament. But maybe remaining with me is what you truly want." I fork another mouthful.

"Monstrous and delusional." She scoffs a barely audible breath. "God, I'd love to know what lies you told my brother to add to his reasons for disowning me."

"Maybe he didn't disown you. Maybe he understands what you need more than you do and left you here to find happiness." *There.* She has the truth. I can't be held accountable for leading her astray.

"Happiness?" Her laughter increases, her breasts jolting with faux mirth. "You're a punishment, Matthew. A sickening, loathsome form of torture."

"You told your sister you were falling in love with me."

The briefest glimpse of pain pinches her features before anger reclaims supremacy. "I fell in love with a man who doesn't exist."

"He could exist, *amore mio*. I can be that man for you. I can be whatever you need." I want nothing more than to be the embodiment of the man she gave her heart to. To be trustworthy. Honorable. A successful businessman instead of a proficient murderer.

All it would take is a little more time to chip away at the brutal default settings that have been cemented in place.

"The only man you know how to be is a pathological liar."

"Pathological is a stretch. I assure you I had a motive for each and every instance of deception." I force another mouthful of spaghetti.

"I'm sure you had a whole string of motives, but none of them would make your actions excusable."

"Without those actions, we never would've existed."

"And the world would've been a far better place."

She doesn't mean that. Her anger is a front for her pain. Her temper is a vain attempt to hide how much she still wants me. And she *does* want me. I can see it in her eyes. The heat remains there, flickering and wild.

"All you need is a reason to forgive me and I can give that to you, too." I place the napkin back on the table and hold her stare. "My actions were a direct result of my infatuation. I would've done anything to keep you close, and I still will, because you're every-thing to me. I'm lost to you, Layla. Life without you isn't some-thing I'm willing to concede to."

5
───────

LAYLA

I STEAL MYSELF AGAINST HIS ADMISSION.

Thought by thought, brick by brick, I frantically build my walls higher against his seduction. I remind myself of what he's done. I relive the hypocrisy. The malignance.

But it's hard.

Even now, with hatred swimming in my veins, I can't switch myself off to his charm.

That's why I stayed in my room for three days. I needed the time to assemble my defenses. It's also why I came out here in my current state of undress.

I'd hoped to distract him from the wicked way he weaves me around his little finger. That my body would leave him tongue-tied and disheveled. That for once, I could be the reigning force. The superior. A victor.

Instead, I've achieved the opposite.

He's far more confident and cunning now. Each retort seems perfectly constructed, as if spoken from a playbook, while I struggle to keep a grip on my hectic emotions.

The conversation I hoped we would never have is now tormenting my ears, his words of adoration stripping layers from my shield.

I'd treasured him. With all my heart, I'd *loved* him.

"You've owned me from the first night we met." He holds my

stare, those dark eyes exuding sincerity I refuse to believe. "I knew it wasn't a coincidence that this beautiful woman walked into Perfezione not once, but twice, to spy on the same man I despise."

"Your *father*," I correct.

"Bishop approached you at my request." He ignores my strike with ease. "I needed to know what you were up to. Who you were. Where the hell you came from. But you looked at him in fear, and the sight sickened me."

"It mustn't sicken you now, because you certainly haven't lost your appetite."

"You don't fear me. A scared woman would never choose to walk out here the way you did. Instead, I'd place a substantial wager that you've enjoyed triggering my desire. And then there's that sharp tongue of yours." He rakes his teeth over his lower lip as his gaze devours me. "I don't like that I've earned your spite, but I'll be honest in admitting how fucking hard it makes me."

"If you ever talk to me about being hard again, I'll make sure your body can no longer facilitate the function." I struggle to regain my synthetic smile. To pretend I'm unfazed. Dauntless.

He grins, calling my bluff. His composure spits in the face of my tumultuous pulse. "If the task involves placing your hands around my dick, it might just be worth it."

I increase the brittle curve of my lips and grab my fork in a clenched fist. "Then get it out, big guy. Let me take a stab."

He takes a sip of wine. "I don't think your viciousness is having the effect you want it to."

I know it's not, and it's fucking killing me. He needs to take me seriously. To be scared of me.

"Give it time, *amore mio*. I'm certain I'll earn your forgiveness."

"And I'm certain I'd prefer to see you dead."

His brows pinch. "You don't mean that."

I know. But I wish I did.

I'd give anything to be able to treat him with the same callous disregard he gave me while I was falling for him.

"You had me mugged." I speak through clenched teeth. "Tell me, Matthew, what would've happened if I didn't give up my purse? Would you have had me beaten instead of shoved into a wall? Did my attacker have permission to rape as well as ransack?"

He raises his chin, his eyes hardening. "He was never meant to lay a hand on you."

"But he did. My face was bruised—"

"And he paid for his mistake. I know that doesn't improve the situation, but the lengths he went to were neither planned nor excused."

Curiosity twists my stomach. I shouldn't ask, yet the words escape my lips without consent. "What did you do to him?"

He doesn't look away. Doesn't flinch or waver under the question. "What do you think a man like me would do?"

A chill sinks under my skin.

"A man who was already irrevocably obsessed with you, Layla. *Enslaved* by you."

I swallow over my drying throat, hating the idiotic thrill that sweeps through me at the stupid thought of him taking vengeance against a man he contracted in the first place. "Forget it. I don't want to know."

"Are you sure? I thought you'd want the truth. *Honesty*. To learn the *real* me." He leans back in his chair. "I made him understand your worth. Your significance. I used the knives and blades that had once been my calling card to ensure—"

"That's enough." I drop my fork, the silverware clattering to the table.

"I disagree. You need clarity for us to get back to where we once were."

"When have I given you the impression there was even the slightest possibility of going back?"

"We *will* get back to where we were, *amore mio*." His voice becomes a threatening growl. "I won't accept any other outcome."

The chill escapes me, the coldness eviscerated by white-hot rage. I shove to my feet, the chair scraping loudly behind me, the stupid fucking tie acting like a pendulum between my breasts. "I'm done with your delusions."

I'm about to storm for the bedroom when he reaches for his cell, subtly tapping the device with his pointer finger

"Are you sure?" He looks up at me. No smirk. No anger. Just pure confidence in those chocolate eyes.

Fuck him.

He knows it's been days since I spoke to Stella. I have no idea what Cole has told her. I don't know where she is. Or if she's protected. I've had to rely on the assumption that my brother continues to cherish her safety even though he's discarded mine so easily.

"There's no going back from what you've done." I stand tall, trying hard to remain confident with my nudity while his tie begins to feel like a noose. "You arranged for me to be mugged. Then had the audacity to sleep with me. And that was just the tip of your duplicity."

"You're wrong." He sits straighter. "I didn't sleep with you that day. I deliberately kept sex off the table even though, if memory serves, you begged for me to fuck you. Instead, I gave pleasure and tortured myself in return."

After everything he's done, he still has the nerve to claim *he* was the one being tortured?

I want to hurt him. *Kill* him.

"Every moment we spent together was a well concocted fallacy." I push the words through clenched teeth. "You acted surprised when I told you about the cyanide—"

"I *was* surprised. Not that you had it. But that you owned up—"

"You lied and pretended and conned," I speak over him. "You deceived and distorted. You were sly and cunning and cruel."

"Because I adore you," he states simply. "And you began to feel the same about me. I gave us a chance at being together and had every intention of telling you the truth. In my own way. In my own time. If it weren't for Remy—"

I slam my fists on the table, rattling the bowls and cutlery. "Remy's appearance changed nothing. His *existence* was the problem. His *genetics*. The fact he's your *goddamn brother* and was involved in my husband's murder." I scream at him, my face hot, my blood boiling. "You made me worship a fictional character. I loved a man that was make believe."

He pushes from his seat, poised and confident. "And I'll make sure you feel the same about the real me."

My heart skips a beat. I'm not sure if it's in fear or frustration. Rage or resentment. But the tempo in my chest pauses a moment only to kick back at a manic pace.

I suck in a slow breath, begging my pulse to calm, my lunacy to ease. "It doesn't matter what personality you present. I won't stop hating you. And once I finally figure out my next move—after you did such a fantastic job of ruining my life—I hope to God I never see you again. Do you understand me?"

His lips thin. His shoulders stiffen. Everything about his expression is tight, especially the skin over the faint swelling on his cheek from my brother's attack.

Could I have finally gotten to him?

"Now I expect you to make good on your promise and let me call my daughter."

He's silent, the quiet palpable until he reclaims his seat with equal poise and confidence as when he left it. He grabs his wine glass, takes a lazy, taunting sip, then raises his condescending gaze to mine. "If you expect me to make good on my promise, you need to make good on yours. The deal was that we would eat together. You've barely lifted your fork."

Fucking bastard.

I'll lift my damn fork. I'll stab it right through his mother-fucking jugular.

He doesn't care if I eat. All he wants is power. *Control.*

"I'm not hungry." I enunciate each word in a slow, drawn out growl.

"And I don't give a shit." He matches my tone, his mood shifting to menace. "Sit. Eat. Or you don't get a fucking phone call." He leans forward, roughly discarding his jacket to throw the heavy material across the table at me. "And the next time you think it's a good idea to parade around naked, be aware I won't restrain myself. I *will* fuck you, *amore mio*. And you *will* enjoy it."

6

LAYLA

I FORCE MYSELF TO EAT, TAKING DAINTY BITE AFTER DAINTY BITE UNTIL most of my meal is gone.

I don't speak a word. I don't make eye contact.

I scoop and swallow, keeping my composure in check, playing the game.

"You will forgive me." His declaration is barely audible and still has the ability to raise the hair on the back of my neck. "I won't stop until you do."

I shiver, the warmth of his coat doing nothing to shield me from the chilling effects of his commitment.

Why did he have to be the devil? Why couldn't I find a normal man to fall for?

"I've upheld my part of the deal." I place my fork down. "Now can I get my phone call?"

I meet his gaze, being hit hard with emotionless eyes. Even sterile and impassive, he's handsome. So goddamn handsome it makes the contents of my stomach churn. It doesn't help that I'm cloaked in his scent, the deliciously woodsy aftershave sinking into my lungs with every breath.

"One phone call." He slides the cell toward me. "While in this room."

I scoff. "You think I'm capable of calling reinforcements? Who could I possibly rely on that hasn't turned against me?"

"Stay in this room, Layla."

I wait until his hand retreats, then grab the device and push to my feet. I don't waste time dialing Stella's number as I walk alongside the wall of glass, Matthew's jacket dwarfing me.

Each trilling ring makes my heart swell with anticipation. My throat burns with the need to hear her voice. But I can't let her know I'm broken. I won't put her through more heartache. Despite Matthew being a voyeur to the upcoming conversation as he begins to clear the table, I have to pretend my life is peachy. That I'm loving my beach escape with a crazed butcher.

"Hello?" Stella says in greeting. "Who is this?"

Emotion clogs my throat. "Hey, little fish." I force a chipper tone, my bravado painfully flawless. "How are you?"

"Mom? Whose phone number is this? I've been trying to call you. Uncle Cole said you went on a last-minute vacation and might not have cell service. But I call bullshit. You wouldn't go away without telling me. You didn't even send a text."

"Don't curse, sweetheart." I close my eyes against the anxiety in her voice. I've failed her for the millionth time. "Uncle Cole was right. I made a snap decision to go to the beach but I lost my phone at the airport and the cell service here is terrible. I haven't been able to call until now. Is everything all right?"

"Everything is fine. It's just not like you to go radio silent for days. I was worried."

I scrunch my nose against the building tingle. "Forgive me. I've been having such a great time that I didn't realize how many days had passed."

It's been four. I could determine the last time we spoke right down to the hour. But she needs to think I'm happy and healthy. Not humiliated and vengeful.

"Who did you go away with?" she asks. "Last time I came home from boarding school, Tobias overheard Uncle Cole talking about a man you met. Are you dating?"

Pain stabs between my ribs, savage and cruel. "No, we're just friends."

"Are you sure? Because I don't mind." She pauses, the silence heavy between us. "It's been years since Dad passed."

I clamp the cell tighter. "I know. But that's not what this is. I've been going stir crazy at home and just needed a change of scenery. Has anything exciting happened at school this week?" *Deflect, deflect, deflect.* "Are you keeping on top of your homework?"

"Nothing has changed here. Some of my friends were actually about to watch a movie together in the hall... so I've kinda gotta go."

My misery increases with every shallow breath. "Already?"

The clatter of bowls and cutlery carries from the kitchen behind me. Pots and pans follow. It's scripted, as if Matthew wants me to believe he's distracted and not devouring every morsel of my anguish.

"I don't want to miss the start, Mom. Can we chat tomorrow?"

The clog in my throat becomes a jagged rock, threatening to take over my stable tone. "I'll try. But like I mentioned, cell service isn't great here. I'm not sure when I'll be able to speak to you again." I don't know when *he'll* let me.

"That's fine. As long as I know you're okay and having fun, I don't mind. Call whenever you can."

"Okay. Enjoy yourself. And say hello to Tobias for me." I hang my head and pinch the bridge of my nose.

"I will. I promise."

"I love you, little fish." My voice breaks. It's only slight. The start of an avalanche that threatens to buckle me.

"I love you, too. Night."

The line disconnects. My heart wrenches.

But she's all right. Cole weaved fiction for me. I need to be grateful for that. He's still doing everything in his power to shield her from my poor decisions.

I delete the call log from the cell, then let my arms fall limp at my sides as I focus on the moonlight reflecting against the inky-black ocean. I have to figure out what the hell I'm doing. How to redeem myself in the eyes of my family.

Cole said I need to fix my mistakes.

How do I do that? Where do I even start?

"Is she okay?" Matthew approaches.

I wrap his jacket tight around me, needing another barrier against him. "Don't."

"Don't what?" He stops a few feet away, his commanding

frame stalking my periphery. "Don't ask? Don't care? Don't speak?"

"All of the above." I hold out his cell.

He takes the device but those calloused fingers linger on mine. "You need someone to talk to. To vent to."

"Are you serious?" I release a low murmur of a chuckle as I drop my arm back to my side, my laughter increasing as he looks at me in pity. "*You're* the reason I need to vent. You get that, right? *You're* the reason I'm in need of everything right now—clothes, money, safety, shelter. I have nothing. Not a dime to my name or a shred of dignity. All because of you."

"You're safe here. And like I've already said, I can give you whatever you need. All you have to do is ask."

I shouldn't have to beg for the things he took from me.

"Ask, Layla," he murmurs.

No. I was willing to demean myself and jump through hoops to speak to Stella, but I'd rather live in the same clothes for the rest of my life than ask him for help.

"I can take care of you." He steps into my personal space, awakening all my nerve endings.

I smile, scoff, then finally sink into a deep sigh. "Do you not understand your role? Why are you acting like a misunderstood victim when you're the villain? You're vile, Matthew." Handsome and brilliant, yet so incredibly vile. "You're depraved, immoral, and goddamn evil."

The pity slowly seeps from his narrowing eyes, his gaze turning predatory.

I fight against another shiver.

He's looked at me like that before. In the bedroom. Between satin sheets. With his fingers gripping my skin and his teeth scraping my heated flesh.

I hate him for stoking those memories to life. I hate even more that my body welcomes it.

I clamp my mouth shut and glare, hoping the action will stop my tongue tingling.

"I'm depraved?" He inches closer, until we're almost chest to chest. "Immoral? Evil?" He quirks a brow. He's so close I can feel the heat emanating off him, can breathe his essence into my lungs.

"Tell me, *amore mio*, what part of that description turns you on the most?"

He's right. I am turned on.

Despite the hatred and fury, he still makes me burn. But that's muscle memory. A miscommunication between mind and body. It won't last long.

"The devil comes in an enticing package," I purr. "That doesn't mean I'm willing to see past all the pretty ribbon now that your true colors have been exposed."

He leans in, those brown irises unfathomably dark as he peers down his nose at me. "But this enticing package knows how to make you feel good."

He does. Oh, *God*, how he does.

The flashbacks play on a loop in my mind. The pleasure he's given. The ecstasy he's produced. Problem is, he also knows how to shatter me beyond recognition. Heartache has never been more potent. Shame consumes my every breath.

"Get away from me," I seethe, my chin high.

"I can't." He reaches out, gliding a lone finger along the jacket lapel.

I stiffen, my head hating the contact, my tingling limbs exhibiting the opposite reaction, and my heart... *Jesus Christ*, the weak, pathetic organ falters.

It's all a game. He wants me to cave. To submit. What I don't understand is why? To prove he's the almighty conqueror? To cement his victory and my pathetic existence?

Fuck him.

Whatever the reason, I can't lose this time.

I straighten my shoulders, allowing the jacket to gape. I won't let him know I'm daunted by a simple touch. By mere proximity. "I said, get away from me."

His gaze lowers to take in my exposure, the slightest rumble of appreciation emanating from his chest. "I'll never be able to walk away from you, *amore mio*." His finger moves to the edge of the lapel, his skin making contact with mine along the inner curve of my breast.

I clench my teeth against the hardening of my nipples. I swallow over the explosion of rage.

I hate him for this. For the pleasure and the pain.

I despise the lust in his eyes. I loathe the confidence in his touch.

This is how he entrapped me the first time. He made me capitulate to adoration. To being wanted. Desired.

"I'll make sure you don't merely walk," I promise. "You'll run."

His mouth lifts at one side, the grin making me see red. "Do I need to remind you your savagery has the opposite effect to your intentions?" His fingertip brushes my stomach, the touch sparking flames in my belly.

Fuck him.

Fuck everything about him—his enviable looks, his commanding presence, his sinful eroticism.

I never understood ecstasy until he entered my life. I hadn't known what one person could stoke within another from mere words or brief glances. But when we were together—actually connected, body to body—the sensation was unlike anything I shared through years of marriage.

Only now, the zing Matthew provides is coated with a dark undercurrent of violence. A sinister, wicked intent, and I'm ashamed to admit it's all the more alluring.

"Forgive me," he murmurs, his hand trailing lower to my abdomen, then my mons.

I remain still, holding eye contact while he attempts to win me over. *Screw* me over.

I keep myself in check. Levelled breathing. Stiffened stance. I don't show a flicker of the flames he's stoking inside me.

I disassociate from my rampant pulse and aching breasts.

He sweeps his touch farther, his fingers parting to tease along the outer edges of my sex. "Forgive me, *amore mio.*"

My denial comes in the form of silence, the rejection loud between us.

"How can I redeem myself?" His breath brushes my lips, the scent of sweet alcohol teasing my senses. "What do I have to do?"

I fight a shudder, my pussy throbbing. I'm wet, my slickness dampening my inner thighs. "Your death is the only way to gain absolution."

He doesn't react. Not a flinch or a smirk in sight. He continues teasing those fingertips around the outside of my sex, increasing my need for oxygen.

He inches closer, his chest brushing mine as his mouth approaches my ear. "I would willingly die for you, *amore mio*." The delicate sweep of his breath awakens a shiver along my neck. "But not without your forgiveness."

"Then we're at an impasse."

"I guess so." His arms swoop around my waist, lifting me off the floor. I gasp, not only at the abrupt movement but the vacuum of pleasure, as he carries me like a rag doll, backtracking me across the room.

I don't protest. Don't speak. Don't fight.

I take another strategy, letting him think he's in control while I eagerly plan my victory.

He places me down on the table, the wall of glass behind him reflecting what a voyeur might consider a loving moment but instead is a power play.

"Spread your legs," he demands.

"Spread my legs?" I ask slowly, taking my time, splaying my hands on the polished wood behind me, the coat gaping to expose my middle, my breasts on display.

He bites his lower lip, the hunger increasing in his eyes. He's starved for me. Ravenous. "Spread those beautiful fucking legs, Layla. Or I'll spread them for you."

"No, you won't."

He's not in charge here. Neither am I. But he doesn't need to know that.

His nostrils flare. He won't force me. Won't hurt me. Not physically. He prefers to do it mentally, *emotionally*, or he'd get someone else to do his dirty work.

He braces his hands on either side of my hips, looming close. "Do you want me to beg? Is that it? Do you need to hear how much I want to make this up to you?"

It's too late for that.

What I want is his agony. His torture.

Slowly, I spread my legs, giving him more room between my thighs. He acknowledges the feigned acquiescence with the slightest clench of his jaw. He thinks he's winning. Maybe he is.

"*Allevia la mia sofferenza, amore mio, perché non posso stare senza di te.*"

"More lies?" I ask. "Speaking in another language doesn't make your words less deceptive."

"There's no more lies. I can promise you that."

I ignore the clench of my heart, the weak organ demanding my submission.

He places his hands on my knees, gradually sliding his palms higher and higher, making my core throb with the promise of pleasure.

He's so close, those hard eyes mere inches from mine. But he doesn't kiss me. Doesn't attempt to make the connection affectionate. He's smart enough to know I'd never allow that tenderness.

I hold my breath as his touch climbs higher, approaching my sex for a second round of temptation.

He doesn't quit staring at me while those fingers skim the sensitive skin at the apex of my thighs. He doesn't even blink when his thumbs reach my folds to part my flesh.

I bite the inside of my lip, refusing to show appreciation for the burst of tingles. But there's definitely a burst. After three days of unwavering heartache, the suffering keeping me bedridden, this indulgent thrill is an undeniable counterpart.

"I'll spend the rest of my life making this up to you," he promises.

I deflect the agony of his vow with a sinister smile. "Then I guess I need to ensure you don't have much longer to live."

He grins, eyes blazing, a dimple teasing.

God, I wish he wasn't so damn gorgeous.

"You underestimate my dedication." He circles his thumb at my entrance. The slightest movement. The harshest tease. "My devotion would only increase in the afterlife. What else would my spirit want to do other than adore you?"

My pulse falters.

I clench my teeth and remind myself how I got here. That the pleasure is only intense due to the preceding pain.

Focus. Focus. Focus.

He gently glides his thumb inside me. I can't stop my pussy from eagerly clamping around the intrusion. I can't quit staring at the gaze that calls to me like home. He's attempting to infiltrate my heart all over again, to decimate what little strength I have left.

"I can read your thoughts, *amore mio*." He curls his thumb inside me, hooking the digit, circling to find the perfect spot that makes me buzz. "You want this."

He's right.

The pulse in my core thunders. My abdomen heats. And my breasts. Dear Lord, how they throb.

It takes all my restraint not to plead for him to make me come.

"You want *me*." He increases his rhythm, stroking with that hooked thumb, delving it deeper inside.

I don't answer with anything other than a gasped breath. I can't hold it in. My pulse is too rampant. My desire too strong.

I claw my fingers against the table, scratching my nails into the gloss.

It's useless to deny what he stokes inside me. I'm not naive enough to even try. Instead, I continue staring into those fathomless eyes as I roll my hips, grinding into his hand. His breathing increases to match mine, each exhale a muted growl of approval.

He doesn't attempt to deepen the connection. There are no kisses. No lingering touches. He's waiting for permission. For me to cave.

I arch my back, the jacket parting farther to barely cover my shoulders as I thrust my breasts toward him.

His gaze treks the temptation. His tongue swipes out to lick his lower lip. He wants to take this further. Wants to grasp and suck and bite. His restraint only makes me hotter.

I cherish his suffering. Devour it.

"Tell me you forgive me," he growls. "Tell me we can move on."

"Never." I grind harder, faster.

With every roll of my hips, I delight in my progress toward the finish line, knowing he won't reach the same pinnacle with me ever again. I use him, cheapening every heated moment we've shared as my pussy clenches around his fingers, the slickness of my arousal coating the inside of my thighs.

His exhales become animalistic. The heavy rise and fall of his chest simulates a beast in battle. I can sense the stiffness of his cock.

Can practically feel how hard he must be throbbing because every ounce of blood in my veins does the same.

"Forgive me." He pulses his thumb, wilder, sharper, demanding submission I will never give. "For the love of God, forgive me, *amore mio*."

I let my head fall back, blocking out his sickening pleas, the mistruths, and allow my eyes to roll with the approaching orgasm.

I relax into the wave of gluttonous pleasure that overwhelms me, and come with a breathy whimper. Over and over, my core contracts, the thrill consuming my limbs. My heart. My mind.

For the briefest seconds, there's nothing but bliss.

Pure. Effortless. Freeing.

The peace I previously found in him returns as if it never left. The world corrects itself for a few brief moments.

I'm at home. Happy. Alive.

Then with each ebbing pulse of euphoria, reality seeps in.

I blink back to the here and now, where the sponsorship deal for my life is still owned by misery, and sit up straight.

He removes his touch from my body, his eyes intense with potent hunger as he raises a hand to his mouth. He swipes his thumb over his lower lip, coating the darkened flesh with my glistening arousal before deftly licking it away with his tongue.

My breath catches as his eyes close briefly and a low rumble of appreciation hums from his chest. I could come again from the visual alone. Not only his enjoyment of my taste, but the adamant bulge against his pants zipper.

I've always been hypnotized by his want for me. It's a weakness I can no longer afford to indulge, but it's perfect to exploit.

"You were right." I sit straighter, placing a hand on his chest to push him out of my personal space. "I'll concede that much."

His brow raises in question. "How so?"

"You told me not to deny my body's needs. And using you for gratification has me feeling invincible." I pause, waiting for the twinge in his expression that exposes his blindsiding failure.

It doesn't eventuate.

Instead, he regains the devil's look, his mouth tweaking in a sly grin. "You think I didn't know you were attempting to use me?" I stiffen as his gaze rakes over my breasts and lower, his focus stopping at my exposed sex with a breathy snicker. "Believe me, I was well aware this was a third-base hate fuck."

Bullshit.

He didn't know. He had no clue.

"The thing is, *amore mio...*" Slowly his attention raises to mine, his smirk increasing. "You can't use someone when their only goal is to achieve what you've just willingly given. Being able to pleasure you—*taste you*—is a blessing. A goddamn gift. So although you consider yourself the victor, I can assure you my gratification far outweighed your own."

My cheeks flame, the heat seeping down my neck, the defeat burning my throat.

"Aww, you're so sweet." I paste on a smile, not willing to surrender. "But for the sake of this awkward post-coital conversation, I think I'll take my needs to Bishop next time."

He snickers, menacing and low. The pinch of his eyes that tells me I've hit a sore spot. "You'd be giving him a death sentence."

"Are you trying to discourage or entice?" I inch forward until our noses almost meet. "Because I assure you, you've done the latter. Two birds with one stone and all that."

His nostrils flare.

Good.

I'm crawling under his skin.

Goddamn perfect.

We stay there. Breath mingling. Gazes locked.

Dopamine floods my system as rage glazes his eyes. My pulse flutters with the win.

"We're done here." He shoves back from the table, his shoulders tight, his jaw clenched. "Sleep well, *amore mio.*"

"I appreciate the well wishes. But in contrast, I'd suggest you rest with one eye open." I scoot from the table. "You never know who might attempt to slit your throat during the early morning hours."

He repeats the sinister snicker, the sound sending a chill down my spine. "As long as you're making plans to climb into my bed, Layla, I don't care what the fuck you do while you're there."

7

LAYLA

I WAKE TO THE COLD MORNING AIR SEEPING INTO MY SKIN. MATTHEW'S jacket gapes over my naked chest, the soft sheets tangled around my legs.

Cigarette smoke teases my senses, the scent faint yet enough to wake me.

It's dark. No sunlight carries from the yard, but birds chirp, signaling the approaching sunrise.

I fling back the covers and slide from the bed to pad to the glass door leading outside.

Bishop stands a few yards away, facing the ocean, his forearms resting against the deck railing. A lit cigarette hangs from his hand, the tendrils of smoke bleeding into the fading night. He's already dressed, his suit pants and buttoned shirt immaculate as usual. Or maybe he didn't change from yesterday. Maybe he's like me, and this unwanted situation is making it hard for him to sleep.

A gun sticks out of the back of his waistband, the weapon sparking dark ideas that are becoming all the more common since being disowned by my family.

I unlock the door, slide it open, then walk out onto the wooden deck, the chill biting into my toes. "I didn't know you smoked," I murmur in greeting, cinching Matthew's jacket tight around my chest, the hem falling to midthigh.

He keeps his stare on the horizon, the cigarette still dangling from his loose fingers. "Only when the situation demands it." He raises the cancer stick to his mouth to breathe deep, the resulting smoke exhaled in a smooth glide from shadowed lips.

I stop a few feet from his side and mimic his position. "And what situation demands it?"

He shoots me a sideways glance, letting me know I'm the situation. "It's nice to see you've ditched the minimalist fashion sense. I assume dinner went well if you're in his jacket."

"You assume wrong. I have very few options when it comes to clothes." My only outfit remains in the dryer, ready and waiting for me to wear for yet another day.

He returns his attention to the ocean and takes another drag. "When you fuck up your life, I guess you're not one to do it in style." He flicks the half-used cigarette to the lawn, then straightens and walks away.

There's no farewell.

He descends the stairs, disappearing from view, his footsteps receding before I hear the whoosh of a sliding door.

"It's always a pleasure, Bishop," I mutter.

I don't know why I bothered talking to him. I've despised that man from the moment we met. But in hindsight, I didn't understand what his warnings to stay away from Matthew meant.

I thought it was for my betrayer's benefit. Not mine.

I stare at the growing sunrise, begging the breaking dawn to bring answers to where I need to go from here. I have to make a move. To find money, clothes, and a more effective way to communicate with Stella.

You need to learn to clean up the mess you create.

Yeah, there's that, too. I just wish I understood what mess Cole was referring to. I've created a junk yard full of trash and don't know which pile he needs actioned.

Do I have to level the playing field with Matthew, repaying him for the humiliation he caused me and my family? Or was it the discovery of my attempted revenge plot against the Costas that caused my brother to disown me? Do I need to make good on my plan to kill Emmanuel?

I'll happily do both. I just have to figure out how to do it without any money.

Another whoosh of the sliding door sounds from the ground level. Bishop's footsteps follow. He comes into view on the stairs, his scowl hard in the dim light as he holds some sort of material in his hands.

"Here." He continues toward me, then flings the clothing at my chest.

I catch two separate pieces from the air. "What's this?"

"Shirts for you to sleep in." He reclaims his position against the railing, his forearms against the metal, his gun teasing my line of sight. "Don't let Langston see you in them. I'm not taking a bullet to the brain for you."

I nod, understanding his gruffness for what it truly is—a peace offering.

"Thank you." I stare down at the soft cotton, running the material through my fingers. "I appreciate it."

He grunts. "At this point, you're welcome to my entire wardrobe if it means I never have to see you naked again."

My cheeks burn, the heat travelling down my neck. "Don't worry; you won't."

"Good. He's not usually the jealous type, but last night…" He shakes his head. "You shouldn't taunt him like that."

"Why? Do you think he'll hurt me?"

"No. He already hates himself for lying to you."

"He didn't just lie. It was—"

"I don't give a shit about the technicalities—that's for you two to argue. What you need to realize is that when he gives his loyalty, he gives it all. It's not half-assed or temporary. He moves mountains, which is exactly what happened with Lorenzo. He became obsessed with allegiance, doing whatever his uncle asked without a second thought, and he'll do the same to get you back."

My stomach hollows. My chest, too.

I breathe a soft chuckle to dislodge the yearning. "He can't win me back."

"Then prepare to watch the world burn to the ground while he spends the rest of his life failing. He won't give up, Layla."

"If that's the case, maybe I should ask him to start burying bodies. He can do my dirty work for me."

"With Lorenzo, there were too many to bury," he states simply.

My hollowness increases.

I've spent days trying to recall what I once thought were inconsequential headlines about the Butcher Boys of Baltimore. They were a threat on the other side of the country. A part of the underworld too far away to take notice of. Now I wish I'd paid more attention.

"Why are you telling me this?" I straighten. "Do you want me to be scared of him?"

"With your lack of self-preservation, I didn't think you were capable of fear. But you're not in danger, Layla. What I was attempting to inspire was concern for those around you. Now and in the future."

I frown as the building sunrise glows across his face. "What does that mean?"

"He's a ticking time bomb." He shoves a hand into his pocket and pulls out a cigarette packet. "Anyone who gets in the way of what he has planned for you won't survive."

"And what does he have planned for me?"

He shrugs. "God only knows. I'm not even sure what he said to get your brother to walk away."

I'm not certain either. All I know is that it wouldn't have been kind.

It's true Cole and I weren't on the best of terms. But leaving me with Matthew like this had to have taken an unwarranted amount of bad-mouthing from my betrayer.

"I won't be here long." I stand tall with the admission. I'm going to leave. To escape this cage without bars. I just need to figure out a plan.

He scoffs. "Sure you are."

I ignore the dismissal and focus on the birds chirping in nearby trees as the sun breaches the horizon. I should go inside and get dressed, but it's peaceful out here. Almost normal, if only I could force my reasons for being in this place to the back of my mind and simply pretend I'm on vacation.

The sun brings warmth. There's no breeze. Only crystal-clear skies filled with a kaleidoscope of orange, red, and yellow.

Behind us, the scrape of tugged curtains skitters along a track, raising the hair on the back of my neck.

I glance over my shoulder to see Matthew standing at the glass door of his room wearing nothing but boxers, his face an expressionless mask as he glances from Bishop to me.

Bishop doesn't move from the railing. He doesn't react to the threat like I do with my straightening posture, my arms crossing over my chest.

My heart shifts pace, too, the once lazy beat transitioning into a staccato.

Matthew pulls the door open, his hair mussed from sleep, his bare torso a masterpiece of temptingly smooth muscles.

"You two are up early." He keeps his focus on me. "Did you sleep in my jacket, *amore mio*?"

"It's not yours anymore."

He chuckles, his satanic smile making my stomach churn. "Have breakfast with me and you'll earn the use of my credit card to order new clothes."

I'll earn it?

I'll. Fucking. Earn. It?

I clench my teeth. "You told me last night you'd give me everything I need."

"I didn't say it wouldn't come without strings."

I switch my attention to glare at Bishop's profile, waiting for him to give Matthew the lecture on taunting just like he gave me. But the jerk doesn't acknowledge either of us, making that gun in the back of his waistband seem so goddamn inviting as he continues to stare at the sunrise.

"What's wrong, *amore mio*? Can't find the words to ask for what you need?"

"Nothing's wrong." I smile and raise the shirts Bishop gave me. "I've got all I need right here. It doesn't get much better than being able to wear an attractive man's clothes."

Matthew continues to grin, only now it's brittle. Forced.

"I'm going to get dressed." I wink at him. "I'm looking forward to smelling like your best friend all day."

8

MATTHEW

She saunters into her room, my jacket dwarfing her frame as she shuts the door behind her, then yanks the curtain closed.

It takes all my control to remain in place. To not stalk after her. To stop myself from killing Bishop.

"Jesus Christ." He lights a cigarette and takes a drag. "It didn't take her long to throw me under the fucking bus."

"Why did you give her your clothes?" I keep my voice level, not allowing a hint of jealousy to spill free.

"I thought that was the better alternative to seeing her tits again." He keeps his back to me as he takes another long drag, his attention on the horizon. "Was I wrong?"

I clench my teeth, picturing her in his shirt, the smell of his aftershave on her skin. Yes, it's a better alternative, but *my* clothes would've been preferred. *My* scent.

I move to his side, resting my ass against the railing, my gaze remaining on her door. "You're smoking again."

"Desperate times," he mutters.

I cringe. I haven't seen him succumb in years. Not since we were in the trenches with Lorenzo. "Has a set of tits got you running scared? I would've thought you weren't so easy to spook."

He scoffs. "It's not the tits. It's the motherfucker who owns them."

I don't own them. Or her. Maybe I had at one point, but nothing of hers is mine now, and I'm not sure if it ever will be again.

Her hatred is impenetrable. I hadn't wanted to believe it, especially last night while her pussy had clamped around my thumb, her arousal dripping to coat my hand. I'd thought I was winning her over. That desire would be the toppling point for her anger. But she'd walked from the living room with just as much vehement superiority as she'd had when she entered.

"Why are you taunting her?" He pushes from the railing to turn to me. "I just told her to quit doing the same thing, then you waltz out here to start shit again."

I don't know.

There's no strategy. I'm riding the waves here. Up one minute. Free-falling the next.

"Answer me," he grates. "Tell me why we're here. Why *she's* here." He glances toward Layla's room and lowers his voice. "What did you say to her brother? Why did he agree to let you abduct his goddamn sister? Did you threaten him? Are we at war?"

"There's no war." Not yet, anyway. Only time will tell.

"Then what's happening? Why am I playing house with homicidal Adam and psycho Eve?"

"Because I won't let her go."

He rolls his eyes. "That much is obvious. But why did he?"

I don't know. Maybe her brother felt sorry for my pathetic ass. Or maybe he knew only death would stop me from leaving without her. "She loves me."

"She *loved* you. Past tense." He points a menacing finger toward her door. "That right there is contempt."

"I'll change her mind." I pivot to the sunrise and bridge the space between me and the railing, grabbing the cold metal in tight fists. "She was somewhat receptive to me last night."

"If you're talking about your hand all up in her cookie jar, then I'm well aware. I had the misfortune of coming upstairs to return my dinner bowl and got yet another front-row seat to you two going at it." His eyes harden. "Tell me something, Langston, do I look like someone who wanted to be signed up to your OnlyFans?"

The bitter taste of jealousy assails me again.

I've never felt this before. Never come close to wanting to poke out the eyes of my closest confidant just for seeing my obsession naked.

"The correct response is no," he answers for me. "And while we're on the topic of your unhinged mating rituals, can you please clarify why you're fucking baiting her into homicide? Why can't you just give her space?"

"I've decided I prefer carnage to apathy." The former is where I'm at home. In my element. It's a fucking default. "I'm not wasting any more time. I won't let her go."

"And Torian is aware of your barbarian mindset?"

I clench the railing tighter, the brightening sunlight making me squint.

"Langston?" His scowl stalks my periphery. "What did you say to convince him to cut ties?"

"He hasn't cut them." I keep my voice low, ensuring Layla doesn't overhear.

"Are you sure about that? She's under the impression her brother disowned her."

"That's not the case. He's given me thirty days."

There's a beat of silence. A pause of building anger where the call of birds echo from the trees.

"Thirty days for what?"

I stand tall, anticipating his reaction before I voice the admission. "To win her back."

There's more silence. More increasing aggression.

"And if you don't?" he grates.

"Failing isn't an option."

"Well, winning won't be either if you continue baiting her, you stupid fuck. What happens after the goddamn thirty days?"

"Lower your voice," I warn. "He didn't say and I didn't ask."

He steps closer, getting in my face, the cigarette smoke hovering between us. "He didn't say? You didn't fucking ask? Am I just meant to—"

"It's an open-ended deal. If I fail, he gets whatever he wants from *me*. I'll be his to own. Not you. Not her. Just *me*."

He glares. Tight-lipped. Nostrils flared. Then he shoves his free hand into his hair and steps away, turning his back. "You've lost your goddamn mind."

"My life is with her," I state simply.

"She doesn't want you." He swings around to face me, livid, muscles tense. "You burned that bridge and pissed on the ashes. How can you not see that?"

"She'll forgive me." She fucking has to.

He shakes his head, incredulous.

He doesn't understand her value. How priceless it is to have someone who can quieten my demons. Without her, the darkness is clawing its way back in. My restraint toward the outside world is nonexistent.

"You can walk," I offer. "I've said it before, and nothing has changed—leave if you need to. I won't hold it against you. You'll always be my brother."

"Walk?" He grows inches taller with the straightening of his posture. "I can fucking walk, can I? With half your fucking gene pool on the attack and assholes already watching us from the shadows, I can just fucking walk?"

I tense. "Someone's watching us?"

"Yeah." He reaches into his pocket and pulls out a business card. It's pure black. Expensive stock. With one word embossed in the middle in rich font—Hunter. "You're lucky I didn't kill them."

"*Them*? How many?"

"Two. A man and a woman, if the smaller set of shoe prints are anything to go by."

I bite back a curse. "Why wasn't I told earlier? Where are they?"

"I only made the discovery during the early hours of the morning when I went outside for a smoke. They were smart enough to set up camp on the beach outside the boundary fence, just out of range of the security camera. They left the card in their hollowed-out bunker and shoe prints in the sand. There was no threat or attack. At the moment, I assume they only want us to know they're watching."

Shit.

I've failed in hiding her. "How the hell did they find us?"

"The same way we would've found them. Bribe airport staff for flight records, then scour the arrival location. They've probably spent the last three days searching every inch of coastline."

Fucking Cole.

"I'll call Torian." I should've known better than to think he would fade into the shadows while our deal was in play. "I'll get them to disappear." Either by threat or violence.

"Yeah, you do that. And while you're at it, maybe ask your new best friend what will happen after the thirty days are up and Layla still wants you dead."

He's pissed, and I get it. I've complicated his life with no benefit.

But he's also worried. For me. For himself. And given the way he handed over his clothes to Layla, it goes without saying he's worried about her, too.

"I'm going to finally get some fucking sleep." He backtracks toward the stairs. "You two are on your own for a few hours. Try not to kill each other in the meantime."

"I'll pay attention to the security system and wake you if something happens."

"Don't bother. I'll keep my notifications on." He turns and descends the first step. "At this point, I don't trust you to pay attention to anything other than your dick."

I scowl at his back, hating his lack of faith. But I still can't regret the choices I've made in bringing Layla here.

Letting her go wasn't an option. It never will be. He'll understand that in time.

I crumple Hunter's business card in my fist and march into my bedroom to snatch my cell from the bedside table.

I dial the only Torian number I have. The call's answered on the second ring.

"Is she okay?" Keira demands without pause.

My anger stumbles over the concern in her voice. Layla thinks her family hates her, that they disowned her, and I'm the sick motherfucker who hasn't assuaged the misconception. "She's fine."

"Then why are you calling?" A bitter edge creeps into her tone.

"I need to speak to your brother. What's his number?"

"Why?"

I clench the phone tighter, my patience thin. "Because his men are watching us, and I want him to have a clear understanding of what will happen once I get my hands on them."

There's no response. No bite of my meaty threat.

"I'll take your silence as a lack of concern," I grate, "and retaliate accordingly."

"No, you won't… Hold on a second."

There's a rustle of noise, the murmur of undecipherable conversation, then, "Calling to renegotiate terms so soon, Costa? Layla's always been a handful, but I thought you would've lasted longer than three days."

I close my eyes, holding my screaming demons at bay. "I've warned you about calling me that."

"My apologies." He snickers. "What can I do for you? Is my sister's fury more than you can handle?"

"I can handle her just fine, along with the men you sent to spy on us. I just wanted to give you prior warning that I don't treat trespassers kindly."

"There's been no trespassing." His superiority is potent. Sickeningly tart. "They've remained outside your property. Out of view. Layla won't see them."

"They left a fucking business card."

"Out of respect."

"Bullshit." I keep my voice low. "It's out of insecurity. Your men are here because you're second-guessing our agreement."

"My people are there because I'm not hanging my sister out to dry." The correction is multilayered, not only reaffirming his commitment to his sister, but confirming it's not only *men* that are here.

Bishop was right. There's a woman.

"And don't worry," he adds. "They're skilled enough to remain safe despite any threat you might pose."

"This wasn't part of our agreement. Tell them to back off."

"Confining my sister to a bedroom wasn't part of the agreement either."

I wipe a hand over my mouth and pace in front of the bed. This asshole is inching me closer toward the edge of rage. Or maybe it's just my compiling failure. Layla's opened me up to vulnerabilities because I can't function until I win her back. "Your sister is free to do what she likes."

"But she prefers to stay away from you for the most part?"

"I'm giving her space because she *prefers* to tend her wounded pride in private, seeing as though her brother cut her off."

"Listen here, you disillusioned Grim Reaper wannabe. I told her she was cut off for *your* benefit. This wouldn't be a fair fight otherwise, and I intend to *own you* fairly."

He's deliberately provoking me, and I have a hunch the timing is deliberate. All of this—the taunts, the blatant proximity from his people—it's because they were watching last night.

Does he think I'm winning her over?

I fucking wish.

"The only ownership will be mine over your sister. I won't fail, Torian. I can promise you that. I'm sure you've already been informed I made substantial headway at dinner." They wouldn't have known Layla sat at the table naked out of spite. They would've seen her fucking my hand and thought I was on the home stretch. "That's why your spies left a business card. You want to throw me off my game."

"All's fair in love and war."

The line disconnects, turning my blood to lava. I won't let those assholes ruin this for me. The threat alone is enough to send me manic.

Cole has no idea how close I am to breaking point.

I stalk to the hall, then straight to Layla's closed door to yank at the handle.

It's fucking locked.

My frustration detonates with my foot launching at the barrier before I can rein it in.

The doorjamb breaks, the door flings wide, and there she is, lazing on the queen-sized bed, hands behind her head, ankles crossed as her face turns to mine with a raised brow.

She's back in her jeans, but it's Bishop's grey T-shirt resting against the curves of her breasts that acts as a starting siren for another skirmish. She fakes calm, rolling her eyes before shifting her attention to the ceiling, pretending I don't fucking exist.

"It's time for breakfast." I glare. Lock my jaw.

"I'll eat later."

Like hell she will.

I storm inside and stop at the end of the bed, her bare feet within reach. I'm tempted to grab her ankles and force them around my neck. To bury my face between her thighs and feast until she admits defeat. "You can have your meal whenever you like, *amore mio,* but you will sit with me while I eat mine."

She meets my gaze, the narrowed slits of her eyes harsh yet so damn inviting. Her venom is invigorating. Exquisite.

I'd love to fuck her like this. To have her hate me and want me in the same breath. To experience the vicious push and pull. The euphoric pain and pleasure.

"And if I refuse?"

I paste on a smile. "Try it and see. I'd love the opportunity to force compliance."

She mimics my expression and reaches under the pillow beside her to retrieve a steak knife. "And I'd love the opportunity to create a puncture wound."

My dick hardens. *Sick fuck.*

The thought of her with a blade to my chest... at my throat... under my skin.

God, help her.

I grab for her ankle, prepared to drag her down the bed, wanting her violent vengeance. But she snaps her feet toward her ass, scrambling backward on the mattress until she's seated, staring and smirking. "Touch me and pay the price, asshole."

"I touched you last night, *amore mio.*" I stalk around to her side of the bed. She counters by scurrying to the opposite side. "My fingers were buried inside you. You came with very little effort."

"I came because I was fantasizing about your death."

I raise a brow. "A woman with a sadistic kink. We're better suited than I thought. Maybe we should exchange notes on preferred foreplay, because wielding that knife of yours is driving me wild."

She growls and raises her weapon, flinging it toward me.

It's a good throw. Strong. On target. But she didn't aim for body mass, so a simple sidestep has it sailing past me to thunk against the wall before thudding to the carpet.

"Nice try. Next time aim for my heart." I place a hand over the thumping organ. "It shouldn't be hard to find. You own it after all."

She laughs. "You're such a contradiction. You claim you have a heart when you don't even have a soul. Tell me, Matthew. How many people did you slice open to become the Butcher?"

"More than you can imagine."

"Delightful," she drawls. "And how many did you kill?"

I stand tall against my sins. "Enough to wipe out a small village."

"So proud. So psychotic."

"I'm not proud." I won't deny the mental assessment though. "You asked a question and I didn't hesitate in giving an answer. I owe you the truth and that's what you'll get."

"And you expect me to fall for a murderer?"

"You already did." I reach for her across the mattress. "Now walk your ass to the dining table or I'll get you there by whatever means necessary. And trust me, I'll far prefer the second option."

She huffs. Glares. Then slides off the opposite side of the bed to stand facing me. "Fine. But first—do you like my new threads?" She grabs the hem of her shirt, her smile seductive as she raises the material to breathe deep against it. "It smells like Bishop. It feels like he's all over my skin."

Her blow hits its target, creating an eruption of envy beneath my sternum.

I grin through the torture. Clench my molars at the pain. "You're going to smell a whole lot like me if you don't get out of this room."

Her eyes sparkle. She delights in her victory as she takes another deep inhale of Bishop's shirt, taunting me.

If the Butcher is what she wants, I'm obliged to give him to her.

I lunge, jumping onto the bed, obliterating the space across the mattress.

Her delight vanishes. Her eyes bug.

She turns. Lunges. But I'm on her in a heartbeat, my hands snatching her wrists behind her back before she can flee.

"Is this what you want?" I drag her hips flush against my crotch, her heat seeping into my hardening dick. "Don't play pretend and tell me you weren't goading me into this."

"Why am I not surprised you think standing up for myself means I'm begging for assault? I should've known forcing women would make you hot."

"Not other women." I walk her forward, each step marked by her resistance until she's pressed against the wall. "Just you."

History repeats itself. I had her up against my front door in D.C. But back then, her anger was mindless. A tart storm to this fine wine of protest. "When are you going to give in to me, Layla? When will you forgive me?"

"Never." She bucks, her ass rubbing against my erection.

"Do it again," I growl in her ear. "I dare you."

"Get your fucking hands off me," she grates. "I swear to God, Matthew, I'll end you."

"Then end me." I release her wrists, placing my hands on the wall on either side of her head. "Because I'm not going to quit attempting to earn redemption until I no longer see hunger in your eyes."

"There is no hunger." She turns to face me with a scowl. But I still see it. It's right there. The flames of her desire warm every inch of me. "And for all the sane people in the room, can you please explain exactly how you're earning redemption?"

"Ruthlessly, *amore mio*. Just the way you like it."

She raises her chin, denying the truth, pretending she isn't tangled up in the heat of this moment just as much as I am. It's fucking clear she still wants me. *Needs* me. But it's also evident she has to see me suffer for my mistakes.

If only she understood how brutal my demons have punished me for the pain I've put her through.

"Do you want me to knee you in the balls?" she threatens. "I've done it before. I can do it again."

"If you want me to bow before you, you only have to ask. There's no need to attack your favorite asset."

She scoffs.

"I'm not kidding. I'd kneel. I'd bow. I'd kiss your feet." I lean closer, making her inch back into the wall. "Want to know what I did last night after you fucked my fingers?"

"No." She crosses her arms over her chest.

"I resorted to fucking my own hand because I couldn't pacify my desire for you." I'm so close I can taste the toothpaste on her breath, can feel the lust mingling between us. "You've reduced me to adolescence, Layla. You're all I think about. You consume me."

"Such sweet lies." Her smile returns, slow and sinister. "How long did it take your father to teach you how to manipulate women?"

"I must be wearing you down if you're resorting to the lowest of blows." There's a growl in my voice. A resentment I can't hide. "Let me guess—next you'll start calling me by my birth name."

"Is that what it will take to get you out of my face?" She inches from the wall, her cheek grazing the stubble of my jaw as she whispers in my ear, "*Dante.*"

I close my eyes against the violence inside me. "Say it again."

"*Dante.*" There's laughter in her voice.

She's playing a dangerous game. Poking a monster.

I should leave. Back away. Flee.

My hands itch to grab her. Sweat slicks my brow.

And my dick—*fuck*—it throbs for relief. For *her*.

"The Butcher," she whispers. "Dante *fucking* Costa."

Each utterance is a spear through my chest. A savage reminder of what I've lost. What I've endured. What I've fucked up.

"I suggest you stop." I raise a hand, grabbing her throat, my grip firm but gentle. I push her back into the wall, her gasp a gift and a punishment in equal measure.

She's rigid. Stiff as a board. But that hunger is still there. Still right fucking there, energetic and erotic in her eyes.

"Don't keep taunting me, *amore mio*." I lean in, a breath from her lips, our noses almost touching. "You won't like the man I become."

"I don't like the man you already are."

I squeeze gently, her carotid fluttering beneath my fingertips. "Then I shouldn't have to repeat myself again, should I?"

I'd bet my life she's wet. That those pretty panties of hers are seconds from being soaked.

Fucking her right now would be a masterpiece. A callously beautiful disaster. I wouldn't be able to think straight through my need to please her.

"Insults and name calling won't change the way I feel about

you," I murmur close to her lips. "You're mine, Layla. So get used to it."

Her throat works over a heavy swallow beneath my palm. Her tongue sneaks out to quickly lick her lower lip.

I could come like this. Her throat in my hand, her eyes on mine, my dick rubbing against her abdomen. It's goddamn pathetic, but my desire for her is that rich. That cloying. Her temper stokes my lust. Fucking douses it in gasoline.

"Now, I suggest you take your sassy little mouth to the dining table," I warn. "Otherwise, you'll be the one on your knees."

9

———

LAYLA

He releases my neck and marches from the room.

I wait a beat before I buckle against the wall, my pulse wild in my chest, my limbs trembling.

I thrum.

Everywhere.

I can't tell if it's from fear, adrenaline, or a third option I don't want to face even though my nipples are hard and my abdomen throbs.

I need to hate him. With every fiber of my being, I want to look into those dark eyes and see my enemy, but whenever he's in front of me my insides turn to mush. My heart flutters. My stomach free-falls.

I can't wring out the love that still clings to me. It's burrowed deep. Tattooed in my veins.

I remain in place as I curse my stupidity, my breathing remaining rampant, my self-loathing thickening. He messes around in his adjoining bedroom, the subtle squeak of door hinges and bed springs spurring my imagination into avenues I despise.

Then his footsteps trek down the hall, the clap of shoes giving me the slightest relief that he must now be fully dressed.

I hang my head, the tide of failure suffocating me.

I have to get out of here, but I want what he promised me first. I need Emmanuel gone. *Dead.* I just can't keep myself calm enough to demand what I'm owed.

Pans clatter in the kitchen. Cutlery, too.

"*Now, Layla,*" he yells. "Don't make me wait."

I glare and shove from the wall. He's such a fucking asshole.

I stalk from the room, going over the mental checklist of things he's done to me in an effort to regain my fortitude. I relive all the lies. The betrayal. I let the memories strengthen me as I enter the living room to find him standing before the cooktop, his immaculately-tailored charcoal suit doing nothing to decrease his physical appeal.

"Take a seat at the table." He grabs a chopping board from a nearby cupboard. "This won't take long."

I bite my tongue and comply, reclaiming the same seat as last night while he confidently makes the kitchen his bitch. Bacon sizzles in a frying pan. Eggs are cracked and scrambled before being poured into another pan. He slices tomatoes, mushrooms, and spinach, the meal becoming a masterpiece I fast begin to regret rejecting.

His performance is deliberate. He's trying to prove he can provide for me. Nurture.

I don't need the reminder.

But when he walks over with a mug of steaming coffee and places it before me, I succumb to the bribe. I take the offering in both hands while he strolls back to the kitchen, not waiting for praise.

"Will Bishop be joining us?" I ask in a weak attempt to show I'm not daunted by him.

"No." He places two plates on the counter and begins to serve the bacon. "You've risked his life enough for one morning."

"Where is he?"

He doesn't pause in serving our meals, dishing up the scrambled eggs alongside the cooked mushrooms, tomato, and spinach. "Keeping his distance for the sake of self-preservation."

I roll my eyes. "You'd never hurt him."

"Your faith in me is misplaced." He dumps the frying pans into the sink, then grabs the plates and walks toward the table. "I'd hurt anyone who dared to come between us."

I tense, clamping down my body's desire to shiver. I'm not going to swoon over his obsessive bullshit. I refuse.

He places my breakfast down in front of me, a meal fit for a queen, and then takes the opposite seat. "You're welcome."

"Excuse me for not being thankful for your dictatorship."

"You're excused." He cuts into his bacon and takes a bite. "Now, I suggest you eat."

I grab my knife, clutching it like a weapon.

His lips kick up at one side. "You're a slow learner, *amore mio*. You're well aware your threats of violence turn me on, yet you persist with them."

My body is a slow learner, too. The heat between my legs sparks to life all over again.

I lower my gaze to the food and force myself to eat. I fork one tiny piece and then another before succumbing to the deliciousness awakening my taste buds.

Neither one of us breaks the lengthening silence.

I use the passing minutes to pull my shit together, stitching the holes in my restraint thread by unraveled thread.

I should ask for what I want. *Demand* his assistance with Emmanuel. But every time I raise my gaze and meet his waiting stare, my courage vanishes.

I need to work with Matthew to obtain my objective, and that's not achievable at the moment. Not when the pain of my emotional wounds are still raw.

He finishes his meal before I do and stands to clear his plate.

I watch from the corner of my eye as he loads the dishwasher, then retrieves something from the pantry and carries it toward me. A laptop he places within my reach.

I stare at the temptation as he slaps a credit card on top of it.

It's a trick. A trap.

"Consider it a peace offering." He returns to his seat. "Buy whatever you like—clothes, shoes, toiletries. I don't care. But I want your civility in return."

"No deal. I'm not going to be here long enough for an order to arrive."

"Is that so?" He raises a lone brow. "And where do you plan on going?"

Nowhere. *Anywhere.*

"Denver." I hold his dark gaze. "I'm going to finish what I started."

"You won't go anywhere near there without me."

"Then when do we leave?"

The muscles in his jaw tic. His eyes narrow. He's trying to think of something to placate me. To tide me over so he can continue playing these stupid games.

"When?" I demand.

He slides his chair back a few inches and leisurely crosses his arms over his chest, a picture of sophisticated relaxation. "Things have changed. We need a new strategy."

"I'm all ears." I finish the last of my bacon, then place the cutlery on my plate. "Tell me what I need to do to speed this up."

"Be patient."

"That's not possible in my current captivity."

"I'm yet to determine if it's best to approach Lorenzo or if we should do this under the radar."

"And I no longer care about the repercussions to your life if you break your uncle's rules." It's a lie. I *do* care. I *hate* how much. "You promised you would help me. Or was that just another betrayal?"

His nostrils flare. "Fine. We'll discuss this tonight over dinner. For now, purchase the things you need because it's going to take more than a few days to work on a plan that doesn't get us killed."

He's stalling, and he'll continue to do so for as long as I allow it.

"Tonight," I confirm, pushing to my feet to grab the laptop. "No excuses."

"I wouldn't think of it."

My smile is brittle, the edges of my lips tight with malice as I start for the hall.

"Stay where I can see you, *amore mio*."

I pause. A cry of potent irritation builds in my throat.

"Take a seat on the sofa." His chair scrapes behind me. "I'm sick of being kept from that pretty face of yours."

He doesn't trust me not to create havoc while on his laptop. I don't blame him. If I had the know-how, I'd get on the dark web and arrange to have him killed. Maimed at the very least.

I divert my path to the other side of the room and sink onto the leather three-seater.

I start my shopping spree on the bare necessities, just in case I'm unfortunate enough to still be stuck here in a few days. I order underwear and casual clothes while Matthew clears the table and stacks the dishwasher.

I'm on my third website by the time he walks onto the deck to make a call. He talks loud enough for me to hear, approving stock purchases and chatting shop with whom I assume are his staff.

Whenever I glance over my shoulder, it doesn't take long for his eyes to meet mine. His subtle smirk always follows.

I want to slap the arrogance off his face. Instead, I divert my internet browsing into more conniving territory. I splurge on a pair of Gucci sneakers. I one-click designer clothes, red-bottom shoes, and expensive makeup.

Every time our gazes clash, I add another over-priced luxury to my cart.

I'm well aware I won't get the opportunity to wear the four hundred-dollar Guerlain limited edition satin-red lipstick he just bought me. My body won't be adorned in the thousand-dollar La Perla black silk camisole with macramé frastaglio. And the La Prairie White Caviar Creme will never kiss my skin. But every purchase coats my tongue with the sweet taste of revenge.

I luxuriate in the shopping spree, drinking coffee with my legs stretched along the sofa while Matthew prowls the deck like a panther.

By brunch, I've spent five figures.

By midday, I'm inching closer to ten.

I invest in limited edition books from authors I haven't heard of. Signed memorabilia gets added to the list from major sporting clubs I didn't know existed. And the pièce de résistance is how I've memorized his credit card details, the digits firmly secured in my mental bank for safe keeping.

"What are you up to?"

I jolt, snapping my gaze toward the sound of Bishop's voice to find him approaching from the hall.

He glowers. "Did I scare you?"

"Not in the slightest."

He continues into the living room, his disapproval raking over the shirt I'm wearing before turning toward Matthew on the deck. "I'm going for a drive. Do you want me to get you something to eat?"

My stomach squeezes. I'm unsure if it's from hunger or trepidation. "Can I come with you?"

He looks at me as if I'm scum on the bottom of his shoe. "You're kidding, right?"

No, not kidding at all. "I don't want to be left here with him."

"Well, you probably should've thought about that before you decided to wear my fucking clothes in front of him after I told you not to."

"He doesn't care." I click the final order button on my most substantial purchase and close the laptop. "He knows I only put it on to annoy him."

"Is that what he said?" He scoffs. "Come on, Layla, you're not that naive. His temper would be soaring beneath the surface."

I follow his gaze to where Matthew watches us from his position near the railing, his cell still plastered to his ear. There's no hint of any temper as he stares inside. There's no hint of any emotion at all with his smirk no longer in place.

"I assure you," Bishop continues, "every second my clothes are on your skin, he's imagining how to rip them off."

Matthew strolls forward, headed for the door.

"See?" Bishop glares at me. "He can't even stand us being alone in the same room. Don't say I didn't warn you."

The door is flung open, Mr. Calm and Casual walking inside. "Yes. I'm keeping an eye on it," he speaks into his cell. "I'm not concerned, but let me know if we approach the limit."

My stomach fills with unwanted butterflies as he disconnects the call and places the device in his inner jacket pocket, his attention fixed on Bishop.

"You're awake."

Bishop juts his chin. "I am. I was about to go for a drive and find something different to eat."

"And I'm going with him." I place the laptop on the seat beside me and stand.

Matthew's lips thin. "No, you're not."

"You're not my keeper."

"Aren't I?" His brow raises, the haughty expression hacking into my restraint. "When you've got no money or support outside these four walls, I wouldn't test that theory. You might not like the outcome."

"I'm leaving." Bishop turns for the entry. "For the love of God, could you two sort your shit before I return? I'm fucking sick of the ping-pong match."

He disappears into the far hall, Matthew's presence becoming all the more suffocating the closer we creep toward being truly alone.

"I'm going to my room." I leave the laptop and credit card on the sofa to flee.

He doesn't answer. Doesn't follow.

Thank God.

I count down the minutes until dinner in my room, lazing on the bed, my back against the headboard, a pillow clutched to my chest while new phone conversations murmur from the living room. I can't even close the door properly to give myself privacy because the super villain broke a piece of the latch with his entrance earlier.

The longer I spend here, the worse it gets.

The increased suffering. The prolonged pain.

But after tonight I'll have a blueprint for freedom. Once plans are in motion for Emmanuel, I can figure out the rest. I'll get home using Matthew's credit card details, and from there I have my own cash stashed in a safe. At least enough to tide me over until I determine how to make amends with my brother.

This is the homestretch.

"*Amore mio,*" Matthew calls in a chastising tone. "I need you to come out here."

"I'm busy."

"Would you prefer if I came to your room and we picked up where we left off?"

I sigh and fling the pillow to the other side of the bed, then storm for the hall and enter the living room with a huffed, "*What?*"

He glances at me from his position near the dining table, his eyes playful as they settle on mine. That's all it takes to rile me up again. My blood turns scorching. My heartbeats are frantic.

"You look tired," he drawls. "Your shopping spree must have been exhausting."

"Not at all." I place my hands on my hips, my fingers clawing into my jeans. "Spending your money came naturally."

His grin is subtle, the softest curve of the most enticing lips. "So I've discovered."

"Checking up on me already? Where's the trust? Where's the love?"

He chuckles, the sound almost friendly as he prowls toward me. Predatory and sleek. I stiffen, my pulse increasing, the closing proximity making my throat dry.

"I wasn't checking up on you. The bank called for a second time, wanting to confirm if your last purchase was legitimate before they approved the transaction."

"It's legitimate." I don't falter even though I've been caught red-handed.

"I didn't take you for a Tesla kind of woman."

"Well, you also thought I was someone who would forgive and forget, so your analysis of me has never been accurate." I hold his gaze, those confident eyes consuming me.

He doesn't flinch. He holds himself in that arrogant state of command while I'm forced to look away, turning my attention to the waves, willing the ocean to consume me.

I despise the exquisite aftershave that penetrates thick and rich in my lungs, the erotic scent of sandalwood reawakening unwanted memories.

I stand frozen as he reaches out, his fingertips the most delicate brush against my skin as he guides a stray strand of hair behind my ear. "How long are you going to keep punishing me?"

The question cuts deep. The vulnerability in his tone. The plea in his words.

"Forever," I whisper.

He takes liberties with more of my hair, brushing additional strands from my cheeks. Excruciatingly slow. With brutal gentleness.

I want to scream for him to stop, to leave me alone, but I can't even back away. His touch is a vise I can't deny.

"Why can't you accept my apology?" he murmurs.

Because it hurts too much. Because his betrayal cut far deeper than any other.

I'd let down all my guards for him. For *us*. I'd handed him my vulnerability in a ribbon-covered package and he'd set the threads to flame.

"I'd kill kings for you, *amore mio*. I'd betray gods." His words are poetry, articulated with reverence, evoking weakness. "I'd slit my wrists if it would make you happy."

I raise my chin and meet his gaze, his regret-filled eyes slicing right to my marrow. "It would."

He holds my stare, reading me, scrutinizing, his hand falling to his side. "Then so be it." He turns and walks for the kitchen, shucking his jacket along the way to throw it onto the island counter.

He pulls open a drawer, the clink of cutlery harsh as he snatches a paring knife and places it on the counter. "You want a physical wound to make up for your emotional pain?" He faces me, his hand aggressively yanking at the button on his shirt cuff. "Then will you forgive me?"

"Stop being dramatic."

"All I'm doing is clearing up any misconception that there are limitations to my apology." He aggressively folds his sleeve to his elbow, then reclaims the knife. "You want my suffering, so I'm offering it to you. Would you like to do the honors?"

I keep my mouth shut. He won't go through with it.

"Layla?" My name is a warning. "You or me? Tell me how to do this right to get you to forgive me."

My heart clenches, the tormented organ threatening to wither and die.

I want him in agony. In anguish. I want him withering with the misery that his lies have created. But I also can't stand to see him in pain. I'm too weak. Too fucking pathetic.

"Don't falter now. If this is what you need, take it. Slice me. Stab me. Cut me into a thousand pieces."

I cross my arms over my chest. "I know you're bluffing."

"Like hell I am. I'm standing here, willing to give you whatever the fuck you need to forgive my sins. And you've seen me naked enough times to know nobody else has gotten close enough to leave a scar. You'll be the first. The only. Then I'll have the privilege of having a physical injury to match my internal misery because even though you don't want to believe it, *amore mio*, I'm fucking suffering just like you."

I glare, unwilling to fall victim to the sincerity in his tone.

He's lying. Manipulating. He's taunting me with the offer of violence because he knows I could never follow through.

"Then do it yourself," I grate.

"As you wish." He swivels the three-inch blade toward his arm and buries it in his flesh.

Bile screams up my throat. Panic takes over my pulse. And all he does is stare at me. Questioning. Silently asking if the steel embedded in his forearm is enough.

"Want more?" He retrieves the knife, sending a trail of blood over his wrist to spill to the tile.

"No." I tremble. Shake.

I'm livid and sickened and weak.

"I can make a lengthy gash this time." He looks down at his injury. "Straight down the vein instead of a flesh wound. Blood loss might be your best friend. There's no hospital within forty miles."

"Stop it." My heart screams for me to go to him, to check the damage and quit this stupidity. It's my head that keeps me in place. My pride. My self-preservation.

"This is what you asked for." He starts toward me, crimson streaming down his arm and along his hands, leaving a spotted trail behind him. "It's what you want." He holds the knife for me to take, the hilt coated in blood.

He knows I won't grab it. He knows I'm a coward.

I hate myself for it. The disgust eats at me. Gnaws.

"Take what you need, Layla."

Tension forms beneath my sternum. "Nothing will fill the gaping hole you created." My voice fractures. "No stab wound. No amount of bloodshed."

His jaw hardens, but his eyes are pained. Pleading.

I wish his vulnerability repulsed me. Instead, his suffering makes mine greater. "I trusted you."

"I know."

My palms itch to slap the undeserving sorrow from his face. "I *loved* you."

His chin raises before he nods.

He's doing it again. Manipulating me. Molding reality.

"*Stop it*," I snap. "Stop acting. Stop pretending like you give a fuck."

"I'm not. I'd do anything for you."

Agony screams inside me, bursting to break free. The pressure intensifies. The insanity builds.

I snatch for the knife. He doesn't protest. The handle slides into my palm slippery and wet. I raise the blade to his neck, his eyes on mine as I hold the threat bare millimeters from his skin.

I could end this with a nick of his carotid. I could kill Emmanuel's golden child. His firstborn. I could do what Cole asked of me and make up for the mistake of trusting a stranger. A *butcher*.

"Do it, Layla." Matthew slides his hand over mine, strengthening my threat against his neck. "If this is what it takes to heal you. If my death is what you need, take it."

My skin awakens with goose bumps, every inch of me shivering despite the mindless adrenaline.

He adds pressure to the knife, digging the blade into his skin.

"Don't." I try to pull it back, but he denies me, his hold adamant and far stronger than my own.

Blood wells along the steel, the tiniest rivulet of red making me hyperventilate.

"I lied to buy more time with you," he admits. "I knew once you found out about Emmanuel, you'd leave, and I couldn't stand it. I hid who I was to quieten my fear of losing you. I hurt you because I can't live without you."

He slowly moves our hands, dragging the blade across his throat. It's only light. The barest slice of skin, but it's enough to carve flesh.

"Stop," I warn.

He holds my gaze, the knife continuing its path of destruction.

"Stop."

Blood seeps down his neck to his pristine shirt, the pure white tainted with deep red.

"You need this." His eyes slay me. Slaughter.

"No. *You* do," I accuse. "You're trying to buy your way out of guilt and that's not how this works. My pain will still be here once your cuts heal."

"At least you acknowledge that I feel guilt." His voice is a whisper. "I guess that's a start."

"I acknowledge that you're doing this to take the easy way out. You want a quick fix."

"Or maybe I'm giving *you* the easy way out. Because as long as I'm breathing, I won't let you go, Layla." He wraps his free hand around the back of my neck, his fingers gripping me tight. "End me or forgive me, *amore mio*. Put us out of our misery."

I shake my head. Glaring. Faltering.

He leans in, his lips approaching mine. For a moment, I'm tempted to let him make everything disappear with the brush of his mouth, the taste of his tongue. But at the last second, I tilt my face away.

He growls, the deep rumble vibrating in his chest. *"End me."* He grabs my chin and forces my gaze back to his. *"Or fucking forgive me."*

"No. You can suffer."

His eyes harden, his lip curling. "Then we suffer together." He smashes his mouth to mine, the kiss harsh and punishing.

I scramble, frantically pulling my hand away from the knife, the weapon clattering to the floor. I fight, shoving, scratching.

He doesn't quit. He keeps attacking me with his affection, slaughtering my defenses with his returned grip on my neck, cutting me down at the knees with the swipe of his tongue against my lips.

It's too much. The passion. The worship.

My mouth tingles. My heart gallops.

I quit fighting his war strategy and attack with my own. I kiss him back with increased ferocity. Our mouths spar. Harsh movements. Vicious lashes of tongue. I shove my hands into his hair. Pull the strands. Claw his skull.

His growling continues, the animalistic rumble living inside my chest as he grabs my hips and turns to walk me back to the island counter. He dumps my ass against the cold marble, then tugs me forward, forcing my legs to part around his waist.

I burn. In my heart. My limbs. No place more fiercely than between my thighs.

It's agony. Potent and tart. It's what I deserve for being so pathetic. So weak.

He yanks Bishop's shirt over my head and possessively reclaims my chin to slam his lips back on mine.

His other hand is everywhere, cupping my breast, my ribs, my ass. He leaves a trail of blood all over me, marking my skin, painting me in his possession.

I don't want this. Not the passion nor the lust.

But I don't want anything other than this either.

I grasp his waistband while our mouths tussle. I blindly undo his belt. Tug his zipper. He does the same with my jeans, yanking the material down my legs along with my underwear.

Everything is a mass of wildfire and licking flames until his cock drives into me, the intrusion making me break away with a pleasured gasp.

We stare at each other, frozen, panting, hating, while his wrist drips with blood. The ruby-red stains the counter. My arms. Thighs. Cleavage. But all I know is the hardness of him inside me. The contact that sends me all the way back to love, affection, and thoughts of forever.

"Don't stop now," I snarl. "Fuck me."

I need this mistake to be over. For the pleasure to come and go so I can start regretting my actions. Because right now, all I want is *more*.

He's slow to comply with a roll of controlled lethargy. It's a meticulous thrill.

I arch my back, thrusting my breasts toward him, my nipples hard through my lace bra. He watches the movement, his gaze devouring every inch of me with ownership I yearn to submit to.

"Harder," I demand.

I can't withstand lazy and loving.

This needs to be a punishment.

Harsh. Fast. Cruel.

I focus on the blood oozing from his neck, the liquid seeping into his collar.

I tug and rip at his buttons, hungry to see more of him. I don't stop until his shirt hangs open, his muscled pecs on display, the beautiful canvas blood free but not for long.

I run my palm over the crimson on his throat, then trail my touch over his chest. I leave a path of carnage, increasing the gore, letting his punishment soothe mine.

"You like to watch me bleed." His stare tracks me with something akin to fascination.

"I like to watch you suffer." I reinforce the lie with a glare.

"*Arrenditi a me.*"

I scoff. "That dreamy Italian has become a crutch, Butcher."

"Really?" He claims my neck in his hand and grins. "You think I need foreign words to make you come?" His hold tightens. Restricts.

The confinement is riveting. Disturbingly delicious. It makes my pussy pulse around his cock.

"You don't understand how perfect you are." He strikes at my heart, each word a punishment I won't allow myself to believe.

"And you don't understand that I'm only using you again," I counter.

"Use me all you like." He smashes another kiss to my lips, speaking into my mouth. "Use me for the rest of my life."

Emotion tears me apart as his thrusts deepen. Quicken.

I could cry from the relief of it. The *pain* of it.

I yearn and despise. Love and loathe. And still, he brings me pleasure, his cock gliding in and out, his adoration seeming to increase with each undulation.

He cups my cheeks. Kisses me tenderly, then ferociously. He digs his fingers into my thighs. Palms a fistful of my hair.

It's chaotic. Wild. At least until a foreign sound breaches my ears. A chink of metal. A thud.

I stiffen. Freeze.

The front door opens in the distance with a squeak.

Shit. Bishop.

I shove at Matthew's chest, jostling and scooting to get out from under him. He stands solid, not budging an inch, his cock remaining buried inside me.

"He'll leave," he grates. "This isn't over."

"Yes, it is. We're done. *Move.*"

He grips my chin, his eyes vicious as he gets in my face. "I'm not letting you go. I won't lose you now."

"You never had me to begin with." I push at his chest only to have his hands lock tight around my wrists.

"That's a lie," he growls.

Bishop's footsteps approach, the rhythmic thud stopping as soon as he comes into view in my periphery. "Jesus fucking Christ, is that blood?"

I twist my arms free, then grab for the T-shirt on the counter, pulling it over my head while Matthew remains plastered between my thighs.

"What the fuck is wrong with you two?" Bishop's steps trek toward the bedroom hall. "One of you better be dying, otherwise I'll be fucking disappointed." He continues out of view, his stomped steps fading down the stairs.

Matthew doesn't acknowledge the anger. Neither do I.

I'm too busy bathing in shame, the carnage soaking me inside and out.

"Stay with me," Matthew demands. "Don't backtrack now."

It's too late. Regret has its hooks in me, the barbs buried deep.

"Don't say it," he warns. "Don't fucking say it, *amore mio.*"

"This was a mistake." I shove at him, using all my force to make him take a retreating step. I scoot from the counter and onto my feet, sweeping my jeans and underwear from the floor. "I can't do this anymore. I won't be baited." I meet his gaze, my chin high, my shoulders strong despite the weakness chipping away at my limbs. "I want what you promised me. Then I never want to see you again."

10

———————

MATTHEW

I CLENCH MY TEETH AS SHE WALKS AWAY, THE CUT ON MY NECK stinging, the puncture wound on my arm throbbing.

The closer I get to her physically, the farther she pushes me away afterward.

It's a ratio I don't understand and can't fucking balance.

I right my pants as her door slams down the hall, then lean my hands against the blood-smeared counter while silence takes over the house.

She's goddamn stubborn. But so am I.

Footsteps echo from downstairs, the noise getting closer until Bishop stalks into the room to throw a brown paper bag at me. "Here's your lunch, you perverted prick."

I snatch the projectile from the air, the soft food inside scrunching on impact.

He stalks to the opposite side of the island counter to glare at me. "I hope you choke."

"Duly noted."

"What the fuck is with the blood?"

I glance down at my torso. Her handprints are plastered over my chest, the crimson beginning to harden and flake. "What can I say? We discovered new kinks."

"That arm is going to need stitches."

"I'll handle it."

80

He scoffs. "So she's forgiven you?"

"Hardly." I open the bag to find numerous paper-wrapped sandwiches. "We need to get back on track with Emmanuel. I promised her we'd make plans over dinner tonight."

"Then go back on your promise. We both know he's a complication we don't need."

"He's a loose end we need to tie." I dump the bag on the counter and trek to the pantry to grab the first aid kit.

"What about your promise to me? You said we weren't going to live like this anymore. We gave up the bloodshed, remember? Now you're having sex in it."

I remember.

All too well.

"Admit you miss the thrill," he demands.

"I don't." I dump the kit on the counter and go in search of alcohol. The only thrill is Layla. She's the one who brings the adrenaline. There's no darkness involved. Only the warmth that accompanies the thought of making her happy.

It's not my fault her happiness revolves around death.

"Bullshit."

"I'm not in the mood, Bishop." I wrench open the liquor cabinet and snatch the last bottle of Macallan. "Take the food to her. Make sure she's okay."

"Hell no. I'm not stepping foot near that woman while you're like this."

I hang my head, the weight in my hands falling limp at my sides. I'm at my wit's end here, and the ache from my compounding blue balls isn't making my impatience to win her back any easier. "She needs to eat."

"And I need to live."

I swing around to scowl at him. He glares right back.

"This shit with her needs to end," he warns. "You're reaching the edge."

"Then don't push me any further." I shove the paper bag toward him, then start for the hall with the first aid and alcohol. "Take the fucking food to her. She doesn't deserve to starve."

. . .

BY NIGHTFALL, my blood is tinged with the faintest hint of scotch, the liquor doing nothing to quieten my demons as I sit on the deck in the dark.

The slight scratch on my neck has hardened. The wound on my forearm has been stitched by my own shitty craftsmanship. I took my time dragging the needle through my skin in the hopes it would distract me.

It didn't.

Every time I close my eyes, Layla's there. There's no escaping the storm we've created.

The sliding door opens behind me.

I already know it's not her. She won't come in search of me.

"She offered to cook dinner." Bishop takes the seat beside me. "Don't worry. I confiscated anything poisonous from under the sink. If she's going to kill us, it won't be through something ingestible."

I glance over my shoulder to the kitchen, finding her at the counter chopping vegetables. "Why would she offer?"

"Maybe because she's sick of staring at the same four walls."

Or maybe she's been snooping and found the sleeping pills in my bathroom.

"You realize those fuckers are probably out here watching us, right?" he asks.

"I don't give a shit." I take another mouthful from the liquor bottle. As long as Hunter stays in the shadows, the blade in my pocket will remain hidden.

"And when we start talking about Emmanuel?" He snatches the scotch from my hand and throws back a gulp. "What then?"

"They won't hear us from the beach." I can barely hear myself think over the waves and sea breeze.

He doesn't respond. He doesn't need to. His judgmental thoughts are loud and clear while the clatter of pans echoes from inside.

He wants to tell me how much I've messed up. To run through the list of my mistakes. And how much I've changed. How much I've risked.

"Hurry up and say it," I mutter. "I've known you long enough to understand you can't hold back from rubbing in my failures."

He settles into the deck chair, the scotch returning to his lips momentarily. "Who's to say you failed? I'm pretty sure that blood ritual of yours was successful. I'm just waiting for the demonic creature you summoned to show."

The reminder of the violent sex has my mind racing back there. To her fingers splayed on my chest, her skin covered in crimson.

"I spoke to her when I took in the food…" He hesitates, as if waiting for me to attack.

"And?"

"And I'm no connoisseur of the female psyche, but you only seem to be pissing her off more. Have you ever thought about doing the opposite of what your instincts suggest?"

"Don't start being a smart-ass." I attempt to snatch the bottle back only to have him yank it out of reach. "I'm on the precipice here."

"I know. That's why you're cut off until further notice. No more alcohol for you tonight. We're making plans for Emmanuel, remember? And you sure as shit won't be doing it with a gut full of liquor."

"I'm not drunk." Not even buzzed.

He raises the scotch along with a brow. "There's barely any left."

"I used it as antiseptic, asshole." I'm well aware I need to be on my game for the dinner conversation. I can't fuck up the only reason Layla's remained here.

"Good." He takes another chug as the outdoor lights turn on, blinding me. "*Jesus.* What the fuck?"

The door opens behind us while I blink. Layla's gentle footsteps head toward the outdoor dining setting. I squint as she brings a stacked tray to the table, then removes placemats, cloth napkins, and cutlery.

There's something different about her.

I scrutinize her as my eyes adjust, taking in the paler shade of her skin, the slightly rounded shoulders. She's lost the rigidity in her posture. The defiance.

She places the salt and pepper shakers down, then turns back toward the house to make for the door. "We're having warm chicken salad for dinner. It should be ready in fifteen minutes."

There's no strength in her voice. Only layers of exhaustion that intensify my guilt.

"Did she say *salad*?" Bishop asks as she closes the door behind her. "She knows we're men, right?"

"She knows *I* am." I return my attention to the inky ocean. "I'm not sure about you."

"Okay. This has gone too far. I took the perverted sex in my stride. I haven't complained about living on a lick of sleep. But salad? Come on, man. Nothing is worth putting up with *salad*."

"Then go discuss it with her."

"I risked it once, but I'm not going anywhere near your girl on my own again. That shit is suicide territory when you're like this."

"Then quit complaining." I grab for the scotch, only to have him swipe it out of reach for a second time.

"I will *never* quit complaining about salad. What am I, a fucking gopher?"

I slide my hand into my pocket, discreetly removing the plastic cover from the knife. I need something to take the edge off.

I creep my fingers along the steel as Bishop continues to mutter nonsense. I tilt the blade, digging it into the material against my thigh, then deeper into my flesh.

The first pinch of pain is cathartic. Sharp and serene.

I drag in a slow breath, leaning into the relief. The clarity.

The tension wanes. The guilt eases.

I close my eyes and dig the blade deeper, more than a scratch, the tip of the knife slicing through skin.

"Are you listening?" Bishop's voice hardens. "I said, are we going to talk about Emmanuel before she gets out here?"

I meditate on the burn in my thigh. The twinge of discomfort soothes. "No."

He falls quiet, the silence condemning me, stealing my tiny glimpse of peace.

"All you need to know is that the dinner conversation has to run smoothly." I release the knife and give him a warning stare. "Don't cause trouble."

"*Me?*" His face scrunches. "I'm not the one who's been—"

"I mean it. Whatever she wants, she gets, okay? Even if it's

Emmanuel's head stuffed and mounted on her wall. As far as I'm concerned, whatever she asks, we deliver."

He holds my gaze, his disgust increasing as he raises the scotch to drain the remaining liquid.

"Whatever she wants," I repeat.

He dumps the bottle beside his chair, refusing to respond. He won't dare to defy me. Not when I'm so fucking volatile.

I return to my meditation. Eyes closed. A hand on the knife. The blade digging into flesh.

I pull myself together. Focus on the end game. On what will happen once I succeed.

I'll take Layla away from here. Out of reach of family. Hers and mine. And we won't return until her feelings for me are stronger than they were before.

We'll make plans.

A future.

"Dinner is ready," she calls from the kitchen.

"Fucking salad," Bishop mutters pushing from his chair.

She returns outside, using her foot to slide the door closed behind her. This time her tray is filled with dinner bowls and sparkling glasses already filled with white wine, along with the remainder of the opened bottle.

I approach as she places one of the salad concoctions at the head of the table. "This is mine." She puts another down to her left. "And yours, Bishop." She shoots me a cursory glance while putting my bowl to her right. "And yours…"

Our gazes barely meet, but there's something different in her eyes. Something that causes tension beneath my sternum.

"And the wine?" Bishop's tone holds blatant skepticism. "Are those already designated?"

She reaches for the lone glass in the corner of the tray. "This one is."

He clears his throat and glowers at me, sending a message that's far from silent.

Specified meals. Stipulated drinks.

If she's striving to drug us, it's far too blatant. But am I careless enough to throw caution to the wind in a vain attempt to show my trust? Maybe.

I take my seat.

Layla does the same.

Bishop continues to glower.

If she wants us dead, I can't fulfil my obligation to kill Emmanuel. But we discussed my commitment before our last fight. Before the sex and violence and blood.

We fall mute. Nobody eats. Nobody drinks.

The meal becomes a game of chicken. A standoff. I don't want to risk being incapacitated if her intention is to run.

"Fine." She scoffs. "You don't trust me?" She grabs her fork and leans toward me, stealing a piece of chicken from the top of my meal to stick it in her mouth. "Satisfied?" She speaks as she chews, then does the same with Bishop's dinner. "That's why you're both not eating, right?"

He nudges his glass of wine toward her. "This, too, kink queen."

She stiffens slightly. "I want Emmanuel dead." She grabs Bishop's glass and takes a sip, immediately following with mine. "And I know I can't do it on my own. What would be the point in spiking your food?"

"You forget that I walked in on your demonic sex ritual," Bishop drawls. "At this point, I think you'd poison me for shits and giggles."

I barely acknowledge their conversation, my interest no longer on the food or wine.

My instincts are tuned in to her. Searching. Scavenging for clues.

She's different. There's no fight in her eyes. No frustration in her posture.

All I see is resignation.

"I'll take care of Emmanuel, Layla." I grab my fork and dig into my meal, the taste of oyster sauce and soy coating my tongue. "Consider it handled."

"That's not what I want." She places my wine down in front of me. "I need his blood on *my* hands. I want to be the one who ends his life."

Icy dread skitters down my spine, my hand itching to reach for the relief that would come from palming the blade in my pocket. "It's too dangerous."

"I'm not asking for permission. I need to do this for myself. For Stella. I won't risk being fooled by your promises again." Her words lack hostility. It's an admission of humiliation, not a taunt.

"In that case, the plan will take longer to organize." I stab a piece of chicken. "I'll want a million contingencies in place for your safety before we step foot in Colorado."

"I don't need a million. You should consider this like any other assassination. I'm sure you know how to be efficient but cautious. No strategy will be foolproof."

But this isn't any other assassination. This is about *her*.

"It's nonnegotiable, Layla. I'll give you what you're owed as long as you're patient while I create a plan that ensures your protection."

She lowers her gaze, remaining poised. "How much time are we talking about?"

A lifetime. Forever. I can't imagine putting her in more danger.

What I've dragged her through already has been bad enough.

"A long fucking while," Bishop cuts in. "Lorenzo is never going to give you permission."

"Forget Lorenzo," I mutter. "I'll deal with the repercussions later."

Her shoulders straighten.

In appreciation? Or merely shock?

"You're going to defy him?" Bishop grates. "Don't be fucking stupid."

"He won't find out. We'll cover our tracks."

"Fucking perfect." He punctures a piece of lettuce, his gaze narrowed on the leafy green as if it's the root of all evil. "Can you explain how we're going to do that when we won't be able to get back inside the Costa property? We've already burned that bridge. And with Emmanuel sick, he might never leave the house."

"I'm sure he'd have doctors' appointments in the city." Layla shrugs. "Rehab at the very least."

"But that's an assumption we need to confirm." Bishop grabs the lettuce from his fork and hikes it over his shoulder to the lawn below. "He may have arranged home visits. So recon is essential."

She doesn't respond. Instead, she takes dainty bites of chicken and salad, then a sip of wine.

The silence stretches. The awkwardness, too.

"How long?" This time her question is a faint murmur as her gaze meets mine, her suffering hitting me head on. "A few days? A week?"

What have I done to you? How do I fix this?

"Let me make some calls." I'm well aware I'm on a tightrope. If I give her a timeline that's too short, I'll risk not winning her back. If it's too long, she'll see it as a deliberate delay. "I'll get a team together. They can watch the house and give us an idea of what we're working with."

"Don't you have someone who could hack their security feed?" She takes another sip of wine. "They could skim over the recordings of the last few days to see when people have entered or left the property. Decker has done stuff like that before."

"Well, unfortunately I'm not Decker, and Langston is far from a tech guru." Bishop punctures another piece of lettuce to hike it over the railing. "Since when have you been impatient to end your life?"

"I'm not." Her eyes narrow, the fiery goddess flickering to life before being quickly snuffed when she lowers her gaze to her meal. "I'm just well aware *someone* is trying to keep me here as long as possible, and it's a waste of all our time. I won't be staying once Emmanuel is dealt with."

I pick at the chicken. Chew on a piece of carrot. Savor the wine.

Our rendezvous on the kitchen counter unsteadied her. But I'm unsure if it was in a bad way. Is she close to succumbing to me? Is her lack of fight the first sign of surrender?

She's definitely shaken. Unsteady. But is she susceptible?

"What about Remy and Salvatore?" she asks after Bishop has thrown half his vegetables over the railing.

Foreboding skitters down my spine. "What about them?"

"They want me dead."

"*Emmanuel* wants you dead," Bishop corrects. "So we kill the king and the empire will crumple."

"And what if we kill the king and his bastard sons want revenge?"

I keep my mouth shut, wondering if she's heading down this path in an attempt to punish me. *Spite* me.

"I don't want to spend the rest of my life looking over my shoulder." She grabs her napkin and dabs at the corners of her mouth. "And I won't allow that for Stella either."

"I'll assure your safety." I keep my tone in check. No instability. No aggression. Just a simple vow.

"You can't do that when I'll be living on the opposite side of the country."

If only she knew what lingered underneath all this pretense. If I don't win her back, her brother will have me in Portland doing his dirty work. Right under her nose.

"We're not getting rid of his brothers." Bishop stabs at his meal. "Those fuckers aren't worth the time it would take to dispose of the bodies."

"They killed my husband." She raises her chin.

"Doubtful." He shoves the forkful into his mouth, chewing as he speaks. "They're not built for violence."

"They had no problem playing a role in the abduction of children. And they were there when Benji was shot."

"So was Abri," Bishop adds. "Yet she was the one who fucked me over by helping you flee Emmanuel's house. I'm telling you, they don't have the balls to kill anyone."

"They were literally shooting at us a few days ago." Her voice raises with brittle emotion.

"No, they weren't," he adds. "The bullet holes on the car weren't above thigh height. They weren't aiming to cause injury. They didn't hit anywhere near the back seat windows. They barely broke a taillight."

She frowns, her attention turning to me. "Is that true?"

She doesn't want the truth. She wants ammunition. Condemnation. But I can't give that to her.

I incline my head. "I assumed they were warning shots."

Disbelief enters her eyes. "Why?"

"Maybe that's something you should find out before planning their cremation." Bishop pushes his bowl away and grabs his wine glass. "Just a thought."

She holds my gaze, attempting to read me. "Why, Matthew?"

I've wondered the same thing myself. They were sent to retrieve Layla yet made no real attempt to do so. Salvatore had a clear shot at Cole. He could've hit Bishop and didn't try. Maybe he was aiming for our tires, but even then, he didn't come close. Which means he's either a pathetically shitty shot or he bailed on Emmanuel's orders for a reason.

"I don't know." My phone vibrates in my jacket. "It's been a long time since I've been able to predict their motives." I retrieve the cell and excuse myself from the table as I answer the call. "Hello?"

"Brother," Abri says in greeting.

I slow my trek across the deck. We haven't spoken since Denver. Since the awkward goodbye at Emmanuel's house.

"I know this is unexpected," she says into the growing silence. "But I thought I should tell you father's men are out hunting for you."

"His men or Remy and Salvatore?"

"Both. I don't think they've got a clue where you are at the moment, but they won't quit. Father won't let them." Certainty strengthens her voice. "They'll find you."

"Well, you can tell him his minions won't return if they do." The admission twists my gut. I don't want my brothers dead, but I'll kill anyone in an effort to keep Layla safe.

"I'd prefer not to tell him anything seeing as though he's unaware I'm making this call. And before you ask, yes, I'm using a burner."

"Why call at all?" I turn toward the house and stare at my reflection in the floor-to-ceiling glass. "Is this to help Layla again?"

"No, it's to help *you*… and *me*. I hate what's become of us. I need you back in my life."

Paranoia and skepticism claw at the back of my thoughts.

I want to believe her, but it's not that simple. She chose the life she's in, just like I chose mine. She accepted her father's behavior. She encouraged it by staying at his side. "Get rid of Emmanuel and I'll see if I can make that work."

"It's not that easy."

I glance to the table, my attention latching onto Layla staring back at me. "Then I'll do it myself."

"You can't kill him," Abri whispers. "I understand it's what he deserves, but please don't be reckless enough to try."

I keep staring at the woman who owns me. The one whose pleas I need to value more than any other. My siblings made a choice. They could've walked away like I did. They may not have known about Grace's murder, but they were well aware of Emmanuel's dark side.

"Look, I've gotta go," she says in a rush. "I don't want to get caught talking to you. But please be careful."

I frown. "What's this really about?"

"We'll speak later."

She disconnects before I can stop her, leaving me to speculate about her intentions.

"Who was it?" Bishop asks.

I slide the device back into my pocket and return to my seat at the table. "Abri."

His eyes narrow. "What did the viper want?"

"To help, apparently. She said Emmanuel's men are looking for us."

"How is that helpful? It's common fucking sense. My guess is that she traced the call."

I reclaim my cutlery, hoping for Abri's sake that she isn't trying to make me an enemy.

"Unless she's still working with you somehow." Bishop pins Layla with a stare. "I never got an explanation as to why she helped you escape Emmanuel's house."

"She was helping herself. Not me." She shakes her head. "She told me she owed Cole a favor. It was something about him showing her kindness the night Benji died."

"And why would he show her kindness?" Bishop asks.

Good question. I don't like the thought of that fucker anywhere near my sister even if she is trying to set me up.

"I don't know." She shrugs. "Maybe if I hadn't been disowned I'd be able to get an answer. Instead, I'm here—potentially being surrounded by my enemies. With no one to trust. Am I even safe? We're out in the open. Everything is—"

"You're safe," I cut in. "There's camera surveillance. And a panic room inside if necessary. I'm also tracking inbound flights from the private airport." At least I have been since Hunter made himself known. "We'll have enough notice to get out of here if anyone arrives."

"And when all else fails—" Bishop finishes the last of his wine and grabs for the bottle. "—we have a reputation for a reason."

She raises a condescending brow. "Is your butcher status meant to be comforting?" It's yet another emotionless question. No heat. No taunt. Just words strung together by apathy.

"It should be," he counters.

I clear my throat. Shoot him a warning glance. Shake my head slightly.

She's been through enough today without his input.

He rolls his eyes and guzzles another glass of wine.

"Well, if there's nothing more to discuss regarding Emmanuel, I'm going to my room." Layla pushes back in her chair and grabs her bowl. "Is it too much to ask to be kept informed? That you'll let me know what your surveillance team finds?" Her gaze meets mine and for a moment, a glimpse of fortitude flickers in her eyes, but it fizzles. With one blink, her confidence vanishes and she dips her attention to her hands.

"It's not too much to ask." I silently beg her to look at me. Talk to me. Give in to me. "Whenever you want an update, all you need to do is ask."

Her expression flinches. "Good." She walks away, opening the door without dramatics and closing it without a heavy slam.

I don't like it.

This whole subdued, peaceful interaction twists my fucking balls.

"I don't know what type of seesaw relationship fuckery you two have going on…" Bishop grabs for the wine for a third time, pouring the remainder into his glass. "But the transition from bloodlust to dreary lethargy has me confused. Did I miss something?"

If he did, so did I, and I need to figure out what that is.

I push from my seat to follow her.

"Come on, man. Leave her the fuck alone." He leans back in his chair and kicks a boot onto the table, crossing his feet at the ankles.

"Remember what I said about instincts? Do the opposite. Stay out of her way instead of trying to get into her panties."

I grab my bowl and glass. "I'll be back to clear the table."

"You'll only push her further away."

He could be right, but she might also be on the precipice of being shoved toward submission.

I stalk inside, dump my bowl in the sink, and continue down the hall.

Her body craves mine. The carnality between us with every interaction is more than enough evidence of that. All that's left to win over is her head and her heart, and maybe now's the time.

I stop at her door, and for a second I think she left it open because she wanted me to follow, until I see the splinters of wood on the carpet from when I broke the latch.

I've terrorized her today.

"Layla—"

"I need to see my daughter." She cuts me off as she peers up at me from her position on the closest corner of the bed. "If this plan with Emmanuel isn't a trick, and we're legitimately going to take action, I want to see her first."

"I can arrange that." I can do anything. Whatever she needs. Whatever she wants. "I'm not tricking you."

"Okay, then when we leave for Denver, can you organize a detour to Chicago first?"

"That's where Stella goes to boarding school?"

She rakes her teeth over her lower lip as she dips her head once in a quick affirmation.

I'm caught off guard by the vulnerability she's just exposed. Completely blindsided with optimism.

"I'll make sure you see her." I step into her room, hungry for more of her trust. "I'll do whatever—"

"Don't." She raises a hand. "That's all I want. Nothing else has changed."

I stop. Stiffen. It's not her words that turn my feet to stone—it's her eyes. The ocean blue fills with desolation. Bleakness takes over her expression.

The woman once alive with aggression and sass is a brittle shell.

"Layla, what we did earlier today—"

"I already told you." She pushes to her feet. "It was a mistake."

"I agree."

Her brows narrow.

"I'm being honest." The pain. The trauma. The fucking blood. It was all a mistake. I pushed her too far. Toyed with her too much. We both craved the violence but I know now that she's too pure to revel in that toxicity. "Everything I've done since we arrived here has been a mistake."

She turns rigid.

"Except maybe giving you space when you first arrived," I amend. "I should've allowed you more time to think over what happened. I regret taunting you into fighting with me."

Her chin raises an inch.

"How do I make you understand the obsession you've created?" I chance another inch toward her.

"Please stop." She lowers her attention to the carpet and shakes her head. "I'm tired."

"Me too."

Me. Fucking. Too.

Her plea only makes it worse.

"I'm tired of not being heard," I admit. "And you're tired of fighting me, *amore mio*. Tired of denying how you feel."

She keeps her focus on the floor, her face the most beautiful inscrutable mask. "Is an admission what you need for this to be over?" she asks. "Is that what it will take? Your ego needs to hear that I still love you?"

Not my ego—my soul.

"Fine," she whispers. "I still love you, Matthew."

My entire body becomes motionless under the weight of her admission.

"But I despise myself for it." She raises her gaze to mine, the misery in her eyes slaughtering my ability to breathe. "I *hate* myself. I can't even look in the mirror without wanting to claw at my skin. And it took having sex with you, while covered in blood, to realize that I can't hold you accountable. At least, not entirely."

"Layla—"

"No, you were right when you said we were both at fault. I kept things from you that put you in danger," she states simply. "And I agree that it's part of the lifestyle we're in. Our secrets and safety are paramount. We do what needs to be done to cover our tracks."

My chest pounds with her sorrow. With her brutal fucking anguish.

"But the difference between our two betrayals is that I never knew your identity. I wasn't aware until Remy told me. Yet you understood Emmanuel was my enemy, and you went right ahead with seducing me into sleeping with his son. The offspring of my daughter's abductor. The same flesh and blood as my husband's killer."

I grind my teeth against the guilt.

"You knew I was in a temperamental position with my family, and still, you ruined what little integrity I had left. You didn't stop the games. You continued to drag me into an emotional entanglement that had no future. You created a world I needed. You gave me all I ever wanted even though you had to have known our lives couldn't coexist the way they were."

"They can coexist—"

"Stop," she warns. "There's no way I can be with you while continuing to respect myself *and* my daughter. You had to have known that. So why were you so cruel in giving me all I ever needed? Why did you make me fall in love with you when it was going to cost me *everything*?"

Because I'm a fucking monster.

"All I've ever wanted was someone to care for me the way you did." Her face crumples.

"The way I *do*," I correct. "You're everything—"

"My mother died when I was young, Matthew. My father pretended I didn't exist unless he wanted something. And my husband..." She winces and looks away. "I think I've already told you it was practically an arranged marriage. I fell pregnant from a one-night stand, and there's no way anyone in my family would've allowed Benji to live if he'd abandoned his responsibilities."

No, she didn't fucking tell me, and the insight is a bitch.

"But that's what I was." She meets my gaze again, the beautiful blue of her eyes swimming in emotion. "A responsibility. A chore. He never loved me. I've only ever been a hindrance. And the worst thing is that I thought you were different. You made me feel welcomed. *Cherished.*" Her voice breaks, the fissures splintering into me like knives. "You spun the most beautiful lies and I believed every one of them. In your presence, I was smart, and brave, and empowered. I had hope, and meaning, and hunger for a better future."

Every word is a punishment for my lies.

Every admission a torturous truth.

"You were so incredibly good at deceiving me that I find it hard not to applaud you for it." She laughs to herself, half-hearted and pained. "You've won, Matthew. I still don't know what you set out to achieve, but I keep losing. I lost in Denver. I lost last night at the dinner table. And again this morning, when I tried to buy a Tesla and ended up sleeping with you instead. But I need to stop losing now. I can't keep doing this."

"I'd never diminish your suffering, but you've got this all wrong."

"Suffering is such an easy word for what I feel." She holds me in place with her hollow gaze. "Do you want to know what I wanted to do once the thrill wore off last night? Once I did the walk of shame from the dining room and came in here to be alone?"

"You wanted to kill me."

"No." She shakes her head, her tongue snaking out to lick her drying lips. "I wanted to kill *me*."

My stomach hollows. Fucking bottoms.

"For a split second, I wanted out of this mess. Permanently." Her face scrunches as she struggles to keep her voice steady. "I wanted to make everyone's life easier by taking my own."

I clench my fists.

I did this.

I did something far worse than Emmanuel ever did to me.

"So, I'm begging you, please stop." She straightens her shoulders. "Quit fighting me, give me what you've promised, then let me go."

LAYLA

"As you wish, *amore mio*."

That's all he says before turning on his heel to leave the room.

I expected him to put up a fight. Or flirt. Or beg for forgiveness.

Instead, he let two days pass with nothing more than murmured greetings or well-mannered questions when we happened to cross paths, which isn't often.

He's kept his distance, allowing me to recover the slightest semblance of pride after spewing my truth at him. He's spent the time on his phone, pacing the deck, his conversations easily overheard from my bedroom as he talks strategy about Emmanuel.

I assume it's for my benefit that he's remained out of reach yet within listening range.

He's assembled a team in Denver. I think it's the same men who helped us get onto the Costa family property last week, but I'm not willing to start a conversation to confirm.

It's best to remain alone.

Whenever Matthew's in the kitchen, I escape to my bedroom. While he's in the living room, I waste hours on the deck.

My packages started to arrive yesterday, giving me something to do while isolated. I've received a mass of cosmetics, books, and lingerie. But no clothes have shown up, which means I've been forced to wear Bishop's T-shirts to bed and the same worn jeans and blouse during the day.

"Your drinking hours are getting longer." Bishop climbs the deck stairs with a judgmental glower.

I glance at my wine glass, the liquid glistening in the beaming sun as I laze on the outdoor lounge chair.

"Should I be worried?" he asks. "Is this yet another attribute I didn't know about like the knife-and-blood kink?"

"Go to hell."

Unlike Matthew, Bishop hasn't given me a wide berth. He's done the opposite, always checking to make sure I've eaten, his annoying face constantly poking into my room to see if I'm still alive.

I take another sip of chardonnay, focusing my annoyance at the ocean. "I don't have kinks." And it's midafternoon, for Christ's sake. It's a socially acceptable time to drink.

"Sorry, am I using the wrong term?" He stops a few feet away and leans his hip against the railing. "Kink… Fetish… Perversion… They all mean the same thing to me."

"What do you want?" I glare.

"I just thought I'd let you know Langston left thirty minutes ago."

My heart skips a beat. "He left? Why?"

"He should be back in twenty. So you might want to ditch the wine and maybe do your hair."

I frown, confused.

"Or you could continue to look like a cheap drunk while on your hundred and fifth day of wearing the same clothes." He shrugs. "It's up to you, but you'll regret it once our visitors arrive."

"Someone is coming here?" I push to my feet. "Who?"

He pulls out his cell, ignoring me.

"*Bishop?*"

"Sorry. I can't hear you." He flicks a finger over his cell screen. "I'm too busy buying my ticket to hell."

Asshole.

"Can you at least tell me if I need to be worried? Did he go back on his word? Has he changed plans for Emmanuel without telling me?"

Who would Matthew trust enough to bring here? Lorenzo? Another mafia connection?

"You've got nothing to worry about." He keeps flicking his cell screen. "Unless you don't brush your teeth. Your booze breath might be a red flag for our guests."

"You want to see a red flag?" I step closer, throwing back the last of my wine. "Keep provoking me and I'll wave one in your bad-boy-wannabe face."

He grins. Snickers.

I stalk to the French doors leading into my room and lock them behind me. I comb my hair. Brush my teeth. Then finish with a touch of mascara, eyeliner, and a thin layer of BB cream in the hopes of hiding my exhaustion.

When I return to the deck Bishop is still in the same spot, his attention fixated on his cell.

"This better?" I ask, heavy with sarcasm.

He flicks me a two-second stare. "You've still got clothes on—that's always a bonus. I guess that means your exhibitionist kink hasn't been initiated today."

My aggression spikes as I reclaim my seat. "I'm not an exhibitionist."

"Tell that to my therapist."

I know he's only having fun. But these cat-fight conversations make me feel more alone. I haven't had a supportive ear in weeks. The diet of ridicule is draining.

"Can I borrow your phone?" My throat aches with the plea. "Just for a few minutes."

He looks up at me with a scowl. "Why?"

"I haven't spoken to my daughter in days."

"Have you asked Langston?"

My fingers twitch in my lap. "No. I think you're well aware I've been trying to stay as far away from him as possible."

"And let me tell you, it's been a blessing not to walk in on another porn act."

My cheeks heat, the flames equal parts rage and humiliation. "Can I have your phone or not?"

"Sorry, kink queen, you're going to have to wait until your guy gets back."

I fight not to give him the bird while the sea breeze whispers past my ears, the ebb and flow of the ocean doing nothing to soothe me.

Once Matthew returns, I'll have to risk speaking to him about our plans in Denver. I won't let him drag this on any longer. Two days has been enough.

"He's here." Bishop pushes from the railing and returns the cell to his jacket.

I stiffen at the faint rumble of a car carrying from the front of the house. A door slams, increasing my anticipation.

Then another.

And another.

And another.

I sit taller. "How many guests are there?"

"Why?" Bishop waggles his brows. "Are you getting excited that it might be a gang bang?"

Fuck you.

"What's going on?" I demand.

"Wait five seconds and you'll find out."

Footsteps carry around the side of the house. Fast. Light. Someone is running.

I shove to my feet and rush to the railing to peer into the yard. A young girl runs onto the lawn, her long dark hair flowing behind her back.

My heart stops. Breath evacuates my lungs. "Stella?"

"*Mom?*" She glances around the backyard.

"Up here, little fish." I tremble, my hands shaking, my throat drying as she swings around, her face tilted skyward.

She beams a smile at me, then runs for the stairs. All I can do is stare while my knees threaten to buckle.

I glance to Bishop in question. In confusion.

He smirks. "Aren't you glad you brushed your teeth?"

"You're such an asshole." A sob clogs in my throat.

He starts for the living room, sliding the door closed behind him as Stella reaches the top step.

Her pace increases. She flings her arms wide while I rush to meet her halfway. "*Surprise.*"

I close my eyes, hugging her tight, nestling my face in her hair. "What are you doing here?"

"Aunt Keira took me out of school. She said I deserve a few days off."

My heart skips another beat. "Aunt Keira?" I pull back to read her expression.

"Yeah." She leans toward the railing to stare into the yard below. "I think she misses you."

My stomach bottoms as I follow her gaze, finding my sister on the lawn. Longing isn't what stares back at me though. It's indifference. Sterility. From her and Decker at her side.

I don't bother glancing toward Hunter and Sarah, who close in a few feet behind them. I'm not wearing enough clothes to withstand their arctic chill.

The only one who looks at me with any civility is Matthew, who prowls around the mini crowd toward the stairs. Watching. Supervising.

I'm not sure if he's trying to determine if I'm okay or if I'm about to run off with my child. Because I could. Skipping town is an option now that Stella is here. But only if I had the intention of letting her live on the streets.

"Well, it's a lovely surprise." I swallow the foreboding threatening to suffocate me and return my attention to the most beautiful girl in the world. "God, I've missed you. How did you get here?"

"The jet. Then *Matthew* picked the three of us up from the airport." She says his name with an exaggerated teasing lilt.

"The three of you?"

There are five new arrivals. Not three.

"Yeah. Hunter and Sarah were already waiting with *Matthew*." She does that teasing, playful tone again, but it doesn't stop the pit of my stomach becoming a cesspool.

"How were they already here? When did they arrive?"

"I don't know." She shrugs. "Please tell me I can stay longer than one night. Aunt Keira said you'd kill her if I missed more school, but it's not a big deal." She bats her lashes. "A few days won't make a difference—"

"You've been here two seconds and you're already blinking those puppy-dog eyes at me?" I kiss her forehead as my firing squad makes its way up the stairs. "I hate to admit you're your mother's daughter."

"Is that a yes?"

"That's a hard no." For starters, I don't know why she's here. I asked to see her in Chicago. A quick reunion before our task with Emmanuel got underway. I don't want her in the thick of this—surrounded by men she would hate if she knew their lineage.

I clear my throat. "School is important."

"School is painful."

"I thought you liked being in Chicago." I hold her gaze as Matthew enters my periphery over her right shoulder. "Has something happened?"

"No. It's just school, Mom. Nobody likes it."

The deck fills with an audience, each approaching footstep chipping away at my confidence.

The majority of people in the vicinity have given up on me. Discarded. Abandoned. And I'm meant to smile and pretend it hasn't happened.

"Hey, sis." Keira gives me a subdued finger wave, playing the amicable role. "I hope our arrival isn't too much of a shock. Matthew said he didn't tell you we were coming."

I turn my gaze to the man in question. "No, he didn't."

"I wasn't sure we could pull it off." He shrugs. "I didn't want to get your hopes up."

My stomach does a sweeping drop. What is this? Has he teamed up with my family to reinvigorate my torture? Has he brought my daughter here to prove he's still calling the shots?

"Well, you definitely succeeded in surprising me." I keep my tone level, my distress hidden. "I had no idea."

Keira beams a smile at Stella. "I'm just doing my best to maintain my status as the favorite aunt."

"You're my *only* aunt." Stella rolls her eyes.

"It's still a tough mantle to maintain, kiddo. And it's also not entirely true. Anissa is your aunt now, too."

"Not by blood."

There's a pause of silence, the awkward atmosphere settling in like a building storm.

I don't have the resilience to play pretend. At least not convincingly. Not when Sarah stares at the house so she doesn't have to meet my gaze, while Hunter and Decker do the same toward the ocean.

"Why don't I get you set up inside, little fish?" I glide a hand around Stella's shoulders. "We haven't spoken much lately. You need to fill me in on all the gossip."

"Sure."

Keira straightens, as if understanding my desire to get as far away from her as fast as possible. Did she expect me to fall to my knees and beg forgiveness? Am I meant to grovel? She'd only despise me more for the show of weakness. Earning my family's respect has only ever been achieved through strength, and that's not something I possess right now.

"Good idea." Keira nods. "We'll get our things from the car and meet you in the house."

Hunter, Sarah, and Decker remain silent. They don't even glance my way.

I wish the rejection didn't hurt, but it does. It festers inside me, weakening limbs and organs.

The three of them have done far worse than I ever have. They've betrayed us all in their own way. But apparently, their sins are forgivable because they've also killed to protect us.

Matthew leads the way toward the living room. I'm loathe to follow as he pulls the sliding door wide and waits for us.

It's Stella who makes the first move, striding toward him with a smile of admiration. "Thank you."

If only she knew his family killed her father.

"You're more than welcome, *principessa*."

I give him a reprimanding scowl, silently warning him not to manipulate her with his dreamy Italian like he does with me. But he doesn't meet my gaze. He's too focused on my daughter, his expression kind, his posture nonthreatening.

"Did you bring your swim suit?" he asks.

"Why?" She balks. "It's too cold."

"You can't come to the ocean and not take advantage of the surf. I've got boards in the garage that haven't seen the light of day in over a year. We can't leave them draped in cobwebs."

"Are you serious?" She glances to me with excitement. "Surfing?"

"She doesn't know how to surf." My friendly expression is fake. My kind tone, too. "It's best to leave it for another—"

"Please, Mom." She clasps her hands in prayer as she hovers at the threshold. "I want to learn."

I hold the dark eyes of the man who has already worked my daughter around his little finger, trying to let him know he's crossing multiple lines.

"Forgive me." He raises his hands in surrender. "If you don't have a bathing suit, it's better to surf some other time."

I keep staring, glaring, because unlike his ignorant ass, I know it's already too late to backtrack.

"I can wear shorts and a T-shirt," Stella counters. "Or we could buy something. Are there shops around here? *Please*, Mom."

I don't know how he does it. Is it the easy smile? The confident posture? The deep, chocolate eyes?

He's won my daughter over faster than he did me. But he doesn't stare back in victory. There's no demoralizing grin or smug smirk. His eyes are questioning. Cautious. Does he actually care that he's betraying me again?

"We'll see." I shoo her forward with a wave of my hand, then follow her inside. "You're not going to be here long, remember? You might find something more exciting to do."

"Like what?"

Good question.

I take the lead toward the hall, leaving Matthew in our wake. "I'm sure there are a million things."

She sighs as I step into my bedroom with the mess of half-opened packages strewn across the floor. I tidy the rubbish, grabbing crumpled paper and plastic as she belly flops on the bed, her body bouncing on impact.

"Time to spill the details." She turns onto her back, her long hair covering her face. "So, Matthew is the guy you've been spending all your time with? I thought you were just friends."

"We are."

"Mom, he's clearly simping over you."

"Simping?" I turn away, hiding from her scrutiny. "Do I want to know what that means?"

"He likes you." The bedsprings squeak with her movement.

"He couldn't stop talking about you in the car, which means he really, *really* likes you."

The words shouldn't hurt, but they do. They lash with the force of a knotted rope.

I'd thought the same thing. I'd *wanted* it, too.

"Where did you meet? What's his last name? What does he do for work?" She peppers me with questions that seem more like accusations, each one harder than the last. "You said you two were working together, right?"

"Calm down, little fish. We've got all the time in the world to talk about me. I want you to tell me about school first."

"Forget school. Something is definitely going on with you two." She grins. "I've been here five seconds and it's already obvious he thinks you're the goat."

"The goat?" I squeeze a tissue paper tighter in my grip, compacting it into an aggression-filled ball to throw into an empty box in the corner. "Where are you getting all these words?"

"You're so old. It means the Greatest Of All Time."

I shouldn't have asked.

"How long have you known each other? Have you met his family? Have you kissed?"

"Stella, please." I turn back to her, my eyes pleading. "I told you, it's not like that."

I don't want to lie to her. Not about this. I also can't stomach telling her even the slightest snippet of truth. Problem is, she's old enough to remember all the things I might lie about if the reality is eventually revealed.

I need to lay low. Glide under the radar.

Distract. Divert. Redirect.

"Do you want to sleep in here tonight?" I force energy into my voice. "There's plenty of room in my bed. We could stay up late and watch the stars like we used to."

Her nose scrunches as she breaks eye contact. "Are there any other rooms?"

"There are plenty of rooms. I just thought…" I don't know… I guess it doesn't seem so long ago that she was crawling under my covers in the middle of the night, her face soaked from tears, her mind a mess from nightmares of her father's murder. She spent months cuddled into me. Almost a year. Now she doesn't even want to spend a night. "Where would you like to sleep?"

"It's just that I kinda like my own space now. And I wouldn't want to wake you if I get up during the night and check my phone. I get good cell reception here, by the way. I don't know what carrier Matthew uses for his phone, but he needs to change."

I smile despite her revealing my first lie. "Well, you better hurry before Aunt Keira takes the best room."

"Are you sure?" She scrambles from the bed. "You don't mind?"

"Not at all." It's more dishonesty. "Go. Claim the comfiest bed."

"Okay." She dashes for the hall, her eager footsteps clapping into the distance.

I don't move. Don't even twitch.

I remain weighed in place while sorrow consumes me.

I thought being with her would strengthen me. That all I needed was to see the one person who loves me unconditionally. But pretending I'm not dying inside has only increased my suffering.

The worst part is that I hate acknowledging I have no fear for her safety under this roof.

Yes, Matthew might worm his way into my daughter's heart, or Bishop could say something highly inappropriate in an attempt to make her laugh. But I don't doubt for a second that the men who have ruined my life will never hurt her.

It's just me that the world wants to bring to its knees.

I force myself to move. To keep busy tidying the remainder of the mess as doors open and close through the house.

Voices murmur from the living room, a low grumble from Decker, a soft reply from my sister, then a sarcastic drawl from Bishop. They should be killing each other. Why aren't they?

Footsteps approach along the hall, the heavy thuds coming from a man.

I pause in the middle of crumpling tissue paper in my hands, hoping it's someone walking to a nearby room. Luck isn't on my side.

The shuffle of movement stops at my door. The heat of attention tickles the back of my neck.

"Your sister brought this for you," Matthew murmurs.

I turn to him standing in the doorway, a small duffle in his hand. "What is it?"

He places the luggage at his feet. "Clothes, I assume."

"How did she know I needed them?"

He shrugs, the collar of his crisp white shirt rubbing over the cut I left on his neck. "I may have mentioned it."

I don't know what hurts more—the fact he's on speaking terms with my family or that they disrespected me enough to let him make plans for my daughter. They couldn't have known I'd trust Matthew around Stella. That the goddamn Butcher Boys of Baltimore could provide a safe space for a child.

"Where is she?" he asks.

I walk for the sheer curtains covering the French doors, needing the peace of the ocean instead of the struggle that comes with staring at his face. "She went to find her own room. Apparently, she no longer wants to share my bed."

"If it makes you feel any better, I know someone who would eagerly take the offer."

I sigh. "I thought we weren't doing this anymore."

"You asked me not to fight with you, and I haven't. Nothing else has changed. I still see hunger when you look at me, Layla. I'm not giving up."

"You're mistaken."

"I assure you, I'm not."

The hot rush of anger adds to my sorrow. I force myself to focus on the gentle waves. *Breathe in. Breathe out.* "You shouldn't have brought her here. I asked to see her in Chicago."

"I didn't want to risk someone following us to her school."

"So you called my family?" I murmur.

"Is that a problem?"

Everything is a problem. Every thought. Every action. Every inhale.

Then there's the paranoia that has me questioning who he spoke to and what was said. Does Cole still hate me? Will my brother ever forgive me? Is he happy that Matthew is now my caretaker so I'm no longer a burden to my siblings? And why the hell were Hunter and Sarah already here?

"I didn't know you were on speaking terms." I pull back the see-through curtain as I glance at him over my shoulder, my fingers clutching the material for support.

"Neither did I, but for you, I asked."

My pulse pounds with the need to know the intricacies of his conversation, but with every second Matthew looks at me with pitiful longing, he chips away at the meager morsels of strength I have left.

"You should speak to your sister." He inches farther into the room, his hands sliding into the pockets of his suit pants. "She might be able to clarify any questions you have."

"No, thank you." I turn to face him. "And you can stay right where you are."

He complies, somehow unbelievably predatory even in his stillness.

"Does Stella's arrival mean you've made headway with Emmanuel?" I ask. "Can we finally get this over and done with?"

"Soon. He's left the property while under surveillance, which is a start."

"It's more than a start. It's enough to warrant going there and watching for ourselves. Any time he leaves the property—"

"I won't budge when it comes to your safety. So don't bother trying."

I turn back to the French doors. "You're stalling, and as soon as Stella is gone, I'll be putting a stop to it."

"Enjoy the time with your daughter, Layla." The soft pad of his steps retreats toward the hall. "Let me know if you need anything."

I swallow over the lump in my throat, his kindness causing more volatility than his aggression ever did.

Everything he does kills me. Every facet of his personality is a direct hit to my heart. I want it all. The possession. The compassion. But there can never be a future with a man who can warp my reality.

I wait until his presence is a brief brush of sound in the distance, then go in search of Stella, finding her in the farthest room down the hall. The bed is perfectly made. The curtains are pulled wide. Sunshine beams in on the beauty of her as she stands at the large bay window overlooking the garden, her finger frantically tapping against her cell. She has to have grown an inch in the past few weeks.

"Like the view?" I walk to her side, wishing she was still at the age where cuddles were all she ever wanted.

She looks up at me with a smile as she pockets the device. "It's so nice here. Why do we never come to the coast?"

Because Uncle Cole prefers the safety of isolation, not the risk of open space. "I guess our family have always been city people. My parents rarely took me anywhere like this either."

"Can we go for a walk on the sand?"

"Of course."

I lead her outside via my bedroom so I don't have to come face to face with my sister.

We don't walk far, maybe half a mile, before we sit on the dry sand. I listen as she quickly chatters about the new boy in class who used to tug her hair whenever he passed until Tobias punched him in the stomach. She tells me how hard her advanced math class has become. And how her grades are improving. Then she diverts the conversation back to Matthew, as if the prior information was a strategic info dump to appease me before she could get onto the only topic she's excited to talk about.

I'm forced to fudge my way through tricky answers.

No, I haven't met his family.

Yes, I know what he does for a living.

He's a nightclub owner. He lives in D.C. He's a good man.

"Do you still think of Dad?" Her tone remains energetic, but it doesn't hide the vulnerability of her question as she digs her toes into the sand.

"All the time, little fish." I slide my hand around her shoulders and pull her closer. "I promise I'll never stop."

"I don't think about him as much as I used to." She digs her feet deeper, breaking my heart with her admission.

"How come?"

"It hurts."

I kiss her temple, buying myself time to respond without breaking. "Do you want to come back home? Would it be easier to return to school in Portland?"

"No. I like the friends I have now. And I can't leave Tobias. Who would keep him out of trouble?"

I scoff. "Tobias shouldn't be getting in trouble."

"Somehow I don't think that's an option." She chuckles, half-hearted as she glances over my shoulder toward the house. "Who's that guy watching us?"

I follow her gaze to the suit-clad monstrosity standing over ten yards away. "His name is Bishop. He's Matthew's best friend."

She makes a noise. A high-pitched questioning humph.

"Before you even ask, I'm not his goat either." I nudge her shoulder. "There's no goat business at all."

She laughs. "What's he like?"

I chance another glance at the man leaning against the white picket fence of a neighboring yard, his arms crossed over his chest. "He's…" I frown, attempting to come up with a way to describe him. "I guess he's a lot like the men you've grown up with."

"Overprotective, grumpy, and always thinks he's right?"

"That's an apt description." I turn back to her with a smile.

"And Matthew?" she asks. "What's he like?"

I look away, wincing at the first word that comes to mind —*perfect*.

Perfect for me. Perfect for my insecurities. Perfect for my soul. If only the things I adored weren't perfectly fictional.

"He's the same."

I sense her eyes narrowing in my periphery, her scrutiny potent. "Why can't you admit you like him?"

Because his family killed your father.

"He's just not the right man for me. We're too different." Or maybe the problem is that we're exactly the same. Either way, there's no escaping the red flags that accompany us being together.

"Different is good, isn't it?"

"It can be. But there's a lot more to it. You know we're not like most people. We need to be careful with who we align ourselves."

"And he's not someone you should be aligning with?" She glances toward Bishop again, giving me the briefest reprieve.

I can't keep distracting her from the truth. I don't want to feed her more white lies. But… *Goddamnit.* I hate this. "He's familiar with some of our enemies."

"Familiar how?"

I turn to her. "It's nothing for you to worry about, I promise. And his familiarity was only part of the issue. The real problem was that he hid it from me. He lied."

She frowns. "Why would he do that?"

I don't know… Because he's cruel. Deceptive. A born liar. "It's complicated."

"Why do you always say that when you don't want to give me the real answer? It's so annoying. You treat me like I'm too young to be told stuff, but I'm not. I know a lot more than you think."

"It's usually a nicer way of saying I don't want to talk about it, little fish."

"Well I *do* want to talk about it. If he's a liar and familiar with our enemies, why am I here? Isn't it dangerous?"

"No, not at all. You're safe. *He's* safe." I brush a hand through her hair. "I'm still working with him. I'm just no longer wanting to be in love with him."

"So you *were* in love?"

Goddamnit. "Stella, please."

She grins. "I want you to be happy, Mom."

"And I want you to stop asking questions, my sweet little pumpkin seed."

She laughs. "I'm just trying to understand because you being in love is huge."

"I don't feel that way anymore," I lie. "So can we please drop it?"

"But if you're still working with him even though he knows our enemies, then your problem must be about him lying… and you lie to me all the time. If I can forgive and forget, why can't you?"

"What have I lied about?"

She lowers her gaze to her toes popping up from beneath the sand. "Everything. You hide things from me, too. I always find out, though, and it's ten times harder to hear it from someone else."

I ignore the icy chill working through my limbs. "Stella, I'm sorry. But sometimes I keep quiet on issues so you don't worry unnecessarily. We have a lot of things that make people envious—"

"I'm not talking about that. It's the things I deserve to know that make me mad."

My pulse increases with apprehension. I don't want to ask.

"You should've told me about Granddad," she murmurs. "I had to find out from Tobias."

All the blood rushes from my face. "What did he tell you?"

"That his dad liked to humiliate women." Her throat works over a heavy swallow. "That he hurt them. *Raped* them. Probably even killed them."

Oh, God. "Stella…"

I don't know what to say.

"He was my family," she continues. "I deserved to know."

I grab her hand, encasing it in mine. "No, you deserved to be free from those horrible thoughts. I didn't want you to feel the way I felt after finding out."

She meets my gaze. "And how did you feel?"

Guilty. Dirty. Vile.

I swallow over the tightness building in my chest. "I was ashamed."

"Of what?" Her nose scrunches. "What he did wasn't your fault."

I wish that were true, but who knows what that monster accomplished due to the secrets I fed him. "He was the man who created me. Whose blood flows through my veins. His soul made mine."

Her face crumples. "Mom…"

"Please forgive me." I squeeze her hand. "I never meant to hurt you."

"I *do* forgive you. I always will. I just wish you understood that I can handle the truth."

No, she can't. Not the real truth. Not the darkest deceptions.

Even I can't handle those, and I'm the one who committed them.

"I'll try to do better in the future." I nestle close against her side, both of us turning our attention to the setting sun. The day creeps toward night in varying shades of orange, pink, and purple, the waves gently gliding across the sand as the breeze dances in our hair.

"Could it be possible that Matthew lied to you for the same reasons you lie to me?" she asks softly.

I lean in to kiss her temple, closing my eyes with the light brush. "It's getting close to dinner. We should head back to the house."

"*Mom*," she begs. "I want to talk about this."

"You've made that clear, sweetheart. But can you understand that it hurts?" I push to my feet and hold out a hand to help her do the same. "I don't want to think about it anymore."

"But you were in love." She wipes the sand from her butt. "Surely if I can forgive you for the things you lie about, you should be able to forgive him."

I start along the beach, wishing I'd put more thought into a plan before I opened my big mouth. "Forgiveness is hard."

"Believe me, I know."

"Well, it's even harder when you're an adult."

She hustles to keep pace at my side. "But not impossible, right? Surely if you both love each other you can work things out."

Vultures take over my insides, picking me apart, scavenging for the mere morsels of strength left behind.

"He doesn't love me, Stella." He never confessed the emotion. That was all on me. *My* assumption. *My* mistake. *My* stupidity. "Now can we please drop it?"

12

———

LAYLA

MATTHEW IS ON THE DECK WHEN WE RETURN, HIS GAZE ON MINE THE moment we walk into the yard.

"I've never seen a man look at you the way he does. Not even Dad." Stella releases my hand. "It sure seems like love to me."

She doesn't give me the opportunity to respond as she takes off across the lawn. "I'm going to freshen up for dinner." She bounds up the stairs two at a time, stealing Matthew's attention once she reaches the deck to share murmured words.

I walk faster, tempted to break into a run to hear what they're saying, but she's already inside by the time I reach the upper level. "What did you say to her?"

He turns to me, raising a lone brow at my tempered aggression.

"And what did you say to her before she arrived?" I hiss. "She has certain misconceptions about us that I don't appreciate."

He scowls, his concern fake. "What sort of misconceptions, *amore mio*?"

He's tempting me to fight with him again. Poking. Prodding.

I want to get in his face. To demand he quit calling me that stupid endearment. To stop being a manipulative prick and toying with my emotions.

"You know exactly what I'm talking about." I chance a cautious glance inside, finding an audience of Stella, Keira, and Decker in the living room. *Shit*. I force a smile and relax my shoulders, not

114

wanting my daughter to realize I'm a prisoner of circumstance. "She's becoming more convinced that I'm here for romantic reasons."

"I think you are, too." He steps toward me, entering my personal space.

I huff a laugh and turn my back to the house so I have the freedom to glare. "Don't push me, Langston. When it comes to Stella, I attack first and ask questions later."

"Langston?" he muses. "I don't think I like you calling me that."

"Then back the hell off," I growl.

He inclines his head. Subtle. Submissive. "I assure you, apart from answering her questions about you on the way from the airport, I've barely talked to her. I deliberately didn't want to step on your toes. And I'm not trying to lay blame, but I'd assume your sister is the one who's given the little *principessa* the wrong idea. You really should speak to her."

I'm almost tempted to believe him if it weren't for his second suggestion—to confront Keira. He knows I won't go there. My pride is too brittle to go crawling to her when I'm yet to make up for my mistakes.

"Stay away from my daughter." I stand taller. Straighter. Attempting to see right through the charm he's laying thicker than glue. "I told her you're a liar. She knows you're not to be trusted."

His face falls. It's a split second of confounded shock before his eyes narrow. "Whatever you say, *amore mio*."

"And don't call me that in front of her. She already thinks you're obsessed with me. I don't need you making things worse."

"Knows," he clarifies. "She already *knows* I'm obsessed."

My hands itch to grasp the fight he's offering. To dive headfirst into it in one rapid release of endorphins. But he'll win. He'll wrap my ovaries around his little finger like always and then I'll be a slave to shame all over again—this time in front of a daughter who will hold me accountable.

"I'm not doing this with you." I start for the French doors of my bedroom.

"I like seeing you like this," he says to my back. "Your protective side is captivating."

I snatch at the door handle and pull it wide. "You act like everything about me is captivating."

"It's not an act, *la mia piccola sporcacciona.*"

I stop myself from slamming the door behind me and continue to the bathroom to douse my face in cold water.

I hold my breath as I splash and splash, attempting to wash away his attention, but I'm already warmed by it. *Heated.* His affects sink under my skin. Delve into my lungs.

He promised to quit antagonizing me only to revert to yet another effective strategy—seduction.

Bastard.

I slump onto the lowered toilet seat, water dripping from my face onto my clothes while the scent of spices filters into the bathroom.

Cutlery clatters from the kitchen. Stella's laughter echoes down the hall. The world keeps spinning while I slowly unravel on a goddamn toilet in a town I don't even know the name of.

"*Mom*?" Stella calls out. "Are you coming for dinner? Hunter bought Chinese."

"Yep." I drag myself to my feet, pat my face with a towel, and suck in a deep breath.

"*Mom*?"

"I'm coming." I meet Stella in the hall, her attention far too scrutinizing as we walk toward the living room.

"You okay?" she asks. "You look tired."

"It's nothing an early night won't fix." I craft a subdued smile while everyone takes a seat at the dining table and begins eating.

I don't make eye contact with anyone.

Not Matthew, who sits to my left, or Keira, who's in front of me on the other side of the table.

I focus on the takeout containers. I fork food onto my plate that I don't have the stomach to consume. I stare at the wine glass someone left at my place setting and wonder how many seconds it would take to drain it clean.

The conversation is smooth around me. Keira, Sarah, and Decker talk to Bishop and Matthew as if they're friends. They discuss the weather. The stock market. The damn NFL, for Christ's sake. Hunter retains his usual air of ice-cold indifference.

To the untrained eye, everything is normal. There's no hitch in conversation or pause of discomfort for Stella to latch onto. Not one hint to trigger her suspicion that the family surrounding her have disowned her mother.

They all play nice—the loved ones who divorced me and the man who betrayed me.

I should be grateful, but the agony builds beneath my sternum with every nibble of chow mein.

"Can we come back to this place sometime?" Stella asks. "I love it here, and I haven't had a chance to look around."

"You're always welcome." Matthew drapes his arm over the back of my chair. "In fact, we can make plans before you leave." His eyes meet mine, taunting in their hunger. "What do you think, *la mia piccola sporcacciona*?"

Bishop clears his throat, the slightest laugh shaking through.

"She can't miss any more school." I hold Matthew's gaze, ignoring the warmth in my belly, the flood of adrenaline in my veins.

"Then summer vacation sounds perfect. You can stay however long you like." He stares me down, waiting for a rejection.

Nobody else speaks. All eyes are on us.

"Our work will be done by then." I grab my napkin and dab at my mouth as I wink at my daughter. "But don't worry, little fish. I'll find us a sugar daddy with a bigger beach house."

Stella snorts and rolls her eyes. "Gross, Mom."

Matthew inches closer, making me tense as his lips brush the sensitive skin below my ear. "You know I can give you all the sugar you need."

I ignore him. The words. The proximity. The contact.

I shut everything out and slowly reach for my glass of wine.

"Well, that's a visual I never knew I didn't need." Bishop grabs for the container of rice. "Did anyone want any more of this before I eat it all?"

The conversation diverts away from me. Away from *us*. But Matthew doesn't move.

He keeps his arm around my chair, his body nestled close as Stella laughs at her aunt's recollection of a childhood vacation at Salt Lake City.

My wine goes down too easily. I punctuate every bite of shame and twinge of regret with a sip of Chardonnay which requires my glass to be filled repeatedly until everyone is finished eating.

"Can I go to my room to check my phone?" Stella places her cutlery on her empty plate and bats her lashes at me. "I'm waiting to hear from Tobias?"

"Sure." I force a smile. "I think we're all finished here, aren't we?"

"I believe we are, *principessa*." Matthew nods at her, and Keira agrees.

Stella hustles for the hall, taking every ounce of fraudulent conversation with her.

The table falls silent. Discomfort suffocates the room.

My skin crawls.

I suck in a deep breath and push back in my chair. "I need fresh air." I don't wait for a reply before I stand and walk for the door.

I leave the fake civility behind, not stopping my escape until my hands clutch the deck railing, my fingers aching from the tight grip.

I barely have a chance to lower my pulse before the door slides open behind me and heavy footsteps approach.

"Everything okay?" Matthew stops a few feet away, awakening the hair on the back of my neck.

I don't want his concern or his questions. I don't even want his attention. But my body continues to respond as if it needs him, warming despite the cool breeze.

"You've done a great job raising your daughter." He moves to stand beside me, his attention on the moonlight beaming a path across the ocean. "I've never known someone her age to settle into adult conversation the way she does."

"She had to grow up a lot earlier than most." I want to inch away, to get out of the intimacy zone where his aftershave plays havoc with my senses. But he'd know exactly why I'd needed to move and I don't want to give him that ammunition. "That growth only increased when your family killed her father."

He sighs and turns toward the house, his arms leisurely crossing over his chest as he leans back against the railing.

He doesn't defend my attack. Doesn't match me taunt for taunt. Instead, he remains quiet, letting me suffocate from guilt.

"I shouldn't have said that." As much as I don't want to be near him right now, I'd despise anyone who used my father's actions against me. "I'm sorry."

"You're forgiven, *la mia piccola sporcacciona.*"

I slump at his quick pivot toward seduction. "What does that even mean?"

"Do you really want to know?" The grin lifting his cheeks tells me my answer should be a hard no. "It roughly translates to 'my dirty little girl.'"

"And you said that in front of my daughter?" I gape. "You're such a jerk."

"I am. But you lied when you said you told Stella I'm not trustworthy, so I guess we're as bad as each other."

"I *did* tell her. She knows you broke my heart by lying to me."

His brows raise. "Interesting."

I want to claim otherwise. That it's not interesting at all. That nothing about my daughter's feelings toward him are even vaguely intriguing.

"She still likes me, Layla. Why is that?"

I don't respond.

"She smiled when I put my arm over the back of your chair," he continues. "She blushed when I spoke to you in Italian. Every time I glance at her, it's as if she's silently giving me permission to keep trying to win you back. Why do you think that is?"

Son of a bitch.

He wasn't testing *me* with his actions at dinner. He was testing *her.*

"Stop manipulating my daughter," I seethe under my breath.

"I wasn't. All I did was investigate the boundaries on what she wants for her mother, and clearly, she wants you to be happy with me."

I glare. "Do I look happy to you?"

He takes the time to rake his gaze over my features—my nose, cheeks, chin. His attention lingers longer than necessary on my mouth before returning to my eyes. "You look like you're still fighting your love for me, and I hate watching you struggle."

He pushes from the railing and closes in behind me, caging me in place.

I stiffen, every part of him awakening every inch of me. I stand taller, shifting my hips away, but all he does is lean closer, pressing his crotch harder against my ass.

"*Matthew.*"

"Yes, *la mia piccola sporcacciona*?" he whispers against the back of my neck.

I swallow over the dryness decimating my throat. "What do you want from me?"

"Everything." His lips burn my skin, sending wildfire over my shoulders. "I want the love you've held hostage. I want the future we deserve. I want your passion without the malice."

I shudder, the low cadence of his words horrifically hypnotizing. "Why? We both know this is a passing phase."

"Is that what it feels like to you?" His question is barely audible. "Is the fire in your lungs burning out? Has your attraction begun to fade?"

I dig my nails into the railing.

"Mine either, *amore mio.* I still want your pants around your ankles every time I see you. Your bite marks on my skin. Your claw marks over my chest." His voice grows deeper, richer with lust. "I want to do things to you that would make a sinner blush. Then afterward, I want to hold you. *Care* for you. *Protect* you."

"You're the only thing I've needed protection from." I turn in his arms, realizing the mistake of my actions as soon as those dark eyes slay me with their proximity.

He stares at me with hunger. With pure infatuation. The potency sizzles through every place our bodies connect. Into limbs. Through organs.

I swallow. "Let me go or I'll—"

"I beg you to say something violent." He leans his waist harder into mine, the length of his cock aligning with my mons. "Your brutality does things to me that keep me up at night. Extremely dirty things."

He smirks and raises his hand to glide a thumb over the cut on his neck. "This is a constant turn on, *amore mio.* A perpetual thrill."

He inches closer, his breath brushing my lips. "I can't wait to have my blood back on your beautiful skin."

"*Move.*"

"Like this?" He grinds his hips into me, the friction electric.

I burn. Heart to hands. Throat to thighs.

"Quit fighting this." His tongue snakes out to deftly swipe his lower lip. Devilish. Sinful. "If your own daughter approves of me, why can't you?"

"I. Won't. Quit." I enunciate the words slowly as movement enters my periphery. I glance over his shoulder, finding my daughter returning to the living room, her attention fixed on me and Matthew as she strolls toward the sofa. "Stella is watching."

"Good." He weaves a hand around my waist.

"Stop it."

He's betting all his chips that I won't lash out. He knows I won't fight him in front of her.

"I won't give up what's mine," he repeats.

The need to scream builds, the tension forming a choking mass in my throat. He has to stop. I can't keep doing this.

"Have you ever wondered why Cole disowned me so easily?" I grate. "Did it ever cross your fucking mind to question how such a notorious family could discard one of their own in the blink of an eye?"

"I don't need to know."

"Yes, you do." I press my forearms to his chest, attempting to leverage a breath of space. "My brother would've been relieved that your ignorance has taken me off his hands. He probably laughed at the stupid asshole who didn't understand he was claiming a traitor. A pariah. Someone who ratted her own brother out to a monster all for a little money."

His eyes narrow. "Nothing you say will change the way I feel about you, if that's what you're attempting to achieve. Your family still care for you, Layla."

"My family despise me, but they'd do anything for my daughter," I correct. "You have no clue who I really am. You've never met the real me. The liability. I'm a threat to whoever remains close to me. Why do you think I'd allow the one thing I treasure most to be sent to a boarding school on the other side of the country?"

"You think I don't know you're a liability?" He stares at me, eyes intense, breathing heavy. He raises a hand, killing me softly as he glides a stray hair behind my ear. "Anything that weakens me is a threat to my existence. And nothing weakens me more than you."

"Are you deliberately ignoring what I just said? I'm not trustworthy. I'm not a good person. I sold out Cole for years. My own flesh and blood. My father wanted information and I willingly gave it. I told him my brother's strategies. His secrets. His plans."

"I'm not ignoring it. But I'm well aware there are parts of your story that would excuse your actions. Why did you give up the information, *amore mio*? Were you blackmailed? Threatened?"

"No."

"Then why?"

Because I wanted affection. Attention. I wanted someone to be proud of me. To love me.

The same way I thought you had.

"You won't answer me because deep down, you know I'm right." He strokes my cheek with his thumb, leisurely back and forth with savage tenderness. "You paint a horrible picture of yourself, Layla. But I see you. The *real* you."

"You see what I want you to see."

"You're many things but a good actress isn't one of them." His gaze holds unflinching confidence. "You can't push me away."

"You're not listening. I betrayed those I love. I did it over and over—"

"You made mistakes. We all do. If it weren't for mine, Grace would still be alive."

"Stop it." I thump my fist against his chest. "You're making excuses for something you know nothing about."

"That's because I don't give a shit." His mouth is almost on mine. So close. A breath apart. "I will never give up on you."

God. But I need him to.

"Well, I've already given up on you." I raise my chin through the lie. "And I'll tell you exactly why—my father manipulated me into stealing Cole's secrets. He used my desperation for love against me. He fed off my need for affection just like you did."

His lips press tight. His nostrils flare.

"I can't be with a man who has that much power over me. I

won't risk doing that to my family again no matter how much they hate me."

"I'm not your father," he growls.

"You're right. You're nowhere near as proficient as he was because you were stupid enough to get caught in your lies. You're a poor man's version of Luther Torian. Now get the fuck out of my face."

He scowls. Sneers. Retreats. "Don't for one second think that I don't know exactly what you're doing."

I stride for the living room door, my heart in my throat, my restraint in tatters.

"I'm well aware you push me to the brink to distract yourself from how you feel," he mutters. "But the time will come when you can't keep kidding yourself. And I'll still be here. Waiting. It's inevitable, *amore mio.*"

13

———————

MATTHEW

I wait outside, dragging the cold night into my lungs, wishing that shit would dull the lust coursing through my veins.

She keeps pushing me away.

There's always a new excuse. Another reason. A different story.

None of it fucking matters. I'm not going anywhere.

I want *her*—mistakes, lies, and all.

I watch her in the living room as she approaches her daughter. She says something that has the young girl moving to her feet, then the two of them head for the hall.

Once they're out of sight, all eyes turn to me—Decker, Hunter, Sarah, and Keira.

I have no idea where the fuck Bishop is, but the family descends on me in a pack, the four of them walking outside with varying degrees of annoyance.

"What was that all about?" Decker asks.

I raise a brow. "You're going to have to be more specific."

"Layla came inside, clearly flustered," Keira says. "What's going on with you two?"

"That's none of your business."

Hunter chuckles, low and menacing. "I assure you, it is."

Bishop enters the living room, his long strides eating up the space to the door that he yanks open, his expression set in stone. "I

124

leave the room for five seconds to take a piss and the scavengers descend."

He's ignored. All scrutinous eyes remain on me.

"Can you at least tell me if she's okay?" Keira asks. "She's barely spoken a word to me."

"And why do you think that is?"

She winces, wrapping her arms around her middle.

"Are you making headway?" Hunter moves to the outdoor setting, cocking his hip against the corner of the table. "Or do we start making plans for you to join us in Portland?"

"He's still got weeks, asshole," Bishop snarls. "Don't get your hopes up."

"I can't help it." Hunter's grin is subtle. "I can't wait to start riding his ass into the ground."

"You sure your bitch won't get jealous?" I jerk my chin at Decker. "He seems like the possessive type."

"I'm possessive as fuck, sweetie." Decker takes a threatening step forward. "But don't worry. I'll get a turn riding your ass, too."

"Stop it." Keira moves in front of him. "We're not here to cause trouble."

Decker glares at me over her shoulder.

"Listen to your boss." Bishop maneuvers around behind them, his attention on my hand as I slide it into my pocket to palm my blade. "You don't want to start a fight you won't win."

I dig the metal into my thigh, deeper, harder, distracting myself from the call of violence.

"We're not fighting," Keira says. "All of you need to go inside so I can speak to Matthew alone."

Nobody moves.

Nobody quits staring at me.

Keira swings around. Not to her man, or the enforcer, but to Sarah. "Get them out of here."

I smirk. It must chafe their balls to be commanded by a woman. Then again, I'd let Layla do far worse to my pride.

"Him, too." She glares at Bishop. "I want to speak to Langston alone."

Bishop leisurely meets my gaze, as if waiting for approval.

"Go." I nod.

His attention lowers to my pocket, his eyes narrowing.

"*Go.*"

He complies, leading the charge inside with Torian's cronies following.

Once the door closes, Keira strolls to the railing, her focus on the inky ocean. "Please tell me she's okay."

I wish I could, but I'm not going to lie to make this bitch feel better about her family's actions. So instead, I keep my mouth shut.

"Can you at least tell me what you've told her about the situation?" she asks.

"Nothing." I keep my voice low, knowing Layla could be right up against the French doors trying to overhear every word.

"So you're still lying to her?"

"No," I mutter. "She hasn't asked questions and I haven't offered information."

"Does she know about your agreement with Co—"

"I've told her nothing," I snarl. "Not a fucking thing. Now lower your goddamn voice before she hears you."

She shoots me a sideways glance—a glare—then slumps her shoulders with a sigh. "She's hurting. But it's obvious she still has feelings for you."

It's true. One hundred percent on both counts.

"I can see it in her eyes," she adds. "She truly believes we've disowned her. That we think less of her. And she already battled with a misconception about our commitment to her before you two met."

"Her self-worth isn't her strongest attribute."

She nods. "This situation is only making it worse. I'm worried this is causing trauma that she might never recover from."

What's her angle? Her game plan? Is she trying to trip me up?

"I'm not lying." She reads my mind. "I can't stomach what damage this is potentially creating. She was already too fragile."

"She told me she ratted out your brother. Is that true?"

"It was years ago, and I wouldn't describe it like that. She was manipulated into thinking she was helping the family. But all she did was strengthen a monster." Her voice lowers to a whisper. "She's never forgiven herself so I'm surprised she told you."

"She's trying her best to push me away."

"Is it working?"

It's strengthening my concerns about the damage I'm creating. That this situation has the potential to break Layla forever. That's why I tried to encourage her to talk to Keira this afternoon.

I drag in a deep breath. "You should tell her."

Keira straightens. "Tell her what?"

"All of it. Everything. She deserves to know the truth."

"She's always deserved to know. What's changed?"

Me. I was too fucking naive to understand how hard it would be to watch her suffer through a false perception. I was an asshole for thinking I could win her back without tearing her apart. "Just fucking tell her, Keira. Do it in the morning."

Her eyes narrow. "Is this a ploy to get out of your arrangement? That if I spill the details it'll somehow nullify the deal you made with Cole?"

"Nothing will nullify the deal. I made a commitment and I'll stick to it. But Layla should know the truth."

"Then *you* tell her."

"I can't. She doesn't trust me. She'll think I'm trying to mess with her somehow."

"Well, neither can I. My brother will kill me."

"Bullshit. We both know her insight will only work in his favor." If Layla knows she has a safe haven back home, she'll leave, and I'll be forced to follow. "She doesn't know how you all feel and that's the only thing keeping her here."

Keira's nose crinkles. "I'm confused. If you know she'll leave, why tell her?"

Because even though Layla loves me, I want her to love herself even more. I can't watch her wallow in self-loathing. I can't put her through more shit.

"Langston?" Keira cocks her head. "Talk."

"All you need to know is that she's suffering from what your brother made her believe. So get it done."

"Do you understand what will—"

"Get it fucking done." I stalk for the door, pull it wide, and ignore every single motherfucker along the way to my bedroom.

I'm shooting myself in the foot. Sabotaging my own goddamn future.

But there's no way around it.

Layla's misery has to end.

I take a shower, letting the water's spray wash the bloodied cuts along my thigh. Then I drag on my boxers, cut the lights, and climb into bed to stare at the fucking ceiling for hours after everyone else has gone to sleep.

Layla will walk. No doubt about it. And when I follow, I won't have access to her on my terms. She could lock herself at home. Or worse, in her brother's house.

Cole won't grant me any more concessions. He's given me enough already. So sinking back into my old lifestyle, this time under Torian's reign, is inevitable.

Given the circumstances, I guess I never left.

A normal man wouldn't spy on his woman. He wouldn't pay to have her mugged. Wouldn't manipulate or mistreat her.

A squeak of noise catches my attention. The sound is faint. Those fuckers are planting bugs while the house is quiet.

I slide from bed, grab my blade from under my pillow, and creep to the door to gently glide it open.

Everything is dark—the hall, the living room, the staircase leading to the lower level. But someone is there. I can make out a frozen silhouette near Layla's door.

"Did I wake you?" Stella whispers.

Shit. I inch the knife behind me, slipping it beneath the waistband of my boxers, the blade digging into my tailbone. "No. What are you doing up so late, *principessa*?"

"I couldn't sleep. So I thought I'd crawl into bed with Mom... But when I got here, I started to wonder if maybe you were already in there... ya know... with her."

She's fishing. Attempting to broach a subject I won't touch with a ten-foot pole.

"Not at all. Enjoy your time with your mother." I backtrack into my room.

Her shadowed silhouette approaches, her footfalls short and sharp. "You don't want to go in there instead of me?"

"I think she'd much prefer your company, Stella. Now go get some sleep." I grab the door handle.

"Wait." She places her hand on the wood. "She said something to me today that I'm hoping you might be able to get out of my head."

Warning sirens fill my ears. Loud. Deafening. "Ask me in the morning."

"Please. I'm obsessing over it. She said you were familiar with our enemies. *Our*," she repeats. "Meaning mine and hers, not my Uncle Cole's. Which got me thinking, because as far as I know, I only have one enemy, and that's the family who abducted me and killed my father."

Jesus Christ.

"So, I'd like to know how familiar you are with them. Because she meant the Costas, right?"

Jesus fucking Christ.

"Stella, this isn't something we can discuss. Any questions you have need to be directed at your mother."

"Why?" Her shadowed face peers up at me, her features unreadable through the darkness. "Because I'm too young? Because I won't understand?"

"Because I don't want you to be scared of me," I answer truthfully.

She falls quiet, the thickening silence wrapping its hands around my throat.

"Go to bed, *principessa*."

"How familiar are you with them?" she whispers. "Are you, like, friends or something?"

I keep my mouth shut, my hand tightening on the door handle.

"Do you work for them? Do you help them? Are you the reason I was taken?"

"Jesus. Fuck. No." *Motherfucker.* This kid is treating my paternal heart strings like a fucking jungle gym, and I never even knew I had any. "I despise the Costas," I seethe. "I hate them just as much as you do."

"Then why would I be scared of you?" She steps closer, her foot nudging my door wider, the proximity exposing the glint of something metallic in her hand.

A knife?

"You looking to stab me, *principessa*?"

"All I'm looking for is the truth, and as much as I love my mom, I know she'll never give it to me."

I could disarm her. With a strike of a hand or the kick of my foot, she would cease to be a threat. But I refuse to upset her.

"It's funny. My mom thinks I'm this innocent little kid, but I've never been that way. I've never been a kid at all. And Tobias hasn't either." She steps closer again, forcing my retreat. "So after we were abducted, and kept in the dark about what happened, we decided to figure it out on our own. We spent a year learning all there was to know about the Costa family. We tracked school records for Abri, Remy, and Salvatore. We got copies of birth records. We hired someone to search newspaper archives. And even discovered an older son of Emmanuel's that nobody mentions on social media. But do you know who did mention him?" She cocks her head. "A girl called Grace in his senior yearbook."

"*Stella,*" I warn.

"I knew who you were the moment I got off the jet. I know all about you. What I don't understand is why you now call yourself Matthew and what you're doing with my mom. Does she know who you are?"

"Yes." I clench my jaw.

"Why are you two working together? Why did you change your name? Why aren't you part of the Costa family anymore?" She lobs questions at me without accusation or emotion. "And what have you been doing since you left them? As far as the internet is concerned, you disappeared after you finished school."

"I'm going to wake your mom." I move to step around her, but she counters to block my path, the knife raising.

"No. Don't. Obviously she knows the truth, if you're willing to wake her. But she said you were working together. Doing what?"

"I'm losing patience, *principessa.* I won't betray your mother by discussing this with you."

"Then tell me I don't have to worry about her while she's with you. Tell me you hate them for what they did to me. Tell me you love her."

"I wish Emmanuel dead for what he did to you."

She sucks in a ragged breath. "What about my mom? Do you regret hurting her? Why did you lie?"

The questions from a barely-known child punish me harder than I could've imagined. I want to protect her. Help her.

"There were a lot of reasons. Safety was one of them. Preservation of what we had was another. I care about your mother, Stella. I never wanted to upset her."

"I figured as much from the way you stare at her."

"You're perceptive." I maneuver around her and approach my bedroom door, waiting for her to follow. "Are you done or am I waking her?"

"I'm not done. I want to know why you changed your name. Why did you disappear?"

I start into the hall, prepared to wake Layla and cause World War III.

"Wait. Fine. I'll stop." She shuffles around me and guides me back to my door with an adamant finger pointed at my chest. "Just answer one more question—what's your new surname?"

I shut the door on the kid's face, her heavy sigh carrying from the other side.

"Night, Matthew," she whispers.

I slink back to bed, blindsided.

I continue staring at the ceiling, contemplating where the fuck I go from here.

Stella is going to get herself in trouble. All she needs to do is dig into the wrong person's past and she'll be snuffed. Which means I still have to tell Layla what her daughter has been up to.

Great.

That conversation will be less enjoyable than a prostate exam. And how the fuck do I broach it? Subtle or sledgehammer?

I spend hours trying to figure out the best course of action as sleep evades me. Then as soon as I pass out, a shuffle of noise wakes me again.

I sit, the bed coverings falling to my waist, the faint hint of early morning sunshine highlighting a silhouette at the end of my bed. "*Amore mio?*"

"It's Stella."

Are you fucking kidding me? "Is something wrong? Is your mom okay?"

"She's fine. Still sleeping. I just thought, seeing as though I was awake and it's really early, that we might be able to go surfing before she gets up."

She's joking, right?

"Where's that knife of yours?" I scrub a hand down my face.

"Back in the kitchen. I was hoping I could make up for last night by getting to know you better."

I blink her into focus—the innocent shadowed features, the goddamn shorts and shirt I assume she's already wearing in place of a swim suit. "I don't think that's a good idea, *principessa*. Your mom already said no to surfing."

"Because she said we wouldn't have time. But I got up early specifically for this."

"I think you're smart enough to know that wasn't the only reason." I slump back onto the pillows and drag my arm over my eyes. "Go back to sleep. We'll surf next time."

"There won't be a next time. Not unless you figure out how to win her back." Her footsteps carry closer to my side. "Come on. Aunt Keira said I could."

"Your aunt Keira said you had permission to go surfing with me?" I ask slowly, as if everyone under this roof is insane. "I find that hard to believe."

"Then ask her yourself. She's already up making coffee."

I'm fucking tempted to do exactly that. To put this meddling little schemer in her place. If only I didn't appreciate her tenacity.

"I'm doing you a favor." Her tone gains an edge of superiority. "This is your chance to get the inside scoop on all things Layla Hart. I could teach you how to win her back. How to gain her forgiveness. Isn't that what you want?"

"I want your mom to forgive me, not kill me."

She giggles, feigning innocence I now know doesn't exist. "Come on, Matthew." She grabs my wrist, dragging it away from my face. "I know you can make her happy. I just need to teach you how to convince her of the same thing."

I growl and sit up as she tugs my arm. I can't deny her any more than I can deny her mother. "Meet me downstairs. The boards are in the garage."

She makes a soft squealing noise—a sound of pure delight as she hustles for the door.

I fling back the covers. "And, *principessa*…"

"Yeah?" She stops at the threshold.

"If your mom wakes up and doesn't approve, I'm throwing you under the bus as hard and fast as possible. Understood?"

She chuckles. "Understood."

I stalk for my walk-in closet and wait until she leaves before changing into swim trunks. When I get downstairs, she stands in the fluorescent light of the garage, her hair pulled back in a ponytail.

"I don't have a wetsuit in your size." I grab the first board from the rack, then open the roller door. "We're going to have to brave the cold."

"If you can do it, so can I."

"Homicidal and an optimist. The world better beware." I jerk my chin for her to walk ahead.

"I think my mom would describe me as more of a harmless people pleaser."

"Which one of us is correct?"

She shrugs. "Both."

We walk around the side of the house where the breaking sunrise greets us, then into the backyard. Hunter glares down from the deck, silently warning.

I wait for him to make a threat. But he doesn't say a word, just watches with narrowed eyes as I lead Stella to the back gate and hold it open for her to walk onto the beach.

"Don't worry about him." She stops a few feet onto the sand to wait for me. "He's always like that."

"An arrogant prick?" I grate before common sense kicks in.

She chokes out a laugh. "Yeah. It's his job. He used to be meaner before Sarah came along."

"Well, I'm glad I didn't meet him back then." I close the gate behind us and continue toward the surf where the breeze is more savage. "You sure you still want to do this?"

Goose bumps cover her arms as she bundles them close at her sides. "Of course. Like you said, I can't come to the beach without surfing. And we haven't even talked yet. I've got a whole heap of questions, like what happened to your arm?"

I glance down at the square bandage covering the stab wound.

"There was an incident in the kitchen."

"And the scratch on your neck?"

"Same thing."

She raises a brow. "You're either a really bad cook or you haven't learned your lesson on lying."

"Believe me, I learned that lesson well."

She sweeps the stray strands of hair away from her face and shoots me a sideways glance. "Will you tell me about your father? What did he do to you?"

I stiffen. "I don't refer to him that way."

"As your father?"

"Yes."

She stops. I do the same, hitching the board higher under my arm.

"He hurt you more than he did me, didn't he?" Her eyes turn somber, but I'm not sure if the emotional display is real. She's a perfect little actress.

"Nothing hurts more than losing your dad, *principessa*."

"But he hurt you, right? What did he do?"

"He killed someone I cared deeply about. Just like he did with you."

"I'm sorry." She gives me an awkward look. Half cringe. Part wince. Then starts walking again. "Was it a long time ago?"

"Sometimes it feels that way. At others, it's as if it were yesterday." I take the lead, wanting to be in front of her before she steps into the ocean in case there are jellyfish.

The first trickle of water is like liquid ice. The second is more punishing.

"That's what it's like with my dad, too." She follows me into the shallows, her mouth gaping as a gasp escapes. "Holy crap. It's freezing."

"I did warn you."

"I know, but…" She bounces on her toes. "It's so cold my feet are stinging."

"Does this mean we're not surfing, *principessa*?"

She drops her bottom lip. Slinks her shoulders.

"Okay, let's get you back inside." I smirk. "Your mom won't forgive me if you get sick."

"Can't we sit on the beach for a while? I haven't told you how to win her back yet." She looks at me with Bambi eyes, making me question whether she came out here to surf at all.

"You sure are manipulative, aren't you?"

"I take pride in my work." She bounds out of the water, her arms wrapping around her middle as she plops down onto dry sand, completely ignoring Hunter and Decker who stand at the edge of the house yard like guard dogs on patrol.

I'm almost inclined to give them a reason to attack just so I don't have to dodge questions from the miniature detective.

"So who did he kill?" she asks as I dump the board out of the way and sit beside her.

"It was the woman who mentioned me in the yearbook. It happened when I was a teenager."

"And you stopped calling him your dad after that?"

"The very same day."

"My mom doesn't like her dad either. You two have a lot in common… in a bad way. And you're kinda like Romeo and Juliet with the whole family rivalry kinda thing."

What a delightful fucking omen of what's to come.

"Family can be a blessing and a curse," I mutter. "We don't get to choose which."

She nods. "Why won't you admit you love my mom? She says you don't but I know she's lying."

I clench my teeth. Glare at the horizon. "It's complicated."

"You sound just like her."

I keep my mouth shut, hoping she'll quit this line of questioning before I have to demand we go back inside.

"You know, my dad never looked at her the way you do."

I clench harder. Glare with more ferocity.

"I don't think he loved her like she deserved," she continues, compiling my anger. "I didn't notice until a few years back when Aunt Keira and Uncle Cole met Sebastian and Anissa. I hadn't really been around other couples before that. But seeing them together made me realize my dad didn't treat Mom the same."

Commenting on her father is a trap. One I don't plan to fall into. Not now. Not ever.

She sniffs, as if emotion is getting the better of her or maybe just the impending Emmy nomination. "Tobias said he heard my dad had cheated on her."

I lean forward, elbows on knees, hiding my fisted hands in my lap.

"Would you ever do that to her?" she asks.

"Never. And I'll take that vow to the grave."

"Why do I believe you?"

God only knows. I don't even understand why she wants to be near me. "Is it time to go back yet?"

A throat clears behind us, the tone feminine.

Yep. Definitely time.

I don't bother glancing over my shoulder. I can already feel Layla's laser focus burning through the back of my head. But Stella turns, her sigh quickly following.

"She's awake," she murmurs. "And it looks like she got out of the wrong side of the bed."

"So much for helping me win her back, *principessa.* You didn't give me any pointers."

"I didn't need to." She pushes to her feet. "You win her back by winning me over. And you did that with flying colors."

14

———

LAYLA

I stare down at the man who defied my orders and my daughter who sits close beside him, their conversation unheard over the ocean.

They're talking though. The two of them converse as if they're best buddies.

Resentment eats through me, the cold breeze nothing in comparison to the chill in my veins.

I cross my arms over my chest, restricting my billowing pajama top, and clear my throat.

Stella straightens as she turns to look at me, her eyes softening with apology. She knows she's done the wrong thing. She predicted my disappointment and came down here anyway. All because of him.

She says something else to Matthew, then stands, wipes the sand from her butt, and starts toward me.

"Morning, Mom." Her arms are covered in goose bumps, her smile wide. "Don't worry. We didn't go in the water."

"I'm glad to hear it." I tug her in for a hug, easing the panic I felt when I woke and found her gone. "Breakfast is ready. I'll see you inside."

"Okay. But before I go…" She glances over her shoulder at Matthew who still hasn't turned to face my wrath and lowers her voice. "Can I tell you how much I think he's perfect for you?"

"Not now, Stella." I kiss her temple and drop my arms from her shoulders.

"But he really is. You two have so much in common and he really adores—"

"*Not now, Stella.*" I add a warning to my tone. An annoyance that I don't want to inflict when she's one meal away from returning to Chicago.

She sighs. "Mom, he made a mistake. Give him a second chance."

"If you don't hurry, Bishop will have eaten all the bacon."

She looks at me with disappointment that smarts.

Matthew gets compassion while I get frustration. It isn't fair.

"I'll be there in a minute." I swivel toward the house where Hunter and Decker remain waiting at the yard gate. "Tell the guys to go eat, too."

I already told them as I passed but obviously they want to watch the fireworks.

She gives another sigh and starts toward them, shoulders slumped. I wait until she's at the gate before I move closer to Matthew, stopping a foot away to watch him stare at the ocean.

He doesn't acknowledge me. Doesn't even spare me a glance.

I want to hate him for it. For everything. And I guess I do. But the negative feelings only dilute the furthest edges of my longing.

"We need to talk," he mutters to the ocean.

"You're goddamn right we do. What the hell were you thinking bringing her out here when I told you not to?"

"That's the least of our problems." He stands like a shirtless Greek god in the early daylight, his dark hair falling around his eyes. "Stella knows who I am."

I freeze. Blink.

My mind doesn't compute.

"My thoughts exactly." He bends over to pick up his surfboard.

"You told her?" I can barely hear my own voice through the static in my ears. "How could you?"

"I didn't do shit, Layla. She knew who I was from the moment she got here. Apparently, her and Tobias have spent a substantial amount of time digging into the Costa family behind your back."

"No." I shake my head. "She's just a girl."

"She's a fucking crafty genius with balls bigger than mine. And she needs a leash. She's going to get herself killed if you don't pull her into line."

He's lying.

He told her the truth to mess with me. Now he's blaming it on her.

"How dare you?" I can't think through the anger.

"Excuse me? What the fuck have I done apart from stay up all night, pandering to her interrogation?"

"Her *what*?" My legs weaken. My pulse trembles.

"Interrogation," he repeats. "She came at me with a million questions all while wielding a goddamn fucking knife, *amore mio*. She said she has copies of birth records and school yearbooks. She knows the family I was born into, and exactly why you're angry with me... Well, part of it, anyway." He stares at me in concern. In *fear*. His features tight, his lips thin.

Oh, God. He's not lying.

I raise a shaky hand to my mouth, my head suddenly light, my limbs heavy.

"*Hey.*" He drops the board and grabs my upper arms. "*Shit...* don't pass out on me."

I sway, unable to blink away the encroaching darkness.

"*Amore mio*, it's okay. I'm sure it's just normal crazy kid stuff. I bet they all do it."

He's willing to bet all kids instigate a dangerous search on the people who abducted them?

No, this is insane.

I can't breathe. I can't get enough air.

"Forgive me." He smashes his cold mouth to mine. Harsh lips. Dominating hands.

He consumes me in an instant, the sizzle jolting through me like lightning to snap me out of my daze.

"Get off me." I shove at his chest.

"You're welcome." He steps back, smug. "Color is already returning to your cheeks."

I bet it is. The heat of unwanted lust races through me in a rush of wildfire.

"You're a son of a bitch." I swipe the tingling remnants of his kiss from my lips with a rough hand.

"I know, but sometimes it's nice to get a second opinion."

He's distracting me. Attempting to divert my attention from Stella's complete and utter lunacy. What the hell was she thinking snooping on the Costas? What if they caught her? What would they have done?

Matthew clears his throat, regaining my attention. "You should get someone to track what she does on her cell. Or any other device, for that matter. Tobias, too. Keeping an eye on what they're searching online and who they're contacting might be enough to keep them safe."

And if it's not? What then?

I pinch the bridge of my nose, trying to stem the forming headache. This can't be happening. I sent her away in the hopes she'd be better protected. But space didn't help. I still failed by sheltering her so much that she went in search of her own truth.

"Do you want me to organize it for you?" Matthew asks. "I can make a few calls—"

"Was she scared of you?" I drop my hand to my side. "Is that why she had the knife?"

"The knife wasn't for protection, *amore mio*. Personally, I think it was because she's a bad-ass like her mom."

"Are you trying to be funny?" I snip.

"No. I'm trying to be honest. Like I said, she knew who I was from the moment she arrived and not once has she acted in fear. Even in front of you—am I right? I think she sees me as an ally against Emmanuel."

I shake my head. "It's not like her to act this way, though. It's so far out of left field, I'm struggling to believe it."

"Kids do stupid shit. I'm sure it's only natural."

"Coming at you with a knife isn't natural, Matthew. As hard as it might be to believe, I never brought her up to be violent."

"And she wasn't. She was confident. Determined. Some might say a chip off the old block."

I glower. *Glare.* "I have to speak to her." I start toward the house.

"Don't." He grabs my wrist. "Not while you're worked up. Stay out here a while. Breathe. Don't go to her until you know what you're going to say because I'd place good odds on her already having a watertight defense prepared for her actions."

"Oh, God." My shoulders slump. "This is ridiculous."

"I haven't even told you the best part yet." He releases me and bends over to grab his surfboard. "For the sake of being entirely transparent, she woke me early this morning because she wanted to give me pointers on how to win you back. Isn't that cute? She approves of me despite the family I was born into."

"I bet a history lesson on the Butcher Boys of Baltimore would change that," I mutter.

"But what if it only made me more of an idol in the eyes of your knife-threatening offspring?" He starts for the house. "It's a crazy world, *amore mio*. Who would've known your daughter would be my biggest support?"

I bite back the need to scream. To shove. To slap.

But I've done all that before without relief. I've snapped. I've fought. I've fucked.

All the things I hope will ease my suffering never do. The mindlessness only continues to build. And I sure as hell won't give Hunter front-row tickets to my breakdown while he remains on his own at the gate. Watching. Judging.

Matthew passes him, then continues through the yard while the breeze whispers through my hair, the pain of my failures building to new heights.

I force my chin high and follow, ignoring Hunter's narrowed gaze as I approach.

"Everything okay, Lay?" he taunts. "It seems like you two have problems."

"You're the only one who's going to have a problem if you don't get out of my face." I stop to stare him down, but his superior expression doesn't falter. "You're not welcome here."

"It's my job to keep an eye on you."

"No. Not anymore. Not after Cole disowned me." I keep my voice strong, my shoulders stiff. "When the jet takes off this morning, I want you on it. I already know you were here before Stella arrived, but you're not sticking around once she leaves."

His jaw ticks. "I'll need to call Torian to—"

"I don't care what you have to do. But you'll take off with everyone else." I push through the gate, stalk onto the deck, and hustle inside before my tough exterior evaporates.

I lock myself in my private bathroom and slump against the counter as I hyperventilate.

I need to talk to Cole, but I don't have a phone.

I have to arrange closer surveillance of Stella and Tobias, but I don't have any money.

Shit.

I pull on jeans and a woolen sweater while laughter and conversation echo down the hall. I chastise myself for not keeping a closer eye on my daughter while the clink of cutlery signals the family meal being eaten without me. And I fight the desire to continue hiding while I put on a bare hint of makeup and a spritz of my new expensive perfume.

Maybe I shouldn't address Stella's actions just yet. Maybe I should let her think she's gotten away scot-free while I do some snooping of my own.

"*Fuck.*" I grip the counter and scowl at my reflection in the mirror. The eyes of a traitorous failure don't spark any bright ideas on how to handle this.

I'm clueless. And running out of time.

I force myself to leave the bedroom, hoping enlightenment will strike me with each passing breath. I paste on the flimsiest fake smile before entering the open living area where everyone is seated at the dining table.

Everyone except Matthew, who is nowhere in sight.

"I saved you some bacon." Stella pulls out the vacant seat beside her. The one that also happens to be next to my sister. "But you're right. Bishop did try to eat it all."

"I'm a growing boy." He shoots her a grin from across the table.

"You can never trust men to be chivalrous when it comes to food," Sarah mutters. "Believe me, I know."

I take the offered seat and ignore Keira as she stalks my periphery.

"Want some eggs?" She leans forward to grab the serving spoon, placing a heap of scrambled mush on my plate before I can respond.

"What's wrong?" Stella leans into me, bumping my shoulder. "You're not angry with Matthew for taking me to the beach, are you? We didn't go surfing, I promise. I barely put my foot in the water."

"I'm not angry." No more than usual, at least.

"Good." She scoops the remaining scraps of her breakfast onto her fork. "I'd hate to think I got him in trouble."

"He does that well enough on his own." Bishop snickers to himself.

I pick at the mushed eggs, unable to stomach food, despising yet another charade. "On second thought, I'm not that hungry." I push from my chair and claim my plate. "I'm going to make coffee."

"I'll help."

I hide a cringe as Keira follows me to the kitchen where I discard my food in the bin.

"Sorry about the whole surfing thing." She grabs the juice and milk from the counter to place them in the fridge. "I didn't realize she wasn't allowed."

I pause in front of the coffee machine. "Given the circumstances, I would've thought it was obvious."

She straightens. Nods. "I guess she twisted my arm like she always does."

"She asked you for permission?" I thought Matthew was the one who'd trampled over my rules.

"Yeah, she said you only denied her because there wasn't enough time. So she deliberately got up earlier to make it work."

Stella is turning into someone who enjoys manipulating authority and the thought of those skills increasing through her teenage years makes me shudder.

"You need to consult me first." I place a coffee pod in the machine and a mug under the nozzle. "I wasn't even told she was being brought here."

"I know." She inches closer, entering my personal space. "I'm sorry about that, too."

But not sorry for disowning me?

"Can we go somewhere and talk?" she asks. "We need to leave

soon, and the two of us really have to hash out a few things before we go."

"No, thank you."

I have no intention of *hashing out* my mistakes.

Or letting her *hash out* a hundred I-told-you-sos.

I press the start button on the coffee machine. "I'd prefer if you left without causing drama."

"Layla—"

"I said no." I meet her gaze. "I'm not perfect, Keira. I've made shitty choices. But I'm not going to relive them with you. I plan to make up for what I've done and prove my worth, exactly like Cole expects. But I don't owe you any more than that."

"That's not what I want. If we could just—"

"It's time to get moving." Decker pushes from the table, the legs of his chair scraping along the tile. "I just got a text that the jet is prepped and waiting."

"I can't." I lower my tone, hiding my words from the rest of the room beneath the gurgle of the coffee machine. "Stella will get curious, and that girl already knows too much. Just let me get on with the ramifications without drawing more attention to how I got here. That's all I ask of you."

Her face falls, her eyes pleading with mine. "I have to speak to you. If not now, then soon."

"Soon. Later. Just not now." I grab my filled mug and turn toward the island counter as Matthew strolls into the room.

He's dressed in one of his pristine suits, his hair freshly washed, his aftershave infiltrating the air. He glances from me to Keira, his questioning gaze lingering longer on her than me. *Why?*

"They're leaving." I raise the mug to take a sip. "Will we all fit in the Lincoln if I come to the airport? I want to be able to say goodbye to Stella."

"Yeah." Matthew pats his suit pockets as if searching for a key. "How many are leaving?"

I pivot to the group, my attention on Hunter to see if he'll dare to defy me.

He glowers, lips pressed, one brow raised in rebellion.

"We all are," Sarah answers for him. "It's time to head home."

"I'll get our bags." Hunter's expression doesn't change as he pushes from the table. Decker follows. Both of them dump their plates and cutlery in the dishwasher as they pass.

"Can somebody grab mine?" Stella asks around a mouthful of juice. "It's already on my bed. I just need to get my phone and charger."

"I can get it." Keira brushes a hand over my arm. "But we really need to talk."

"Later." *Never.*

Matthew stalks for the coffee maker as my sister leaves the room. I watch him watching her. His attention isn't casual. It's cautionary. Questioning.

They're up to something.

"I need to have a quick shower." Sarah takes the remaining plates from the table while Stella begins clearing the condiments.

They flitter around, tidying up while I sip my coffee, remaining silent until they both disappear down the hall.

"Did you say something to her?" Matthew asks.

"No. And I don't think I will. She needs to think she still has freedom while I put added security measures in place."

"Are you sure that's the right move?"

No. I have no clue. "It's all I've got right now."

He raises his brows. "Then in that case, be careful, *amore mio*. I lost the woman I adore by using the same tactics."

I fight against a wince as Bishop pushes from the table.

"What are we talking about?" He throws a bite of crispy bacon in his mouth and walks toward us. "I heard something about tactics."

Matthew turns to him. "You need to sweep the house while we're gone. I want every inch of this place searched."

"Why?" The reply drips with sarcasm. "You don't trust our guests?"

"Just get it done." Matthew dumps his remaining coffee in the sink, then starts for the entry, his gaze brushing mine. "I'll be waiting at the car."

"Did I miss something?" Bishop narrows his attention on me. "The tension between you two is different."

"I don't know what you're talking about." I place my empty mug in the dishwasher and go in search of Stella, even more unsure what to say to her after Matthew poked at my plan with brutal logic.

She's in her room, on the bed, her focus riveted on her cell.

Who are you spying on now, little fish?

"Reading something exciting?" I ask.

"Nope." She pockets the device and smiles up at me. "Just messaging Tobias to let him know we're leaving soon… unless you've changed your mind about letting me stay for one more night."

"Maybe next time." I open my arms, wordlessly beckoning her forward. "But nice try."

She walks to me, nestling her head against my shoulder, her arms around my waist.

She's not a little girl anymore. She's not a child, despite her age.

My heart hurts over the playful years she was denied. I ache for all the innocent years she's missed.

"He told you, didn't he," she murmurs into my neck. "I knew he would. He learned his lesson about keeping things from you."

I close my eyes and squeeze her tighter. "Stella, it's dangerous to dig into the lives of powerful people."

"I know. But it's also wrong for those same people to get away with murder."

My pulse falters. What is this beautiful girl planning?

"That's true." I swallow over the dryness taking over my throat. I need to appease her. To temper her thirst for revenge. "But I would never let that happen."

She pulls back, her eyes questioning as they meet mine. "It's been years, Mom. Nothing has happened to them."

"It will."

Her gaze narrows. Her head cocks to one side. "Is that why you and Matthew are working together?"

I give a somber smile. "I need you to trust that we've got this under control."

"What are you—"

I shake my head. "I'm not discussing this with you, little fish. I'm your mother. I was Benji's wife. It's my duty to take care of them, and I will. But you need to be aware you're risking your life and mine by snooping. If you're caught—"

"I'll stop," she vows. "We won't do it anymore. I promise."

I want to believe her. I wish I could. But as I stare down at her, I struggle to recognize my little girl in the woman she's growing into. She's far more independent than I've ever been. A lot more cunning, too.

"Good." I lean in to kiss her forehead. "Because I'd hate to have to drag you back to Portland to keep a closer eye on you."

"You won't. I'll speak to Tobias. I'll tell him you're handling it."

Her statement strikes through me, her words making it clear they had plans of their own.

"Stella, do you realize what could've happened if you were caught? If Emmanuel—"

"We weren't going to get caught. Tobias has a whole heap of money in his savings account from Uncle Cole, so we've been paying someone to do the digging for us."

"You can always get caught. If they found the person you paid, they could find you. Everything is traceable."

"It's just information, Mom. It's not—"

"Listen to me." I cup her cheek with my palm, calm yet determined as I force her to hold my gaze. "If something ever happened to you, I wouldn't be able to live through it. Losing you would kill me. So I need you to be safe for the both of us, okay?"

Her face falls. "I know. And I already promised. I won't do it again."

"Tobias either."

She nods. "Tobias either."

"It's time to go," Decker shouts down the hall.

I ignore him, my palm still cupping her cheek, my eyes holding hers.

"I wish I could stay," she whispers. "At least until you and Matthew make up. I really like him."

You wouldn't if you'd been snooping more in his direction.

"No more matchmaking, little fish." I kiss the tip of her nose and step back. "Go say goodbye to Bishop. You heard Decker. It's time to leave."

15

———

LAYLA

I keep my attention on Stella as I endure the long drive to the airport, the two of us squished into the very back seats while Hunter rides up the front with Matthew, and Sarah, Decker, and Keira take the middle row.

Stella's hyped, the energy in her voice making me realize how incredibly tired I am as she conspiratorially whispers all the things that would make Matthew and I a great couple.

"You have the same lifestyles… He has an awesome beach house… He thinks you're the goat… I bet he'd treat you like a queen, too. Just look at the way he's staring at you in the rearview mirror.

I don't look. I don't dare.

But I'm sure everyone else does because even though she's whispering, her voice is frustratingly loud through the silent car.

"Do you have any assignments due this week?" I ask.

"Mom, don't try and change the subject."

"I'm not."

Sarah clears her throat as if punctuating my lie.

"How much longer until we get to the airport?" I direct the question toward the front of the Lincoln, still not daring to glance toward the rearview mirror.

"Five minutes," Hunter mutters.

Damn it. Stella will have our wedding vows written and the rest of our married lives planned before her departure.

"Our time is almost up, little fish. I'm going to miss you so much. Don't forget to start thinking about what you want for Christmas. I'll need you to write me a list soon."

"Christmas?" she drawls. "Really? Do you want me to change the topic that badly?"

Like you wouldn't believe.

"It's not that far away. You know how fast time flies." I keep her busy with innocuous conversation while praying that I'm financially back on my feet by December. "We should plan a surprise escape. Maybe even take a trip to somewhere on the coast."

She rolls her eyes but reluctantly plays along, naming potential holiday destinations until Matthew pulls into the small private airport and stops at the gate leading to the tarmac. A jet is already waiting, the whir of the engines humming through the vehicle.

The ignition is cut. Hunter and Matthew climb out to get the bags. Sarah, Keira, and Decker follow, and once the side middle seat is lowered, Stella and I do, too.

"Do you need anything at school?" I cling to her free hand as she closes the car door. "Socks? Underwear? New uniforms?"

"I'm all good, Mom."

I'm not sure what I would've done if she'd said otherwise. I don't have the funds to help her.

"Don't get all emotional." She turns to face me, wrapping her arms around my waist. "You know I hate when you do that."

"I don't get *all emotional,* thank you very much." I squeeze her tight, breathing in the scent of her hair. It's always jasmine. Sweet and pure.

"Yeah, you do. I can already sense the waterworks about to take hold."

I mimic her laughter, doing my best to lighten a situation that tears me apart. The encroaching isolation. The torturous defeat. "I love you so much. You know that, right?"

She pulls back to look at me. "Even after last night?"

"Of course. You're everything to me, Stella. You always will be."

She nods, solemn with her half-hearted smile. "I wish you'd give Matthew another chance. With me living on the other side of the country, you need someone else to love. And to love you back."

She glances to the front of the Lincoln where the man in question waits, his ass pressed against the hood, his arms crossed over his chest as he stares at the jet. "I like him."

"You've made that abundantly clear."

She engages those puppy-dog eyes of hers. "Let him love you. You deserve it."

"Be good at school." I guide stray strands of hair behind her ear, fervently ignoring her. "Make sure Tobias behaves."

"I will."

I kiss her forehead and close my eyes. "I miss you already."

"I miss you, too." She retreats, each step squeezing more air from my lungs.

"Be safe." I raise my voice over the jet engines. "Be sensible. Don't kiss any boys."

Her beautiful smile beams before she pivots away, her stride leading her to Matthew's side. I hold my breath as she engulfs him in a hug—one that's reciprocated. He's so good with her. How does he do it?

"I'll be on the jet." Hunter grabs the suitcases at his feet and starts toward the aircraft.

I don't acknowledge him. Or Decker and Sarah, who follow his lead with the remaining bags as Stella pulls back to say something to Matthew.

I can't hear what she says, but I witness her adoration. It kills me. She's naive and dauntless.

It's a dangerous combination around a man like him.

With an infectious smile, she swivels toward the aircraft and jogs to catch up with the group. The only one left behind is Keira who remains within reach, watching them from beside me, her silence increasing the awkwardness.

"Can we talk now?" she asks. "I need to say I'm sorry."

She wants to apologize?

"I let you down." She speaks softly over the roaring engines. "You told me you were in love and instead of showing support, I judged you."

"You didn't just judge me, Keira—you *disowned* me. And I get it. If anyone else made the mistakes I did, I'd hold them accountable, too. But right now, I don't need another reminder."

"That's not what this is." Her eyes plead with me as Matthew climbs back into the Lincoln. "I never disowned you. Nobody did."

"Tell that to our brother." I walk for the car only to be stopped by her hand around my wrist.

"Our brother is a fool. All men are. You know that." She hustles in front of me, blocking my path. "We *haven't* disowned you. Okay? We still love you. Nothing has changed."

"Everything has changed. I'm *stuck* here. I was running for my life in Denver and Cole refused to help. I had no phone. No money. He *made* me leave with Matthew."

She winces, her gaze cutting to the man behind the wheel. "Has he treated you well?"

My stomach lurches as my mind does a painful recap of his so-called treatment—the encounter on the dining room table, the blood-smeared kitchen bench, the seductive words, the heated arguments.

"Layla? How has he treated you?"

I can't answer.

I won't lie and say he's treated me well. I've been engaged in a constant battle against the heart-wrenching tactics he's used in an attempt to win me back. But he hasn't treated me horribly either.

"Listen." Keira sighs. "I understand that you don't want to talk to me, but you need to know you haven't been disowned. Matthew made a deal with Cole."

My blood turns cold. "Excuse me?"

"He convinced Cole to give him thirty days to win you back. That's why you're here. That's why Cole let you leave with him in Denver."

"He didn't *let* me leave. I was *forced* to go. Cole cut me off financially, then took delight in informing me I would be reliant on the Butcher Boys of Baltimore while ignoring all my pleas to return home. He stood by while the man who lied and betrayed me was left to be my only support."

"He stood by while the man you loved was allowed a second chance to win you back," she counters.

My pulse becomes erratic.

"I'm sorry. I should've said something sooner, but..." She reaches for me, her fingers gently gliding over my wrist. "You two seemed like you were getting along when we first arrived. Maybe not perfectly. But it looked to me like you were trying to make things work. You were close on the balcony last night, and Hunter had already said you'd hooked up on a more—" She bites her lip. "—explicit level."

I raise a hand to my mouth as disgust burns the back of my throat. "I can't believe this."

"All any of us want is for you to be happy. And you *were* happy with him, right?"

"I was happy when all I knew were lies. I didn't know who he was back then."

"But you didn't fall in love with his name. You fell in love with the man."

I glare. "Well, I sure as hell would've thought twice if I'd known who he really was."

"I understand. And I should've spoken to you as soon as I arrived. I just…" She shrugs. "I didn't want to get in the middle of the deal they made. But you can come home. There's nothing stopping you from flying out of here with us."

My stomach hollows. My chest, too.

I turn my attention to the aircraft, trying to determine if that's what I want—a way out, an escape.

"I realize leaving would mean Matthew lost the deal and would have to face the consequences," she continues. "But if you're not—"

My gaze snaps to hers. "What consequences?"

"Well, obviously Cole didn't go into the agreement without a potential reward. You know him as well as I do. He isn't someone who would let an asset like Matthew slip through his fingers."

Matthew sold his soul?

I glare at him. Glare so hard my temples ache. But he stares straight ahead, not paying me attention as his hands hold the steering wheel in a white-knuckled grip.

"You still love him," she murmurs.

"No." My denial is instantaneous. "I was a fool—"

"You weren't a fool, Layla. You were in love. With a man who clearly adores you."

I turn my glare to my sister, my pulse thunderous. "He lied to me."

"No man is perfect."

"When I wouldn't disclose my full name, he had me mugged in a successful attempt to steal my identification."

She cringes. "While I'm not condoning his tactics, I will admit Sebastian did far worse to me before we hooked up."

She doesn't understand. What she went through with Decker isn't the same. "Matthew's family abducted Stella and Tobias. They killed Benji."

"His *family*," she reiterates. "Not him. He showed the goodness in his character by disowning them years before the Costas crossed our path."

"The goodness in his character? Keira, he became the Butcher of Baltimore."

"Then abandoned his role," she argues. "How many men do you know who have been dragged into our world, then fought to get out? How many men do you know who would be *allowed* to walk away? I might be on my own with this opinion, but I think what he achieved shows a level of integrity well beyond anything we're accustomed to."

I rake a hand through my hair, tugging tight on the strands.

"Leave with us," she repeats. "It's what he expects."

"He knows you're telling me?"

"He asked me to. He said you'd suffered enough, thinking we no longer loved you."

"Then why not tell me himself?"

"Because he thought you'd assume it was a trick. That you wouldn't believe him. He said I was the one who needed to break the news."

Is that why he told me to speak to Keira? Was he trying to push me toward the truth?

"I'm sorry." She gives a sad smile. "I wish I wasn't making this more difficult for you."

"You're not. I just don't understand. He has to have motives I don't know about."

Her forehead creases, her pity hitting me with force. I step back, needing space. Needing answers. Needing… *God*, what the hell do I need to stop this train wreck?

"*Keira,*" Decker shouts from the jet. "*How long are you going to be?*"

She doesn't move, just keeps staring at me. "Are you coming with us?"

I should.

If I'm not truly disowned… If I don't have to fix my mistakes… If all of this was an opportunity for Matthew to win me back, I should just board the aircraft and put what he did behind me.

But…

I glance at him sitting in the driver's seat, his intense eyes now on mine, his expression tight.

He knows I'm no longer clueless.

The thinly veiled panic in his gaze says he's waiting for me to flee.

"I can't." Even if I don't have to earn my family's forgiveness, I still need to deal with Emmanuel for my own sake. For Stella's. I turn back to Keira. "There's something I have to do first."

"That's what I thought you'd say." Her lips lift in a teasing grin as she steps forward, engulfing me in a hug. "I love you, sister. Have faith you're making the right decision."

I haven't made a decision. All I'm doing is sticking to my original plan. "Before you go, I need to ask a favor."

"Anything." She pulls back.

"I found out this morning that Stella and Tobias have been doing some digging on the Costas. From what she told Matthew, they've obtained birth certificates and school information. But who knows what else they've come up with?"

Her eyes flare. "Those sneaky little shits."

"Exactly. They're lucky they didn't get caught. So I need you to stay a while in Chicago and arrange to have some sort of cloning and tracking software put on their devices. Even though she promised to stop, I don't want to risk her doing anything else behind my back."

"Of course. I'll get it organized as soon as we land."

"Make sure they don't find out."

She nods. "No problem. Consider it done. Is there anything else?"

"No, that's it." Even though she claims I haven't been disowned, I still don't deserve to be asking for blessings I haven't earned. There's a lot of drama to make up for.

"If something else comes up, call me." She treks backward toward the jet. "No matter what it is."

"I can't. I don't have a cell."

She grins, then swirls toward the jet, shouting over her shoulder, "Then maybe you should've checked the duffle I brought here for you."

16

———————

MATTHEW

Layla climbs into the car. Without a word. Without acknowledging me.

For once, I don't have the balls to break the silence.

Instead, we remain locked in the calm before the storm as the aircraft approaches the runway, then finally takes off into the overcast sky.

I don't need to ask if she knows. The shock, anger, and wince of betrayal were written all over her face as she spoke to her sister. What I don't understand, though, is why she's still here.

I placed all my bets on her boarding the jet to leave me behind.

I even messaged Bishop to tell him I might not make it back to the house because I planned to follow her, but that fucker is ignoring my theatrics.

I start the ignition, giving her more time to perfect the verbal barrage she's about to assail me with, and drive from the parking lot.

She keeps her gaze on the sky, her hands in her lap, her shoulders stiff.

Each second of silence eats away at me. Gnaws.

Until she finally says, "Why didn't you tell me?"

"And have you convince me I was wasting my time, *amore mio*?" I indicate onto the quiet road leading back toward the beach. "No, thanks."

"You make no sense to me, Matthew. You tell me how you don't want to return to your old lifestyle, but what exactly do you think will happen when you're not successful?"

"I have no intention of failing."

She shakes her head. Slow and steady. "I won't be guilted into changing my mind, if that's what you're thinking. I only stayed because you promised me Emmanuel's death."

"I don't need guilt when you still love me."

She stiffens. Huffs.

"Have I not proven my loyalty?" I ask. "Have I not shown sincerity? Can't you see I'd give up everything for you, even a future with freedom, all for the sake of calling you mine?"

"You've told me conflicting stories. If you were me, you wouldn't believe any of it."

"I've shown you every side of me. The good, the bad, the vulgar. The facets are conflicting because that's who I am." I clench the steering wheel tighter, my palms sweating. "I'm a cold-blooded killer, Layla. Yet knowing I hurt you has filled me with more guilt than a thousand deaths. I can't fucking think straight through my want for you."

"Yet you still get angry at me."

"I get angry at my obsession with you. At my mindlessness. At my mania." I press harder against the accelerator, needing to get home to speak to her face to face. "I don't know how to win you back and it's destroying me."

She sucks in a long breath, the exhale shaky.

"Layla, what do I have to do to—"

"Pull over."

The demand cuts through me, her aggression a bad fucking sign. "I'm not trying to make a scene out of this. I just—"

"I said *pull over*." She reaches for the door handle.

Shit. I slap my foot against the brake, not willing to let her risk her life just to spite me.

As soon as the car stops, she shoves the door wide and escapes.

"What the hell are you doing?" I shout.

She slams the door in response.

For fuck's sake. I unclasp my belt and follow.

"Layla." I storm after her, fists clenched, pulse thunderous. "Stop."

She doesn't. The woman born of fire and brimstone continues striding away like she's on a marathon mission.

"*Fucking stop.*" I lunge, grasping her upper arm to haul her back to face me.

The moment her glassy eyes meet mine, I'm done for.

Winded.

Broken.

Her tear-stained cheeks punch right through me.

She doesn't fight my hold. Doesn't yell or wail. She merely stands there, skin pale, lips trembling.

"Talk to me," I demand. "*Scream* at me." Because I can't stand her silent suffering a moment longer.

"I don't get you." She shakes her head. "For the life of me, I can't work you out. And the worst part is that the more I try, the more I blame myself for this mess."

"It's not your fault."

"It definitely is. My father *always* told me he loved me. It was the prelude to every manipulation. He used the emotion like a weapon. He knew it was all I needed to do his dirty work. All I wanted was his love. His pride. And that's originally how I thought you manipulated me, too. But you know what, Matthew? You never said those words to me. Not once. Not when I confessed my feelings to you. You didn't even attempt to use love against me during this shitshow when you've apparently been trying to win me back."

She throws her hands in the air and scoffs. "You've said you're obsessed. But you've never whispered a hint of that one enslaving word apart from that stupid fucking endearment. So I must be here for another reason. Something important enough to have you throwing away your future, because Cole will make your life a goddamn misery."

"My life is with you, whether I'm free or under your brother's control."

"*Bullshit.*" She blinks up at me. Stark. Vulnerable. Another tear spills free, the trail racing to her chin to be quickly swiped away. "What do you want from me? Why can't you let me go?"

I don't know how to tell her. The thought of fucking this up one more time suffocates me.

"Forget it." She wiggles her arm from my grip and turns to continue along the roadside, the black tar to our right, the dense shrubs to the left. "Like I said, I blame myself. You never loved me. I created this mess all on my own."

"Layla…" I follow. "Give me a second to figure out how to explain this in a way that—"

"In a way that what—lets me down gently?" She raises her voice. "Why start now?"

"Jesus Christ, would you fucking stop?"

"No. Just give me some space to figure this out. I need to think."

"You need to fucking listen." I grab her again, latching onto her elbow. "You didn't create anything. You know how strongly I feel for you. That was never a lie."

She raises her chin. "But you don't love me."

I wince. I can't help it. That word pisses me off.

Emmanuel *loves* me. My uncle *loves* me. Yet one killed the first girlfriend I ever knew, and the other had me killing men as if they were flies.

I would never do that to her.

I would never place my feelings for her in the same category as the affections those men inflicted upon me.

I open my mouth to tell her why I can't say what she needs to hear, but she raises a hand in warning.

"Don't play pretend. I can see it in your eyes." She pastes on a smile so fake, it's painful to watch. "I hate those words anyway. I despise what they've made me into. The weakness they induce. I never want to hear them again."

"Good." I tighten my grip. "Because I'll never fucking say them."

She sucks in a breath, heartbreakingly fragile despite the show of strength.

"I don't love you, Layla. I never will."

She attempts to yank free from my hold. Once. Twice. Each tug is more vicious than the last. "Let me go."

"I'm not finished." I drag her closer so we're foot to foot. "I need you to hear me out."

"I don't want to." She twists her arm from my grip, then runs.

I chase, catching her in two steps to haul her off the ground. "You're going to fucking listen."

"Let me go." She wiggles in my hold. Thrashes. "*Stop.*" She screams as I carry her back to the car, fighting me, pummeling my chest.

I dump her on her feet beside the Lincoln, caging her against the metal with my body. "You're going to hear me out, because we both know this moment is either sink or swim for us." I grab her chin, forcing her face to mine. "And I'm going to need you to look me in the fucking eye while I talk to you, because if I mess up my words, at least you'll be able to see my goddamn sincerity."

She refuses.

I tilt my head into her line of sight, smothering her harder against the car's exterior. "I don't love you, Layla. What I feel for you isn't close to what other people describe. I say I'm obsessed because I am. I'm consumed by you. I'm infatuated and intrigued. I'm fucking captivated and enslaved. I can't think past you. You're all there is. All I have. And that's not love. There's no way it could be, because the fucking world couldn't function if everyone felt the way I do." I pause, catching my fucking breath, imploring her with my goddamn eyes. "Do you understand me?"

She doesn't respond. All I get are more tears and a deeper tremble to her lips.

"I'll never tell you I love you, Layla. That's a vow. From now on, I won't even call you *amore mio*. Because you're *la mia ossessione. La mia vita. La mia anima. Il mio santuario.*" I cup her cheeks, wiping away her tears with my thumbs. "My obsession. My life. My soul. My sanctuary. I'll spend every day making sure you know your value is worth so much more than three fucking words."

I lean close, my mouth a breath from hers. "Every time I look at you, you'll know you're valued above any other. That you're cherished and adored. If you fall asleep at night thinking you're anything less than perfect, then I've failed you, and I expect you to hold me accountable. Because that's what you are to me. It's all you've ever been."

She swallows, her eyes remaining pooled in moisture as she licks her lips.

"Talk to me," I beg. "Tell me you understand."

Her nose scrunches, bringing a new trail of tears down her cheeks.

"Tell me what you're feeling. What you're thinking."

She drags in a shuddering breath. "I'm thinking that I want to hate you."

I wince, taking the hit to the chest. "I know. I want to hate me, too."

"So why don't I?" she whimpers. "Why am I so weak?"

"Weak?" I swipe those fucking tears away. "How can you be weak when you're the only one capable of bringing the Butcher to his knees?"

She shakes her head.

"It's true. You destroy me, *la mia stella polare*. You tear me apart. Don't you understand how powerful that makes you?"

"You have all the power. You always have."

"That's not true." I brush my nose over hers, my chest heating with the contact, my dick hardening. I can already taste her, her heated breath filling my lungs. "You rule over me. You always will."

"I don't want to." She sniffs. "I don't want any of this."

"Yes, you do. Your problem is that you think succumbing to me makes you vulnerable. But it's the opposite, Layla. Nothing is stronger than the two of us together. I promise you that."

She closes her eyes, a trail of tears escaping her closed lashes.

"Kiss me, *mia dea*. Tell me you're mine."

She drags in a shaky breath, her hands moving to grip my arms.

"Kiss me." I wait for her to push me away. To destroy me with her rejection.

Her inhales become ragged. Fractured. Broken.

I don't know what else to do. What to say. So I repeat what she means to me, whispering her value against those fragile lips. "*La mia ossessione. La mia vita. La mia anima.*" I close my eyes, resting my forehead against hers. "*Il mio santuario. La mia stella polare. Mia dea.*"

She sobs, killing me with her suffering.

"Forgive me," I demand. "Absolve my sins. Let me spend the

rest of my life making this up to you."

She shakes her head, denying me.

"Layla," I beg. "You're killing me."

"No, you're killing *me*." She opens her eyes, the bloodshot depths drowning in sadness. "I can't take it anymore." She wraps a hand around my neck and smashes her mouth to mine.

Euphoria hits me like a motherfucker, blinking the world from existence.

I devour her, tasting her tears, surrendering my soul.

She clings to me, her nails in my skin. Our tongues dance, parry, attack.

I've never felt more overwhelmed with relief.

"I need you," she pants into my mouth.

I'll give her what she wants, just not on the side of the road against a dusty car. Not after waiting this long. "Let's get back to the house."

The next time I pleasure her, she'll be in a comfortable bed where I can give her the attention she deserves.

"No. Now. Here," she pants.

"I want to fuck every inch of you. But I'm doing this right." My dick thrums in protest. I succumb to temptation, grinding my cock against her abdomen. "You need to get in the car."

She moans, reclaiming my mouth.

We kiss as if we're starved. Desperate. Our bodies grind. Our breath gasps.

"This isn't something you're going to walk away from again, is it?" I pull back to stare at her, trying to see sense through the lust. "You're mine now, Layla." It sounds like a statement but it's not. It's a question. A fucking pathetic plea.

"I'm yours." She nods, her brows pinching as if she's in pain.

She's mine, but she's torn. She's succumbed to fate but hasn't been convinced of her decision.

"I'll make it up to you." I palm her throat, using pressure to guide her head to the side to expose her delicate neck. "I'll make this right."

She mewls, her eyes fluttering shut as I lean in to kiss the sensitive skin below her ear.

I lick and bite and suck. I taste and savor and consume.

I'm so fucking hard for her. My dick throbs against my zipper. My chest pounds like thunder.

I want to be inside her. To be all over her.

"Matthew." Her back arches, her phenomenal breasts brushing my chest. "We need this."

I hold her tighter. Kiss her harder. "*Sei perfetta. Così fottutamente perfetta.*"

She whimpers.

My dick takes note of every sound. Every movement.

I don't understand the hold she has on me. The consumption. The mindlessness. We're dry humping on the side of the fucking road, like teenagers, and I can't drag myself away.

I'd kill for her.

I'd die. I've never been more certain.

"*La mia ossessione,*" I whisper. "*La mia vita. La mia anima. Il mio santuario.*"

Her throat works over a heavy swallow beneath my palm, her chest rising and falling under ragged breaths.

She releases my arms, her neck craning away so she can meet my gaze. "Remind me what that means."

"My obsession. My life. My soul. My sanctuary."

Her gaze regains the sheen of moisture as her nose crinkles. Then she quickly glances away.

I've upset her again. "Tell me what's wrong?"

She shakes her head.

"Tell me." I palm her chin, brushing my mouth over hers. "*Trust* me."

"I can't." Her shoulders slump. Her entire body weakens. "I want to. I *need* to. I just don't think I can."

I stiffen, taking the punishment I deserve.

She winces, understanding my suffering. My guilt. "Matthew, I need you to promise me this is real. That it always will be. That you'll never lie again. But as much as I need those promises, I won't believe you. I *need* those words, but I don't know how to accept them."

"Then it's my job to convince you." I kiss her gently. Reverently. "Nothing has ever been more real, Layla. And I plan on spending the rest of my life proving that to you."

17

MATTHEW

I keep my waist pressed into hers, our gazes tangled for long silent heartbeats while she contemplates me with sorrow.

I've got a lot of work ahead of me. I have to prove myself without force.

But I will.

I'll make her believe.

"Let's go." I check my watch, annoyed that Bishop hasn't responded to my last text. "We'll finish this at the house. Then we need to pack."

"We're going to Denver?"

"Not yet. I still need a few more days. But I don't want to risk your safety by staying here." I retreat, mourning the loss of her heat.

"Why would it risk my safety?"

"Because I didn't give our address to your family. They found us on their own."

"But I thought you arranged for Stella to come here."

"I did." I pull her door open and help her climb inside. "Problem is, Hunter and Sarah were here before that, meaning someone at the Denver Airport needs to be taught a lesson on manners."

She frowns as I close her door, then trek around the hood to climb in the driver's side.

"What were they doing here?" she asks as I start the ignition.

"Checking on you. Making sure you were safe."

"Oh." Her mouth forms the subtlest circle. An almost shy expression of surprise.

"Your brother always cared about you. He never stopped."

She rests back into her seat, shifting her attention out her side window to the wild shrubs bordering the side of the road. "He's always had a funny way of showing it."

I reach for her hand as I pull onto the road and drag her knuckles to my lips. "I want you to know I didn't ask him to act as if you were disowned. I didn't know he was going to go down that path until it was too late."

"And you couldn't tell me afterward because I would've run straight home." She keeps her gaze diverted. "I get it."

"But do you forgive me?" I turn her arm to kiss the inside of her wrist.

She doesn't respond. I'm asking too much.

"Ignore me." I focus on the road. "I know it's too soon to ask."

She sucks in a breath, letting it out gradually. "I need to take this slow. I know I'm probably giving you mixed signals, but I'm still hurting."

"There are no mixed signals, *la mia stella polare*. And you don't need to explain. I understand completely."

She squeezes my hand. "I like the sound of that endearment more than *amore mio*. What does it mean?" She shoots me a glance. "Or don't I want to know."

I grin, unable to stop myself from kissing her again, this time in the middle of her palm. "It means 'my northern star.'"

She sits taller. Her chin higher. "I definitely like that one better."

"*Sei la mia stella polare. L'unico posto che chiamerò mai casa.*"

"Not fair," she drawls. "You're trying to seduce me all over again, aren't you?"

"I wouldn't dream of it."

She smiles, subtle, slow, and so fucking stunning.

"*Così fottutamente bella.*" I smirk at her. "*Non vedo l'ora di averti sotto di me.*"

She grins right back, raising her brows in challenge.

"Do you want more, *mia dea*?"

"What does that one mean?" She turns her body, giving me her full attention.

"My goddess. But from memory, I think your favorite is *la mia piccola sporcacciona.*"

Her eyes narrow in a faux glower. "I remember that one, Matthew, and I assure you, it's not."

I keep smirking. Keep holding her hand. Keep thanking my lucky fucking stars as I drive us toward the place where I plan to spend hours cherishing her.

"Tell me more about the terms you agreed to with Cole." She leans her cheek against the edge of the seat. "What did he ask of you?"

"Does it matter?"

"I guess not. But I'd like to know exactly what you were willing to risk."

"And if the terms weren't generous enough? What then?"

"Somehow, I don't think that was the case." Her gaze narrows, her appraisal gentle. "What was it? What were the exact terms?"

"We didn't have any. As far as I was concerned, it was all or nothing."

Her brow furrows, her confusion potent. "And there's really nothing else you want from me? No insider knowledge or Torian family secrets?"

"There's only ever been you. I don't need anything else in my life."

"But you wouldn't have had a life if Cole got his way. How could you risk your future like that?"

I focus on the road, slowly kissing her knuckles, her wrist, her palm. "Because you are my future, Layla. I hope I can prove that to you one day."

She releases a heavy breath as I kiss her again and again. Lazy, lethargic worship. Quiet and content affection.

"And nothing has changed with our agreement on Emmanuel?" she asks. "We're still on the same page?"

"Always. The particulars haven't changed. Your safety remains my priority, with his death being the goal."

"I don't think I can wait much longer. I've been striving for this outcome for two years, and I'm more tired than I've ever been. I need it to be over."

"Then let me do it on my own." I meet her gaze. "I can leave this afternoon. He'll be dead by morning."

She swallows. Bites her lip.

I can't tell if her hesitation is because she still doesn't trust me, or because she's battling with her desire to concede.

"You'd never have to worry about him again." I turn my attention back to the road. "And I wouldn't have to risk your safety."

"But you'd risk my sanity." She drags her arm away but latches her hand around mine to take it with her. She mimics my affection, kissing my knuckles, my wrist, my palm. "I'd go insane worrying about you. I need to be there to make sure you're okay."

"Then we do it together. We just need to do it right." I turn onto the road leading to the beach house. "Two more days should be enough. In the meantime, I want you to rest. Relax. And *eat*. Don't think it hasn't skipped my attention that you haven't been looking after yourself."

"Heartbreak doesn't make for a healthy appetite."

I stifle a wince. "Well, there's no more heartbreak now. I promise to keep you fed and rested. In fact, I don't think I'll let you leave the bed."

Her chuckle is breathy. "How selfless of you."

"I can be extremely generous."

"And single-minded," she adds.

"Always. There's only you, *mia dea*. That's all there is."

Her smile turns solemn as she diverts her attention back to the road. She's still not all in, and that's okay. I can't expect her to get to my level of obsession within minutes of reconciling.

But she'll get there.

I'll make sure of it.

She keeps hold of my hand as we reach the property. She doesn't let go as I enter the pin into the panel at the gate. And our palms remain united while I shift into park and kill the ignition.

She doesn't move to get out. Doesn't release her belt.

"You okay?" I ask.

She nods, her expression a gentle statement of peace as she

looks back at me. "I just want a few more seconds of this before I have to deal with Bishop."

"Don't worry about him. I'll keep him occupied."

"Promise?"

God, she's beautiful. With playful eyes and a slight tweak to her lips, I could die a happy man with her as my final image.

"Cross my heart." I strike a finger across my chest.

She snickers, her attention diverting over my left shoulder.

Her posture stiffens. Her humor evaporates. Her hold on my hand tightens.

She's scared.

Panicked.

Someone's in the yard.

"There's a gun in the glove compartment." I lower my voice. "Can you grab it?"

She shakes her head. Swallows. "He's right there."

A silhouette enters my periphery, making my blood surge.

"Who?" I slowly release my belt. No sudden movements. No risking her safety. But the question becomes redundant when Remy creeps into view on her side of the car.

He meets my gaze, his navy suit and matching tie boasting professionalism while the Glock in his grip awakens my demons.

"Salvo's behind me?" I ask.

She nods. "What do I do?"

"Nothing. Stay still. It's going to be okay. I won't let anything happen to you."

Her attention returns to mine, her eyes silently screaming for help. "They want me dead."

"They won't succeed." I squeeze her fingers. "They're not going to hurt you."

She continues to nod, the action short and sharp. She's in shock. A breath from fight or flight.

"Don't make any sudden movements, okay, *mia dea*?" I release her hand, gradually lowering my fingers to my thigh. Then my pocket.

"Get out." Remy taps the barrel of his weapon against her window, only pausing a moment before he yanks her door open.

Salvo does the same on my side, his gun entering my line of vision.

"Proceed with caution," I warn. "If you touch her, there will be hell to pay."

"We don't want trouble." Remy places his barrel at the back of her skull. "We just need you to get out of the car."

She could be gone in a blink. Without hesitation or remorse.

"Move the gun away from her." I can barely hear through the roar of blood in my ears. "If you hurt her, I swear to God it'll be the last thing you do."

"Get out of the fucking car," he repeats, nudging the weapon into her head.

She whimpers. Flinches.

I grind my teeth. Clench my fist around the blade.

"Get your hand out of your pocket." Salvo steps closer, thrusting his gun toward the side of my face. "Start moving."

I can't be separated from her. But I also can't start a gunfight in the fucking Lincoln when all I have is a blade.

"Why don't you help me, asshole?" I stare at her. I don't take my eyes off hers as Salvo creeps closer.

"You want me to drag you out, brother? Because I will." He grabs my suit sleeve with his free hand and tugs.

I lunge, twisting my body toward the gun, forgoing my blade for his barrel. I grip the metal. Shove it downward.

He recoils. Panics. Pulls the trigger.

Layla screams, her limbs flailing as Remy drags her from the vehicle.

I elbow Salvo in the face. Capture and twist his wrist hard. Then charge while he's reeling from the impact, throwing myself out of the car to shove him off-balance.

He stumbles backward, the gun loosening in his grip.

We fall. The weapon does, too. All three of us clatter to the pebbled drive.

My body slams onto his. My forearm finds his throat. My hand finds my blade.

"You're dead." I stab the metal into his upper arm and his roar explodes in my ringing ears as I retrieve it. "But not before you suffer."

I scramble to my feet, dragging him with me by the front of his suit, needing to get eyes on Layla.

"*Fuck*." Salvo clasps his shoulder as I lever him backward into my chest, my blade at his throat. "You stabbed me."

"You're lucky I haven't blown your fucking brains out." The gun is right there. A few feet away. He'd be dead if he hadn't dropped it.

I would've killed my own brother.

Without thought.

Without hesitation.

That's why I don't fucking carry.

"Let her go." I drag Salvo to the hood until Layla is in full sight on the other side of the Lincoln.

Remy copies my stance, his arm around her neck, but his gun is trained on me.

Big mistake. I'd risk a bullet for her. I'd chance death.

"Let her go." I drag Salvo farther, making him stumble to the other side of the car, getting as close as I can to Layla whose chest heaves with rapid breaths as her fingers cling to my brother's arm for stability.

"Matthew," she begs.

"It's okay." *It's not fucking okay.* "You're going to be fine." *He's going to kill her.*

"Stay where you are." Remy drags her backward, his hold tightening on her neck. His forehead beads with sweat. He's fucking scared.

I'm petrified. "*Let. Her. Go.*"

His eyes widen as if I'm insane. "Do you really think I'm going to do that when you've got a knife to his throat?"

"We just wanted to fucking talk," Salvo grates through clenched teeth. "Jesus. Dante. You fucking *stabbed* me."

"I'm going to do far worse if he doesn't let her go."

"Listen," Remy snarls. "If you calm down, we can explain."

Where the fuck is Bishop? I glance to the house, searching for a sign of life.

"Your man can't help." Salvo stumbles along with me, one hand clutching his shoulder as I continue to stalk after Layla. "But he's fine. He isn't injured."

"Then where is he?"

"In the house."

"Just chillin', watching TV?" I drag him farther. Harder.

"He's taped to a fucking chair in one of the bedrooms." He groans. "God, can you stop for a minute?"

"No." I can't stand the sight of Layla's fear. She's tearing me apart one frantic blink at a time. "If you want to talk, then talk. But for your sake, you might want to hope baby brother doesn't make one wrong move, because if he does, you're both dead."

Salvo mutters a string of profanities, then raises a hand in surrender. "Let her go."

"Are you fucking serious?" Remy's face is wild with disgust.

Layla remains quiet, her attention never leaving me, her hands clutching at my brother's arm as he continues to lever her backward.

"Do it," Salvo demands. "Now."

"*Fuck*." My youngest brother licks his lips. Swallows. Then finally, he loosens his hold around her neck.

"Run for the house, Layla." I keep hold of Salvo, my blade remaining at his throat. "Get inside."

She's hesitant, slowly inching away from her attacker as her gaze darts between my brothers.

"Now, *la mia stella polare*. Find Bishop." I point the blade at Remy. "Remove the magazine. Then kick the Glock away."

He shakes his head. "Not until you release him."

"Fucking do it," Salvo snarls. "Before I bleed out."

"You're not going to bleed out, you goddamn pussy." I keep leading him forward. Shoving. Pushing.

"Excuse me for not having firsthand knowledge of stab wounds," he snips. "Not all of us have extensive experience like you."

"You've got more experience being stabbed than I do, asshole. I've never been careless enough to be wounded."

"Maybe not, but you've inflicted more than your fair share."

"Then maybe you should be fucking thankful you're still breathing. It would've been easier to plunge my blade into your throat."

Remy releases the magazine, then drops the weapon.

"Throw the bullets." I get closer as he complies. Five feet. Four. "Then kick the gun away." I chance a glance at Layla over my shoulder, finding her at the bottom step. "Keep moving, *mia dea*. Don't stop." I bridge more space. Three feet. Two. "I said kick the fucking gun."

I don't wait for him to follow orders. As soon as I'm in lunging distance, I coldcock Salvo with a closed fist. He topples to the grass, senseless, as I throw the blade at Remy. Hard. "I warned you." I aim low, hitting him in the thigh.

He yells as I charge, launching my fist at his cheek. The impact knocks him backward. He falls. I follow.

I straddle his chest, my hand gripping his neck, the other grabbing the knife from his leg to raise it to his throat. "I told you not to touch her."

He inches his chin away from the blade, his breathing ragged.

"I fucking warned you." I press the tip of the knife into his skin, my vision red, my mind violent.

"You're the one who attacked," he snaps. "We didn't come here to fight."

"Instead, you started a war." I dig the metal deeper, drawing blood.

"*You* started it, you trigger-happy motherfucker." He glares at me, eyes stark, skin flushed. "This is on *you*. *Your* actions. *Your* knee-jerk impulse. So what are you going to do? Murder me? Is that what we've come to?"

"Maybe," I snarl. "It's what you deserve."

It's what he's earned for scaring her. *Threatening* her.

"Matthew." Layla's plea whispers through my rage, her light footsteps approaching.

I keep staring at Remy, devouring his suffering, feeding off his fear.

"Don't kill him." Her gentle hand comes to rest on my shoulder. "Use him instead. He can give us information on Emmanuel."

She's such a treasure. A fucking godsend in a moment of madness.

"Did you hear that?" I sneer. "My woman just saved your life."

"Probably because your woman has more fucking brains than you." His nostrils flare as he remains rigid.

Salvatore groans from a few feet away, regaining consciousness.

"Get behind me." I shoot Layla a glance and wait until she complies before I push to my feet. I drag her close, one hand on her waist as she stands at my back, the other holding a tight grip on the blade at my side.

Both brothers remain on the ground. Remy clings to his injured thigh. Salvo clutches his head. Both of them sit with knees bent and shoulders slumped. Defeated but far from punished.

"Are you here to take me back to Emmanuel?" Layla asks. "Or just to kill me?"

They don't acknowledge her. Don't even wrench their gazes from me to pay her the respect she deserves.

"Answer her," I demand.

"We've already explained why we're here." Salvo raises his chin, his eyes hard. "We told you we came to fucking talk."

"You came with raised guns," she counters.

"For self-fucking-preservation." Remy looks to her, finally, with resentment. "After what we've done to you in the past, we didn't think a gift basket would've been a sufficient peace offering."

Peace offering? "What the fuck are you two playing at?" I keep my hand on her, not letting her away from my touch. Not trusting them for a second.

"It's a long story." Salvo labors to his feet.

"Find a way to make it short."

"As if we fucking wouldn't if we could." Remy removes his belt and wraps it around his thigh. "A lot has happened since we were kids."

I tense, not understanding why they need to delve that far in history. "Who's this about. Me? Or Layla?"

"It's about all of us, you psychotic fuck." Remy struggles to stand, the blood on his leg soaking into his suit pants. "We wanted to get away from Emmanuel and thought our long-lost brother might help. I just didn't anticipate it being in a fucking body bag."

18

———

LAYLA

I keep the shock bottled inside my chest.

Matthew became someone else while I was under threat. Sterile. Calculated. Cold. He was the Butcher, and I'm ashamed to admit I'm as drawn to his dark side as I have been to his seduction.

The way he fought for me was exquisite. His severity profound.

"You ambush us, dare to hold Layla hostage, then have the balls to ask for help?" He's a predator ready to pounce, his anger tightly corded into every muscle.

"It wasn't meant to be an ambush." Salvo continues clinging to his injured shoulder. "We just wanted to get you in a position where you'd listen without us being slaughtered."

"You had a gun to her head."

"I fucking panicked." Remy clings to the belt strap around his thigh. "You're a scary son of a bitch when under threat."

"Then you'd better hope Bishop is okay, because you're going to see some next-level shit if he isn't."

"He is. Go check for yourself." Salvo jerks his head toward the house. "He's in one of the downstairs bedrooms."

"Is he hurt?" I ask.

"Barely. I swear to God, we never wanted any of this shit. Not the guns, or the violence, or the threats."

"Tell that to my dead husband." The bitterness spills from my lips before I can rein it in.

Salvatore cringes. Remy quits playing with his belt and straightens.

That's all I'm given for my loss. For my daughter's nightmares.

I should be ending their lives. Repaying what they did to Benji. Instead, my mind is stuck thinking about Matthew's hesitation when I spoke to him days ago about killing his brothers.

He'd been stricken. He may have hidden it well, but I'd known.

He still feels loyal to them. No matter what they've done to me.

At least, he did before today.

"I swear it wasn't us." Remy meets my gaze. "That night was out of control, but we were firing air shots for cover. We didn't kill anyone. It was Emmanuel's guards."

The hatred I've let fester for two years doesn't budge. It's bone deep. Embedded.

"You shot at us in Denver," I counter.

"And I could've hit your brother without even trying. But didn't." Salvatore shucks his suit jacket, exposing a white button-down with a sleeve stained in blood. "Or at a bare minimum, your car tires. Those shots were warnings to get you to hurry up and skip town."

Matthew doesn't deny their claims.

He doesn't say anything at all.

I slide a hand over his. Questioning. Searching for insight.

He squeezes my fingers and drags me to his side. He doesn't look at me. Doesn't dare to take his attention off his brothers, but I see his struggle.

He wants to believe them.

"Why?" I ask Salvatore. "Why didn't you aim at my husband? Or at us in the alley? Why pretend? Why play games?"

"It's not a game."

"Not a fucking fun one, anyway," Remy drawls. "This shit has gotten old real fucking quick."

I don't understand.

"They weren't willing participants, *mia dea*," Matthew mutters. It's not a question or speculation. There's confidence in his voice. Certainty in his expression.

"Meaning?" I ask.

"Emmanuel forced them to participate in the abduction of your daughter." He meets my gaze. "And they never wanted to be a part of your husband's death."

I frown. Shake my head. "How do you know?"

"I didn't. I only had suspicions until now."

"Suspicions since when?" I can't hold the accusation from my tone.

"Denver. When you took off in Abri's car." His eyes seek my understanding, his hand loosening around mine. "If she was loyal to Emmanuel, she never would've aided your escape. Then she spoke to me as if she wanted help but seemed too scared to ask. I didn't know why. I thought her fear may have been over your brother's possible retaliation. But I always wondered if it was because she hated her father's actions as much as I did."

"You should've told me," I whisper.

"You wouldn't have listened." He cups my cheek, rubbing his thumb over my lower lip.

He's right. I would've denied any leniency toward his siblings. I still want to now.

"Give us a chance to explain." Remy limps forward. "We'll tell you everything."

I don't stop looking at Matthew. Don't stop trying to read his thoughts.

"It's up to you, *la mia stella polare*." There's no inflection in his tone. He doesn't beg for them. Doesn't show weakness or attempt to sway me with guilt. But I feel it regardless. I sense the yearning for understanding over a family he lost. "They hurt you. Threatened you. It's your choice how we proceed."

No, it's not.

He's already made the decision for me.

"Please, Layla." Remy stands tall. "Give us a chance to explain that we're not your enemy."

"But are you an ally?" I raise a brow. "If we hear you out, will you willingly give information to help us kill your father?"

The brothers exchange a look. A tense visual standoff.

"It's not a trick question," Matthew growls. "There shouldn't be any hesitation if what you're claiming isn't a setup."

"There's no setup, but there's also no easy way to answer."

Remy rakes a hand through his hair, inching forward. "If you're willing to talk this through, we can explain."

"Stay where you are." Matthew slides in front of me. "Don't get any closer."

Remy sighs. "I'm not going to hurt her. I think we've unintentionally done enough of that over the years. I just want her to see my sincerity. We never wanted to be a part of your darkest days, Layla."

They weren't merely a part of it. They were the creators. The instigators.

"One conversation," I concede, "that can be ended at any time."

Matthew looks at me over his shoulder. "Are you sure this is what you want?"

No. But it's what *he* wants. What he *needs*. And I'm willing to give it to him. "I'm listening. That's all. I'm not offering forgiveness."

He frowns. "Layla—"

"It's okay. I promise." I paste on a half-hearted smile. "I trust that you'll allow me to end the ceasefire at a moment's notice if I change my mind."

His shoulders straighten. Stiffen.

I know he's thinking about the most important word in my statement—*trust*.

He's earned it, at least a little, after almost killing his brothers to protect me.

"You heard her." He leans in, planting a smacking kiss to my lips, before swinging back to my enemies. "You've got one chance. So make it good."

Salvatore relaxes. "Where do you want to do this?"

"Inside." Matthew points his knife toward the stairs. "Lead the way."

Salvatore starts for the house, his injured shoulder hanging low while Remy limps a few feet behind.

I wait until they're halfway to the front door before I step away from my human shield to grab the Glock from the ground, then the magazine. I load the gun as Matthew watches, then shove it into the back of my jeans.

"Are you sure you're okay with this?" he asks. "You've already been through enough."

"We both have. But if what they're insinuating is true, I want all the details. Who knows? Maybe they're innocent."

"It's been years, Layla." His brows furrow. "If they weren't willingly complicit with Emmanuel's actions, then they were weak for far too long."

"You're right. But I know what that weakness feels like, because I was someone who did horrible things in the hopes of my father's love, not realizing the cost until it was too late."

His eyes harden. "You're not like them."

"That's beside the point." I grab his hand and entwine our fingers. "We need to hear them out."

"They don't deserve your kindness, *la mia stella polare*."

"Maybe not. But you do." I bring his knuckles to my lips. "The truth will set us free, right?"

He falls quiet, his thoughts loud behind his piercing stare.

I hear his affection through the silence. His adoration. His concern.

"Come on." I tug him toward the house. "I'll find Bishop while you organize first aid supplies."

"First aid supplies?" He scoffs, following along beside me. "Now you're just being soft. They're fine. I stayed away from arteries and the blade is small." He holds it up in front of me. "Barely big enough to require a Band-Aid."

I chuckle at his immunity to carnage. "Humor me. I don't want to be left cleaning up a blood trail. And besides, we can't get their side of the story if they bleed out."

He pauses before the bottom step, his brothers already poised at the front door.

"Whatever you say, *mia dea*." He kisses me softly. Warm lips and gentle affection from such a brutal man. "But just so you know, they're probably going to need a lot more than a first aid kit once Bishop gets hold of them."

We continue inside and part ways in the living room.

His brothers approach the kitchen sink. Matthew heads for the bathroom. I hustle downstairs to pause on the bottom step.

The silence is eerie. Unsettling. "Bishop?"

A smothered yell carries from a nearby room. Then a clatter of furniture.

"I'm coming." I jog toward the sound and stop in the doorway to a darkened bedroom, the curtains closed and bathing the room in shadow.

I flick on the light, illuminating Bishop, bound to a wooden chair by thick, grey electrical tape.

He's mummified, ankles to torso, his suit barely visible beneath his bindings, with a lone strip over his mouth. I'd almost feel sorry for him if it weren't for the glare aimed my way, his eyes tiny slits of rebellion.

He's livid. Bloodthirsty.

He yells beneath the tape gag. It's aggressive. Clearly insulting or threatening.

"I don't like your tone." I scan the room for something sharp. A knife. A pen.

He scoots the chair forward an inch, reclaiming my attention, and jerks his chin at the bedside table.

"There's something in there?" I stalk for the drawers, pulling the top one open to claim the pocket knife inside. I flick the blade open, walk to him, then remove the tape over his mouth with a quick rip.

"*Motherfucker.*" His lips are red. His eyes furious. "Did you stop to contemplate, even for the slightest second, that you could've removed the tape from my mouth the moment you walked through the fucking door?"

I crouch at his side and start cutting the bindings at his wrist. "Did you stop to contemplate how much your silence is preferable to your attitude?"

"*Funny,*" he snaps. "Where the fuck is Langston?"

"Upstairs." I saw through the heavy tape from his hand to his elbow, not caring if I'm destroying his suit.

"And those fucking pussies?"

He yanks his arm free and begins clawing at the tape on his chest as I work on his other wrist.

"They're up there with him."

We work in silence, the shredding of stitching and tearing of bindings filling the room before he finally asks, "Did they hurt you?"

I pause, not sure why he'd care. "No."

He pulls his second arm free. "Did they touch you?"

Apprehension trickles through my veins. His concern is unsettling.

"Layla?" he growls. "Did they touch you?"

"No. Why?" I kneel before him, turning my attention to the tape at his ankles. "Have you grown a heart all of a sudden?"

He yanks harder at his bindings, wobbling the chair. "What I've grown is fucking attached to a stellar reputation that I have no intention of losing."

Of course. Silly me.

I slice harder at the tape, dragging the blade between his legs, moving past his knees, then toward his upper thighs.

"I appreciate the help." He snatches the blade from my grip. "But the last thing I need is you with something sharp near my dick."

"Are you sure?" I lean back on my haunches. "I could teach you some manners."

"If that's what you call the shit you've been doing with Langston, then it's a hard pass from me. All I need right now is revenge."

I stand as he stabs the tape to shreds. "How did they get you down?"

"From my lack of memory and one hell of a fucking headache, I'm assuming those sons of bitches sucker punched me when I was doing a perimeter check." He throws the last of his bindings to the floor and shoves to his feet, his suit in tatters. "You might want to stay down here a while."

That's not going to happen.

I follow as he stalks for the hall. He pounces up the stairs three at a time, arms swinging, posture rigid.

He storms into the open living area and straight toward Matthew's brothers at the island counter, who are tending to their wounds.

Salvatore is shirtless, the muscles on his chest smeared with diluted blood as Remy sits on the counter, one leg of his suit pants cut open as he affixes a bandage to his thigh.

My gaze turns to Matthew in panic, already anticipating the

carnage that's about to ensue. But he doesn't move from his settled position against the far counter. He doesn't even change his lazy stance, his arms and ankles crossed.

"*Fuck*." Remy scoots from the counter.

Salvatore pivots toward the threat.

Bishop storms forward, shoulders broad, face menacing, and launches a fist at Salvatore's cheek.

The blow isn't defended. My enemy takes the hit, his head flinging to the side as he stumbles into the counter.

Bishop strikes Salvatore's chin. Mouth. Jaw. Each punch is fast and precise before he pivots to Remy, grabbing the younger man by the shirt to drag him forward. Chest to chest.

"Your turn, cockroach." His knuckles pound Remy's nose. Eye. Cheek.

Matthew barely blinks as my pulse thunders, his thoughts almost perfectly hidden if it weren't for the way he unfolds his arms to clutch the counter behind him. He white-knuckles the marble. His chin hitches higher.

"That's enough," I warn Bishop.

He doesn't stop. He swings again and again as Remy ducks into the blows.

"I said, *that's enough*." I raise my voice. "We need them in a position to talk, and they can't do that without teeth."

Bishop hesitates, his back stiffening as he pants, chest heaving, nostrils flared, his grip still tight on Remy's shirt.

"Let him go." I walk to his side, tilting my head into his line of vision. "Now, Bishop."

Remy doesn't move. Doesn't speak.

He stands there, fearless in the face of another deserving blow as Bishop snarls, then finally shoves him away.

"Are we good now?" Remy limps, his blotched face pinched while he struggles to regain footing on his injured leg.

"Not even close, you fucking bitch." Bishop swipes rough hands down the front of his shirt, smoothing the crinkles. "I'll never be *good* with someone who throws cheap shots."

"Cut us a break." Salvatore licks the cut on his bottom lip, then prods at the swelling flesh with a gentle finger. "We waited until the kid was gone. We didn't want trouble. We just needed you out of the way."

Stella. They were watching while she was here?

"You waited until you weren't outnumbered," he corrects. "You knew Torian's men would've killed you without hesitation."

Salvatore glowers, denying the obvious.

This could've turned out so much worse. They could've approached while my daughter was around. Could've petrified her like they have before.

"Hey." Matthew draws my attention, his palm patting the counter at his side. "Come here."

I drag my feet toward him, thankful for the support while Bishop marches to the fridge, muttering under his breath. He yanks the freezer drawer open and grabs a handful of ice.

Matthew drapes a protective arm over my shoulder, nestling me into his side. "Is he okay?" he murmurs in my ear.

"I think so." I assume, aside from a headache, the only thing wounded is his pride.

He kisses my temple, then sucks in a long breath. "Okay, motherfuckers, now that the welcoming party is over, you two need to start talking."

"Can't we do this without your guard dog?" Salvatore keeps his death stare on Bishop as he grabs his blood-stained shirt from the counter to pull it back on. "It's a family matter."

"He *is* family. *My* family. And you wouldn't be in any position to talk if it weren't for his leniency. So I suggest you quit asking for more favors."

"Hear that, boys?" Bishop's expression turns smug as he holds the ice on his knuckles and leans over the sink. "My beating was lenient. Next time I'll have far more fun."

Remy rolls his eyes, grabs his belt from the island counter, and begins threading it through his pants. "Like we said outside—we want to get out."

"Out of what exactly?" I ask.

"The family." He looks to Matthew. "We want to walk away from Emmanuel like you did."

Bishop scoffs. "Like he did? So you're prepared to become

homeless, form a drug addiction, then earn your living by slaughtering strangers?"

Salvatore gives Remy a pointed look. "I told you this was a bad idea."

"You're damn fucking right about that." Bishop's jaw tenses. "You should've listened to your brother."

"I thought you'd understand." Remy keeps staring at Matthew, undaunted by the judgment. "That you'd have sympathy."

"Sympathy for what?" Matthew drawls. "Your wealth? Your career? What part is my heart meant to bleed for?"

"We don't have wealth." Salvatore shakes his head. "Not a fucking penny. None that we can access anyway. It all goes into a trust that we can't touch." He turns his attention to me. "Maybe you'll understand our position better than anyone. I'm told our father learned his tactics from yours."

A chill skitters down my spine. "Meaning?"

"Emmanuel has always said Luther Torian used his children like pawns."

I try not to flinch, but I'm not strong enough. His arrow makes a direct hit to my pride, the shame exploding through my chest.

"Like *weapons*," Remy clarifies. "And that's exactly how Emmanuel treats us. We never wanted to be a part of this mayhem. We were manipulated into it, and the fucking humiliating part is that we should've seen it coming"

"Pathetic is another accurate description," Bishop mutters.

I have a million questions, each one locked behind a cage of trauma and pain.

I don't want to believe them. I don't want to be sympathetic or obliging or lenient. But I can't help wondering if our lives could possibly be carbon copies. If they're dealing with emotional wounds like mine.

Salvatore returns his attention to the man at my side. "After you left, Dad lost his fucking mind knowing he could no longer control you."

Matthew's jaw twitches. "It was lost well before that. Otherwise Grace would still be alive."

"Well, it avalanched from there. He began to script every part of our lives. From the classes we attended, to after-school activities.

And every time we fought back against his control, he used your disappearance to justify his actions. He said he wouldn't allow us to ruin our lives the way you did."

"That's it?" Bishop asks with incredulity. "Dear ol' Daddy picked economics instead of trigonometry so now you're throwing a tantrum?"

Remy's expression tightens. "The classes were an example, asshole."

"Well, it wasn't a fucking good one, was it?"

"How's this for a better example?" Salvatore bristles. "For Rem's fifteenth birthday, he was forced to go to a strip club where a woman was paid to take his virginity."

"That's not your fucking story to share," Remy snarls.

Matthew turns rigid. "Is it true?"

My stomach hollows as Remy's nostrils flare. His fists clench.

"Is it true?" Matthew demands.

"Yeah, it's true." Remy pins us with a judgmental stare. "But don't look at me like that. I was a fucking teenager with a twenty-four-seven hard-on. It wasn't like I didn't get my kicks."

Breath escapes my lips in a rapid vacuum. He's excusing the abuse. Rationalizing rape.

"What else?" Matthew pushes from the counter to pace in front of me. "Tell me every-fucking-thing he's done."

"You name it, he's done it. We've been threatened and manipulated. We've been part of a multimillion-dollar fashion label for years without seeing a penny of income."

"How?" I drag my gaze down his tailored suit, all the way to what look to be polished Dior shoes, then back up to his designer watch and styled haircut.

"You think this means something?" He indicates his appearance with a wave of a hand. "Everything we earn goes into a trust that's guarded by legal loopholes we don't have the money to defend. We survive through the accounts Emmanuel has opened at a long list of businesses. We can spend whatever we want as long as it's within the parameters of his control. He knows what we're buying and when we're buying it. There's no freedom. We can't do anything without his knowledge."

"That Cartier watch would cost more than my housekeeper's

yearly salary." Bishop drawls. "Ever heard of a pawn shop?"

"Ever contemplated that Emmanuel has spies everywhere?" Salvatore sneers.

"You know what? I'm getting really sick and fucking tired of your attitude." Remy straightens to his full height. "Do you think we want to ask for help? Do you think we'd be here if we weren't scraping the bottom of the—"

"Did all your friends turn you away, pretty boy?" Bishop matches his posture, taking a threatening step forward. "You can't even crash on someone's sofa while you pull your shitty life together? Or better yet, go public with your father's manipulation and let cancel culture take the wheel? Social media will dismantle his empire quicker than any of us can."

They stand toe to toe. All madness and malice.

"There are no friends," Salvatore mutters. "The only people who have permanent access to our lives are those that Emmanuel allows. And going public isn't an option either because every illegal action we've been forced into has been documented. He's kept the fucking receipts. So when we say he's gained control over everything, we mean it. He *knows* everything. Influences *everything*."

"If that's the case, then he knows you're here." Matthew plants his feet. "And you've placed Layla in more danger."

"No." Remy shakes his head. "We were strategic. We fed him information to stay off our tail. We told him we bribed an airport official for details on your flight out of Denver. We said you landed in Charleston, and that's where we flew into, then hired a car so we weren't pinned in your actual vicinity. But it's only a matter of time. If we don't give him results soon, he'll send more men."

"I'm not fucking convinced." Bishop throws the ice into the sink and stalks for the floor-to-ceiling windows. "All this smells like bullshit to me."

The room falls silent.

I don't know what to say. Or think. Yet there's a part of me that leans toward belief. I hear truth in their words. I see it in their pained expressions.

I hate it, but it's there.

Matthew rubs a rough hand down his face.

Bishop stares at the ocean.

Remy braces his hands against the island counter and hangs his head.

Salvatore sighs.

None of us want this. And all of us know something needs to change.

"Tell me about your role in my daughter's abduction." I swallow over the weakness in my voice. "Was it planned? Did you know our children were going to be taken?"

"We didn't know a damn thing until after Emmanuel had us board a jet to Sacramento and those kids were on our doorstep." Remy looks up at me through hooded lashes, his dark eyes intense.

"Until after your brother was in that penthouse," Salvatore corrects. "Even after the kids arrived, I thought we were just looking after them until Torian came to pick them up. But Emmanuel blindsided us again with the blackmail."

"And the guy your brother killed…" Remy cringes. "It was the first fucking time we'd had to dispose of a dead body."

"It was the first time I'd *seen* a dead body," Salvatore mutters.

Matthew walks to my side, gently maneuvering me away from the counter to stand behind me, hands on my hips. "Was it your last?"

"No." Remy shakes his head. "Dear ol' Dad has put his dirty fingers into some pretty fucked-up pies of late—extortion, guns, drugs. We've had to learn how to cover our tracks better so he couldn't get as much ammunition against us as he did that day. We made so many fucking mistakes back then. He has security footage of us handling the body and buying the chemicals to clean the crime scene."

"Because every penny you use is through his accounts." Matthew lets out the faintest huff of a laugh. "He's smarter than I gave him credit for."

"But those smarts only work to his advantage while he's breathing," I murmur. "So why is he still alive?"

Remy gives a bitter smile. "I don't appreciate having to state this word for word. But seeing as though you haven't already realized, he's fucking smarter than us."

"He already has a system in place that ensures we'll never gain access to the family trust if he dies of anything other than natural causes." Salvatore presses on the swelling at his cheek. "That's hundreds of millions of dollars, all down the drain. And as much as I want him dead, I want a fucking future more."

Are they saying they want to take murder off the table?

I wrap my arms around my middle, my unease building as Matthew tightens his hold on my hips.

I won't live in a world where Emmanuel isn't punished for what he's done to me. What he's done to my daughter. Stella deserves to be free.

"What about Abri?" Matthew asks. "Is she treated the same?"

Remy nods. "If not worse. The money and control is no different. But he's got something over her that she won't discuss. Or even admit."

"Then how do you know it exists?" Bishop swings back to face the group.

"Because she's always been the most defiant out of the three of us until a few years ago when she disappeared off the face of the earth. He took her somewhere. For months. One minute, they were fighting over family dinner—the next, she was gone. He left her God knows where. And when she returned, she wasn't the same. She was fucking compliant."

This isn't happening.

I'm not caving to the plight of my enemies. I can't be.

It's anger that claws at my throat. Rage that burns my eyes.

I walk toward the sofas, needing space, craving hope. I stare at the black television screen, attempting to visualize a future that isn't a continuation of this nightmare. But their situation is changing everything.

"So let me get this straight." Bishop stalks back toward the island counter. "You're here for Matthew's money, right? You want him to pay for the mistakes you were too pathetic to escape from and bankroll your future."

I drag in a breath, despising that image.

Their future is reliant upon Matthew. Meaning, if I stay with the man who owns my heart, I'll become a part of their picture, too.

"We don't know what we want." Remy's voice is hostile. "We just know we need to get out."

19

MATTHEW

I RUB THE BACK OF MY NECK, EVERY MUSCLE TENSE AS LAYLA STARES AT the blank television.

She's suffering again. We both are.

I don't know how to help my siblings without hurting her.

Hell, I'm still not sure if I fucking believe them. But I want to.

I want them back in my life—if only it wasn't at the expense of her happiness.

"Honestly, Dante." Salvo's voice weakens. "We wouldn't be here if we weren't—"

"That's not his name," she warns. "That's not who he is anymore. If you're here begging for help, the least you can do is offer him the respect he deserves."

I raise my brows, not expecting her passion. Her defense.

"I meant no disrespect." Salvatore clears his throat. "It's habit."

I keep looking at her. In pride. In gratitude. "Everyone, out. I need to speak to Layla alone."

"You don't have to tell me twice." Bishop stalks for the hall. "I'm tired of this shit show. I'll be downstairs."

Salvatore and Remy exchange a troubled glance.

"I guess we'll go for a walk on the beach." Salvatore heads toward the deck door.

"Walking is going to be a hard pass for me." Remy limps after him. "I'm going to find somewhere to sit."

They leave without protest, their murmured words filtering into the quiet of the house until they slowly descend the outside stairs and head out of sight.

Layla watches them leave, her arms wrapped around her middle, her shoulders rigid.

I want to go to her. I'm fucking drawn to her side. But the anguish woven into her posture is enough to give me pause.

Anguish *I* caused.

If only I'd killed Emmanuel when he took Grace from me. If only I'd had the balls to give him what he deserved all those years ago, nobody else would've had to suffer.

"How do you want to proceed, *la mia stella polare*?"

"You can't ask me that." Her voice is frail. "This isn't my decision."

"Yes, it is. You're in control here."

She shakes her head slowly. Solemnly. "No, Matthew." She turns to face me. "I need to leave."

"Like hell you do." I stride for her, not stopping until we're foot to foot, my hands claiming her waist. "I just got you back. If you walk out on me now, I'll tear the world apart to find you again."

"We both know you have to help them. And I can't be around when you do."

"Why not?"

She lowers her gaze to my chest. "You know why."

Because of Stella. Because of her husband. Because history is cruel and understanding doesn't equate to forgiveness.

"I'm sending them away." I start for the deck.

"Stop it." She grabs my jacket, clenching her fingers in the material. "They're your family."

"They *were*. A long fucking time ago."

"Matthew…" Her big blue eyes blink at me in sorrow. "You've spent a few days trying to win me back. But I bet you've spent years trying to gain closure over walking away from your siblings."

Her accuracy is pinpoint. An arrow straight through the heart.

"See?" She winces. "You can't leave them again. You can't give up this opportunity to bring them back into your life, especially if they've been manipulated this whole time. Think about

Abri. Think about what her future might be like without your help."

I clench my jaw, denying the imagery that fights to be seen.

"You understand where Emmanuel could've taken her, right?" she whispers. "If he's anything like my father, he could've sent her to a human-trafficking hub. She might have been forced to spend time with sex slaves. And what if he has that hanging over her head if she defies him again?"

I clench harder.

"Even I can't live with that." She gives me a sad smile, her hand raising to graze the stubble along my jaw. "And I hate your family more than anyone. So there's no way I'll let you deal with that guilt."

"But you'll allow me to suffer through losing you again?" I capture her wrist, lowering it to her side. "You underestimate what I'm willing to live with if it means keeping you."

"I'm not yours to keep." She makes another direct strike with her gentle honesty. "And I know you're not that callous. You've told me before that you have no one. There's only Lorenzo and Bishop—"

"I have you."

"*I* don't even have *me*, Matthew. I'm not someone anyone can rely on. I've made too many mistakes. I've hurt everyone I know. Basing your future on me isn't good for either of us. You need to choose your family."

"I choose both."

She shakes her head. "You can't."

"Like hell," I growl. "*I. Choose. Both.* And I get what I fucking want, *la mia stella polare*. So don't think I can't figure this out, because I will. You're not walking away. I'm not letting you go. I know this is a hard fucking crossroad, but we'll find an outcome that works for us. Trust me."

She glances away.

I drag her close and press my lips to her temple. "Trust me. Okay?"

She sighs and nods as she nestles into me, her palms resting against my waist, her hips leaning into mine.

I hug her to my chest, resenting the fact that she's trying to emotionally slip away while still in my arms. She's giving up too easily when I'm sure I can figure this out.

My resources are unlimited. My contacts extensive. My determination lethal.

"Our agreement hasn't changed, *mia dea*," I murmur into her hair. "Emmanuel will die and we'll be the cause."

Her exhale is long. Ragged. "I need to lie down for a while. I'm getting a headache and I can't think straight."

If she's lying, it doesn't matter. We both need space to contemplate our next move. Just as long as that move is together, I don't give a shit where she draws her conclusion.

"I'll make sure the house remains quiet." I kiss her temple and drop my arms to my sides, fucking despising Emmanuel more than ever as she walks away without a backward glance.

I return to the kitchen, grab a glass of water, and Tylenol from the first aid kit sitting on the counter, then follow her.

She's in the bathroom when I enter her room, the door closed, the faucet running.

I place my offering on the bedside table and continue downstairs to Bishop's room, stopping at the threshold.

He stands with his arms crossed over his chest, glaring at the wooden chair at the end of his bed, electrical tape littering the floor around it.

"It's a good thing we quit working for Lorenzo when we did." I lean against the doorjamb, despising how far we've fallen. "We became complacent too damn quick."

His lips thin. "Then why does it feel like you're worming your way back in?"

"It's temporary."

"Is it, though?" He raises a brow. "First, there's your agreement with Cole. Then the promise to kill Emmanuel. Now, you're contemplating playing Mr. Fix-It with your brothers' lives, or have you already committed to helping them?"

"I haven't decided."

He scoffs, his smile vindictive. "Like hell you haven't. You just don't want to admit it because you know it's a fucking mistake."

"You need to find a new catch phrase. The 'mistake' lecture is getting old."

"I guess that means you're right on cue to tell me I can walk whenever I feel like it." He turns to me. "But I swear to God, if you say that one more time, I'll kill you myself. I'm sick of being insulted, especially since I'm the only one who's ever had your back."

"What part of this pisses you off?" I stroll toward him. "Is it Layla gaining all my attention? Do you resent her?"

"Your attention is the last thing I need, asshole, so why would I fucking resent her?"

"If it's not resentment, then what is it?"

"How I feel about her doesn't matter when she's going to be dead soon. There's no way she'll outlive Emmanuel. He's fucking smarter than we thought, and we've already been found. *Twice.*" He points a hand toward the outside wall. "Who's to say he didn't follow those roaches here? He could be a mile down the road, waiting for us to fall asleep, and your dumb ass still won't carry a gun."

"If I carried, my brothers would've been dead the moment they pulled Layla out of the car."

"Now that's a conclusion I can get behind." His arm falls to his side. "I'd much prefer to be disposing of their bodies than helping fix their fucking lives."

I don't buy it.

We've spent years spying on my family. Not once has he shown enough investment to react this emotionally toward them. They've always been a job. A task.

Not only that, but he's never shied away from an adrenaline fix. Bishop loves anything with a hint of danger. I'm the one who had to convince him to leave Lorenzo, even though he's always craved a return to the darkness.

"What's up with you?" I scrutinize him, taking in the tightness of his expression, the way he keeps working his fingers as if he's overrun with energy. "Why are you pissed off about this?"

"Because you're making a mistake."

"By helping them?"

"By getting more involved. You're going to get her killed."

He's said that twice now.

This is about Layla. Her safety. Her life.

"This is you being protective," I muse. "You're worried about her."

"Like I give a fuck about the bitch you're banging."

"That's it, isn't it?" I grin, letting the slur slide because I now understand the glimmer in his eyes is fear. "You care about her. You want her to be safe."

"Like I said," he snarls, "I don't give a fuck about the bi—"

I launch my palm at his throat, my fingers digging into his jugular. "I let you insult her once. We both know I won't let it happen again. You're deliberately goading me into a fight and I'm not in the mood."

"Fuck you." He shoves my arm away. "Her death is a complication I don't need. You're obsessed with her. So what happens when she no longer exists? Where does that leave us? Where the fuck does it leave our investments and staff?"

It's a cop-out.

He can't admit he's worried about her because he's never been inclined to feel that way about a woman before. All he's ever known are the escorts he's paid to share his bed.

"If she dies, I die with her," I state simply. "Then everything is yours."

"There you go, insulting me again." He gets in my face. "If I wanted your money, I would've slit your throat a long time ago, *stronzo*."

And there's no way my body would've been found.

"So what's the plan?" he asks. "What should I expect in this next episode of How Much Can Langston Complicate My Fucking Life?"

"She wants to leave," I admit with a shrug. "She thinks I should help my brothers, but she doesn't want to hang around while I do it."

"Can you blame her?"

"No." I step back and rake my hands through my hair. "But I think I can figure out a strategy that works for all of us."

"Since when did your lizard-sized brain grow big enough to do that sort of shit?"

"Since when did you stop reading me well enough to determine when I'm ready to choke you out?" I start for the door.

"Where the fuck are you going? We're in the middle of a conversation."

"No, you're in the middle of a tantrum and I need to speak to my brothers. Are you coming to lay the ground rules?"

"Do I have to play nice?" he growls.

"Not at all."

He follows with a huffed breath. "In that case, I'm in."

We walk through the laundry and into the backyard. Remy sits perched near the top of the deck staircase, his injured leg outstretched, the hole in his pants gaping while Salvo stands close to the bottom.

They eye us as we approach, their pinched expressions more focused on Bishop than me.

"I'm going to make one thing emphatically clear." I stop before them, Bishop doing the same at my side. "I'll help but only while Layla's happiness is at the forefront of everyone's thoughts. Her life won't be complicated by this. You will consider everything you've put her through before you make the slightest decision, and if your assessment concludes that your intentions will give her even the tiniest discomfort or heartache, you will stop whatever the fuck you were planning and thank the heavens that she's allowed you to live long enough to make any plans at all."

Salvatore stands taller.

"You will treat her with respect," I continue, "and acknowledge that she is your ticket out of this. Not me. Your future is in her hands. Not mine. Is that understood?"

Remy jerks his chin. Salvo inclines his head. Their expressions remain pensive.

"Is it understood?" I repeat, my tone lethal.

Salvatore raises his hands in surrender. "Yeah, it's understood."

"Loud and clear," Remy adds.

"Good. Because we already have plans for Emmanuel, and those aren't going to change. So get used to the idea of starting over."

"Starting over? Meaning we'll lose access to the family trust?"

"He's going to die. That's nonnegotiable."

Salvo scrubs a hand over his face, muttering something unintelligible as he breaks eye contact.

They want him alive. Or they're not willing to risk their money for their freedom. Either way, the hesitancy to kill the man enslaving them doesn't sit well with me.

"Layla must mean a lot to you." Remy struggles to his feet, the skin on his left cheek already turning purple as he stares at me. "How long have you two been together?"

"Five seconds."

I ignore Bishop's snappy retort and incline my head. "She means everything. The first of those five seconds was enough to determine she'd be mine till the day I die."

"But what about D.C.? She didn't know who you—"

"Bringing up D.C., where you royally screwed me over with her, isn't the best move. What you need to concentrate on is your complete and utter respect for her moving forward."

"What about Abri?" Salvo asks. "Where does she stand in all this?"

"We'll help her, too, as long as she agrees to the terms."

Remy hangs his head and nods. "I don't think we should tell her. Like we said before, she changed after she was sent away. She won't approve of an attack on our father."

"Then she gets kept in the dark." Bishop claps me on the shoulder. "But what I'm concerned about, which my man here seems to be ignoring, is that this could all be a setup. Who's to say you two aren't buying time until Emmanuel gets here?"

Remy looks up with hard eyes. "Call the house. As of this morning when we spoke to Abri, he was still there with his men. He's barely back on his feet. The fucker can't walk more than ten yards without hyperventilating."

"It's no secret he taps your phones."

"That's why we got new ones." Salvatore reaches into his pocket and pulls out a cell. "It's turned off but feel free to check it. Only Abri has the number. The phones our father knows about are waiting back at a hotel in Charleston."

Bishop ignores the device. "And you trust Abri not to rat on you? You admitted she's got secrets. Who's to say she won't stick with Emmanuel when this all blows up?"

"There's nothing to rat on. She doesn't know where we are or what we set out to achieve. And we haven't called her within twenty miles of this place." Salvo's tone hardens. "She's not the threat here. What you need to worry about is Dad growing tired of waiting for you to be found. He'll send more men. And that snitch on the Denver runway will lead them right here."

"I've got eyes on the local airport. We'll know if anyone flies in. But we'll leave in the morning." I glance at them in turn, waiting for a protest. "I suggest you strap in for a bumpy ride because your lives are about to get hectic."

"Where are we going?" Remy grabs the railing, shuffling on his good leg.

"You'll find out once we get there. For now, sit tight and stay out of Layla's way." I start for the laundry, Bishop following a step behind.

"Wait," Salvo calls out. "Can't you at least tell us how this is going to work? Is this a long-term reunion kind of thing? Or merely transactional, where you give us money and we part ways once we're on our feet?"

I tense. Stop.

I don't have a clue about the family situation. A lot of our future depends on Layla. But one thing's for sure. "I'm not giving you a damn cent. I started from the bottom without a dime to my name, and you can do the same. But I'm working on a plan that might get you places faster than I ever did."

20

———————

MATTHEW

The house is quiet when I return through the lower level.

"Tell me about this plan." Bishop stays on my six.

"Give me a chance to speak to Layla first. I'll find you once I'm done."

"I'm relegated to second-string already?" he mutters.

"What can I say? She's got better tits than you." I make a beeline for the stairs. "I'll find you once I'm done."

"I guess I'll be in the kitchen eating all the leftovers then."

"Have at it. But organize the jet while you're there. Have it ready midmorning for Virginia Beach."

"I'll get it done."

"Just keep it quiet. If Layla's asleep, I don't want to wake her."

We part ways at the top of the staircase, my steps slowing as I approach her ajar bedroom door. I anticipate the relief of seeing her resting, snuggled on her side like she always slept in my D.C. apartment.

But she's not there.

The bed is made. The covers flat and crisp. The curtains open.

I don't have to move any farther to determine the atmosphere in the room is hollow. Her floral scent doesn't linger. I can't feel her presence.

I drag my feet inside, finding the glass of water and Tylenol untouched on the bedside table. "Layla?"

There's no response. Nothing other than the rabid beat in my chest.

I continue to her private bathroom, my blood heating in rage.

It's empty. Her toothbrush is gone from the counter. Her makeup and deodorant, too.

Fuck.

I pivot, swinging back to the bedroom, scanning it from top to bottom.

The duffle her sister brought is gone. The clothes. The shoes. All that remains is a box in the corner with the trash from her packages compacted inside.

She ran.

She fucking left me.

"Jesus goddamn Christ."

She's risking her life out there on her own.

I palm the knife in my pocket, digging it into my skin as I storm for the hall. I have to find her before anyone else does. Before I lose my goddamn mind.

I trek for the living room, passing my bedroom, my steps skittering to a halt.

Did I close my door?

I backtrack, my temples pulsing, my palms sweating as I reach for the handle. I'm holding my fucking breath for a miracle as a faint brush of noise carries from inside.

"Layla?" Adrenaline has me by the balls as I open the door, gut clenched, chest tight.

She sits on the far edge of the bed, staring toward the ocean, her back to me, her duffle on the floor near the dresser, Remy's gun on the bedside table.

"Gesù dannato Cristo." My pulse takes off, wild and unrhythmic. *"La mia stella polare,* you scared me half to death. I thought you left me."

She glances at me over her shoulder, her smile forlorn. "Sorry. I didn't feel comfortable in my room with the door lock broken. Not while they're here."

I decimate the distance between us, falling to my knees in front of her, clasping her hands in her lap. "I'll speak to them. We'll find them somewhere else to spend the night."

"No. It's okay. I want this for you."

I want this for you. Despite her fear. Despite her enemies being under the same roof. *She wants this for me.*

She wants my happiness. My closure.

"*Mi dispiace che tu ti sia guadagnato l'ergastolo con me.*"

"What does that mean?" she asks.

"It means you're mine." I drag her toward me, taking her mouth with my own. Hard. Fast. Frantic. "That you're stuck with me. That I'm never letting you go."

Her reciprocation is meek. A gentle palm presses on my sternum.

I lean back, seeing the torment she doesn't try to hide. "I can't live through another betrayal, Matthew. If you hurt me for a second time, I'll…"

"You'll kill me," I answer for her. "You'll realize that none of this was your fault and that I'm a pathetic son of a bitch who deserves to die, and you'll fucking kill me. Is that understood?"

Her nose scrunches, the scars of my past transgressions still raw as she lowers her attention to my chest.

"But it won't happen." I grip her chin, tilting her head upward, reclaiming her attention. "I swear it to you. I make mistakes, Layla. But I never repeat them." I drag my thumb over her lower lip. "I promise your heart is safe with mine. We'll make this work."

"How?"

I move to sit beside her, sliding an arm around her waist to pull her close. "We'll leave in the morning." I follow her gaze to the waves sweeping the shore, my lungs filling with the scent of her shampoo.

"I already know that part."

"We're no longer going back to D.C."

She turns her gaze to mine, her eyes questioning.

"We're going to Virginia Beach."

"To see Lorenzo?" She pivots toward me, reading me. For long moments she stops and stares, quiet in her appraisal. "You're going to ask for his permission to kill Emmanuel instead of hiding our plan."

"Of sorts."

"But if he says no—"

"He won't."

She gives me a wary look. "But you said he has for over ten years now. And besides that, your brothers expect to lose millions if their father is murdered."

"I have an idea that will ensure they bounce back quickly. Trust fund or not. They'll have their own income and influence. They'll slide straight into a position of power far greater than Emmanuel ever had."

Her face slackens. "Matthew…" She's figuring it out. Putting the puzzle pieces in place. "You can't be serious."

My lips kick with pride. She's smart. Or maybe she has the ability to read me like a book. Either way, she's fucking perfect. "It's a win-win for all of us."

"You want them to take over from Lorenzo so he can retire?" She pushes to her feet. "Don't tell me they agreed to do that. It's crazy. Their father's schemes are one thing, but this is…" She shakes her head. "This is insane."

"They don't have a choice."

"So they *did* agree? Or they *didn't*?"

"We haven't discussed it yet."

Her eyes bug. "You haven't told them? Matthew, this isn't the type of situation you spring on someone. Their lives will be changed forever."

"For the better." I reach for her, sliding my fingers around her wrist to pull her between my legs.

"How can you say that when you worked so hard to get out? You hated that lifestyle."

"I hated being alone," I counter. "I went from having a girl-friend and a family to being an orphaned, drug-addicted teenager who killed for a living. I had nothing. But they'll have everything."

"They'll be in danger."

"They already are. They've dabbled in the drug and gun trade for years. They've abducted kids and disposed of bodies. God only knows what else they've been involved in." I slide my hands around her hips. "Yes, there will be teething problems. But it's the perfect fit. They're getting exactly what they want. Protection. Money. Security. A career—"

"Taking on a criminal empire isn't exactly a career."

"*Mia dea*, they're already in this lifestyle whether they like it or not. And the only two options they have are to start from scratch with no money and prospects or slide straight to the top of the food chain. Because either way, Emmanuel is going to die, and they're not going to see a cent of what they're owed."

She peers down at me, her brow furrowed, her teeth digging into her bottom lip.

I hate seeing her like this. I fucking wish we could go back to when she didn't know who I was. When she was all smiles and shy seduction.

I'd do everything differently.

"It won't work," she whispers. "You're going to set this up with Lorenzo and then your brothers will back out, leaving our plan with Emmanuel exposed."

"It will work."

"If you're so confident, then what's worrying you?" She cocks her head. "There's something you're not telling me."

"I'm not worried."

"Don't lie to me," she warns. "I can see it."

"It's not concern for the plan. I'm convinced all parties will understand the favorable opportunity this provides."

"Then what?" She narrows her gaze. "There's something—"

"It's guilt, Layla."

She balks, pulling back. But all too soon her shoulders slump, her tension easing. "You blame yourself."

"Wouldn't you? I left my siblings to be extorted and abused. I walked out on them, and Remy was sexually fucking assaulted."

"No." She shakes her head. "You couldn't have known what Emmanuel was going to do."

I scoff. "But I knew what he did to Grace. I knew what he was capable of and left them anyway. If I'd stepped up and done the right thing when she was murdered, nobody would've suffered. My family would've been without a patriarch, but it would've been better for it. Stella wouldn't have been abducted. Your husband would still be alive."

"Matthew..." She beseeches me with pleading eyes.

"At the very least, I should've gone back for them." I tug her onto my lap. "Once I had a stable life with Lorenzo, it was my duty to save them."

"When did you ever have a stable life? When you were the Butcher? When your days were spent catering to Lorenzo's demands?" She places her hands behind my neck, her mouth close, her breath teasing my lips. "You told me you wanted nothing more than to get out. So why are you blaming yourself for not dragging them into hell with you?"

"It wasn't hell—"

"But it wasn't a life you wanted either. You can't take responsibility for this." Her voice becomes a whisper. "This isn't on you. It's on him. *Everything* is on Emmanuel. Both your hardships and mine."

I cup her jaw. "You don't believe that either. I know you still blame yourself, too."

She lowers her arms to her sides, her attention falling to the bedcoverings.

"*Mia dea*, how can you lecture me on blame but not listen to your own advice?" I rub a thumb along her cheek. "You wanted your father to love you. There's no shame in that."

"There is if I wanted that love despite the cost." She tilts her face away from my palm. "I hurt so many people."

"We all do. It's part of life."

She turns her back to me, straddling my thigh to return her attention to the ocean. "Well, I don't like it."

"Me neither." I press my face into her hair, breathing her in.

We stay like that while Bishop tinkers in the kitchen. After Remy and Salvatore return inside. For long minutes and quiet moments of nothing but contemplation.

She nestles into my chest, returning to the woman who was comfortable in my presence, not protesting when I wrap a slow, possessive arm around her waist.

I try to forget the guilt. To ignore it and focus on gratitude.

I've reclaimed my woman.

She's all I need in this world.

"Once the dust settles…" I graze my lips down the side of her neck, "How do I make you happy?"

She doesn't respond, not in words. There's only a weary inhale.

"La mia stella polare?" I nuzzle her ear. "Tell me what your perfect future looks like for us."

"I'm not sure I understand what happiness is anymore, let alone being able to imagine it."

Her sadness stabs through me. She wasn't like this before I betrayed her. She still had hope.

"What if I tell you mine?"

She sighs and sinks farther into me. "I'm listening."

I circle her waist, my hands resting on her stomach. "We live together in D.C. Just you, me, and Stella when she's home from school."

"What about Bishop?" she murmurs. "Your boy will be devastated."

"He can visit on weekends." I snicker against her hair. "We'll holiday in Italy. I'll take you to fashion shows in Milan and spoil you in Florence."

"And will you call me your dirty little whore like you did in front of my daughter?" she drawls over her shoulder.

"You were never my whore." I kiss her jaw. Her cheek. "You were *la mia piccola sporcacciona*—my dirty little girl."

Her lips tweak before she turns back to face the ocean. "Apparently, not all Italian words turn me on."

"Are you sure?" I grin against her neck. "We'll make love under the Sorrento moon and I'll remind you why *gli Italiani* have such a great reputation in the bedroom." I slide my hands over her abdomen to the apex of her thighs.

"You've already shown me more than enough of your bedroom skills to have formed an unshakable reputation."

"But there's still so much to learn about the intricacies of your body, *mia dea*." I rub a thumb over her jeans zipper, my dick hardening at how she inches up to meet the friction. "We have years of discovery ahead of us."

"Not if Emmanuel gets his way."

"He won't. We'll bury him. We'll bathe in his blood if you like."

She cranes her neck, giving me better access to the sensitive skin below her ear. "I just want to be free."

"Then we'll find freedom together." I scrape my teeth along her carotid. Release the button on her jeans. "We'll find everything your heart desires."

She swallows as I lower her zipper. "We shouldn't. Your brothers are here."

I cock my ear toward the hall, listening. "I don't hear much of anything. Do you?"

There's only her shaky breathing.

She slowly shifts against my thigh, nudging her ass against my cock. "What about Bishop?"

I kiss the base of her neck, the skin awash with goose bumps. "What about him?"

"Is he still in the house?"

"I don't know." I turn my face toward the door. *"Bishop, are you still here?"*

"Yeah?" His shout carries from the living room, his footsteps following as I slide a hand beneath the waistband of her silken panties.

"What are you doing?" She grabs my wrist.

"What we've always done."

Bishop enters the doorway, meeting my gaze with a roll of his eyes. "You couldn't have waited for a more appropriate time to summon me?"

"Where are my brothers?"

He strolls into the room, his hands casually sliding into his pockets as he approaches. "They said they had a car nearby and needed to borrow the Lincoln to retrieve it. I respectfully declined their request, so the gimp and his sidekick are now walking to get it. Hopefully never to return."

"See? You have nothing to worry about." I nuzzle Layla's neck. "We're all alone."

Her nails dig into my wrist in warning.

Bishop rounds the bed to stop before us, his attention pinned to Layla who turns rigid under his appraisal. "I suspect we have differing interpretations of 'alone.'"

"We have differing interpretations on a lot of things." I delve my hand lower. "But I think, when it comes to the woman in my arms, we have similar views, too."

"Meaning?" she pants.

"Meaning the heartless son of a bitch standing before us was worried about you earlier. In fact, he was downright territorial and aggressively protective." I graze my touch over her clit, earning a jolt in response.

She gasps. "I find that hard to believe."

"It's true. You've won him over. So having him here is a great opportunity to ease his concerns." I part her folds, her slickness coating my fingertips. "Tell him you're okay, *mia dea*. Tell him he no longer has anything to worry about between us. That we've reconciled and all plans for our future will be made together. As one."

She whimpers, staring Bishop down as I glide two fingers into her heat, the eroticism hidden from view beneath her tight jeans.

"I'm all right," she pants.

He raises a brow.

"I don't think he believes you." I slide those fingers deeper, curling them in a slow rhythm as my other hand snakes under her blouse toward her breast.

He inches closer, right up to her, his expression tight, his gaze transfixed. "She isn't very convincing."

"I'm fine." She cranes her neck to maintain eye contact, her head falling back to rest against my shoulder as I play with her.

"You're more than fine, Layla." He reaches out, cupping her jaw. "But my concern is for your wellbeing. Do you understand your life is at greater risk if Langston helps his brothers?"

She nods. "He has no choice."

"Yes, he does. He could steer you toward a future with less danger. One that doesn't include their bullshit."

"I wouldn't want that future. Not when he would be left to wonder what could've been. He deserves his family, if that's what they really are."

His thumb strokes her lower lip, his attention fiercely trekking the movement. "You don't want them to suffer?"

"If what they're saying is true, then they already have." She slowly grinds into me, rocking her ass against my dick as she blinks up at him. "Or do you disagree?"

"I'm undecided." His thumb delves into her mouth, her lips tightening around it, her cheeks hollowing as she sucks.

Jesus.

I could come just grinding against her.

"*Lei è perfetta. Vero?*"

He makes a noise. A grunt. Neither a confirmation nor denial of her perfection.

"*Ora capisci la mia ossessione.*" I curl my fingers faster inside her, rubbing the heel of my palm against her clit.

He drags his thumb back to her bottom lip, not taking his gaze off her as her breathing increases. "*Sì. Sei un uomo fortunato.*"

"Tell me what you're saying." She whimpers.

"We were merely discussing how fortunate I am." I bite her neck, then suck to soothe the sting. "*Chiudi la porta mentre esci.*"

"And now?" she whispers.

I taste her skin, graze it with my teeth, my fingers twisting and pulsing inside her. "And now, he's going to close the door on his way out."

She shudders, rapturous and exquisite.

Bishop drags his thumb over her lower lip. Slow. Rough.

He's hard for her. He *wants* her. And if she was interested in experiencing sex with more than one man, I would be happy for him to oblige. But today is about rekindling what we lost. It's about strengthening her position at my side.

"Enjoy yourselves." He steps back, his gaze lingering on her before he turns on his heel and strides for the hall.

Layla pants. Grinds. Her tempting pussy squeezes my fingers so fucking tight. And once the door closes behind him, she scrambles off me in a flourish, stumbling to her feet. She turns to me and climbs straight back onto my lap chest to chest, her cheeks and lips flushed.

Her hands cup my jaw. Her mouth smashes into mine.

She devours me. Savage. Starving. Then frantically tussles with the top buttons of her blouse, swipes the material over her head and throws it to the floor.

"Slow, *mia dea.*" I grab her waist. "I want to savor you."

"And I want to fuck you." She slams her lips back on mine. Crazed. Mindless.

I'm a slave to her demands.

I let her fumble with my belt, releasing the clasp as I casually loosen my tie.

"Why do you do that?" She unfastens the button on my pants.

"Do what?" I pull the slip of material over my head, keeping hold of it while I palm her ass.

She moans, her eyes rolling. "Publicize our sex life."

I grin. "Because, *mia dea*, it's a sin to hide a beauty like yours, and I've already earned enough tickets into hell."

"So sharing me with the world is your penance?"

It's more than that. It's my validation. My proof of worth.

Without her, I'm nothing.

"Sharing you is my salvation."

She looks at me as if I've told her the secret to life. Amazed and captivated. "You say such pretty things."

She lowers my zipper. Delves beneath my waistband. As soon as her touch grazes my cock, I tense, every inch of me already prepared to explode.

"I said, slow, *la mia piccola sporcacciona*." I snatch her hands, making her gasp. "Don't make me restrain you."

21

———

LAYLA

"WE CAN SAVOR LATER." I NUZZLE HIS NOSE, SNAKING MY HAND inside his boxer briefs to palm his shaft.

He's so incredibly hard. Thick.

I need him inside me.

"Not this time." He grabs my wrists, clamping them together. "We're taking it slow."

"Please." I sweep my hips against his.

"*Slow*, Layla." He uses his tie to bind my wrists, the silk tight against my skin as he weaves the material in, out, and around.

"But I need you." I attempt to distract him with my mouth on his neck. His stubbled jaw. I work my way up to his ear and whisper, "I want you fucking me so damn hard."

A hint of a growl emanates from his throat. Feral and fierce.

He stands, making me squeal as I'm hefted upward, his arm cradling my ass when he turns to place me on the mattress.

"You'll get that soon enough." He crouches, removing my shoes with leisurely care, giving my cravings time to smolder.

Next, it's my socks. Then those talented hands are gripping my waistband, tugging me close to the edge of the bed to wrangle my jeans. He strips me, dragging the restricting material down my thighs as I flop backward and wiggle to speed things up.

My jeans are thrown to the floor while his gaze fixates on the apex of my thighs.

208

He devours the sight of my sheer white underwear. The material hides nothing. My peaked nipples are on display. I bet there's a damp patch between my legs, too. A blatant show of how hot he makes me.

"You're so fucking exquisite, Layla." He stands, peering down at me as he shucks his jacket, then starts on the buttons of his shirt.

I fight to free my bound wrists, needing to touch. To taste.

"If that tie comes loose, I'll make sure your next bindings don't. And it won't just be your hands, *la mia stella polare*. I'll have your ankles strapped to the corners of the bed with your pretty little ass stuck in the air." He throws his shirt to the floor. "Now be patient."

I groan, eager to get my fingers on all the sculpted muscles displayed before me.

He's suave. Flawless. And I don't even get to touch.

He lowers back to his knees, spreading my thighs with forceful hands. "I've been denied this for too damn long."

"You were denied because you were undeserving." We both were. We made so many mistakes.

He pauses. "And now, *mia dea*? Have I earned your taste on my tongue or would you prefer to be fucked hard and fast so you can pretend this is still lust and nothing deeper?"

That's why he wants to go slow?

I know it's deeper. I feel it in my bones. I always have.

He leans in, placing a kiss on my inner thigh. "Let me worship you." He moves to my other leg, placing another kiss, then another. He creeps higher and higher with the affection, inching closer to the part of me that burns. "Let this be the beginning of my penance."

I divert my gaze to the ceiling, my bound wrists itching to break free as they rest on my stomach while his lips ascend. "I know this is more than lust. I'm just..."

"Scared." His mouth hovers near my pussy. "Don't worry. I am, too. I'm fearful of your hold on me." He places another kiss near the elastic around my left leg. "Of how you control me." Then my right. "How you can destroy me."

"I don't want to destroy you."

"I never wanted to destroy you either, *mia dea*."

He grazes his teeth across the inside of my thigh. So damn close to my pussy.

"God, you smell good." He places his mouth over the crotch of my panties and sucks on the material. "You're so fucking wet."

He slips his fingers beneath the waistband, slowly dragging, torturously sliding them lower and lower until they flutter past my ankles to the floor.

Those palms grip my knees, spreading me wider, leaving me entirely on display. I tingle under his gaze. Burn.

He repeats the trail of kisses up my thighs, killing me with his listless affection.

Each press of lips makes it harder to breathe. Each inch he creeps toward my heat results in an excruciating struggle to think straight.

"Matthew," I plead, raising my hips off the bed.

He uses the leverage to slide his hands under my ass, digging his fingers into my flesh. I clench as he creeps closer, manipulating my legs wider, until he's poised at my entrance.

He kisses each side of my slit. Then my mound.

It's torture. Pure and decadent. "God, *please*. I need you."

"I'm the opposite of God, *la mia stella polare*. You know this." That mouth clamps over my pussy, his tongue delving deep. He licks me from top to bottom, thoroughly tasting. "If it were legal, I'd tie you to my bed and never let you leave."

"Since when have you obeyed the law?"

He snickers. Licks. Laps.

His stubbled jaw grazes the inside of my thighs, providing the most delicious friction.

"You taste like home, Layla." He releases my ass, sliding a thumb to my entrance while his lips finally move to my clit. "You taste like you were made for me."

And his mouth feels like it was created with the sole purpose of bringing me pleasure. I whimper at his mastery while he concentrates on that tiny bundle of nerves, flicking and sucking as I roll my hips with his penetration.

I'm greedy. Senseless.

I reach for his hair, sliding my hands through the strands,

pulling tight. He's exactly where I need him. His thumb right on that spot.

Over and over he hypes the perfection, building it higher and higher.

I burn for him. Blaze. And not once does he deviate from what he's doing. He *knows* how good this is. He listens even though I don't speak.

I'm already so close. Too close.

I pulse my hips against his thumb. I pull his hair with each delicious suck.

I'm going to come.

"Not yet." He pulls back, reading my mind, kissing my inner thigh, taking away his heat.

I mewl. "*No*. Please. I was right there."

He grins, kissing a trail to my abdomen, then over my stomach toward my breasts. They ache for his attention. All of me does. Every single inch of my body wants his lips. His hands. His gaze.

That smile tweaks higher. He's devouring my torture.

"You're enjoying this," I muse. "You like watching me suffer."

"I like watching you want me." He mouths my breast above the sheer bra, his tongue flicking my nipple, nibbling it against the fabric.

"It's more than want," I pant. "It's urgency. Necessity. I have to have you, Matthew."

"And you will." He grabs my bound wrists as he moves higher, dragging my arms over my head while his face meets mine. "You'll *always* have me."

He plasters our lips together, his free hand delving back between my thighs, his fingers sliding to my pussy, straight to my core.

I buck as we kiss, frantic and breathless.

He savors me like a treasure, like a gift, his hard cock adamant through his pants.

I can't take anymore. My veins thrum. My head screams.

"*Please*," I whimper. "*Please*."

"*God*, that sound," he murmurs against my lips. "You have no idea how much I hate denying you, but I fucking *love* that you need me."

"I do." I nod, our noses nuzzling. "I need you. Inside me. *Now.*"

He slides off me in a sweeping vacuum of pleasure and stands. With intense eyes and rough movements, he shucks his pants, then his boxer briefs.

He towers before me, a man carved in muscle and held together by volatility. A beast scarred by trauma and built with strength.

I drag my gaze over every inch of magnificence—the light sheen of hair across his chest, the chiseled stomach. My exploration stops at the top of his right thigh.

"What happened?" A multitude of cuts mar his skin. Small. Savage. Deep.

He leans down to crawl back over me, taking one of my legs with him, hooking it over his shoulder to expose my sex as he bends me like a pretzel.

"Matthew? What happened to your thigh?"

"*I* happened."

I push my bound wrists against his chest, demanding his attention. "What does that mean?"

"They're reminders, *mia dea.*"

"Of what?"

"That I don't deserve you. That I'm too weak to walk away."

I stare at him. Shake my head. I don't understand. "You deliberately hurt yourself?"

"I was hurting you more."

Another piece of me becomes reclaimed by him. Imprisoned. My heart forgives him a thousand times over.

His hand returns to my mound, his lips to my neck. I close my eyes, drowning in longing, my chest burning with hope. We're going to make this work or die trying. I vow it.

His fingers slide through my slickness as he nuzzles my jaw. "*Sono fottutamente duro per te,* Layla," he murmurs against my skin. "*Non ci sarà mai nessun altro. Solo tu.*"

I mewl with every word. Whimper. Gasp.

He works me into a frenzy of pants and moans, my limbs heavy with anticipation. My heart full from his worship.

"Please fuck me," I beg. "I want you more than anything."

"Have I earned my place inside your sweet cunt?" His thumb rubs my clit. His fingers twist with the same rhythm.

"You know you have."

He licks my neck. "I need to make sure, because there's no regretting this, *mia dea*. Once I'm inside you, that's all there ever is."

I nod. It's all I'll ever want.

"Are you sure?" He slides higher, aligning the head of his cock with my pussy, the hard length teasing my entrance.

"Positive."

"To forever then, *la mia stella polare*." He plunges inside me, effortlessly. Sinking. Stretching.

I moan, my hands seizing the coverings, my back arching off the bed. He gives me what I asked for. Hard and so incredibly fast.

He keeps my leg pinned over his shoulder as he plunders, our eyes locked, his expression fierce.

His reverence roars at me without sound. His devotion is felt through every harsh thrust. His worship consumes me through the slap of flesh and build of pleasure.

The organs he severed with his lies regenerate. The limbs he broke become renewed. He builds me back stronger. More determined.

"Matthew." His name is a gasp. A plea. A prayer.

I can't hold on much longer.

He groans, driving me to the precipice. To the point of no return. "*Mia dea.*"

"I'm close…So close…" I grasp tighter to the coverings. "Whatever you do, don't stop."

He guides a hand between us, reclaiming my clit. "*Non mi fermerò mai.*" He adds pressure, sending me over the edge, making me cry out as I come. "*Non quando sei mia ora.*"

22
———

LAYLA

I RAKE A HAND THROUGH HIS HAIR, OUR LEGS TANGLED, OUR NAKED bodies splayed on the bed as I stare into his eyes.

We've been like this for almost half an hour.

Quiet. Relaxed. No words. Just touch.

But bliss can't last forever.

I suck in a deep breath, letting it out on a long exhale. "What about my family?"

"Hmm?" He raises a brow, his fingers continuing their lazy circles along my hip. "What about them?"

"You painted a picture of our future earlier, but only Stella was involved. What about the rest of my family?"

"I didn't mention the rest of your family because I don't want to play a role in dictating that part of your life. It's yours to decide."

I push onto one elbow. "And if I decide I want to live in Portland?"

"Then we figure out how to live in Portland."

"Is that possible? Can you be civil with Cole after everything that's happened?"

"Sure." He smirks. "As long as I'm heavily medicated for the duration. But I'm more worried about how you're going to get along with him."

Me too.

I'm going to have to call him. And soon.

"Don't worry. I can be civil for you." He grabs my hand, dragging it to his lips to kiss my fingertips. My palm. "I can be civil because although I don't respect most of the decisions he's recently made on your behalf, we wouldn't be here without them."

I rest back into the pillows and snuggle into him. "He hurt me."

"I know. I'm sure he regrets it as much as I do."

I become lost in contemplation, our lazy silence stretching until his brothers return, their voices carrying from the living room.

"I need to check on them." Matthew pushes from the bed to tug on his clothes. "I'll bring you something to eat."

"It's okay. I'll follow you after I take a shower."

I make an effort not to hide in the bedroom for the rest of the day. I lounge on the sofa, my gaze affixed to the news broadcast on the television while my ears stay attuned to Remy and Salvatore's conversation at the dinner table.

They haven't discussed anything to trigger my paranoia. They speak loud enough to be heard, but always on topics that reaffirm their story.

They contemplate their future. They worry about the fallout. They fret about Abri.

The more I listen, the more I buy in to their situation, despite hating every step I take toward belief.

Matthew makes a million calls, his excursions out to the deck for privacy always bringing him back to me where he murmurs intel to validate their claims.

He finds supporting evidence of a substantial family trust. His bank contacts verify none of the Costa siblings have access to cash accounts. And someone Matthew knew in high school confirms there were once rumors that Remy lost his virginity in his early teens at a strip club.

Their story checks out. For the most part. But I still try to pick it apart all afternoon.

By the time night falls, I'm neck-deep in brain fog, my mind entirely exhausted when the doorbell rings.

"Who's here?" I push from the sofa, the gun in the back of my jeans digging into my spine.

"It's not who, but what." Matthew starts for the front door. "Dinner has arrived."

He disappears down the entry hall, returning moments later with both arms carrying cooking trays covered in foil.

"Who delivered this?" I walk with him to the island counter, salivating over the scent of meat and herbs.

"I bribed the housekeeper." Matthew winks at me. "That woman knows how to cook."

His brothers join us in the kitchen, pulling plates from cupboards and cutlery from drawers. The three of them work in a conga line of food service like they've been doing it for years. Like nothing ever came between them.

Matthew cuts the meat. Remy plates it while Salvatore does the same with the baked vegetables. It's nice to see Matthew at home with someone other than Bishop. But it hurts too. These are the men who devastated my life.

"Can I get you a glass of wine, Layla?" Remy wipes his hands on a new pair of pants he must've had in his rental and walks to the fridge for a bottle of red.

I meet his gaze, sensing his optimism. The alcohol is a peace offering. One I'm not ready to accept.

"No." I clear my throat, reluctantly adding, "Thanks."

His expression slackens. It's only a flicker of change, but his disappointment is clear as the room remains quiet.

We all know I subtly snapped the olive branch he offered. Forgiveness will take time.

"You can pour me one, little gimp." Bishop pushes from the sofa, his smile dripping with venom. "I'm always happy to have your bitch ass waiting on me."

"My bitch ass will spit in your drink."

"Do that and I'll skull fuck your sister."

"*Hey,*" Matthew warns. "That went from banter to crossing the line too fucking fast. Abri is off-limits."

I hide my grin as I grab a glass from the cupboard and fill it with water from the faucet.

"Everyone grab a plate. I'm starving." Matthew slides his from the counter and claims a seat at the head of the table.

I wait until everyone has taken theirs before I grab mine and head toward the sliding door with my water. "I'm going to eat on the deck. I need to clear my head."

Matthew pushes to his feet. "I'll come with you."

"No, please don't. You have catching up to do." I'm just not in a place where I can listen.

He remains standing, his expression forlorn.

"It's okay." My smile is honest. "Don't worry about me."

He inclines his head in appreciation as I walk outside, not returning to his seat until I close the door behind me.

I eat alone, the bitter fall breeze my only companion through delicious bites of crisp potato and juicy mouthfuls of meat. Then the door slides open, and I glance over my shoulder to find Bishop approaching.

"Mind if I join you?"

I turn back to my meal. "Is that a rhetorical question? Because I doubt you'll listen if I decline your generous offer."

"Look at you proving how well you already know me." He takes the seat opposite me, placing down his meal and a glass of red wine. "Are you doing okay?"

My cheeks heat at the memory of the last time he asked. "Yeah. I want them to figure this out. I just can't be a part of it. Not yet anyway."

"And in the future?"

I stab a roasted carrot and take a bite. "I don't know. I've hated them for a long time. Stella has, too. I can't begin to imagine how I'd explain this to her."

"She's a smart kid. I'm sure she'll understand whatever view you take on this."

"Whatever view?" I raise a brow. "There's more than one?"

He shrugs. "I'm not convinced they have good intentions."

"You think they're trying to set us up?"

"Maybe. And usually, Langston would tend to agree. But his judgment has been clouded lately." He gives me a pointed look. "He's not listening to me."

"Did he listen to you when plans were made to have me mugged?"

He scoffs. "None of this mess would've happened if he'd taken my advice and smoked you the first night we met."

I blink. Blink again.

"I'm joking." He rolls his eyes. "I didn't tell him to snuff you until you turned up in D.C."

"It's always a delight to speak to you, Bishop." I stand, preparing to eat elsewhere.

He pushes to his feet and reaches across the table to grab my wrist as I pick up my plate. "Sit down," he grates. "It was a joke."

"You expect me to giggle about how shitty you've treated me?"

"The only thing I expect from you, little exhibitionist, is a promise you'll start fucking behind closed doors. I'm getting damn tired of seeing private parts best kept hidden."

I stare him down. "Anyone would think Matthew does it on purpose to make you jealous."

"It takes more than a willing victim and a firm rack to trigger that response, princess. I prefer my women less lippy."

"And I prefer my men with more than a two-inch dick. So I'm glad we both agree your earlier involvement in the bedroom has been confirmed as a one-time event."

He chuckles, his grip loosening on my wrist. "Yeah, nothing but a one-time event." His touch becomes gentle, the sweep of his thumb seductive. "But fun all the same."

He reclaims his seat. "I didn't mean to insult you, Layla. You already know I was hard for you. Any sane man would've been. But fucking you isn't something I think about unless it's shoved in my face."

"It's never been my intention to shove—"

"I know. He likes to show you off. I can understand that."

"I'm glad you do, because he still confuses me. A few days ago, I couldn't talk to you without him being jealous. Now he's…"

"Now you're back together, his confidence has been restored." He jerks his chin toward the house. "Look. He doesn't feel threatened because he trusts you."

I glance over my shoulder, meeting Matthew's gaze.

Heat stares back at me. Hunger.

"He might have earned a savage reputation, but Langston will worship you till the day you die."

I sit, lowering my attention to my meal, shuffling vegetables around with my fork while I contemplate the bliss of that type of future.

"You realize you're stuck with him for life, right?"

My heart falters.

I think I knew the length of my commitment this morning at the airport. Maybe even the night he drew me a bath in Denver—the day he had me mugged. Or right at the very start, when his dark eyes met mine in Perfezione and he offered to help me take down my enemies.

"Yes," I admit. "I'm well aware."

"An exhibitionist and a sadist." He scoffs as he stabs a cut of meat. "You two are going to have a colorful future."

"Wait. Which one am I?"

His brows pull tight in fake contemplation. "Which category does stabbing someone then fucking in their blood fall into?"

"He stabbed himself."

He gives me a quizzical look. "I'm not sure that makes the situation any better."

"Could it make it any worse?" I place my cutlery on the middle of my plate, my appetite lost to the explicit topic.

"I guess not." He snickers. "But it seems our conversation has had a negative effect on your hunger, so I'm going to leave you to clear your head in peace. I do want to clarify one thing first, though." He pushes to his feet. "I might not want to fuck you, Lay, but I will protect you. I'll do my best to make sure you're always safe."

I lower my gaze, awkwardly humbled. "Thank you."

"In return, all I ask is that you keep your private parts out of my line of vision."

I press my chin to my chest, hiding a grin. "I'll do my best."

"For the love of God, please do." He takes his plate and wine glass, then returns inside, leaving me to chuckle into the sea breeze.

After dinner, I stack the dishwasher while Matthew and his brothers reminisce about childhood memories. I shower. Dress. Then climb into bed to contemplate the danger that will arise tomorrow.

It isn't long before Matthew comes in to kiss me goodnight. A long, suggestive kiss that has me panting by the time he pulls away.

"As much as I want to spend the night with you, I won't be in here long. Bishop and I will take turns staying awake to make sure my brothers aren't up to something."

"And if they are?"

The muscles in his jaw tense. "Then the problem will be resolved before you wake in the morning."

Those words leave me unsettled for hours.

I toss and turn, wondering if I should call Cole for guidance. For security.

I fall asleep alone.

Sometimes I wake cold and isolated. At others, I have a possessive arm wrapped around me, with Matthew sleeping peacefully at my back. He isn't restless. He's calm in the face of what lies ahead.

I need to trust that he knows what he's doing. That he can predict how Lorenzo and his brothers will react to his suggestion.

When I wake in the morning Matthew is spooned behind me, his gentle breathing brushing my shoulder.

I haven't lost the urge to reach out to Cole. If anything, the compulsion has increased. I'm anxious over what's to come. And fearful of the possibilities.

I want Cole to know he lost the deal with Matthew. That the Butcher won my heart and no action can be taken against him.

And I also need a reminder that no matter what my future holds, my family will take care of Stella. That she will be looked after and cherished if anything were to happen to me.

I inch out of bed, careful not to wake Matthew, and tiptoe to the duffle to silently feel around the interior for the cell Keira stowed.

I take the device outside, sneaking through the French doors to turn it on and scroll through the two numbers already stored in the contacts. The first is *K*. The second is a devil emoji.

It isn't hard to pick which one is my brother. The tiny little graphic should be enough of an omen to make me second-guess my actions. But I don't allow myself time to pause.

I dial his number, my bare feet freezing to the wooden slats of the deck as the ringtone carries through the device. Then it stops, along with my pulse.

"Good morning, sister," Cole says in greeting. "I didn't expect you'd want to speak to me for quite some time."

"Keira told you she gave me a phone?"

"Who do you think told her to plant it?"

"Why?" Why offer support when all your other actions are cruel?

"Because I want you to be safe."

"Yet you're the one who trapped me here with the son of my husband's murderer." My words are barely audible. It's the pounding pulse in my chest that's loud.

"Did I make a mistake?"

For the sake of my pride, I wish I could lie.

For once, it would be nice if Cole was wrong and I wasn't the one always messing up.

"No. But did you do it for my sake or yours?" This isn't the conversation I planned to have. I don't want to fight again —especially since I'll be walking back into the heart of the Italian mafia within hours. But now that we're here, I need answers.

"I did what I thought was best for you."

"So it wasn't to gain power over a man who has skills you could exploit?" I ask. "You didn't want him for yourself? To use the blood on his hands to your advantage?"

"I'll admit, the strategy had benefits no matter the outcome. But my intent was your happiness."

"You had no idea how I felt about him, Cole. All you knew was that he was Emmanuel's son. That he'd lied to me. That he was the Butcher. How could you—"

"That's not true," he cuts me off. "I knew that when you came home with a bruised face while being with him, you lied for his protection. You *lied*, sister, even though you'd come close to being ostracized for the same actions in the past. I *knew* that you were risking the very little forgiveness we'd given for your mistakes. And after all the shit you've been through in your life, I fucking *knew* it wouldn't have been easy for you to trust any man, let alone a lover."

I clench my stomach to counteract the tightness consuming my chest.

"You fell for him, Layla. And once I spoke to him, I knew he'd done the same for you. There aren't many men who would threaten to start a bloodbath for a woman, but he's one of them."

A bleak smile pulls at my lips, my sorrow and gratitude circling like vultures.

"Did I make the wrong choice?" he asks.

I should say yes. I should make him suffer for the days I went to hell and back wondering where my future might lead. I should give him a taste of the medicine I had to swallow while being stuck under the roof of a man I had to hate while still being neck-deep in love. "No."

"Good."

The conversation pauses, the waves of the ocean filling the thickening silence.

He clears his throat. "Is that all you called for? To set the record straight?"

"There's more." There's so much more I struggle to formulate the right words. "I just… I guess with all that's gone on, I'm struggling with my mortality and want to make sure you'll always be there for Stella. No matter what happens in the future."

"Why?" Sharp curiosity enters his voice. "What's going to happen?"

"Nothing… Then again, who knows when it comes to my track record on shitty choices, right?" I fake a chuckle. "I guess my parental instincts are feeling a little frazzled now that I've made the decision to be with someone who has a past as checkered as ours."

"*Layla*," he warns. "Tell me what's really going on."

"I just did." The lie stings, the bitter taste coating the back of my throat. But I won't risk him getting involved in our plans for Emmanuel. I'm sick of delays and roadblocks. "I'm emotional, that's all."

"Then come home. Bring Langston. We can sit down and discuss arrangements for your future."

"My future isn't up for discussion." And besides, after Matthew cast a vivid picture yesterday, I've found it hard to imagine my life if I return to Portland. I want D.C. I want fashion shows in Milan and seduction in Florence.

"Then come home and properly introduce your man and his punk-ass sidekick."

I snort. "Bishop is far from a punk. A thug maybe. But he can be a good guy, too. He reminds me of you sometimes. They both do."

"Are you trying to flatter or insult? Because I assure you, you've done the latter."

"If you knew them you'd think differently. You'd approve of the brutality of their protection and the underhanded calculation. They have no fear, just like you."

"I have fear, sister. And right now, the biggest part of it revolves around Langston dragging you into something that could risk your life."

"He'd never drag me into anything I didn't want to be a part of. I've always made my own decisions. Even the horribly bad ones. They were all my doing. And that won't change. Whatever happens in the future is mine to own. Never blame Matthew, okay?"

"*Layla*." My name is a more ominous warning this time. "What the fuck is going on? You're talking as if—"

"I'm talking as if I'm at a crossroads, and I'm sure you can understand that given my situation. I want to be with Matthew and that's going to mean a lot of disruption to my life. But before I take the first step, I'd appreciate your forgiveness for all I've done in the past. I never meant to betray you, Cole."

There's a pause. A temperamental build of silence.

"Come home," he demands. "I'll send a jet. You can—"

"No. Please don't." The gentle whoosh of a door opens behind me. *Matthew.* "I shouldn't have called. I'm sorry for confusing you. But I promise I'm fine."

"Layla, get that fucker to call me. I want to know—"

"He's not going to call you." I speak over the top of him. "I'm not your problem to deal with anymore. Okay? We'll speak again soon." I disconnect as Matthew settles in behind me, his arms circling my waist.

"I hope you didn't end the call on my account," he murmurs against my neck, placing one gentle kiss after another.

"Not at all." I turn, my breath hitching in my throat at the sight of him shirtless and stunning. "You don't seem surprised I have a cell."

"I'd be more surprised if you didn't. Your family are cunning."

I grin. "When they want to be."

Something vibrates. Short and sharp.

Matthew glances at his watch, the display alighting with an incoming call from a private number.

"I assume that's my brother." I wrap a hand around his neck, holding him close. "Please don't answer it."

"I didn't plan on it." His hands glide over my ass, dragging me closer.

I wait for his interrogation. For him to question if I've betrayed our plans.

But he doesn't ask. Instead, he stares at me like I'm his next meal, one side of his mouth lifting in a predatory grin.

"I wanted to set things straight." I run my nails along his nape. "He knows where I stand with you now."

"You don't have to explain. Your family is important. What you discuss with them is none of my business."

"But I want it to be your business." I inch back. "I don't want there to be any secrets between us."

"In that case, I'm all ears, *mia dea*." He leans back in, nuzzling my cheek, kissing my jaw. "Tell me all the details."

I shudder as his stubble tickles my skin. "You're in a good mood today."

"Why wouldn't I be? You're in my arms and were in my bed. And by nightfall, Emmanuel will be dead."

"What?" I push against his chest, needing space to understand. "That soon?"

"That soon." He stands tall. "Isn't that what you want?"

"Yes…" I just didn't think things would happen so quickly. "I thought we were leaving for Virginia Beach."

"We are. We'll meet with my uncle straight away, and once all parties agree with my plan, we'll take the jet to Denver."

Apprehension and anticipation swirl inside me. There's nervousness, excitement, hope, and terror, too. "So you trust them?"

"I'm trying to. I did a lot of digging overnight and I can't find anything to discredit their story. Remy even asked for his gun back and I'm contemplating whether permitting it would be a good test of his loyalty."

"You're not worried they'll kill us?"

"They could've yesterday. But today, Salvo can barely raise his arm and Remy couldn't run to save his life. And he'd need to if he ever contemplated betraying me, Layla. He knows I'd flay him alive."

I know it, too.

"Are you okay if I hand their guns back?" He glides my loose hair behind my ears. "It isn't a problem if you don't want to."

I definitely don't want to.

Remy's Glock remained on my bedside table all night. Protecting me. Comforting me. "Can you take the bullets out? Maybe make them carry them separately?"

"Of course. I can keep hold of the magazines until you're ready. That isn't a problem."

It isn't really testing or trusting them. But it's all I can allow right now. I'm not willing to trial their sincerity as much as he is.

"Do it." I swallow over the unease. "As long as you handle the magazines."

"Okay, *mia dea*." He places a kiss to my temple and entwines our fingers. "You better start getting ready. We leave in less than an hour and there's a lot to do before we go."

"Like what?"

He smirks as he leads me toward the bedroom. "I'll give you one guess."

23

MATTHEW

We're in the air within ninety minutes, the flight smooth as we coast toward Virginia.

My brothers have barely spoken a word. There have been no concerns, objections, or speculations. Their level of trust is unnerving.

They should be asking questions. Demanding answers.

"Do they know yet?" Layla murmurs over the rumble of jet engines.

"No. It's best kept quiet."

"What about Bishop? What did he say?"

"I haven't told him either."

She glances over her shoulder at him farther back in the cabin, then returns her gaze to mine. "Why?"

"He wouldn't approve. He doesn't trust them." I slide my hand over hers, bringing her knuckles to my lips. "I also didn't want to risk him feeling obligated to give Lorenzo any prior warning. I'm keeping my cards close to my chest until we get there."

"But he knows where we're going, doesn't he?"

"He would've assumed, yes, and probably speculated that we're going there to use my brothers' stories to gain permission to kill Emmanuel."

"You could do that?" she asks.

"We could. But putting my brothers in power would mean I

don't need his permission at all. It takes away the risk of being denied."

She lowers her gaze, her brows knitted.

"It's going to be okay. I'll keep that card up my sleeve if Lorenzo decides they're not the right candidates to take over." I squeeze her fingers as the jet starts to descend. "Once we're on the ground, I'll give him a call and let him know we're on our way. Don't worry. It's all under control."

She nods, her nervousness hidden behind her confident posture as she sits back in her seat. It's her eyes that betray her. She's anxious, and our upcoming meeting is merely the prelude to our venture.

The danger begins in Denver.

"I believe you." She turns her attention to the window, the ground creeping closer beneath us.

As soon as the wheels hit the tarmac, I pull out my cell and dial Lorenzo's number.

"*Figlio*," he greets in thick Italian.

"We've just arrived in town. I need to see you."

There's a pause. A sigh. "I assume the late notice means it's not a casual visit."

"No. This is important."

"In that case, come to the house after lunch."

A faint vibration carries from somewhere in the cabin. Somewhere along the sofa-style seat to my right where my brothers are.

I glare. Then shoot a glance at Bishop, who's already doing the same.

They said their phones were off. That there was no way for them to be tracked.

"This can't wait," I tell Lorenzo. "I'll be there in half an hour."

"Now isn't a good time, Matthew."

My anger increases as Salvatore nudges Remy in the ribs, the incriminating cell still vibrating.

"Make it a good time, *zio*. We're already on our way." I disconnect the call, pocket the device, and pin my youngest brother with a scowl. "I thought your phones were turned off."

"They are. But—"

"But what, asshole?" Bishop stands, the jet bobbing as it taxis through the airport. "You've risked our safety."

They've risked *her* safety, and the potential threat to Layla's life is inexcusable.

"Answer it," I snarl. "Put it on speaker."

"Only Abri has this number." Remy retrieves the device from inside his suit jacket. "Nobody else knows it exists."

"Answer it," I repeat.

"Okay. Fine. No problem." He taps the screen. "Hey, Abri. What's up?"

"Where are you?" she asks.

"Still in Charleston. Why?"

"You have to come home. The gala is on this afternoon and I don't trust the men Dad has arranged for my security. I'm freaking out." She's rambling, her words building in pace. "I don't think I can do this again. I'm so sick of his goddamn shit, Remy."

Do what? I frown at Salvatore in question.

His only response is the tic in his jaw.

"It's going to be all right." Remy wipes a rough hand down his face. "I'll call Phillip and get him to tag along."

"Phillip isn't answering his cell. None of them are. I think Dad already gave up on you finding Matthew and sent them your way. The entire team is gone."

"Do you know where he sent them exactly?"

"No idea. I booked into the Four Seasons yesterday. I can't stay at the house with him any longer."

Layla's hand slides over mine.

"It's okay." I squeeze her fingers, my eyes remaining on Remy. "We got out in time. We'll be safe here."

"Please come back," Abri begs. "I don't think I can get through today without you."

"We can't right now, Bri. But we're working on a way out. You just need to hold on for a few more days."

"A way out of what?" she asks. "What do you mean?"

"I mean—he can't keep controlling us. We're going to set up a new life. He won't be able to use us anymore."

She doesn't respond. There's silence. Thick and foreboding.

"It's going to be okay," Remy repeats. "Just get through the gala and—"

"No. Whatever the hell you're doing, you need to stop." She's angry now. A fucking kaleidoscope of emotion. "I can't believe you haven't discussed this with me first. And where the hell is Salvo?"

"I'm right here," Salvatore answers. "We've got everything under control. Tell me about the gala. What's he got you doing that requires more security?"

"You know what the hell he's got me doing, you selfish fucking asshole. But forget that shit. You've successfully switched my panic to whatever the hell you two have planned. Why was I kept in the dark?"

"You weren't. We haven't done anything."

"No?" She raises her voice. "That's not what you said a few seconds ago. You told me you were working on something to get us out. Something I haven't been informed about, *Salvatore*."

Both brothers look at me. For guidance. For permission.

They want to tell her what we're doing but that's not a fucking option.

"Not over the phone," I warn. "If you want to tell her, it gets done in person."

"Who was that?" she asks. "Someone else is with you?"

They keep staring at me. Glaring.

I unclasp my belt and lean forward to snatch the cell. "Abri?"

"*Dante*?" she asks.

I ignore the offense. "Is this a safe connection?"

"What are you doing with Remy and Salvo? Where are you?"

"I need to know if this connection is secure first."

"Yes. The phone is new. Salvo gave it to me the day you showed up with Torian's sister. As far as I'm aware, Dad doesn't know I have it."

Salvatore inclines his head in confirmation.

"Tell me what's going on at the gala," I mutter. "What's the event? What is Emmanuel making you do?"

The line goes silent, the quiet stretching as the jet pulls to a stop.

"Abri?"

"Put Remy back on the phone." Sterility enters her voice.

"In a minute. Right now I need to know what's going on with you. Are you alone? Are you—"

"*Put Remy back on the phone*," she demands. "*Now.*"

My youngest brother holds out his hand and nods.

She's not going to talk to me. She doesn't trust me. I concede, handing him the device.

"Sis, you need to have faith in us." Remy pinches the bridge of his nose. "Can you hold out for tonight and then we can—"

"Come home." Her tone is vehement. "You have no right to make plans without me."

"They're only plans. We haven't taken action."

"I don't care."

"I'm done living under his dictatorship." Salvatore leans closer to speak into the cell. "We all are. We can't go on like this."

"*Please.*" The aggression leaves her voice, the layers of anger stripped back to expose her fear. "We need to talk about this. We can't just 'get out.' It's not that easy."

"Why?" I ask. "Give me details."

"Get me off speaker," she snaps.

I shake my head, warning my brothers not to comply.

"Listen." Remy keeps pinching his nose, the skin beside his fingers turning pink. "We'll get home as soon as we can. I promise. But we can't leave right now."

"You *can*. Or I'll never forgive you."

My brothers exchange a glance. A pained, regretful stare.

They're going to bail. They're going to fucking walk.

The pilot leaves the cockpit to open the cabin door, allowing a gush of cold air to glide in as he lowers the staircase. "Was it a smooth enough flight, Mr. Langston?"

I ignore him, keeping my attention on the paused conversation.

Remy stares at me. Stares right through me. "Abri, give me a second to call you back, okay? We've gotta work a few things out."

There's no response.

"Abri?" he asks louder as a chime sounds, announcing the disconnected line. "*Fuck.* She ended the call." His hand falls from his nose. "We need to return to Denver."

Layla's hand slides away from mine. It's the only sign of heartbreak over a plan that was meant to bring her happiness.

"It's okay." I squeeze her thigh. "This changes nothing."

"It changes everything," she whispers. "Without them—"

"We're not doing anything without them. They gave their word." I return my attention to my brothers. "Do you hear me? If you leave, you're breaking a vow that won't be forgiven. You won't be allowed a second chance to fuck us over."

The pilot slinks back into the cockpit, silently closing the door behind him.

"And what about Abri?" Remy accuses. "She doesn't get upset for no reason." He switches his attention to Salvo. "We can't abandon her."

"I know. But what if this is the only opportunity we get? Are you willing to risk it?"

"You're one conversation away from a new life," I warn. "Choose wisely."

"And that conversation could mean our sister is left to suffer alone through a fucking nightmare. We don't know what he's got her doing at this gala, but it's obviously something more fucked-up than usual."

"What's the usual?" Bishop asks. "What does Emmanuel get her to do?"

My brothers fall silent.

"What the fuck does he get her to do?" I demand.

"Whatever the hell he likes. Entrapment. Blackmail. Extortion," Remy barks. "He uses her like a goddamn whore on retainer." He heaves the phone across the cabin, the device splitting as it hits the wall, then splinters to the floor.

Layla gasps.

Bishop mutters a curse.

Everyone functions around me while I'm stuck on pause, barely able to think through the rage tightening my skull.

"Let them go back to Denver," Layla whispers. "We'll figure out another way."

I can't fucking allow it. If they leave it means more delays. More torture. More punishment for Layla, who needs closure.

My brothers are the gatekeepers to an easy slaughter.

But my sister…

"Let them go," she repeats, her calm expression forced. "We'll figure it out."

My lungs tighten with the failure. My temples fucking throb.

"I'll go," Bishop mutters. "You don't need me here, right? I'll fly to Denver and get Abri to calm her tits. You guys can meet me there by nightfall."

Nobody speaks.

Is his suggestion mindlessly reckless or the perfect alternative? He'll be on his own in Emmanuel's territory. But on the other hand, he isn't needed for the conversation with Lorenzo.

"She won't talk to you." Remy stands and faces my right-hand man. "You won't get anywhere near her."

"Let me worry about that while you concentrate on remembering the terms you agreed to yesterday and how you gave your fucking word. I don't take kindly to liars."

"We didn't—"

Bishop's lip curls. "Get off the fucking jet and let me deal with your sister."

They glare at each other. Two grown-ass men trying to win a testosterone building competition as they stand hunched in the cabin.

"He's right." Salvo pushes from his seat to move between them. "We gave our word. We need to see this through."

"And what about Abri?"

Salvo sighs. "We're going to have to trust that he'll take care of her."

"He will," I vow. They might not trust Bishop, but they're here because they trust me. "He'll handle her until we can get there."

"And *how* will we get there?" Remy looks at me with hostility. "You're making snap changes to a plan we don't even know about and expecting us to sit here without complaint."

"I never asked you to remain silent. You could've asked questions."

He points at me in accusation. "You made it clear yesterday that you weren't going to tell us what the fuck was going on. And when it's my fucking future on the line, forgive me for not daring to push."

I release my belt and raise a placating hand. "Everyone needs to calm down. We've got this under control. Bishop can take care of Abri. We're going to speak to Lorenzo, and we'll catch his jet to Denver as soon as we're done."

"Can you tell us what we're going there to talk about?" Salvo asks.

"You'll find out in twenty minutes if you don't hightail it out of here." I'm not ready to give them full transparency. They need more time to calm down before the storm. "But it will mean a future where Abri can have freedom and nobody will be able to use her again."

Remy glances away, his jaw clenched, his eyes narrow slits.

"I don't think we have a fucking choice." Salvatore rakes a hand through his hair. "Running back to Abri is a temporary solution to an escalating problem. We can't keep letting Emmanuel win."

"Well, you all better pray this fucker can look after her." Remy stalks toward the staircase. "Because if he doesn't, I'll hack his fucking face off with a crowbar." He disappears outside as the jet engines whir to a stop.

"I'm a little disappointed nobody scolded him for stepping over the line," Bishop drawls. "Surely that threat was worse than me promising to skull fuck his sister."

I glare.

"What?" He screws up his face. "I'm just sayin' what Layla's thinkin'."

She clears her throat beside me. "I assure you, you're not."

"I better go after him." Salvo holds my gaze. "Can I call Abri back?"

"Yeah. Just don't tell her where we're going." I push to my feet. "The driver should already be out there waiting. We'll follow in a minute."

Layla moves to stand behind me as he walks hunched through the cabin, her hands resting on my hips while I turn to Bishop. "Are you sure you're willing to go on your own?"

He shrugs. No fucks given. "I was willing to do whatever it took to get those two fuckers to stop whining. That shit drives me insane."

Layla snickers under her breath.

"You need to be careful." I clasp his shoulder. "Keep a low profile. Don't do anything reckless."

"I don't appreciate a lecture from an asshole who doesn't carry a gun."

"*Touché*," Layla murmurs.

I pat the blade in my pocket. "I have all I need. It's never failed me before. But you need to keep your head on straight," I warn Bishop. "Don't mess around. Emmanuel will have men everywhere."

"You heard Abri. His posse are out looking for you. If anyone is in danger here, it's not me."

"Don't make assumptions." I drop my hold on his shoulder and start for the stairs. "And stay on your toes with my sister. If memory serves, she's feisty when blindsided."

He scoffs. "I have a feeling she's feisty regardless."

24

———————

MATTHEW

Layla is rigid beside me as we drive toward Lorenzo's Keeling Cove property. Salvatore sits up front with my usual driver while Remy meets my gaze with trepidation whenever I look to him in the row of seats behind us.

Abri hasn't answered her cell despite the calls we've made, and all Layla can do is stare at hers.

"What is it?" I peer down at her phone, only to have her lock the screen.

"Nothing." She shakes her head.

"It's something." I drag my attention back out the window. "Whether or not you want to discuss it with me is a different matter."

"I've made my brother worry. That's all." She places her hand on my thigh, a gentle, reassuring gesture. "He keeps calling. I think he has a sixth sense that something is going on. I'll need to speak to him once we're finished here."

"Are you asking permission?" It sounds like she is. "You know that's not necessary."

"No, I'm not. I just wasn't sure what I should tell him."

I place my hand on top of hers, impatient for Emmanuel's death so I can have her to myself. "He won't stop our plans regardless of what he knows if that's what you're worried about."

She gives me a skeptical look.

"*La mia stella polare,* your brother is a man with a city." I lean close to whisper in her ear. "And I'm a monster who decimated a state. I promise he won't get in our way."

She shudders. In fear or pleasure, I'm not sure. But it makes me fucking hard.

I'm still hungry for her. Always ravenous. Even after the half-hour session in the shower, my tongue in her slit, her hands in my hair.

I'm not sure I'll ever be sated. Or if I want to be. The constant craving is an addiction I'm eager to remain bound to.

"You got the code, sir?" My driver pulls up at the wrought-iron gates blocking us from Lorenzo's estate.

"Yes. And you already know I'm not willing to share." I climb out and round the hood to the security panel, entering the digits to allow us entry.

The gates groan, bounce, then slowly slide aside as I circle back and climb into my seat.

"This is where Lorenzo lives?" Salvatore inches forward in the front seat as we continue down the curving drive. "I always imagined he'd live in a dark, high-rise penthouse for some reason."

"He's got one of those, too." This place is more of a sanctuary. His hideaway.

"It's beautiful," Layla whispers.

I struggle to see it through her eyes.

To me, this place is a fortress.

The tall trees providing a canopy over the yard act as a shield from the outside world. The creeper vines twisted around the trunks hide the mass of mounted security cameras. And once we get outside, the air will be alive with the call of tropical birds from the massive aviary—nature's own alarm system to back up its state-of-the-art counterpart.

The car stops in front of the sprawling house and the middle-aged Italian guard at the front door approaches the vehicle.

"What do I do?" Salvo lowers his sun visor and stares at me through the mirror. "Is there a certain protocol I need to follow? A secret handshake?"

"I'll handle it." I get out before the guard reaches the car. "Hey, Aldo. It's been a long time."

He inclines his head. "The boss wasn't expecting you until later."

"This couldn't wait." I reach toward Layla, helping her to slide across the seat. "Where is he?"

"In the backyard last time I checked. You can wait in the house until he's ready."

"Thanks." I help Layla to her feet, keeping her close with a protective arm around her waist as Remy and Salvatore climb out.

"Is the car going to stay here?" she asks as the driver lowers his window.

"No. I might be the only one with Lorenzo's gate code, but that doesn't mean he favors me enough to allow my driver to loiter." I jerk my head for the chauffeur to leave. "I'll call you to get us once we're done."

He nods and shifts the car into reverse while my brothers stare at the grey brick mansion, their expressions masked, their shoulders taut.

"My hands are sweating," Layla whispers.

"There's nothing to be nervous about. It's only a conversation."

"One that could cause major problems." She starts toward the house, following Aldo up the three steps leading to the front doors. "What if your brothers don't appreciate your plan?" she whispers. "Or Lorenzo shoots us down in flames? What then?"

I glide my hand under the hem of her top, brushing my thumb against warm, soft skin. "After living through Emmanuel's reign, my brothers should be used to doing what they're told, and Lorenzo needs a successor. I don't expect any of them to be enthusiastic, but they'll know it's a strategic way forward."

"I understand that part... I just..." She huffs a pained breath. "Something doesn't feel right."

I feel it, too. "It's because Bishop isn't here." I kiss her temple. "Once you get used to his bullshit, it becomes a crutch."

She huffs a chuckle. "Maybe that's it."

We reach the front doors, one side of the thick, glass-paneled wood opening with Lorenzo's housekeeper filling the open space.

"*Matthew.*" The older woman opens her arms wide as she marches forward, descending the steps to clasp my cheeks, planting air kisses on both sides of my face. "It's been too long."

"Forgive me, Maria. I've been busy convincing the most beautiful woman in the world to be mine." I indicate Layla with a wave of my hand. "I'd like you to meet Layla Hart."

"Oh, *mio dio*." The housekeeper places a hand to her heart. "You have outdone yourself."

Layla blushes. "It's lovely to meet you."

The women exchange a casual hug where Maria murmurs something I can't hear. Whatever it is makes Layla laugh.

"He's a perfect gentleman." She shoots me a grin. "*Most* of the time."

"Only most?" Maria clucks her tongue, backtracking toward the house. "Come, come." She directs us inside the lavish entry and waits at the door for my brothers to follow. "I hope you're hungry. I've made enough food to feed a small village."

"I could always eat." Remy cranes his neck up at the glistening chandelier beneath the overhead skylight.

The five of us walk down the long hall, passing the study, then the library, to the open entertaining area. Sunlight streams in from the wall of windows overlooking the backyard, the lawn perfectly cut, the pool pristine blue.

"Help yourself to a drink from the fridge." Maria continues across the room. "It's so nice to have you all here. The house hasn't seen this many guests in a long time."

"This many?" I meet her gaze. "Lorenzo used to have more than the four of us over all the time."

"Oh, no. Everyone else is on the pool house deck." She stops at the door leading to the yard and pulls it open. "Isn't that why you're here?"

I pause, tightening my hold around Layla's waist. I don't want her exposed to any of my uncle's acquaintances. Remy and Salvo follow my lead, stopping a few feet behind.

"I didn't realize Lorenzo had visitors." I inch forward, exposing my gaze to more of the yard, narrowing my attention on the people under the cover of the deck on the far side of the pool.

Layla snaps taut. A gasp escapes her lips.

A mass of volcanic emotions erupt in my chest as I take in what's scared her.

Lorenzo sits across the outdoor setting from Emmanuel and

Adena. Two guards from each party stand a few feet behind them, positioned like corners on a protective square.

My mentor and my nemesis are face to face for the first time in more than a decade, with Emmanuel in a wheelchair, an oxygen mask over his mouth, his posture still holding the fortitude of an ox.

The call to violence suffuses me. Every thought. Every heartbeat.

Rage becomes a mindless demon inside my chest, the demand to take action roaring inside my skull.

The world will burn for this.

My brothers will die.

"What do we do?" she whispers.

I turn, guiding her behind me as I face the betrayers at my back. "You set us up."

Salvatore remains mute.

"I've gotta hand it to you. This took some balls." Smarts, too. They came at me crying for help, anticipating I'd go to Lorenzo in return. But their effortless ability to manipulate Bishop into leaving for Denver so I didn't have backup was a tactic even I would've struggled to pull off.

"What are you talking about?" Remy stalks around me, taking in the backyard.

"Is everything all right?" Maria asks from the door.

"What's the play?" I ask. "Is this where you plan to hand her over, because no matter what shit he spins out there, Lorenzo will always be on my side?"

"Jesus fucking Christ." Remy's eyes widen as he backtracks, grabbing Salvatore by the arm. "Emmanuel's here. We need to leave."

Salvo yanks free from his hold, storming forward to check for himself. "*Fuck.*" He rakes rough hands through his hair. "What do we do?"

He turns to me, his face full of fear, his eyes cold as ice. Is it a bluff? More sabotage?

"Come on." Remy strides for the hall. "*Move.* We've gotta get out of here."

"I don't know what's going on." Layla's hands cling to my

waist. Her shuddered breath tortures my ears. "Did they know?"

I don't know. The aggression coursing through my veins is turning everyone into an enemy. I'll kill them all. Emmanuel, Adena, Salvo, Remy. I'll kill Abri, too, if her phone call was part of the scheme. Fuck Lorenzo's rules.

"Are you going to pretend you didn't set this up?" I snarl.

"I told you that son of a bitch is always one step ahead." Salvo's face turns pale as he starts backtracking with his brother. "He *always* fucking knows."

"*How*? How would he fucking know anything if you covered your tracks like you said you did?"

"You tell me." Remy raises his voice. "You think I'd dare to betray you after you fucking stabbed us both?"

I palm the knife in my pocket, the devil on my shoulder screaming for a repeat of history.

"Call the driver." Layla tugs on my jacket. "We need to run."

We can't.

We're safest under this roof. Under Lorenzo's protection.

If we leave, we're on our own to outrun any men Emmanuel might have circling the property.

"We didn't do this." Salvo holds my stare. "And we're in just as much danger as you are now that we've shown our faces with you."

"We're fucked," Remy seethes. "What do we do now?"

Maria clears her throat. "I'll get Lorenzo." She hustles from the open doorway as my brothers look to me for guidance.

Jesus Christ. Unless they've mastered flawless poker faces since we were kids, they didn't fucking know.

"Why would he be here if they weren't involved?" Layla whispers. "What would he want with Lorenzo?"

I dig the blade deeper into my thigh, the steel edge bringing temporary relief to the mindlessness. "He must know his days are numbered and the only thing keeping him safe from me is our uncle."

"Will Lorenzo support him?" Salvo asks. "How the hell do we get out of this?"

"I need a gun." I won't have Emmanuel around Layla while I'm unarmed. I don't care how easy it is to pull the trigger.

Neither of my brothers acknowledge my request.

"*Give me a fucking gun.*" I lunge for Remy, grabbing his shirt. I shove my hand beneath his jacket, find his holster, and take the weapon.

Lorenzo strides across the yard and storms inside, his displeasure at my arrival adamant in his condemning eyes. "I told you this wasn't a good time."

"And it seems, for once, I should've listened." I load the magazine from my pocket into the Glock. "Why is he here?"

"He hasn't made that clear… but I assume it has something to do with the three of you reuniting, no?" His attention lowers to the weapon. "That gun is to remain unused, *figlio*. Are we understood?"

He knows I can't commit to that promise. I won't.

"*Matthew*," he warns. "Don't forget my rules."

"Your rules are why I'm here."

His jaw clenches, the wrinkles of an ageing man growing deeper with his annoyance. "We will discuss this later." He treks his gaze to Layla and pastes on a welcoming smile. "It's a pleasure to see you again." He steps forward to take her hands, kissing both knuckles.

"I wish I felt the same." Her eyes shimmer with unease. "But it seems we've been blindsided by your guests."

"Consider this Switzerland, *bella*. There is nothing to fear." He releases her, turning his attention to Remy and Salvatore. "*I miei nipoti*, it's been a lifetime. You were young boys the last time I laid eyes on you. Now you're strong men."

Remy doesn't respond as Lorenzo approaches, grabbing him by the shoulders to drag him close, planting a kiss on both his cheeks.

"I wish it were under better circumstances," Salvatore grates.

Lorenzo waves him away and gives him the same affectionate greeting. "We will discuss circumstances later. For now, we will join your parents in the garden."

"No." I shake my head. "That's not—"

"You have already defied me once by your unscheduled visit." He raises his voice. "Don't do it again."

I grind my teeth, my blood searing through my veins.

"You *will* join us, *figlio*. And you *will* mind your manners."

"That's not an option. Layla's not safe around them."

"You dare to insult me?" His expression fills with contempt. "While on my property, she is under my protection. Since when have you questioned me?"

Since her safety became more valuable than the air I breathe.

"There's nothing to fear, *bella*," he reiterates. "I will look after you."

Her smile is fragile. "It's not me I'm worried about."

He raises a brow, giving a faint chuckle. "Don't worry about Matthew. He's stubborn. But he also understands the etiquette we live by." He starts for the door. "Now come join us. Maybe we can put past differences behind us."

"I'm sorry, Lorenzo." She remains in place by my side. "I understand the etiquette, and none of us are here to be disrespectful. It's the opposite actually. We wanted to offer you a solution to your problem. We only need a few moments of your time."

He pauses, shifts, then rakes us all with a narrowed stare, his attention finally coming to rest on me. "And what problem do I have, *figlio*?"

He's annoyed. Disappointed. He thinks I've fallen into old habits with my hatred for Emmanuel, but he'll understand once he learns the truth. "We're here about your retirement."

His brows raise. "You've decided to take over?"

"No." I clutch tighter to the gun, prepared to fight this with words but extremely tempted to use bullets. "But I've found someone who will."

25

———

LAYLA

Lorenzo falls silent, the stretching bleakness making my stomach churn. He needs to say something. Anything. This quiet is torture.

"My sons," Emmanuel's rasped call carries from the yard. "Don't be rude. Come outside and say hello to your father."

Salvatore curses under his breath.

Remy stands rigid as if one wrong move will end his life.

"We will discuss this later." Lorenzo sucks in a long breath and sighs. "For now, I need to return to my other unexpected guests."

Matthew's fingers tighten around mine. "*Zio*, this is important."

"All the more reason to discuss it later when we won't be interrupted." He continues toward the door. "Come. Be civil. I'm sure we're all familiar with biting our tongue in front of our adversaries." He casts one last look at the weapon in Matthew's hand, then continues outside. "Get rid of it."

Adrenaline suffuses me, intoxicating every nerve. "What do we do?"

"For starters, you can clarify who the hell you have pegged to take over for our uncle," Salvatore demands. "Because I've a sinking fucking feeling I'm the lamb being brought to the slaughter."

Matthew shoves the gun into the back of his pants, hiding it beneath his jacket.

"Well?" Salvatore ping-pongs an aggressive look between us. "Talk."

Matthew squares his shoulders. "It's true."

"Fucking Christ. You can't be serious."

"That's why we're here?" Remy's voice drips with venom. "*That's* your plan?"

I lick my painfully dry lips and start praying.

"It's the best option," Matthew states simply.

Salvatore balks. "For who? Because it sure as shit isn't me."

"Do you really think you still have the option to start fresh?" Matthew slides a protective arm around my hips. "What do you think this is? Disneyland? You don't buy a one-day ticket then kiss this lifestyle goodbye. You've committed crimes. Disposed of bodies. You've made enemies—ones like her family." He clings tighter to me. "You don't get to walk away from that. Taking over from Lorenzo is the only path that gives you some semblance of freedom."

Salvatore's nostrils flare. He's livid, his brow breaking out in a sweat.

"Matthew's trying to protect you," I say softly. "You'll be safer with Lorenzo's name and reputation behind you. And at least this way, you'll be in control."

"And what do you both get out of this?" His vehement eyes turn to me. "Apart from ruining any hopes for my future."

"We get Emmanuel's death," Matthew answers. "Lorenzo has forbidden family blood to be spilled, but if he's not in charge, he doesn't make the rules. So you vow to take over and I convince our uncle there's no point delaying the inevitable."

Salvatore's laughter is cruel. "Great. Not only am I meant to become some illustrious mafioso, but my first act of notoriety is to kill my father? That's fucking perfect."

"*I'm* killing him. You only need to be in the position to give the order."

"Is that meant to be comforting?" Remy asks. "Because I can assure you it doesn't dull the edges of this fucking nightmare. We don't know the first thing about this side of the family."

"You'll work it out. It won't be easy, but at least you'll be free."

"*Free?*" Salvatore asks. "We'll be in prison before the year is out."

"Remy. Salvo." Emmanuel calls again. *"Outside. Now."*

My pulse wavers with the fluctuating beat of my heart. I hate his voice. I despise his existence.

"What's it going to be?" Matthew asks.

Remy shoves a hand behind his neck, clawing at his muscles with tense fingers. "Abri will fucking kill us."

"She won't." I shake my head. "She'll be protected here. Nobody will dare to touch her."

The brothers exchange a glance, troubled and bitter.

"I know it's a shock." Matthew reaches into his jacket pocket, retrieving the second magazine. "But I'll trust you with our lives if you trust me with this decision."

I hold my breath, the oxygen festering in my lungs as Salvatore focuses on the offering.

We all stare at him. Watching. Waiting.

"I can't believe this," he mutters to himself. "I don't know the first thing about Lorenzo's business."

"You won't need to." Matthew inches the magazine closer. "You'll be taught what to do. You both will."

My heart pounds painful beats as Salvatore falls quiet. Contemplative.

We can't just stand here. We need to do something.

"Let's fucking do this." Remy steps forward and snatches the magazine. "But there's no point giving this to him. His shoulder is wrecked." He holds out a hand to Salvatore, wordlessly demanding the gun. "I guess it's my job now to guard the future director of all things underhanded and illegal, right?"

Salvatore mutters a curse. "This isn't happening."

"It is." Matthew releases my hip, taking my hand instead. "But not right now. First we need to confirm everything with Lorenzo, then we get to hunt Emmanuel down."

Remy shoves the weapon into the holster beneath his jacket. "Well, time's ticking, and we still need to get back to Abri, so let's get this shit done." He starts for the yard, his shoulders strong, his head high in the face of fear.

"You won't regret it, Salvo." Matthew reaches out to squeeze his arm. "It's the right choice."

"I find that hard to believe."

"Give it time." He leads me toward the door, but I'm slow to follow.

I can't walk out there like this.

"What's wrong?" Matthew turns to me.

"I can't hold your hand out there." I wince. "I don't want to look weak in front of him. I need to stand on my own. To walk without you."

He straightens in offense. "We're not weak together, Layla."

"He doesn't know that. And I don't want him interpreting my affection as vulnerability."

"Okay." He waves a hand toward the door. "Whatever you need. Just remember, your safety is my priority, Layla. And if, for one second, I think Emmanuel is becoming an imminent threat, I won't just be holding your hand, I'll be using my body as a shield. Agreed?"

I don't answer. I don't want him putting his life on the line when we both decided to weather this storm.

"*Agreed.*" This time, his tone isn't questioning. It's a statement. A demand.

"Yes. Okay." I walk for the door, reaching out to drag a hand across Matthew's stomach when I pass. I need one last touch. One lingering contact before I'm on my own.

"I'll go first." Salvatore strides around me to lead the way—a move of dominance or protection, I'm not sure.

I follow, Matthew close at my back, practically walking in my shoes.

A water fountain trickles somewhere in the distance. Birds squawk an occasional song. My thundering pulse drowns it all out.

The scene we approach is picturesque, the outdoor table adorned with food fit for a high tea with ceramic three-tier cake stands littered with assorted baked goods. There's coffee and juice. A water jug with crystal tumblers. Bread plates are covered in half eaten treats. Exquisite bowls are piled with jam and cream.

Then there's the devil who sits on the far side, his eyes sparkling as he lowers his oxygen mask to leer at me. His placid wife sits to his left, a portrait of excessive prestige. Two of their guards stand at attention a foot behind them.

Lorenzo has already reclaimed the seat opposite his brother-in-law, his profile stony to match the security duo flanking him.

"Father," Remy snarls as he stops a few yards from the table. "Mother."

Salvatore claims the space to his brother's left. I stop on the right, with Matthew close at my side. We're a wall of defiance. Of pure hatred.

"You brought her to me," Emmanuel addresses Salvatore with a grin. "I'm proud of you, son."

"Don't be. I think we both know what this really is," Salvatore says.

Emmanuel feigns a look of ignorance, but I swear, he already knows. Behind the confused blink of his eyes, he hides his volatile anger. "What do you mean? Didn't you follow me here to hand over your pretty bounty?"

"Make one more comment about her, old man, and it'll be your last," Matthew warns.

"Enough." Lorenzo claps a hand on the table, rattling plates and cutlery. "I don't want to ask anyone to leave, but I will if you don't behave. You are all well aware she is my guest."

"You made that perfectly clear." Emmanuel inclines his head. "My apologies."

Rage heats my cheeks.

He doesn't care about Lorenzo's rules. He doesn't even care about his own children.

"I do have one concern though." Emmanuel raises his oxygen mask, takes a long inhale as we all wait, then lowers it again. "Should we hide the knives, boy?" His attention shifts to Matthew. "We've all heard you're quite adept at using them, and it sounds like your restraint is a little shaky."

"I'm more than happy to give you a demonstration." The words are grated beside me, every syllable hostile.

"Emmanuel. *Figlio*," Lorenzo growls. "We're family. Treat each other accordingly."

"Unfortunately, *Zio*, not all of us have the same standards of treatment," Matthew stretches his neck from side to side as if preparing for battle. "Isn't that right, Emmanuel?"

There's no response, only the quiet hiss of his oxygen mask and the slight narrowing of Adena's eyes.

"Explain." Lorenzo reaches for a tea cake, leisurely placing the delicacy on the plate in front of him.

"I've recently found out my siblings have lived for years in a lifestyle more accustomed to slavery."

"That's a lie," Adena sputters. "You're always lying, Dante, and I can't understand why. We gave you every—"

"You gave me nothing but pain. But you've treated my brothers with far more contempt. You've held them hostage from their own finances."

Emmanuel rolls his eyes. "Do they look destitute to you?"

"You've tapped their phones," Matthew continues. "Black-mailed them with crimes you forced them to commit. You've enslaved your own children because we all know they would've left you long ago if you didn't."

"Is that true?" Lorenzo asks.

Nobody answers.

"Is it true?" he growls, his focus turning to Salvatore.

"Yes." Remy winces. "We've been without freedom for years."

Emmanuel sighs and pulls out his phone to tap nonchalantly at his screen. It's a subtle snub at the accusations. He doesn't care. He's not ashamed.

"We handle their finances." Adena dabs at the corners of her mouth with a cloth napkin. "We contracted the best financial planner in the state to help them invest in their future. The money is in a trust. They all know that."

"Their money is used as a weapon," Matthew snarls. "Isn't it, Emmanuel?"

The old man chuckles into his oxygen mask, still preoccupied with his phone.

"You're not going to address the allegations?" Lorenzo places his cake down on his plate.

"I have a feeling he knows his hours are numbered." Matthew inches forward and edges toward me, becoming a partial shield. "Isn't that right?"

"My hours aren't the concern." Emmanuel lowers the mask. "It's your whore who will be dead before nightfall."

I open my mouth but my snappy retort is lost to an erupting

melee.

Lorenzo shoves to his feet. Matthew drags me behind him, then lunges for the table. I stumble, Salvatore's hand reaching out to stabilize me as the man of my heart grabs a butter knife and flings it in a blinding flash of silver toward the guard over Emmanuel's right shoulder.

A scream lodges in my throat as the blade skewers the guard's eye, sending his head backward, his body following in slow motion.

He hits the deck with a nauseating thwack. Emotionless. Dead.

Adena scrambles to her feet with a wail as guns are drawn from every angle—Emmanuel's remaining guard, Remy, Matthew, Lorenzo's security—all of them in a mass standoff while my heart becomes a jackhammer.

"*No more bloodshed,*" Lorenzo roars over the deafening squawk of birds. "*Lower your weapons.*"

I'm jostled from all angles as Matthew shields the front of me, Remy and Salvatore closing in on my sides.

"The time for peace is over, *Zio.*" Matthew keeps his barrel trained on Emmanuel. "He no longer deserves your protection. Either support me or become my enemy."

My stomach nosedives. "Matthew," I whisper.

He doesn't want this. Making an adversary of his uncle wasn't the plan.

"What you need is time to air your grievances without an audience." Lorenzo holds a hand out to me through the protective shield of men, his gaze kind. "*Bella,* I think it's best if we wait in the house. Let the family vent their injustice in private."

I wait for Matthew to protest. For him to demand I stay by his side. But he doesn't say a word. He keeps his back to me, his body stiff.

"Matthew?" I whisper, unsure what to do.

A man lays dead on the deck. The remaining guard has his aim pointed right at me through Salvatore's shoulder. And those birds, *my God,* they scream for the tension to stop.

I have no weapons. Nothing to protect myself with apart from the masculine wall surrounding me, most of whom were my enemies only yesterday.

"I will stay with her, *figlio*." Lorenzo reaches around Remy for my hand. "She will be far safer in the house. She won't trigger you in there. Or be a temptation for others."

A trigger? A temptation?

I don't want to be either of those. But I know I am.

I'm Matthew's greatest weakness and I'm going to get him killed.

"I'll go." I squeeze his hips.

"No." He reaches behind his back, grabbing my wrist, his fingers punishingly tight as his attention remains on the threats. "You stay with me."

Emmanuel chuckles beneath the oxygen mask as he tugs Adena back to her seat. "Yes, let her stay. It's much more fun this way."

I ignore him.

I ignore *everything*. The fear. The panic. The hysteria.

All I focus on is Matthew and how to get us out of here alive.

"*Please.*" I press my forehead to his back, begging him to understand. We can't risk him breaking Lorenzo's rules by murdering Emmanuel. I won't let him steer his life back toward everything he's tried to escape. "Don't let him get to you."

"What is she saying?" Emmanuel asks. "Is she pleading for you to save her? Begging for her life?"

Every second I remain here, I'm giving that monster more power.

"What are we doing?" Remy mutters under his breath. "What's the plan?"

"I'm going inside." I squeeze the hand holding my wrist. "Get whatever you need off your chest, because as soon as we have permission, this will be over." I twist my arm from Matthew's grip and maneuver between his brothers.

Lorenzo opens his arm to me, his guards protecting us with raised weapons as I'm hustled toward the pool.

My escape is narrated by the rustle of leaves from the canopy above, and the gradually dwindling caw of birds. My frantic heartbeat, too.

"*Wait,*" Matthew shouts.

I pause. Turn.

He storms toward me, gun clenched at his side, eyes predatory.

But it's not Matthew anymore. The man stalking toward me is the Butcher. The savage.

Lorenzo gives us space as my face is cupped between a weapon and punishing palms, the ferocity of Matthew's manic stare bearing down at me.

"Give me permission," he demands.

My heart crawls into my throat, cutting off my ability to breathe.

I don't need to clarify what he's asking. He wants to end this now. Without our plan in place. Without Lorenzo's approval.

"No." I shake my head. "We do this the right way so you don't have to live with repercussions later."

"I'll handle the repercussions." He leans closer, his nostrils flaring as his lips hover so close to mine. "Give me permission."

"No. You don't have it. You're not going back to that life."

"I won't need to," he growls. "This is temporary. Salvatore will be in power. Let me end this now."

I want to believe him. I want to trust that he can predict what's going to happen. But I've made so many bad decisions in the past. I'm not going to do it again. If I can wait for closure, so can he.

"Talk to him," I plead. "Get whatever you need to off your chest. Because the time is coming to end him. But it isn't now."

He straightens his shoulders. Raises his chin.

"Please, Matthew." I inch into him, clutching his shirt. "You're *la mia vita. La mia anima. Il mio santuario.*" I recite the words he spoke so reverently to me yesterday, trying not to wreck the beautiful language. "I can't lose you."

The Butcher wavers, my Matthew returning for a blink of pained vulnerability before the severity slips back into place. "Then you need to take this." He grabs my hand, placing the gun in my palm.

I hesitate. "What if—"

He cuts me off with a harsh shake of his head. "If I have this, I'll kill him. I'll break my promise and do it without thought." He smashes his lips to mine, his free hand clamping tight around the back of my neck. "But don't worry—I'm handy with a knife. I just need to know you're safe."

26

LAYLA

Lorenzo locks the door behind us, putting the key in his inside jacket pocket.

"Is that necessary?" I ask

He gives me a wolfish grin. "*Bella*, I'm an old man and far too tired to chase you if you decide to run back outside." He pats his jacket pocket. "This ensures those boys get the time they need with their father."

Maybe I should feel threatened. Confined.

I don't.

His smile is genuine. His eyes kind.

"Coffee?" He makes his way to the kitchen. "Juice?"

"No, thank you." I can barely stomach breathing, let alone liquids.

I remain before the wall of glass, scrutinizing the meeting outside. Lorenzo's guards followed us to the house and remain at attention outside the doors, their guns palmed at their sides, their expressions blank.

"Watching them won't make the situation resolve itself any quicker." He opens a cupboard and pulls out a mug. "Sit. Relax. Let them converse without scrutiny."

"I think we both know Matthew has more than conversation on his mind."

"I understand." He moves to the coffee machine, pressing buttons until it gurgles and splutters.

I turn to him. "You understand? Does that mean you approve?"

He has his back to me, his focus on the filling mug.

"Lorenzo?" I step closer, placing the gun on the dining table as I pass. "After all these years denying him what he wanted, are you now okay with it?"

He twists, leaning his hip against the counter as he meets my gaze. "I wasn't denying him. I was *delaying* him." His accent is thick, his words slowly articulated. "After all these years, I think he might finally be ready."

He shows no sign of the hostility he harbored when we arrived. No temperamental concern or demand to respect authority.

"You look at me in confusion, *bella*, but I assure you my intent was quite clear. I forbade Emmanuel's murder because up until now, I was certain Matthew couldn't handle the repercussions of killing his own flesh and blood. He already harbors a heavy burden of regret. I didn't want him to take action then spend the rest of his life punishing himself for it."

"You did it out of protection?"

He inclines his head. "*Sì*. And I never regretted it." His lips curve in an apologetic smile. "At least, not until I met you and discovered what you mean to him. I'm sorry my decision took so much from you, *mia cara*."

I breathe through the emotion beginning to fester beneath my ribs, refusing to show weakness. "Your decision didn't take anything from me. Emmanuel did."

He nods. Solemn.

"Tell me what changed?" I take another step closer, chancing a glance over my shoulder to make sure the situation outside hasn't devolved into chaos. "Why do you think Matthew is capable of this now and not before?"

"Because a ship in a storm needs a tether. And now he has you."

"Is that what it's always been about? You've wanted someone by his side before he took action?"

"I already ensured he had someone by his side. But a brother wasn't enough. The darkness still haunted him."

I take another step. "Bishop?"

He grabs the filled mug of coffee from the machine. "Yes."

"You *ensured* it?" I shake my head, not sure I want confirmation on the assumption whispering through my mind.

"Don't look at me like that, *bella*. Bishop has not betrayed Matthew and neither have I. He was paid to protect the fiercest soldier I ever had because I hoped Matthew would one day return to take over."

"You paid him to stay at Matthew's side?"

He sips his coffee, eying me over the rim of the mug. "Bishop never would've left otherwise. This lifestyle is in his blood, but Matthew needed a companion. A brother. So I made a compromise —he would work for me from afar and return when he was ready."

I raise a hand to my neck, the betrayal tightening my throat. "Matthew will be devastated. He won't forgive you."

"He's a smart man." He lowers the mug to the counter. "I doubt he will be surprised. But I strongly advise you to keep this to yourself. It can be our little secret."

I hear the threat. I don't see it through his kind eyes and gentle smile, but it's definitely hidden in his words. Even the birds seem to hear it, their siren call squawking louder from outside, the cacophony growing as if they sense the rising hostility.

"I take your silence as judgment, Layla, but I assure you my heart has always been in the right place where Matthew is concerned. He means more to me than my own children, and I've never shied away from that admission. What I've done for him has been out of protection and love."

"But what you did went behind his back. It was without his consent."

"And sometimes it's better to ask for forgiveness than beg for permission."

The doorbell rings, the loud chime startling me.

"More unexpected visitors?" Lorenzo frowns, his gaze trekking to the hall. "Is that Bishop?"

"It shouldn't be. He was on his way to Denver."

"Maybe he sensed the hostility and changed his mind."

Fast footsteps shuffle nearby. I assume Maria is on her way to open the door.

"Should I be worried?" My nerves are on edge.

"No. Cars can't enter without a code or approval from the guards on patrol." Lorenzo pulls his cell from his suit pocket, along with a pair of spectacles. "These damn security apps will be the death of me. Too many notifications and not enough peace." He starts for the entry. "Excuse me, *bella*. I'll be back in a moment."

I saunter back toward the wall of glass as he leaves the room, dragging my fingers over the gun on the table while I pass, needing a touch of confidence. Outside, Matthew stands tall, his shoulders tense.

I wish I knew what he was saying. How he was feeling.

Aggressive conversation carries from the front door and I cock my head to the hall to listen. Lorenzo admonishes someone in Italian, his vehemence raising the hair on the back of my neck.

The birds caw and crow over their owner's voice. The cacophony grows louder. Screeching higher.

I start toward the hall, curious to hear more clearly when a piercing scream ricochets through the house.

I freeze. Panic.

A muted blast pummels my ears. *Silenced gunfire.*

I sprint for the table, lunging for the gun.

"*Hide*, bella," Lorenzo shouts. "*Run.*"

Another muted pop echoes off the walls as I scramble for the doors leading outside, my hands slipping against the lever that won't budge.

It's locked.

I'm trapped.

I bang against the glass, desperate for Matthew's attention. My fist pounds harder and harder to be heard over the shrieking birds.

He swings to face me, his eyes stark, his hand in his pocket.

The guards near the door raise their weapons. Remy does, too.

But nobody's attention remains on me. They all shift their fixation to the side of the house. On the armed men who storm the yard.

A pop sounds. Lorenzo's guard is shot in the head. Right in front of me. His blood splatters the glass.

"Oh, God." My hand shakes around the gun. "It's an ambush."

27

MATTHEW

"Put the phone away." My tone brooks no argument.

"I'm not much of a follower, boy." Emmanuel continues to play with his cell screen.

"You weren't much of a father either." I palm the blade in my pocket as he chuckles into his oxygen mask, the sound barely heard over the squawk of birds.

"You know, at one time you were my greatest hope for the future, Dante. Now you're my biggest disappointment."

"The feeling is mutual, but at least you won't have to dwell on it for long. We all know how this ends."

He cocks his head. "Do we?"

"Cut the shit, Dad." Salvo pulls out a chair, dragging it away from the table to take a seat. "We're done. Remy. Abri. Me. We're all out."

Adena's gaze cuts to her husband, her eyes desperate. "No."

"Don't worry, my darling." Emmanuel smiles at her, all arrogant confidence. "They won't survive without us."

"We don't need your fucking money," Remy spits. "We'll make it on our own."

Emmanuel lowers the mask, his expression turning feral. "I don't mean the money, *son*. I mean pure survival. You won't outlive defying me."

Remy flinches. It's an innocent backlash of movement that makes it fucking clear he still hasn't comprehended the sickening level of his father's malice.

"Death threats don't go down nicely around these parts." I glide my pointer finger over the tip of my blade, drawing blood, seeking restraint. "Lorenzo won't stand for violence against family. His rules are the only reason you're still breathing. But I'm sure you know that."

"Then maybe I don't start with family. Maybe I start with your girl."

His confidence turns my veins glacial. "You won't get a chance to hurt her."

He flashes his teeth. "I can't wait to see the look on your face when I prove you wrong."

I glance over my shoulder, needing to see Layla after he's effortlessly triggered my paranoia.

She stands with her back to me, her focus on Lorenzo who walks for the hall. She's safe behind the bulletproof glass, the guards close by with weapons at the ready.

"Your days of toying with us are over." Salvatore crosses a leg over one knee, feigning relaxation that isn't shown in his tight posture. "And I'll make sure all the money you stole from us is reclaimed tenfold. You'll be destitute."

Lorenzo's parrots screech louder.

"I'm not toying with you." Emmanuel places the oxygen mask on the table beside his cell. "I'm defeating."

The noise grows, the panicked birds shrieking.

We need to get out of here. I'm done having patience for his shit.

"Come on." I lean forward to clap Salvatore on the shoulder. "This is pointless. We need to finalize our plan with Lorenzo."

"Wait." Emmanuel pushes to shaky feet. "I have something for you."

"Whatever it is, we don't want it," I raise my voice over the crow. The caw. The flutter of wings. But there's something else, too. Something subtle. A rhythmic thud.

Footsteps.

A faint banging carries from the house.

I swing around. Layla's fist hits the glass, her eyes screaming for help.

"*Fuck.*" Remy draws his weapon, but his attention isn't on her. It's on the men rushing around the side of the house, dressed in black, guns in hand.

A shot is fired.

Salvatore shoves to his feet.

"My gift to you." Emmanuel grins, raising his arms at his sides. "Purgatory."

"*Get to Layla,*" I yell at my brothers, lunging for the table. "*Help her.*" I snatch a butter knife and heave the projectile over Adena's shoulder at the guard raising his weapon toward me.

I hit him in the gut as Salvatore runs for the house. The guard drops his weapon, clutching at the silver protruding from his stomach.

Adena cries out and launches to her feet.

Gunshots erupt behind me, the blasts blazing in all directions.

I flip the table, needing cover, making Emmanuel and Adena skitter backward. Then I pounce at that fucking asshole, my shoulder charging into his chest, sending us both toppling toward the floor, taking the wheelchair out along the way.

Kill the king. Crumple the empire.

Once he's dead, Layla will be okay. These men won't fight without a leader. Without payment.

I climb over him as he struggles, pinning him to the deck to the soundtrack of Adena's screams, the birds wailing louder.

"I've waited a lifetime for this." I get in Emmanuel's face. Eye to eye. Man to man. "Until Layla, I wanted nothing more than your blood on my hands."

"No," he rasps. "Wait."

"Did you wait for Grace?" I snatch the blade from my pocket, my chest pounding as I sink it into his gut. "Did you listen to her beg?"

He jolts with the impact. Mouth agape. Eyes bugged.

I thought this would feel victorious. That the energy-rich adrenaline I'm accustomed to would smother me in relief. But there's only fear. Blinding. Terrifying.

I need to get to Layla.

"Did you?" I sneer. "Did you listen to her plead for her life?"

Adena surges toward me with a wail, her fingers clawing for my face. I grab her wrists and backhand her, sending her toppling to the deck floor.

Emmanuel snatches for the blade, but I reclaim it first, pressing harder into him, digging the knife deeper.

He closes his eyes, his chest jostling. Over and over.

With the discord pummeling my ears, I can't tell if he's coughing, choking, or fucking crying. But it disgusts me all the same. Right up until his lips curve, a smile breaking through to make it known I was wrong on all assumptions because he's not struggling at all. He's fucking laughing.

"Yes, I listened to her beg." He flashes his teeth now tinged with the slightest hint of blood. "And I dreamed about it for years. She was such a pretty little bitch. With a tight fucking pussy. I bet Layla will be the same once my men get hold of her."

I yank the blade free and roar as I plunge it into his neck.

I steal his humor, snatching it away with a strike so clean and hard he falls silent.

"*No.*" Adena scrambles from me, coming at me from behind as I saw the blade, cutting through his throat, coating my hands in his blood.

He gapes, clutching for his throat as weight slams into my back. Then agonizing pain. I launch from his chest, swinging into a crouch behind the table, the corner of my eye catching sight of a shard of porcelain plate embedded in my shoulder near my neck as bullets ping off the pool house.

"You fucking bitch." I snatch the blade from Emmanuel's throat, pointing it at Adena as his arms fall limp to the floor. "You realize you're as much at fault here as he is. You let him get away with everything—with using your kids, with torturing them. His death is on your hands."

Her chest rises and falls, while tears course over her cheeks. "All of you had everything you ever needed," she screeches, her gaze trekking to her lifeless husband, her face crumpling. "You're the one who deserves to die. Not him."

She's delusional.

Unhinged.

"You need to get out of here." I keep low, hunched to protect myself from the continued gunfire as Remy shoots at men who round the corner of the house.

"You're the one who deserves to die," she repeats, oblivious to the danger surrounding her.

She's going to attack. I can see it in her eyes. In her tightly coiled posture.

"Don't do it," I warn.

"I wish you were never born," she wails, running for me.

I drop the knife and brace for contact. I feel the impact a second before she hits. Her barrage strikes me in the gut. Her fists aim for my face. I grab her arms, rolling onto my ass with her momentum, sending her sailing over my head.

She clatters into the table, the collision hard, her cry loud.

I keep rolling, gravity pulling me farther backward until my shoulders hit the deck, sinking the shard deeper into flesh. "*Fuck.*"

Nausea hits.

Vertigo decimates me.

I climb onto my hands and knees as men shout and birds squawk, my shoulder pulsing like a motherfucker. But Adena doesn't make another attack. She crawls past the slayed guards near the pool house wall, rises to her feet, then runs.

"Make sure we get them all," Remy yells.

I struggle to stand, blinking through clouded vision.

"Matt, you okay?" Salvo calls across the yard.

I'm fucking peachy and entirely ripe for the field day Bishop is going to have with my injury. Who gets stabbed with a fucking plate? By their own goddamn mother?

"Matt?" Salvo shouts.

I hear him. I even raise my head to look at him. But my eyes act as if I'm high as a kite. The world blurs. Darkens into obscurity. And my gut. *Fuck.* It burns.

"Where's Layla?" I squint toward the house. Stumble from the deck. "*Shit.*"

I can't even keep my legs locked. They're too heavy. Too fucking weak.

Something isn't right.

"Matthew?" Remy jogs toward me. "You okay?"

No. I'm not.

My heart beats out of my chest. And my head. *Jesus*. What the fuck is wrong with me?

I collapse to my knees. Then my hands. "Save Layla."

28

———

LAYLA

I scream as Matthew tackles Emmanuel to the ground.

"*Bella,*" Lorenzo shouts as the front door slams. "*Hide.*"

I don't know what to do. Where to go.

I have to get outside.

My grip sweats around the Glock as I aim it toward the glass, preparing to shoot.

"Layla, *no.*"

I turn toward Lorenzo's voice. He stumbles from the hall, his face grey, a gun in one hand, his cell in the other.

"Maria's dead." He pockets the phone. "But the house is safe for now. I have to get you in the panic room before that changes."

"I can't leave Matthew."

"Help is already on the way." Lorenzo beckons me with a wave of his weapon. "Come. Hurry."

A thud hits the glass behind me, making me scream.

I swing around and Salvatore is there. On the other side of the door. Peering at me through the blood splatter.

He grasps the handle, frantically working the lever.

"It's locked," I yell, then twist toward Lorenzo. "Give me the key."

He shakes his head. "I can't risk the threat getting inside. Matthew would never forgive me."

"I don't care." I run to him, prepared to claw through each of his pockets to find which one hides my freedom, but I skitter to a stop at the blood dripping from the hem of his black pants to pool beside his foot. "You're hurt."

"It's a scratch." He limps toward the hall leading away from the entry. "Follow me."

"No. Wait." *Shit*. He's bleeding too much.

"Layla," he grates.

"Please. Let me take a look. You can't help me if you die. Now sit."

He raises his chin, stubborn.

"*Sit*." I grab his shoulders and add pressure as gunfire carries from outside. I want to cry. To scream. But I hold it in. I push it down.

"I understand why he's infatuated with you," Lorenzo murmurs.

"You won't for much longer if you don't sit."

He heaves a sigh and leans into the hallway wall, sliding down the plaster to come to a hard stop on the tile. He hisses in pain, his face scrunching into a mass of weathered wrinkles.

I place my gun on the ground and rip at the hole in his suit pants. He's been shot. I push at his leg, twisting the limb to find the exit wound. "It went straight through. In and out within a few inches."

"See? Nothing to worry about."

"You're still losing a lot of blood." I yank off my sweater, wrap it around his thigh above the injury, then knot it tight.

"*Figlio di puttana*," he growls.

"Sorry." I meet his gaze. "You said help is on the way?"

He rests his head back against the wall. "My men and my surgeon."

I swallow and lick my drying lips. "I don't know what else to do for you until they arrive. But I can help Matthew."

"You'll only get in the way."

"Please don't argue with me." I grasp his hands, the blood on our skin making the contact slippery. "I don't want to have to hurt you to get the key, but I think you know I will. I'll do whatever it takes."

His lips press tight. Offended or stubborn I'm not sure.

"*Please*, Lorenzo."

He glares. Snarls. Then leans to one side, wincing as he reaches into his pants pocket to retrieve the blood-covered key. "Shoot first and ask questions later. At least for my sake. I have a feeling I'll be the next person on Matthew's kill list if you don't survive."

I snatch the offering along with the gun and prepare to scramble to my feet.

"Wait." He clutches my wrist, his head cocked toward the yard. "Listen."

I frown, not hearing anything but the screams of wildlife and the shout of men.

The screams of wildlife…

The shouts of men…

No gunfire.

No battle.

"It's over?" I push to stand, gripping Lorenzo's forearm to help pull him up with me.

As soon as he's stable, I run for the glass, taking in the bodies strewn across the yard.

Salvatore remains at the door, his back to me, his attention focused across the pool.

"Matt, are you okay?" He stalks away from the house.

I follow his line of sight and watch as Matthew stumbles from the deck.

He's ghostly white.

Hurt.

I fumble to put the key in the lock, my fingers trembling, my limbs shaking. I miss the hole over and over, my heart contracting like a vise. "Help me." I don't know who I'm pleading with. Myself? God? "I can't get the door open."

"Let me." Lorenzo limps forward, taking the key from my quivering palm. He inserts the metal into the lock, twists it, opens the door, then pushes it wide as Matthew collapses to his knees in front of Remy.

I run for him. Oblivious to any danger. Unconcerned about threats. "*Matthew*."

I reach him alongside Salvatore, both his brothers guiding him to the ground, turning him to his side to expose the shard embedded in his back.

"It's okay." I kneel next to him, cupping his face. "Help is on the way."

"What help?" Salvatore asks. "This place is a bloodbath."

"Lorenzo said a doctor is coming." I keep my eyes on Matthew, drowning in the bleakness of his expression. "You're going to be fine."

He doesn't look fine.

He looks like death.

"Don't wimp out on me, brother." Remy crouches behind him to inspect the injury. "This is a far sight less than the stab wound you gave me yesterday."

"No." I shake my head. "There has to be something else." Something more. Matthew is too pale. Too quiet. Too still.

"Tell me what's wrong?" I scan his body. His jacket. His suit pants. But he remains motionless, one arm limp on the lawn, the other resting over his middle. "I can't see where you're hurt."

"Forgive me, *mia dea*." He winces. "I failed you again…"

"No. You never failed me. You always *fought* for me." Fought to have me. Fought to cherish me. "Talk to me. Tell me where you're hurt."

His eyes roll. He's losing consciousness.

"What's wrong with him?" I scream at Salvatore. "What's happening?"

"Not… my shoulder." Matthew raises the hand resting on his abdomen, revealing the blood soaking the white shirt beneath his jacket. "I'm sorry, *la mia stella polare*. I thought we'd have more time."

No.

No.

My throat burns with the need to scream. "Everything is okay. I'm going to get you to a hospital." I shove to my feet, attempting to drag him with me. "Someone help. I need to get him to a car." I pull on his uninjured arm, trying to leverage him to his feet. "*Someone help*," I cry.

Remy and Salvatore grab his arms.

"Layla," he groans. "I can't."

"Don't you fucking leave me. I already lost a husband. I won't lose a soul mate."

"You will never lose me." His eyes turn solemn. "Even in death, you'll be my obsession."

"Stop it." I can't get enough air. My lungs are too tight. "Do something," I demand of Salvatore. *"Help him,"* I scream at Remy. I glance around the yard, finding the remaining guard. "Help." Then Aldo stumbles around the corner, his face bloodied. "Why isn't anyone helping?"

29

LAYLA

"Bring him into the house," Lorenzo shouts from the door. "Backup has arrived."

"Help me lift him." Salvatore moves behind Matthew. "Grab his legs."

Remy complies while Lorenzo barks harsh Italian into the yard, inspiring his men to hustle toward us.

They assist in lifting Matthew as he loses consciousness, carrying him across the lawn, past the dead guard near the door, then Lorenzo, until they're inside. I follow like a rickety train wreck, my mind running a mile a minute while my body functions on autopilot.

"The surgeon is already preparing in the basement." Lorenzo squeezes my shoulder as I pass the threshold into the living area. "Everything will be okay."

I don't believe him. I don't think anyone does.

I shadow the men across the room, my attention fixated on the blood being trekked over the pristine tile. I focus on each droplet. The contrasting crystal-clean white against the deep red of death chills me to the bone.

He has to survive.

He can't leave me.

They charge for the far hall, away from the entry, taking him to a door that's kicked open by the unfamiliar guard holding Matthew's left shoulder.

I'm led down to the lower level, my feet stumbling over the stairs to an open space resembling a hospital operating theatre. An older man and a middle-aged woman wash their hands in the far sink. Both are in scrubs and surrounded by cabinets of medical supplies and monitoring equipment. There are metal trolleys. Display screens. Wires and vials and fluid.

But all I see is Matthew and the blood he *drip, drip, drips* on the floor.

"Place him on his side." The doctor stalks toward us, the woman doing the same as she rushes to pull on gloves. "Be careful of the protrusion in his back."

The men dump Matthew on the operating table beneath the huge dome of a surgical light affixed to the ceiling and step away, allowing the woman to hold him in place.

"Be careful with him." I take Matthew's limp hand, his brothers at my sides.

"What am I dealing with apart from the shoulder injury?" The doctor wields a pair of scissors and cuts at Matthew's clothes.

"We think it's a bullet wound to the stomach," Salvatore says.

"Any known allergies?"

"IV contrast." Remy's voice is weak as he rakes a hand through his hair. "He had it as a kid and blew up like a puffer fish."

"Blood type?"

Remy shakes his head. Salvatore, too.

God, I don't know either.

"Don't worry. We'll figure that out." The doctor slices at Matthew's jacket. "That's all I need. You can leave. We don't work with an audience."

Lorenzo's men start for the stairs.

I don't move. I keep clinging to Matthew's hand, wordlessly begging his eyes to open. "I'm not going anywhere."

"Then he dies." The old man stops decimating clothing to stare at me, emotionless, giving no hint that he's sworn an oath to help the sick and injured.

"I won't get in the way," I promise. "I won't say a word."

"You'll leave or he dies," he repeats. "All you're doing at the moment is stopping me from arranging the units of blood he's going to need to survive this."

"Come on." Salvatore slides a hand over my shoulder. "Let the doctor do his job."

I don't know how.

The thought of walking away... Of not being here if something happens...

"*Please.*" I peer down at Matthew, his skin ashen, his chest barely moving.

"Layla, come on." Remy grabs my hand. "We'll wait upstairs together."

"I don't want to wait upstairs." Fire burns my lungs. "He needs to know he's not alone."

"He doesn't need to know shit right now, lady." The doctor glares at me. "Get out of here. *Now.*"

Salvatore gives me an apologetic smile. "It's okay."

"*Please,*" I beg. "I—"

Remy grabs me around the waist, hauling me off the ground and over his shoulder.

"*No.*" I push against his back as I'm carried up the stairs. "Please take care of him. Don't let him die."

I beg.

I plead.

I pray.

Nobody listens.

I'm taken into the upstairs hall, the door to the basement closed behind us by a guard who shifts to block any chance of my return.

"Put me down." I wiggle against Remy's shoulder. Push. Thump.

"In a minute." He continues into the living room where Lorenzo snaps Italian at a line of people streaming in through the front door.

I'm placed on my feet as men in suits pass by carrying over-sized duffles toward the yard. Women begin cleaning, the pungent scent of bleach already infiltrating the air.

"*Bella.*" Lorenzo limps toward me, my sweater still tied around his thigh. "How is he?"

I open my mouth, but nothing comes out. No words. No sound. I'm hollow. Empty.

"We don't know," Remy answers. "We were told to leave."

Lorenzo inclines his head, turning his attention to the people entering the room. "Flores prefers to work unsupervised. But I will check on him once my team is under control. I need to get everyone moving before the police arrive."

The conversation filters in, but I don't hear it. I don't care. How can I when Matthew might be dying?

I walk for the front door as Salvatore volunteers to help with the crime scene.

"Hey," Remy calls after me. "Where are you going?"

"I can't breathe in here." I follow the trail of blood to the entry, where Maria's lifeless body is being rolled onto a rug by two men. They flop her around. Without a care. With no compassion.

"Don't look." Remy hobbles to my side, grabbing my arm to lead me through the open front door, shielding me from the view of her sightless eyes. "Don't stop until you get outside."

He drags me past the threshold where a man lays dead, his gaping head wound bleeding all over the polished cement.

Remy tugs me farther, down the three steps, not letting go until we're on the drive. "You're not going to pass out on me, are you?"

I'd give anything to close my eyes and not wake up until Matthew is better. But no, I'm fully awake, my ears ringing, my brain a mess. "You can go back inside. I'll be fine."

I focus on the men storming around the front of the property, the energy out here just as bustling as it is inside. Cars line the drive. Numerous men scan the yard, combing the lawn. Another carries a pressure-wash machine and a bottle of bleach.

"Lorenzo would have the cops in his pocket, right?" Remy murmurs. "My leg isn't in the best position to make a run for freedom."

"I'm sure he has it under control." I don't give a damn though. Not about the cops. Or the bodies. Or the evidence.

All I want is Matthew.

I wait for the men to carry the rolled rug through the door, Maria and the dead intruder bundled inside, then walk for the front of the house. I slump onto the top step, legs bent, elbows on knees, my face in my hands.

I stay there as the whir of sirens approach in the distance. I don't move when men pass me, muttering about the crooked cops accepting the story of kids playing with fireworks.

I keep my head buried and relive every moment of the past hour. The gunfire. The blood. Emmanuel.

"What happened to your father?" I raise my gaze to Remy, still standing a few feet away.

"He's dead. Matthew took care of it."

I swallow, wishing I felt relief instead of desolation. "And Adena?"

"I don't know." He shrugs.

Torment dances in his eyes—a torment I'm all too familiar with. I suffered through enough of it when my own father was killed. It's a horrible sensation. The grief of losing someone you despise. The mourning for what should've been.

I'd pity Remy if I wasn't so numb.

"You should find out." I wipe my blood-stained hands on my jeans, wishing they were clean, wishing even more that I had the energy to wash them. "If she's still alive, someone needs to be looking for her."

He breaks eye contact to glance back at the house. "Are you going to be okay on your own?"

I keep staring at him, the man I once considered my enemy, the person I held partially accountable for my daughter's abduction and my husband's murder. "Yeah. I'll come inside when I can."

He staggers toward me. Up the stairs. To the threshold.

"You realize I still hate you, right?" I say over my shoulder.

He huffs a laugh. "Yeah. Nothing says hatred quite like signing someone up to run a mafia enterprise."

I wince as his footsteps fade down the hall.

I return my head to my hands while the cleanup continues around me. Each second seems like a year without word on Matthew. Every heartbeat feels like it could be his last.

My emotions sprint through different stages of grief—shock, anger, denial.

I try to think about what I'll say to him once he wakes up, but pessimism takes over and all I can picture is his lifeless body. His funeral.

I drown from the weight of it.

I curse myself for wasting the time we had. I should've forgiven him sooner. Cherished him longer. Why the hell didn't I?

"*Layla?*"

I snap upright, stunned by my sister's voice. "Keira?"

She sprints up the drive, Decker, Hunter, and Sarah jogging close behind her.

I struggle to breathe as I shove to my feet and scramble down the stairs to engulf her in my arms. "Why are you here?"

"Why are *you* here?" she counters, embracing me, holding me close. "What happened?"

"I don't know." I shake my head, trying to clear the white noise. "We came to speak to Lorenzo, not knowing Emmanuel was here. There was an ambush."

She pulls back, her grip tight on my arms as she scans me from head to toe. "Are you hurt?"

"No. But Matthew is. It's bad, Keira. I think he might be dying."

"Where is he?"

My throat tightens. "There's a makeshift hospital in the basement. I'm not allowed in there."

She drags me back into her arms and doesn't let go.

I want to cry. To sob. But the tears won't form. They're trapped in my chest, building like a hurricane, pummeling me from the inside out.

"Are we safe here?" Hunter asks.

I glance up at him over Keira's shoulder. "With Lorenzo's men, yes. But against another ambush? I have no idea."

He looks around the yard, taking in the cleanup operation. "Seems like these guys have shit on lock."

"Yeah." I release Keira and take a step back. "How did you get past the gate?"

"I can be persuasive." He shrugs. "And it helps when Torian called ahead to make sure we had safe passage."

I frown, my gaze switching from Hunt to Keira, then Decker and Sarah. "How did you know where…" I sigh as clarity dawns. "The cell, right? You tracked me here."

Decker gives me an apologetic smile. "Not here exactly. The software only gave an approximation, but the mass of cars outside the property helped. Cole had us in the air from Chicago first thing this morning. You scared him with that phone call."

My stomach clenches.

They rushed to help me. They *care*.

Their concern shouldn't have this effect. Keira told me yesterday that she loved me. Cole explained this morning that he feared for my safety. But seeing it... feeling it...

After I've spent so long being the black sheep of the family, their support is overwhelming.

"I'm going to do a walk around the perimeter and offer my services." Hunter closes in and grabs my wrist for a quick squeeze. It's the most sympathy he's ever given me. The most I've seen him give anyone apart from Sarah. "It looks like this shit with you and the Butcher is a permanent thing, so now's as good a time as any to pave the way with Lorenzo."

"Lorenzo's busy being stitched up," Salvatore says behind me.

I stiffen. My family does too.

Shit.

Decker and Hunter reach for their weapons.

"Wait. Stop." I rush to move in front of them. "It's okay. He isn't a threat."

"No?" Hunter sneers. "But I am to him."

"Please don't." I raise my hands in front of me. "Emmanuel tortured his sons more than us."

"They killed Benji." Decker glares.

"*Emmanuel* killed Benji. It wasn't Matthew's brothers. They wanted out. That's why we're here." I glance at Salvatore over my shoulder, waiting for him to back me up. "Tell them."

"Now isn't the time. I'm sure we'll hash this out in the future." Salvatore crosses his arms over his chest. "Until then we can be civil, right?"

Hunter doesn't answer. Decker's lip curls.

"Any expertise is appreciated, though," Salvatore adds. "We've got a lot of shit to clean." He speaks with authority. With power.

"You've spoken to Lorenzo." I turn to him, trying to read what his stony expression hides. "Have you come to an agreement?"

"We will."

He's going to take over. Maybe not today, but soon. He already exudes more confidence than when he shuffled off the jet earlier today.

"I don't like this," Keira whispers. "We shouldn't be here with him. We need to speak to Cole."

I swing back to face her, finding the other three nodding.

"We have to leave." Hunter grabs the crook of Sarah's arm. "Let's go.

Keira steps forward, her fingers sliding over mine. "Come on. We can wait at a hotel nearby. Get someone to call you when there's news on Matthew."

"There already is news," Salvatore says.

I freeze. Panic.

"I'll be waiting inside when you're ready to hear it."

30

LAYLA

"Go." I squeeze Keira's hand. "I can't abandon Matthew."

"Then I'll stay, too."

"No. I understand why you have to leave." I release her and retreat toward the house. "I'll speak to you later." I swing to the door and stride after Salvatore, my heart in my throat. "*Wait.* Tell me. Please."

He stops before the library and turns to face me. "It isn't much."

"I don't care. Whatever it is, I want to know."

"They got the bullet out. It wasn't deep, which the nurse said was good news. It means the damage was minimal. But his blood loss is an issue. They're waiting on units to arrive, and until then, his heart is under pressure while they try to stitch him up."

I drag in a deep breath, trying not to fall back into the pit of despair.

It's hard though. So goddamn hard as I stare at the dark eyes that look so much like Matthew's.

"He'll make it through." His throat works over a heavy swallow, belying his statement.

"But he might not either, right?" My voice cracks. "He could die. The trauma and blood loss could kill him."

His lips press tight. His jaw tics.

Oh, God.

He grabs my arm and drags me into his chest, one hand cradling my head, the other nestled against my back.

My enemy and my comforter.

I'm petrified, and Salvatore is right there with me.

But I still can't break. All my tears continue to compile in my chest, the pressure building like an impending explosion.

"Story of my life," Remy drawls from nearby. "I get the hatred, he gets the hugs."

Salvatore releases me, his arms drawing back to his sides as he ignores his younger brother. "You should pour yourself a stiff drink. I've already taken a shot or two."

"They still won't let me downstairs?" I ask.

"Not until they're finished." He glides a hand around my waist and leads me to the kitchen to drag a bottle of Macallan across the bench.

Someone should call Bishop. He deserves to know… But without insight on Matthew's health, making him worry isn't the right thing either.

I stay there for hours on a stool at the island counter, cradling a finger of scotch and a heart full of fear.

A shady courier with a cooler of blood comes and goes. The team of cleaners pack up and leave. The men clear out, taking the dead bodies with them.

By midafternoon it's just me, Salvatore, and Remy, with a large contingent of guards manning the property.

The house is silent, the atmosphere eerie, which makes the door opening down the hall deafening.

I push to my feet and hustle across the room as the doctor comes to stand in the archway, now dressed in a T-shirt and jeans, his surgical gear nowhere to be seen.

"I've done all I can," he offers in greeting. "Evelyn will stay overnight and keep watch. But for now, the only thing we can do is wait and see if he wants to live."

"Can I go to him?" I ask.

He nods.

My heart catches. I hustle around him, down the hall, and straight into the basement, Remy and Salvatore following. I jerk to a stop on the bottom step.

Matthew is unconscious on a portable bed in the corner of the room, his large frame dwarfing the single mattress, a white sheet resting over his abdomen while sensors connecting him to an EKG machine are plastered across his chest.

"*Bella*." Lorenzo pushes to his feet from the chair at Matthew's bedside. "Come. Take my place."

I'm not sure I can move any closer. I've waited all this time to see the man I breathe for. To get confirmation he's alive. But he still looks like he's clinging to this world by the tips of his fingers.

"It's okay." Lorenzo waves me forward. "He's stable."

The label doesn't fit. Matthew is frail. Fragile.

"Come on." Salvatore leads me forward with a hand around my wrist, his hold releasing me at the foot of the bed.

Lorenzo murmurs questions, at me or the brothers, I'm not sure.

I don't answer. I don't listen.

My attention is fixated on the beeping of Matthew's monitor while his chest slowly rises and falls.

"Why don't we give them some time alone?" Lorenzo says. "Yell out if you need us."

I nod in appreciation and move behind the chair as the men ascend the stairs.

"I'll go, too." Evelyn approaches me. "He's heavily sedated. He won't wake up for a while, and when he does, he'll be groggy. But you should talk to him." She gives my shoulder a quick squeeze. "Some say that helps recovery."

I wait until the door squeaks shut behind them before I crumple into the chair.

"Matthew," I whisper.

He lays there, eyes closed, his dark lashes resting against pale skin.

My vision blurs, my caged tears finally ready to break free. I weep as I drag a hand over his body. Across the remnants of blood. The cut I caused on his neck. The stab wound on his wrist.

Heat trails my cheeks as I lower the sheet, dragging my touch farther past his boxer briefs to the slices on his thigh. Then I finally lead my fingers to circle the surgical tape surrounding his bandage along his abdomen.

He was a blank canvas before he met me.

Now he's a man riddled with scars.

"Forgive me." I lean forward, draping an arm over his chest, resting my tear-slicked face against his bicep as I succumb to heaving sobs. "You always seem so invincible. And now that you're like this—" My throat dries. "I can't live without you, Matthew."

I hear the echo of his voice in my mind, the words he said earlier coming back to haunt me. *"I'm sorry,* la mia stella polare. *I thought we'd have more time."*

I thought we would, too.

I thought we'd have a future. That I'd finally found happiness.

"Please come back to me," I beg. "I'll do anything."

I remain nestled against him, clinging tight, my tears finally ebbing to dry against my cheeks.

I stay there when the nurse reappears to check his stats and don't move once she returns upstairs.

Remy brings me food, the sandwiches and bottle of water remaining untouched all afternoon.

I fall asleep at one point. Nightmares keep me company. I see snapshots of the shard in Matthew's back. The blood staining his shirt. But I hear him. His voice is there, so clear and tangible in my ears.

"I'd never leave you, *la mia stella polare.*" His touch glides over my shoulder, the contact light. "*La mia ossessione. La mia vita. La mia anima. Il mio santuario.*"

I startle awake, my pulse alive at the sound of his voice. But when I look at him, he remains lifeless.

"He's been in and out of consciousness for the last hour," Lorenzo murmurs behind me.

"He was awake?" I shift, taking in the shadowed room, the lights dimmed.

Lorenzo leans against the surgical table, dressed in a fresh suit. "Not entirely. He's trying to get back to you, *bella.* I think the drugs are making it difficult."

I grasp Matthew's hand and bring his fingers to my lips. "I'm here." I kiss his knuckles like he's done so many times to mine. I do it over and over. Not daring to blink in case I miss a sign that he's returning to me. "I'm with you."

There's no response. Not even a flicker of consciousness.

"How do you say, 'I need you' in Italian?" I ask Lorenzo.

"*Ho bisogno di te.*"

I groan. "Trust me to pick a difficult translation."

"I don't think he has to hear it in Italian. He'll value whatever you say no matter the language."

I nod, my eyes watering as I lean close, my cheek brushing Matthew's. "Please come back to me." I kiss his jaw. His chin. The corner of his lips. "I'm right here waiting for you."

I hold my breath, impatient for something. Anything.

"I'm begging," I whisper.

His fingers twitch against mine. The movement ricochets through me. I pull back as his brows furrow.

There's a moan.

"Matthew?" I inch closer.

"*La mia stella polare,*" he croaks.

Relief steals my breath as those dark eyes flicker open, his lips lifting in a faint smile.

"*Mia dea.*" I cup his face.

"That means 'my goddess' but I'll take it." He snickers, wincing. "Do you have any water?"

I grab for the bottle Remy brought and crack the lid. "Here. Take it slow." I help raise his head while he takes a sip, then slowly rest him back against the pillows.

"Now I need that mouth." He wraps a weak arm around me, dragging me close. Our kiss is delicate, fragile, before his hand falls back to the bed. "How long have I been out?"

"It feels like a lifetime. But maybe seven or eight hours." I scoot back to the chair. "It must be night by now."

"It is," Lorenzo confirms.

"Fuck." Matthew rakes a shaky hand through his hair. "Have you heard from Bishop?"

Shit. I forgot about him. And Abri. "No. I haven't heard a word." I turn my attention to Lorenzo. "But I bet you have."

"*Bella,*" Lorenzo murmurs the endearment, his tone holding a warning.

"You haven't then?" I raise a brow. "I would've thought you'd be the next person he'd call if he couldn't get hold of Matthew."

He doesn't answer, just stares at me, his expression masked.

"What's going on?" Matthew cups my jaw, his thumb delicately brushing my cheek to draw my attention back to his. "Has something happened?"

I hold his gaze, questioning what good can come from being honest when he's bedridden. But *God*, do I feel territorial. Matthew was messed over by his real father. Lorenzo was meant to be the devoted replacement.

"Layla?" Matthew's scrutiny sharpens.

"Bishop never stopped working for Lorenzo," I say softly, patiently, allowing the information to sink in and the shock to take hold. "They've worked together since you left all those years ago."

His hand doesn't move from my jaw, but his eyes stray, their attention turning to Lorenzo for a pointed look.

I wait for persecution. For another volcano to erupt.

"I know." Matthew's gaze returns to mine, heartfelt and warm. "Bishop told me a long time ago."

"He did?" *Shit.* I outed Lorenzo for nothing. Right in front of the mafioso's face.

I straighten, cautiously shifting my focus to the older man who grins down at his polished shoes. *Grins.* As if my lack of loyalty was a comedic performance.

"I told you Matthew was a smart man." He pushes from the gurney and staggers toward me on unsteady feet.

"Then why threaten me to keep quiet?" I ask.

"You threatened her?" Matthew growls, his hand falling from my face.

Lorenzo's grin widens.

"No," Matthew murmurs to himself. "You were testing her."

"*Sì, figlio.*" He shuffles forward, making me hold my breath in caution as he approaches. "And you passed, *bella.*"

He drags me in by the arms, kissing both my cheeks. "I don't usually approve of loyalty above *la famiglia* but in this case, I couldn't be more forgiving." He releases me and slides a comforting hand across Matthew's wrist. "When the time comes, you have my blessing."

My pulse skips. Races.

"I'll let you two have privacy." Lorenzo limps to the staircase. "But I'm sure there will be eager visitors soon." He walks into the upstairs hall, closing the door behind him.

I stare at the bedsheet through lengthening silence, my heart warmed by a blessing I would've presumed was far too premature.

"I need you beside me." Matthew pats the tiny stretch of mattress next to his hip. "Let me hold you."

"I don't want to risk hurting you."

"Your denial is hurting me. Not having my hands on you is fucking torture." He reaches for me, his touch light against my arm.

I climb onto the mattress in slow increments, taking my time to make sure I don't bump him. I nestle my hip against his, my cheek to his chest, his arm cradled around my back. "This isn't hurting your stab wound?"

"I can't feel my face, let alone my back."

I smile, but those tears threaten to return.

I never thought I'd have this again—his warmth, his affection. I truly believed I'd lost my only chance at happiness. That God's plan was to make me suffer for the rest of my life.

"I didn't think I'd get to hold you again." His hand glides through my hair in the most gentle kiss of contact. "I was so fucking scared of losing you, Layla."

"It was my fault for taking your gun." For denying him Emmanuel's death. For being a distraction and a trigger. "I'm sorry."

"You have nothing to be sorry for."

Yes, I do. But I'll make it up to him. I'll spend the rest of my life chasing the happiness we both deserve.

"Are you sure I'm not hurting your back?" I reposition myself, trying not to rest too heavily on him.

"Not at all. I think the pain of that injury will always be more emotional than physical."

"Why?" I whisper. "What happened?"

"Adena."

My stomach twists. "She's the one who stabbed you?"

He nods against my head. No words are needed.

"I'm sorry." I hug him tighter. "Is she the one who shot you?"

"No. I don't know where that came from. She was running at me when it happened. All I felt was a punch to the gut. I thought I was anticipating her barreling into me, that my instincts were predicting the impact. It wasn't until I tried to stand and get to you that things went south."

He continues to play with my hair. Nurturing. Comforting. "Is everyone else okay? You weren't hurt, were you?"

"No, but Lorenzo was shot in the leg."

"Shit," he mutters. "I didn't even notice."

"I don't think he wanted to notice it himself. He wasn't entirely cooperative when I tried to tourniquet the wound."

His chest jostles with a chuckle. "That sounds like him."

"But your brothers are okay. They're waiting upstairs."

"They didn't go to Denver to help Abri?" His hand pauses in my hair.

"No. I assume they were too worried about you."

"Have they spoken to her? Is she all right? *Fuck*. I need to find my phone and call Bishop."

"I'll look for it." I push onto my elbow only to have him drag me back down.

"Give it a minute. I'm not ready to let go of you yet." He holds me, the seconds folding into minutes. The constant *beep, beep, beep* is a soundtrack to our quiet reunion.

I can't go through this again.

I lost Benji. I thought I was going to lose Stella. Now Matthew. Our lives have to change moving forward.

"Are you still awake?" I ask softly.

"Yeah."

"What are you thinking?"

"Just about what Lorenzo said earlier." He plants a kiss to my forehead. "I think it's time, *mia dea*."

I close my eyes. *Oh, God.* My heart hammers.

"Marry me," he whispers.

I squeeze my eyes tighter, clinging to his words for precious moments before I'm forced to let them go.

"Layla?"

"You're high on pain meds." I place a gentle hand against his chest. "Ask me again once the drugs have worn off."

"*La mia stella polare*, you already know I spent some dark days jumping from one drug high to another. I might not be able to feel any pain but I'm not wasted."

"Even so, this is a conversation for another time." A vibration carries from the other side of the room, saving me with its distraction. "Do you hear that?"

"All I hear is rejection."

I climb off the bed. "I think it could be your phone."

"And I think you're dodging the subject."

I walk across the room to the sink as the vibration stops. "Forgive me for thinking it's an inappropriate time to discuss a lifelong commitment while you're so dosed you can't feel your face."

"I can feel all the body parts that matter," he drawls. "Come back here and I'll prove it."

I keep my back to him, attempting to hide a smirk as I open a metal drawer. "I'm sure that nurse of yours will return any minute to check your stats."

"Since when has an audience ever stopped us?"

A laugh escapes me. "We're not having sex. Now or in the near future. You'd die."

"A happy man," he counters, then pauses a beat before saying, "Marry me." It's not a question this time. It's an order. A possessive demand.

"Matthew, my life is with you. I don't want anyone else, and I can't see that ever changing. So my response is already determined, but it won't be given until you're back on your feet. I want to save this moment for when you're healthy enough to get down on one knee. Doesn't a future wife deserve that?"

He sighs in defeat.

I don't feel victorious.

I shove the drawer closed and lift things off the counter, moving discarded cardboard packages and plastic gauze wrappers until I find his cell.

"Look." I turn to him, holding up his device crusted in a flaky red film. "It's filthy, but it's still working. You have a heap of notifications."

"Check them for me. The pin code is five-seven-two-one."

"Give me a sec." I grab a paper towel from a dispenser near the sink, dampen it under the faucet, then begin cleaning what looks to be dried blood from the casing as I unlock the screen. "Twenty-three missed calls from Bishop and one voicemail."

"Listen to the message."

I dial into his voice mail and turn up the volume as bed springs squeak behind me.

"*Langston*," Bishop barks down the line. "Where the fuck are you? Call me. My patience with your sister is growing thin, and I fear for her safety if you don't get your fucking ass here. And I assure you, the danger isn't coming from anyone but me."

"*Shit*," Matthew mutters. "I need to get to Denver."

"You're not going anywhere for a while." I throw the damp paper to the sink as the EKG machine stops beeping and shifts into an alarm shriek.

My heart plummets with the high-pitched tone. I turn to Matthew.

He's climbing off the bed, the cords from his chest monitors clenched in a tight fist before he throws them to the floor.

"What are you doing?" I race to him. "*Stop*. You'll hurt yourself."

He collapses, falling to hands and knees with a grunt.

"*Matthew*," I cry. "We'll send your brothers. You don't need to go—"

"I'm not going anywhere."

The alarm keeps ringing. I start panicking.

I grab his shoulders, helping him upright.

"Did you really think I'd delay this once given clear instructions?" he asks. "You know me well enough to understand I wouldn't waste time making you mine."

"I'm already yours." I use all my strength to try and move him, to no avail. "Please let me get you back into bed."

He places one foot on the ground, stabilizing himself as he wavers on one knee. "Marry me."

"How can you be so careless as to risk your life over a question you already know the answer to?"

"I'd risk the world to make you mine."

The door swings open and a rush of feet clambers down the stairs. Evelyn is in the lead, then Salvatore, followed by Lorenzo and Remy both limping behind.

"*Sir.*" The nurse gasps. "You need to get back in bed." She runs for him, grabbing his other arm. "Did you remove the heart monitors?"

"Of course I removed the fucking monitors," he growls at her, not taking his eyes off me. "Make that damn ringing stop."

"Sir, please. Your stitches—"

"He's fine," Lorenzo warns her from the stairs, Remy and Salvatore remaining nearby. "Give him a minute."

Matthew looks up at me, his dark eyes intense as he tugs my grip from his arm and cradles my hand.

He's so much more than fine.

He's protective and brutal. Intelligent and loyal. Devoted and courageous.

He's everything. My hopes. My dreams. My future.

"*Mia dea,*" he murmurs. "Marry me."

IF YOU HAVEN'T ALREADY READ *the book that started the Hunting Her world, check out Hunter's story here.*

These men don't build bridges…
They bury bodies.

Turn the page for a devilish preview.

For more information on this series, join the Eden Summers' Newsletter or join the fun-filled Facebook Reader Group.

You can also receive new release notifications from BookBub.

ALSO BY EDEN SUMMERS

Hunting Her World

Hunter

Decker

Torian

Savior

Luca

Cole

Seeking Vengeance

Ruthless Redemption

Start the Reckless Beat series

Blind Attraction (Reckless Beat #1)

Start the Vault series

A Shot of Sin (The Vault #1)

Information on more of Eden's titles can be found at www.
edensummers.com or your online book retailer.

ABOUT THE AUTHOR

Eden Summers is a bestselling author of contemporary romance with a side of sizzle and sarcasm.

She lives in Australia with a young family who are well aware she's circling the drain of insanity.
Eden can't resist alpha dominance, dark features and sarcasm in her fictional heroes and loves a strong heroine who knows when to bite her tongue but also serves retribution with a feminine smile on her face.

If you'd like access to exclusive information and giveaways, join Eden Summers' newsletter via the link on her website.

For more information:
www.edensummers.com
eden@edensummers.com

www.ingramcontent.com/pod-product-compliance
Lightning Source LLC
Chambersburg PA
CBHW050805190726
48285CB00005B/1797